### "You win. I'm an asshole."

"I didn't say that," she said.

"Not in so many words, no." His gaze raked her body much the same way it had back at the bar, making every alarm in her head go off. Spending any more time in this man's presence was dangerous, though she couldn't say for sure what she was most afraid of. Olivia lifted her chin in challenge, demanding...She wasn't sure what she was demanding. Her gaze dropped to his mouth, and she licked her lips.

He murmured, "If the shoe fits..."

And then he gripped her jaw and kissed her.

She was so surprised that she opened for him—or at least that was what she told herself when his tongue slipped into her mouth and stroked hers. It should have stopped there. He was even in the process of leaning back when her too-long-denied hormones got the better of her and she fisted the front of his expensive shirt and yanked him back to her. *This.* This *is what I came out here for.*

# Acclaim for Katee Robert

*The Marriage Contract*, 2016 RITA Award Finalist

"Robert easily pulls off the modern marriage-of-convenience trope...This is a compulsively readable book! It's more than just sexy times, too, though they are plentiful and hot!...An excellent start to a new series."
—*RT Book Reviews*

"*Romeo and Juliet* meets *The Godfather*...Unpredictable, emotionally gripping, sensual, and action-packed, *The Marriage Contract* has everything you could possibly need or want in a story to grab and hold your attention."
—Nose Stuck in a Book (ycervera.blogspot.com)

"Teague O'Malley—can I get a swoon?!? I adored him from the first time he was on the page, and he just got better and better."
—BJsBookBlog2.blogspot.com

"A definite roller coaster of intrigue, drama, pain, heartache, romance, and more. The steamy parts were super steamy, the dramatic parts delivered with a perfect amount of flare."
—ALoveAffairwithBooks.com

"Had me hooked from the first page to the last."
—HarlequinJunkie.com

"I couldn't put this book down until I was finished and then had to go back to read the last chapters again because... WOW. I really cannot wait for the next book!! Five stars."
—TheLiteraryGossip.com

"Sexy, fun, and intense."
—LovinLosLibros.blogspot.com

"This series is a hit all around, and I'm already loving it."
—TheBookCellarx.com

## The Wedding Pact

"I loved every second. A–"
—All About Romance
(likesbooks.com)

"Fun, fast-paced, and sexy."
—AlphaBookClub.org

"Katee Robert really shines in this series with her incredible storytelling, romance, and characters."
—TheGirlwiththeHappilyEverAfters.blogspot.com

## ALSO BY KATEE ROBERT

**The O'Malleys Series**
*The Wedding Pact*
*The Marriage Contract*

**Come Undone Series**
*Seducing Mr. Right*
*Two Wrongs, One Right*
*Chasing Mrs. Right*
*Wrong Bed, Right Guy*

**Out of Uniform Series**
*His to Take*
*His Lover to Protect*
*Falling for His Best Friend*
*His to Keep*
*In Bed with Mr. Wrong*

**Serve Series**
*Protecting Fate*
*Betting on Fate*
*Mistaken by Fate*

**Sanctify Series**
*Queen of Wands*
*Queen of Swords*
*The High Priestess*

**Other Novels**
*Meeting His Match*
*Seducing the Bridesmaid*

# AN
# INDECENT
# PROPOSAL

## KATEE ROBERT

FOREVER

NEW YORK   BOSTON

Copyright © 2016 by Katee Hird
Excerpt from *Forbidden Promises* copyright © 2016 by Katee Hird

Cover design by Elizabeth Turner
Cover photography by Claudio Marinesco
Cover copyright © 2016 by Hachette Book Group, Inc.

Forever
Hachette Book Group
1290 Avenue of the Americas
New York, NY 10104
forever-romance.com
twitter.com/foreverromance

First Edition: August 2016

Forever is an imprint of Grand Central Publishing.
The Forever name and logo are trademarks of Hachette Book Group, Inc.

The publisher is not responsible for websites (or their content) that are not owned by the publisher.

The Hachette Speakers Bureau provides a wide range of authors for speaking events. To find out more, go to www.hachettespeakersbureau.com or call (866) 376-6591.

ISBNs: 978-1-4555-9052-0 (mass market), 978-1-4555-9053-7 (ebook)

Printed in the United States of America

OPM

10 9 8 7 6 5 4 3 2 1

*To the Rabble. Thank you for the
inspiration and the amazing support!*

# ACKNOWLEDGMENTS

First and foremost, always to God. It's been a wild ride and it only seems to be getting wilder the longer I'm in this world. Thank you for the chance to keep doing what I love and the unending inspiration to keep me writing.

A big thanks to Leah Hultenschmidt for helping me polish this book into a truly amazing story. Cillian and Olivia wouldn't be the same without your input and insight. Thank you! I can't wait to work on more books with you!

Thank you to Laura Bradford for another great year under our belt. Here's to many more books and another awesome year!

Thank you to the whole team at Forever. You all have made this experience such a positive and amazing one every step of the way! Cheers all around!

Hugs and thanks to Jessica Lemmon, PJ Schnyder, Julie Particka, and Trent Hart for being sounding boards and plot wranglers, and listening to me ramble on about the voices in my head. You're awesomesauce.

Thanks and drinks and all the chocolate to the Rabble. Your support and enthusiasm and just downright amazingness never fail to make my day and inspire me to write all sorts of dirty things just so I can share them with you in teasers. This one's for you!

Thanks to Tim (yeah, I know you were looking for this) for being there day in and day out and always being willing to be the one to feed us so we don't starve while I'm under deadline. I would totally put Baby in the corner for you. Kisses!

As always, more thanks than I can express to my readers. I love hearing your responses to this series, and your excitement never fails to make my day. Thank you!

# AN
# INDECENT
# PROPOSAL

# CHAPTER ONE

Need another drink?" The words were clear despite the general ruckus of the bar, the voice like whiskey on the rocks. If Cillian O'Malley put a little imagination into it, he could almost taste her tone. It was the closest he'd come to having an actual drink in ten months.

*Olivia.*

He looked up, straight into night-dark eyes that made him think reckless thoughts about leaning across this bar and kissing the hell out of this woman. It was something the old Cillian would have done, and if the look on her face was any indication, he would have gotten the shit kicked out of him for the effort. He smiled despite the dark mood that had brought him wandering into Jameson's to begin with. "Hey, gorgeous."

The guarded look on her face was the same as the first time they'd met, like she expected him to whip out a gun and start shooting or threaten her or some shit like that.

Since he knew for a fact he'd never so much as raised his voice at her in the two times they'd interacted previously, it stung a little that *that* was her knee-jerk reaction to him.

And it made him want to show her how wrong she was.

"You know, I'd pay good money to know what I did to piss you off so much."

Olivia's expression iced over in a way that would send a smarter man running. It just made Cillian more intrigued. He'd been caught up in his family's dramas for so long, it was refreshing to having an unconnected interaction—even if it was with someone who hated him. Hell, it was almost better this way.

It just added to the tangled mess inside him caused by sitting in this bar. Jameson's and he had a complicated history that he'd never be able to escape. It was the last place his family had felt whole. He'd been here with his brothers, Aiden and Teague and Devlin, on the final night when they'd been celebrating Teague's impending marriage. Devlin had been shot in a drive-by on the way home, and the O'Malley family had lost the closest thing to an innocent they could call their own. Cillian hated this place as much as he loved it, but it was here his feet brought him when he wandered.

Olivia crossed her arms over her chest, which only served to accent the way her breasts pressed against her shredded T-shirt. It wasn't ripped enough to be truly indecent, but he could see several slices of her dusky skin beneath the black fabric, and it was distracting as hell. She cleared her throat, but he still gave her body a slow look, taking in her spiked combat boots, tiny skirt, coming back to that shirt, and then settling on her face. She was beautiful in the way good models were—a little too sharp for strictly traditional good looks, but all the more striking because of it. The mass of dark hair and the anger in near-black eyes took her over the edge into devastating.

She looked like the kind of mistake he would have jumped at a year ago. He *had* jumped at her six months ago when they'd first met, and it had gone in the same direction their current interaction was headed. She'd taken an instant dislike to him, and nothing he could say seemed to convince her that he wasn't this monster she seemed to label him as.

So much had happened between then and now, so much that weighed him down and threatened to drag him under for good. He hadn't even been out by himself since he was shot—the same night he'd last seen Olivia. He rubbed his shoulder, half-sure he could feel the scar beneath the fabric of his shirt.

What would it be like to be that carefree and crazy version of himself, just for one more night?

"Do. You. Want. Another. Drink?"

*Maybe I could let it all go—the stress and the guilt and the sick feeling I can't quite escape—just for a little while.* He leaned onto the bar. "You want to get out of here after your shift?"

Her mouth tightened. "I don't know why I bother. Never mind."

"Wait." He took a deep breath and let go of the wild impulse that had driven him to offer. He wasn't that guy anymore, and trying to reclaim it was like spitting on Devlin's grave. Cillian sighed. "I'll have an apple juice."

She blinked. "Apple juice."

"Yes, please."

He thought he'd sounded perfectly polite, but she frowned harder. "You come in here a couple times a week—or at least you used to from what Benji says—and you've been sitting here, nursing an *apple juice*?"

"Yeah." He hadn't touched alcohol since the night his youngest brother was killed in a drive-by shooting. He was the reason they'd been on that street to begin with, walking home in an effort to sober him up a little. If they'd just called a cab, Devlin would still be alive and...Cillian exhaled harshly. It was pointless to wish for things to be different, but the truth was that he was at least partially responsible for his brother's death, indirectly or not. He could barely stand the thought of drinking again and potentially putting someone else he loved in danger.

Olivia seemed to realize she was staring and shook herself. She bent over and grabbed the apple juice, shooting a look at him like she'd never seen him before. "Why don't you drink? Alcoholic?" It was almost amusing watching the horror appear on her face. "Shit, sorry, it's none of my business."

Maybe not, but a perverse part of him liked that she wanted to know more about him, even if it was morbid curiosity. "It never brought me anything but trouble." *There are plenty of other ways to get into trouble.*

"It doesn't stop most people from doing it." She finished pouring his juice and slid it across the bar.

"Has anyone ever told you that you're something of a pessimist?" The edges of her lips quirked, and Cillian cocked his head to the side. "Holy fuck. That was almost a smile. I think you might not hate me as much as I thought."

Instantly, her amusement was gone. Olivia stepped back, as if the two-foot bar between them wasn't nearly enough space. "Are you opening a tab or paying now?"

He hadn't set out tonight planning on coming here, but

it was the first time he'd left the house without the muscle his father and brother usually insisted on, and he hadn't wanted to waste the opportunity. He nodded. "Benji knows me. Have him put it on my running tab."

She hesitated like she wanted to argue, but then turned and stalked to the giant owner of the bar. Benji had been operating on O'Malley territory before it was O'Malley territory, and Cillian always got the feeling that he'd still be here twenty years from now, regardless of the power struggles that ran through Boston like fault lines. As expected, the big man nodded, and Olivia walked back to him, her permanent frown firmly in place. "Who the hell are you?"

"Cillian O'Malley at your service." He held out a hand, waiting for a full five seconds for her to take it before he lowered it. "Usually a handshake takes two people."

"O'Malley." She glanced around, but the bar was unusually loud tonight, and there was no one within easy eavesdropping range. "I know that name."

Just once in his godforsaken life, he'd like to meet someone and not see that light bulb go off behind their eyes, but the chances of *that* happening in a bar in his family's territory was nonexistent.

Suddenly tired, he sat back. "You know what? Never mind. I'm heading out." He slid the coaster he'd scrawled his number on across the bar. "If you change your mind about letting loose, you give me a call." He downed his drink and dropped a wad of cash onto the bar. The surprise on her face was almost reward enough as he pushed to his feet and strode out of the bar.

Almost.

\* \* \*

Olivia Rashidi watched the O'Malley walk out the door
and told herself to leave it alone. She'd figured out all she
needed to know about him after they'd first met six months
ago. He'd had trouble written all over him, from his tattoos
to his ridiculously expensive suit to the way he'd carried
himself, as if he was waiting for someone to give him
the excuse to start a fight. Exactly the kind of thing she
avoided—and for good reason. Men like that created chaos
and then walked away unscathed, leaving the people around
them floundering in their wake.

It didn't matter if she hadn't seen much of this O'Malley
in the meantime or if he'd had new shadows in his dark
brown eyes. She had other priorities right now, and jumping
from the frying pan into the fire wasn't her idea of a good
time.

"What are you still doing here, Olivia?"

She turned to face Benji, trying to keep the guilty look
off her face. He'd told her to head home ten minutes ago,
and she'd stopped to poke at Cillian O'Malley. *Good job
staying away from that guy.* She held up her hands. "I'm
leaving, I'm leaving."

"Don't forget your tip."

So he'd seen that and known the reason she hadn't immediately left was because she'd let her curiosity get the
best of her. *Awesome.* Olivia worked to keep a smile on her
face. It wasn't Benji's fault that she had a nasty attraction to
trouble, even though she knew better. She snatched the cash
off the bar and froze when she realized how much Cillian
had left her. The bills weren't ones.

They were twenties.

*Goddamn it.* She stared at the money in her hand and, for
a long second, actually considered keeping it. But then real-

ity reared up and kicked her in the teeth. She couldn't keep it. *But...*

*No.* She wasn't the type of woman who could be bought, and she wasn't going to give him the wrong idea that she was. He might not have asked for anything in return, but being in his debt was bad no matter which way she looked at it.

*And maybe you're just looking for trouble in all the wrong places...just like you always do.*

*Shut up.*

"See you later, Benji." She was moving before she decided on a course of action, grabbing her jacket from behind the bar and heading out the front door. A quick look down the street showed a familiar figure striding away. "Hey!"

*What are you doing?*

She ignored her inner voice and started after him. "Hey! Cillian, wait!"

He didn't turn around, and she cursed him in both Russian and English. Growing up the way she had, she knew plenty of creative phrases in both languages.

"Hey, stop!"

She ran after him, thankful she'd put on her badass studded boots instead of the pair of heels she'd been jonesing after. An eight-hour shift on her feet would have her hating herself if she'd gone with the pretty shoes—and they would have made it impossible to catch up with the O'Malley.

She grabbed his arm and froze at the feel of his muscles flexing in her grip. *Holy wow.*

He finally turned to face her and it struck her that, without the bar between them, he was so much larger than she was. Not large like her ex, Sergei—this man was built lean instead of for brute strength—but he still dwarfed her. And he smelled good, like some kind of spicy men's cologne that instantly had her thinking thoughts she had no business entertaining.

Like what it would be like to bury her nose in his neck and inhale deeply. The insane desire to do so almost overwhelmed her.

*Everything* about him was overwhelming, from his beautiful face, to his impeccably styled dark hair, to the tattoos peeking out of his clothes at the neck and wrists. The ink creeping up the side of his neck was like a wild thing trying to escape from his insanely expensive suit, a strange combination of brute strength and poised polish that she should have known better than to be attracted to.

Except, apparently, her body hadn't gotten the memo.

She realized she was still clutching his arm and made herself let go so she could offer back the cash. *Right, because that's why you chased him down a dark street.* "I don't want your money."

"It's called a tip, sweetheart. It's just good manners."

"I don't want it." Even as she said it, she wondered why she was being so damn stubborn about this. He hadn't asked anything of her. All he'd done was throw too much money at a bartender, which was something plenty of drunks did from time to time. Except he wasn't drunk. She should be elated at having the extra cash—God knew she needed it. Instead, there was a growing recklessness in her chest, one she'd thought she'd outgrown a long time ago. "Just take it, okay?"

"No." His gaze narrowed on her face, giving her the sudden thought that he saw too much. Before she could decide what to do with that, he moved closer, giving her another whiff of that cologne that made her whole body break out in goose bumps. Or maybe it was the man himself, the streetlights creating a skeleton's mask of his face, turning his eyes into dark pits of shadows. "Why do you care so much?"

"Oh my God, just take it back." She should drop the cash and head for home. Or, hell, at least take a few steps away so that she wasn't in danger of brushing against him if she took a deep breath.

But she couldn't force her hand to unclench or her feet to create any distance between them. She cleared her throat, trying to get her thoughts back on track. "I didn't ask for your charity."

"Yeah, I got it. You win. I'm an asshole."

"I didn't say that."

"Not in so many words, no." His gaze raked her body much the same way it had back at the bar, making every alarm in her head go off. Spending any more time in this man's presence was dangerous, though she couldn't say for sure what she was most afraid of. She lifted her chin in challenge, demanding... She wasn't sure what she was demanding. Her gaze dropped to his mouth, and she licked her lips. *What am I doing? Walk away. Walk away right now.*

*No. Not yet.*

He murmured, "If the shoe fits..."

And then he gripped her jaw and kissed her.

She was so surprised that she opened for him—or at least that was what she told herself when his tongue slipped into her mouth and stroked hers. He didn't touch her anywhere else, and somehow that only made their point of contact that much more erotic.

It should have stopped there. He was even in the process of leaning back when her too-long-denied hormones got the better of her and she fisted the front of his expensive shirt and yanked him back to her. *This*. This *is what I came out here for.*

He froze for one endless moment and, frustrated, she nipped his bottom lip.

She barely had a chance to register his going tense before he dug one hand into her hair, tipping her head back so he could get better access to her mouth, taking her as if he had every right to it, his tongue stroking hers. He tasted of apple juice and cinnamon, making her head spin. She should stop this. She would. Really, she would.

*No, you won't. You've never been able to stop yourself once the recklessness in your blood takes over.*

She didn't care. She didn't care about anything other than maintaining the pleasure his touch brought her for just a few minutes longer. Her back hit the brick wall, his free hand hooking the back of one of her knees and hiking it up and around his waist. And then...*oh my God*. There was only his slacks and her panties between them, his cock a hard ridge that lined up perfectly with her clit, the contact so good, it temporarily overstimulated her.

He broke the kiss, resting his forehead against hers. "This isn't what I planned when I kissed you."

No, she had no one to blame except herself for the desperation beating in time with her heart. She *knew* she should stop. She knew too many men like him. She didn't like anything that he represented—a pampered son of a family grown rich on the backs of others and their own illegal activities. Hell, she didn't even like him.

But she didn't want to stop.

It was like the last two years had her turning into one giant snowball of need, and Cillian just happened to be in the right place at the right time to shred her perfect record of self-control. *That's all this is. He's beautiful and he's here. Nothing more.*

She was reaching and she knew it, but she didn't want to stop.

He sighed, the same world-weary sound he'd made at the bar. "Another time."

"Wait." She clung to him, her inner voice screaming that this was a mistake, but she wasn't listening.

He went still, but it wasn't with surprise like the last time. No, this was a predator ready to pounce. "Say what you want, sweetheart. I need you to be perfectly clear."

Again, her common sense tried to say this was an awful idea. *Two years of being good and keeping to the straight and narrow. If I'm going to jump off a bridge, it might as well be with this man. There's no chance of feelings getting involved and me making the same mistake I did with Sergei.*

*One night.*

*One time and then I walk away with no strings attached.*

She reached between them and cupped the front of his slacks. "I want this." She stroked him, the feel of his thick length in the palm of her hand making her entire body perk up even further. "Just this once."

He didn't back up, his lips brushing hers with each word. "This is a mistake."

"Yes." There was no way she could pretend otherwise.

"Fuck." He nuzzled her neck, making her shiver. "Just...fuck."

And then he lifted her off the ground, waiting until she wrapped her legs around his waist to walk a few feet down the street to an alley. It was cleaner than the one behind Jameson's, but not by much. She didn't care, as long as he didn't stop touching her. Cillian readjusted his grip so he could wrap a fist around her hair, tilting her head back so she was forced to meet his gaze. "You're sure?"

"Stop talking before I change my mind." She kissed him, rolling her body against his until he cursed and kissed her back. The barely controlled desperation in every muscle of his body made her feel wild and free in a way she hadn't in a very, very long time.

He guided her to stand, his hand going to the hem of her skirt. When he hesitated, she took his hand and guided it up to cup her between her legs. "You have a condom?" she asked.

"I don't get you."

"You don't have to. Just don't stop."

"You don't like me."

"Nope."

His thumb dipped beneath the band of her panties, stroking her so lightly, she was half-sure she imagined it. She made a sound of frustration and the bastard chuckled. "Damn, sweetheart. I think I like being someone you don't like."

He pushed a single finger into her, cursing when she clenched around him. She had the wild thought that it'd been too long and too much had happened and it would never work, but he pumped a few times, her pleasure building with each stroke.

She kissed him for everything she was worth, needing this more than she needed her next breath. A second finger joined the first, spiking her desire. "*Yes*." She rolled her hips, trying to take him deeper, but he apparently wasn't about to let her drive things.

Cillian's whole hand dipped into her panties, cupping

her even as he continued working her. "When's the last time—"

She reached down and squeezed his cock. "Are you really going to ruin this?"

"Hardly." He slipped an arm around the small of her back, holding her in place while he stroked her, his thumb sliding over her clit, teasing her until her breath came in gasps and her whole body was strung so tight, it was a wonder she didn't fly apart at the seams.

"The condom."

He didn't argue, just shifting enough that he could withdraw it from his pocket. She had the wild thought that he'd expected to take someone home tonight, but it didn't matter. He had protection and *that* was the most important thing. He freed his cock and rolled the condom on. "How do you want it?"

*Has anyone ever asked me that?*

*Stop thinking so much.*

She turned around, shoved her panties to her knees, and braced her palms on the brick wall. Cillian's chuckle curled her toes, and then he was there, pressing against her back, his lips on the sensitive spot behind her ear as he notched his cock at her entrance. "You think if I take you from behind that you won't know it's me." He shoved into her, drawing a strangled cry from her mouth. His hand snaked around to stroke her. "Please, sweetheart. It's *my* cock inside you, *my* hand on your clit, and it's *me* who's going to make you come. Right. Fucking. Now."

He filled her impossibly, the feeling of him sliding in and out of her almost too much. And he was right—there was no escaping the knowledge of him, like he was imprinting himself on her skin. He circled her clit as he fucked her, surrounding her until her entire world narrowed down to Cillian and the orgasm that drew closer with every stroke.

"Now." His free hand came up to cover her mouth, his words in her ear a dirty fantasy she never knew she had. "Let go."

It was too late to go back, even if she wanted to. She came, crying out against his hand as he pushed her over the edge, her orgasm so intense, her knees actually buckled. He kept her pinned to him as his strokes became ragged, and he followed her over the edge, muttering her name as he did.

Olivia opened her eyes and tried to find her place in the new order of things. She took a deep breath, and then another. *Nothing has changed. It can't.* But that was okay. He'd allowed her an escape, no matter how brief.

She withdrew and straightened her clothes, watching him out of the corner of her eye as he did the same. "Thanks."

"Did you get what you wanted?"

She inhaled sharply. "That's not what this was."

"Don't insult me." He took her elbow and walked her out of the alley. "That's exactly what this was. You had a need and I fulfilled it—gladly." He flagged down a cab that had just deposited a group of men in front of Jameson's. She started to protest, but the look he gave her stopped her dead in her tracks.

Still, she made herself keep going. "I'm taking the red line."

"Sweetheart, you can barely walk straight right now. Put your pride in the backseat and let me get you a cab."

"But—"

He gripped her chin exactly the way he did when he

first kissed her, those dark eyes seeing entirely too much. "You'll be seeing me again, Olivia."

He didn't wait for an answer, opening the back door and guiding her inside. Then he shut the door before she could formulate a response, shoving some money at the cabdriver and stalking away. Olivia watched him go, her body still aching from his touch, her mind terrifyingly blank.

*Oh my God, what did I just start?*

# CHAPTER TWO

Cillian didn't go straight home after leaving Jameson's. He had too much pent-up energy—and anger. He shouldn't have let things get so out of control with Olivia. All he'd meant to do when he kissed her was shock her into not arguing about the stupid tip anymore, and the next thing he knew, he was carrying her into an alley and...

*Fuck.*

She just wanted a onetime thing. He should be happy that she wasn't expecting more—or trying to weasel her way into his life under the mistaken impression that his family's power would rub off on her.

*I shouldn't have had sex with her. That was unbelievably stupid.* It was something the old Cillian would have done and to hell with the consequences. The woman obviously wanted nothing to do with him, and that was just fine by him. He didn't need another goddamn complication in his life when he was up to his neck and sinking fast.

He turned another corner—and stopped dead. It was the one place he'd gone out of his way to avoid, and it was a token of just how distracted he was that he'd found his way back here.

To the spot where Devlin died.

Cillian stared down at the concrete. It didn't look different from any other sidewalk in Boston—a little scuffed up, a little dirty, but nothing special. There was something so fucking wrong with that. This was the very spot where his brother passed from this world into the next. Where he'd bled out while Cillian stood by, too drunk to be worth a damn. There wasn't even a stain to mark it. He turned, surveying the street. Even at this relatively late hour, it was nowhere near deserted, and the headlights of each passing car only made the muscles along his spine tense further.

Any one of them could be the enemy.

He tried to take a deep breath, but there was no air. He tried to walk away, but his feet were rooted in place. He tried to reason through what was no doubt another fucking panic attack, but reason had no place here.

He kept seeing the events of that night, over and over again in slow motion. Walking behind Teague and Devlin, singing that stupid goddamn song at the top of his lungs. The SUV screeching to a stop in front of them. The doors opening. The second he realized the guy had a fucking gun in his hand. He'd stumbled back, sure that this was it. The end. His life didn't flash before his eyes like everyone said. No, all he could think was, *What a fucking waste*. And then Aiden hauled his ass to the ground and it was over.

A few minutes later, Devlin was dead and Cillian's entire world was turned upside down.

*Jesus*. He slammed back into the brick wall, the impact

shocking the stalled breath from his lungs. He wheezed, the black spots dancing before his eyes slowly abating. *God-damn it. First time in a month, and it happens in the middle of the fucking sidewalk.*

By some miracle, either no one had seen it happen or no one gave a fuck that it was happening. He didn't care which it was. All that mattered was that he could pick himself up and head home without having to answer any uncomfort-able questions.

*Home.* What a joke.

The town house on Chestnut hadn't felt like home in a long time, and he didn't see that changing anytime soon. Things had been heading in that direction for a long time, but it seemed like he'd only woken up to it in the last few months. His siblings were near-strangers these days. His parents? They'd never been close to begin with, but his fa-ther now had a wall between him and the rest of the family that no one could get through. And his mother...Well, he barely exchanged two words with her these days because she was so busy throwing herself into one project after the next. She was there, but she wasn't present.

And now he was getting maudlin. Some days he could barely stand to live inside his own skin, and today was shap-ing up to be one of them. Cillian scrubbed a hand over his face. Jameson's might be uncomfortable for him to spend time in, but at least it held one of the happier memories. It was there that he'd spent the last hours of Devlin's life bull-shitting and fucking around.

Now that he thought about it, it was probably the last time he'd spent actual time with his other brothers, too. Sure, they'd all been present for Teague's wedding, but that hardly counted. They'd been avoiding each other, and it didn't take a genius to figure out why. The only one of them he saw with any regularity was Aiden, but as soon as the work was done, his oldest brother hightailed it off to God knew where. And Teague...Teague was fully occupied with his new wife. Cillian didn't blame him for that, but there were days when he missed the bastard.

He focused on putting one foot in front of the other, each step creating some much-needed distance between him and the past. A fine sheen of sweat covered his skin, but there wasn't a damn thing he could do about that right now. First, home. Second, a shower, as hot as he could stand it. Then...well, if the last nine months were any indication, then he'd spend most of the night lying on his back, staring at the ceiling. It was fucking pathetic.

The only time he'd actually slept through the night was when they had him drugged to the gills after he was shot. He reached up and touched the new scar. He might have slept, but the nightmares were worse while on meds than they were normally. Two nights of that was all he could take. After that, he chose to deal with the physical pain instead.

*Enough.*

The memory of what he and Olivia had done might be enough to get him through the night, though. She'd been so hot and free in his arms, and for the first time in longer than he cared to remember, he hadn't been thinking about alliances or politics or death. He'd been so focused on making her go wild around his cock that there was no room for anything else.

It had been fucking glorious.

He walked through the front door of the town house, bracing himself for running into someone in his family.

Sure enough, as soon as he got to the top of the stairs, he was nearly run over by his baby sister, Keira. Baby? She was nineteen years old now.

"Keira." Then he did a double take. "What the fuck is this?"

She wore shredded skinny jeans and a tank top that started its life as a T-shirt, nothing that would make him give her a second look...But the size of her pupils *did*. She was on something. He'd bet his favorite suit on it.

She lifted her chin. "I'm going out."

"The hell you are." He took in her bedhead that had to have taken her a hell of a long time to create, the dark eye shadow, and lipstick that on any other woman he would have called fuck-me red. Seeing it on his sister made him break out in hives. The reckless look on her face was even worse. "What are you on?"

Keira laughed. "Please. You're not our father, and you can't tell me what to do." She shoved past him and wobbled down the stairs, bumping into the wall as she went. Cillian inhaled sharply. *Vodka*. That's what he smelled on her breath. *Drugs* and *alcohol*. *Shit*.

"Keira!"

But she was gone, disappearing toward the back of the house—the better to sneak out without an escort. *Fuck*. He started to go after her, but his legs chose that moment to remind him that he was still shaky from the stupid goddamn panic attack. And what the hell was he going to do? He couldn't help her. Hell, he could barely help himself.

He couldn't just let her go by herself, though. He already had the blood of one sibling on his hands—another one might actually kill him. Cillian fished his phone out of his pocket and texted Liam. *Keira's heading out the back door.*

A few seconds later, it chimed. *On it.*

Cillian sighed and walked to his room, managing not to run into anyone else. He stripped, leaving the clothing wadded up on the floor as he headed for the bathroom. He'd given up a lot of things since everything went to hell, but his suits were one thing he still clung to. There was nothing on this earth that could fool him into thinking he was in control like shielding himself in a perfectly fitting suit.

He turned the shower as hot as he could stand it and stepped beneath the spray. The shock of it hitting his skin centered him, which only made it clearer just how off-balance he'd been since he left Jameson's. He wished he could blame it on Olivia and that goddamn sex. It wasn't the truth. The snarly bartender, the panic attack, and his run-in with Keira were just the icing on the shit cake.

It didn't matter.

Tomorrow was a new day, except nothing would change and he'd just be going through the motions all over again. Sometimes he felt like he was in a particularly brutal version of *Groundhog Day*, stuck in a wheel that would never stop spinning.

\* \* \*

Olivia climbed out of the cab in a daze. She couldn't believe she'd just gone *there* with Cillian O'Malley. She licked her lips, still tasting apple juice and him, and shivered. *It was a onetime thing. It'll never happen again.*

As good as it was, he was the kind of trouble she couldn't afford, even if she was in the market. Which she wasn't. She nodded to herself and headed for the stairs up to her apartment. She had other priorities.

She was so tired, she almost missed the shadow detaching from the wall across from her apartment door. Olivia froze. "What are you doing here?"

"I wanted to see you." Sergei's low voice with his thick Russian accent used to make her feel safe. He was just as big and blond and brutal looking as he had been when she'd fallen in love with him, his nose broken one too many times to be rakish, his face that of a warrior. His sheer size was something that had attracted her to him in the first place, a wall between her and the speculative looks she started getting from Andrei Romanov's men as soon as she turned eighteen. Sergei was the only one who'd looked at her like she was a person, and a special one at that. He made her feel like more than the bastard daughter of the patriarch of the Romanovs—what was left of them.

She'd been such an unforgivable idiot.

She crossed her arms over her chest, shifting so she could get to the gun in her purse if necessary. "Why don't we try that again? What are you doing here, Sergei?" She went ramrod straight, all the lingering looseness in her body from her encounter with Cillian going up in smoke. "He sent you, didn't he?"

"Your brother is worried about you."

"Half brother." A vital distinction. They might share the same father, but Olivia would never be a Romanov. The old hurt rose, the feeling of having no place of her own, but she forced it down. She wasn't in that life anymore, and she wasn't about to be dragged back in because Dmitri suddenly decided to remember that they were related. The Romanov name came with more strings attached to it than Pinocchio. She'd dodged a bullet by her father never officially acknowledging her as his child—and she fully planned to keep on dodging it for the rest of her life.

She had to figure out what Sergei—and by association, Dmitri—was here for so she could get them both back out of her life. "For the last time, what do you want?"

"You know what I want." The look on his face said it all. *Her*. But that ship had sailed two years ago, and it wasn't coming back—ever. He knew it. He had to know it. He might pretend he could go back in time and regain her trust, but it wasn't happening. Olivia had been fooled once, but she'd never put him in the position where he could hurt her like that again. From his muttered curse, he read that knowledge from her expression. "I want to see Hadley."

*No way. Not* my *daughter.*

Olivia stopped short, clamping her lips shut around the instinctive denial. Hadley was *hers*. Where had he been for the last year while she'd been struggling to make ends meet? *Off with Dmitri, probably torturing small animals and beating the crap out of helpless people.*

Okay, that wasn't fair, but she wasn't feeling all that fair when it came to Sergei. She had no doubt that he loved their daughter as much as he was able, just like she had no doubt that he'd loved her, too. She also knew that he'd put a bullet in both their brains and throw their bodies into the river if Dmitri commanded it. Sergei might—*might*—feel bad about doing it, but he'd do it all the same. The Romanovs were his end-all, be-all, and nothing could compare to that.

*If he was really here to see Hadley, he wouldn't be showing up at one in the morning.* "She's sleeping. Her bedtime is eight." Olivia hesitated. Every instinct demanded that she do whatever it took to see the last of him once and for all, but she was afraid that was *her* hurt talking. Like it or not, he was Hadley's father. She cleared her throat. "If you really want to see her, you can come by in the morning."

"I will." He looked away, his Russian accent getting thicker. "But I am not here only for you."

Of course he wasn't. She should have known better than to think he'd shown up after twelve months of silence just to say hello. "Tell Dmitri to leave me alone. He doesn't want me in the damn family any more than I want to be there. He needs to let it go." Maybe if she said the words enough times, he'd actually listen. She wasn't holding her breath.

"He can't do that and you know it." Sergei still didn't look at her. "He is not a patient man, Olivia."

She knew that. Hell, she knew that better than most people. "I left all that behind when I moved away from New York." She didn't *want* it—any of it. She didn't care that Andrei got terminally ill and suddenly had a change of heart about the bastard daughter he'd spent the last twenty-two years ignoring. She had no desire for a position within the Romanov empire or any of the so-called perks that came with it. The only thing Andrei had done that was less than despicable was making sure she had a roof over her head and didn't starve while growing up. The bare minimum for survival. She didn't owe him anything, and she sure as hell didn't want any of his guilt-driven gifts.

Was she being stubborn? Hell yes. She and Hadley were doing just fine without touching the money Andrei had put in an account for her—especially since she couldn't touch it without agreeing to everything else he'd wanted from her before he died.

"I don't want the money, and I don't want anything to do with the Romanovs."

"That's not what Andrei wanted."

And that was the crux of it. Dmitri loved his father. It was one of the only redeeming things about him, for all that Andrei hadn't been a saint. He wanted to honor Andrei's last wishes, whether he agreed with them or not. She got that. She just wasn't willing to sacrifice both her and Hadley's future to please a dead man.

Olivia took a deep breath, counted to three, and exhaled. Yelling at Sergei wasn't going to do a damn thing. She looked up at him, suddenly so tired she had to fight to keep from weaving on her feet. "Tell Dmitri that my leaving is the best thing that could have happened for either of us. He doesn't want me in New York. I don't want to be in New York. He tried to bring me into the fold like our father wanted, and as far as I'm concerned, he's done his duty." There would be no going back—not for her, and certainly not for Hadley. She'd fought too long and hard to put that life behind her, and get to a point where she could raise Hadley in a household that didn't think everything from tax evasion to torture to downright murder was acceptable as long as their bottom line was met. A family who'd do anything for a little bit more power. She might not be rolling in the cash the way Dmitri and his people were, but it was an acceptable tradeoff as far as Olivia was concerned.

Sergei shook his head. "Livie...that's not good enough, and you know it."

Yeah, she did. But she had to try. All Olivia had ever wanted was to grow up *normal*, and she had the chance to do that for her daughter. Going back to New York wasn't an option. She slid past him to her door. "Good night, Sergei. I don't want to see you around here again unless you're actually deciding to be a father. Dmitri can send someone else to be his errand boy." She walked into her apartment without another word and quietly closed the door behind her.

It wouldn't be that easy. Dmitri excelled at pushing people's buttons, and Sergei was a giant one when it came to Olivia. She could barely look at his face without being transported back to that idiot girl she'd been when she thought that he'd leave with her. That he'd step up as father to their child after the initial surprise of the pregnancy. That he'd be the only person in her life who'd actually put her before the Romanov bottom line.

He hadn't, and she'd barely gotten out as a result.

Except she hadn't gotten out. Not really.

# CHAPTER THREE

$B$y the time dinner was ready the next night, Olivia felt like she'd run a marathon. Two marathons. She'd spent the day with Hadley, cleaning and doing laundry and trying her best to stay busy so she didn't keep double-checking to make sure the lock was secured on their front door. She knew all too well that the flimsy mechanism wouldn't do a damn thing to stop Sergei if he put his mind to it, but it still helped. "Dinner's ready, baby girl."

Hadley toddled into the kitchen, a bright grin on her face. "Mama!"

*This is why I'm doing it. This is why I can't take the money and I can't let Dmitri have his way. Not this time.* "We're going all out tonight. Chicken nuggets and apple slices." She lifted Hadley onto her booster seat at the small two-person table and set her sippy cup full of milk and her plate in front of her.

It didn't matter how hard her life was sometimes—it was

all worth it when her daughter gave her that smile, like chicken nuggets were the greatest gift she'd ever received.

She sat down across from Hadley, nibbling on a piece while she monitored her daughter's progress. Sometimes she ate like she was starving to death, but more often than not lately, she seemed to pick at it or half the food would end up on the floor. *It's just a stage.* Knowing that didn't stop the worry from lingering in the back of her mind that Hadley wasn't getting enough to eat.

A knock on the door had her climbing reluctantly to her feet. Their neighbor Mrs. Richards watched Hadley when Olivia was at work. She wanted to sit here all night and just *be*, but that wasn't an option.

She had to go so she could pay their bills.

Because she was absolutely not taking any money from Dmitri. *Goddamn Romanovs and their goddamn money and power plays.*

She slipped out while Hadley was occupied, pausing to whisper, "Thanks," to Mrs. Richards. Some days Hadley was fine with her leaving—or barely noticed at all—but Olivia didn't want to make things harder on the older woman than she had to. Mrs. Richards squeezed her shoulder and smiled, and then headed for the kitchen.

Olivia grabbed her purse and headed out. She locked the door behind her, the small hairs on the back of her neck rising, though she didn't actually see anything suspicious. That didn't stop her from looking over her shoulder more times than she could count on her way to work. There was no sign of Sergei, but she swore she could feel his eyes on her.

*Maybe I should have called in and stayed home with Hadley.*

"Hey, Olivia."

She pasted a smile on her face for Benji. It wasn't his fault she was in a foul mood. Not to mention—as if she needed yet another reminder—this job paid her bills. Pissing off her boss was a good way to get her ass kicked to the curb. "Hey, Benji. Slow night?"

"It'll pick up." He filled a drink order, each movement so natural it was obvious he'd spent years behind this bar. "If you want to grab another case of Bud, that'd be great."

"Sure thing." She didn't mind hauling things from the industrial-sized walk-in fridge in the back. It gave her some much-needed time to compose herself. Olivia ducked through the door leading back to the supply rooms and then into the fridge itself. She closed her eyes and inhaled the icy air. It would be okay. She'd figure this mess out. She just needed time.

The problem was that time might be the one thing she *didn't* have.

Her phone buzzed in her pocket, and she cursed when she saw Sergei's name on the screen. *I don't have it in me to deal with this tonight.*

She headed back out to the bar area. A group of tourists huddled around a table, pressed closely together as they flipped through pictures on a tiny camera screen, and a set of businessmen at the bar who'd obviously just gotten finished with work, though they hadn't left the job at the office if their conversation was anything to go by. And, finally, tucked in the back corner was a couple so focused on each other, Olivia was pretty sure she could dance naked around the room and neither of them would pay her the slightest bit of attention.

The thought of dancing naked brought back memories

of *him*. Cillian. She'd been so busy with the mess of Sergei and worrying about Hadley being a picky eater that she hadn't had a spare minute to really consider the possible consequences of her actions.

Okay, that was a lie.

She crouched down behind the bar and started unloading beer bottles. It was mindless work, for which she was grateful. She wasn't ready to face actual customers yet.

"I know you don't like me much, sweetheart, but hiding behind the bar is a new low."

*Oh God.* She closed her eyes, took a deep breath, and opened them again. Sure enough, Cillian was still there, peering over the bar at her, his dark eyes lightly mocking. Her body burned, the taste of him filtering through her memory as if it had been seconds since he'd kissed her, minutes since he was inside her, instead of a little less than twenty-four hours.

She shoved to her feet. "What are you doing here?"

"Your customer service is seriously lacking." He leaned back, his gaze skating over her in a move she could almost feel. It made her reconsider her clothing—a worn pair of perfectly faded shorts over black tights, her spiked knee-high combat boots, and her favorite white T-shirt—which only served to irritate the hell out of her. She'd been comfortable when she left the house, and now she wasn't. The fact that he didn't have to say a single thing to make her skin heat just aggravated her further.

She crossed her arms over her chest. *First Sergei, and now this*. It wasn't fair to compare the two, but she wasn't feeling particularly fair right now. She was feeling cornered. "You're in my bar."

His eyebrows rose. "I was under the impression this was Benji's bar."

"It is." She couldn't tell if the heat pulsing beneath her skin was from embarrassment, or the fact that he'd left a few buttons undone on his perfectly pressed blue dress shirt and she could see that the tattoos on his neck extended south. *How far south?*

Why in the world had her hormones decided to wake up for *this* guy? She'd been doing just fine on her own—with regular assists from her buzzy toy BOB. Her life had been going okay until yesterday and, sure, she had so much pent-up desire that she'd been the one to jump him after that initial kiss, but that didn't change the fact that O'Malley's presence here now heralded all sorts of trouble for her. Last night she'd let herself get out of control and then, less than an hour later, Sergei had been on her doorstep. Blaming that on Cillian didn't make the slightest bit of sense, but she couldn't help linking up the two in her head. Both were bad news. She wanted no part of their family entanglements.

*If Dmitri found out you were even talking to him, let alone that you had sex with him…*

The thought was like a bucket of cold water on her insane desire. This guy was nothing but complicated, and her life was too complicated as it was. When she spoke, she managed to sound halfway normal. "Apple juice?"

"You remember. I'm touched."

*Maybe touched in the head.* She busied herself getting a glass and ice and the juice, watching him out of the corner of her eye. He'd looked rough last night, but tonight he looked absolutely haggard—while still being unbearably hot. Hell, whatever burden he seemed to carry around only made him more attractive. It didn't make a damn bit of sense. She'd never had a thing for the dark and brooding types before, and she wasn't about to start now.

Even if a part of her did wonder what put that lost look on his face when he didn't think anyone else could see.

She slid the apple juice across the bar to him. "Last night was a onetime thing."

"You said that already."

She had, hadn't she? There was that damn heat again, pushing against the inside of her skin in a way she *knew* he could see. "All the same, I don't know why you're back here, but you're not getting a repeat."

"I didn't ask for one."

If embarrassment could kill a person, she would have turned to ash on the spot. She opened her mouth, and then closed it. Why had she assumed he'd want to hook up again? He might have said as much afterward, but guys were known for saying things they didn't mean before, during, and after sex. She should have known he wasn't interested. For fuck's sake, *she* had practically strong-armed him into going there with her. He probably thought she was . . . She didn't even know, but definitely not a woman he wanted to spend more time with.

*Which is exactly what you want.*

"Right. Of course." She grabbed a rag and started wiping down the bar, hating how tangled up she felt inside. Twenty-four hours ago she'd had a clear picture of what she wanted and how she was going to get it. There had been no distractions, and her past was firmly in the rearview. Now everything had changed and she felt like the world was shifting beneath her feet.

"I do, though." He tilted his glass, watching the liquid move in the low light.

She blinked. "What?"

"I want a repeat—preferably somewhere a little less public." He looked up and pinned her in place with his gaze. "Somewhere I can take my time, until you come so many times you lose count."

The world stopped spinning so suddenly, she had to grip the bar to keep from keeling over. She couldn't tear her gaze from his, no matter how hard she tried, but she wasn't even sure she was trying at all. She wasn't sure of much of anything except that Cillian could do exactly what he was promising. He'd more than proven that last night.

Why the hell couldn't someone else show up and demand drinks? At least then she'd have a legit excuse to end this conversation in a way that didn't look like she was running away—even if that's exactly what she would have been doing. "No."

"Why not?" He asked the question like he already knew the answer.

"Because, frankly, it wasn't that good." *Liar, liar, pants on fire*.

"Funny that you say that, because it sure as fuck felt like you were having a good time. Especially when you made that little moaning sound when I—"

"Shut up." She looked around, but Benji was on the other side of the bar, chatting with the businessmen, and there was no one else close enough to hear his low words. *Thank God*. But she couldn't keep scrubbing at the bar and pretending that she was busy while he was talking like this. She had to lay things out for him, and hopefully he'd take a hint. Olivia straightened and made herself look him in the eyes.

*He's seriously wounded.*

She shook her head, not sure where the thought had come from. It didn't matter. Cillian O'Malley would be off-limits even if he weren't part of a notorious crime family.

She didn't do damaged, and she didn't do complicated. She didn't do *anything* these days that would take away from Hadley, and maybe if she told herself that enough times, her body would finally get the hint. She pressed her lips together for a long moment, striving to come across unaffected and ice cold. "I'm not interested."

"Okay."

*What?* She'd been so prepared for him to argue that it took her a half second to catch up. "Okay?"

"Yeah." His gaze was intense on her face despite his relaxed body language. "I feel like you've gotten the wrong impression about me somehow." He took a drink of the juice. "Maybe because of my last name."

She jumped, guilt beating in time with her heart. "My life works right now." Sort of. "I don't need the kind of trouble that comes with dating the son of an Irish mob boss."

"Sweetheart, you don't have to convince me. I'm not exactly a catch." If anything, his attention only got more intense. "But I'd be lying if I said last night didn't make me stop short and take notice. I know you felt it."

Was still feeling it, even with the bar between them. Her skin tingled and her nipples tightened just from the look he gave her. *The sex was so good. Maybe one more time couldn't hurt...*

*No. Absolutely not.*

She twisted the rag, realized what she was doing, and dropped it. "I didn't feel a thing except a mildly pleasant orgasm that took the edge off. I don't want anything more from you."

Her words didn't faze him. If anything, he looked even more interested. "I'm not offering to take you home to my parents, sweetheart. I'm talking about sex—the hot and sweaty kind—where we fuck until we can barely remember what day it is, and then both walk away better off than we started. Simple. Uncomplicated."

"That's some line." And it was—a seriously good one. A date didn't tempt Olivia—or at least that was what she told herself when loneliness became too much to bear—but a few hours? *What could go wrong with a few more hours of escape?* It was all too easy to picture what he meant. Maybe he had a place around here where they could slip off to after her shift. He'd shove her against the door and kiss her and... She realized she was pressed against the bar, as close to him as she could possibly be without climbing over the scarred wood.

*What the hell is wrong with me?* Last night was a onetime-only kind of thing. Doing it again was too dangerous to even consider. Too selfish.

She had Hadley to think about. It was one thing to have Mrs. Richards watch her daughter while she was working to bring in money that they desperately needed. It was entirely another to request a babysitter so she could go get her rocks off with an O'Malley, who was just a different shade of Romanov. She knew the type. She'd grown up surrounded by them. This man might seem like he had the weight of the world on his shoulders, but he'd cleave to his family's wishes time after time. Nothing else would be permitted to get in the way.

*He's not asking for forever. He wants to blow your mind a few more times and get his blown in the process. And it would be good. You* know *it would be good.*

Yeah, she did. It didn't matter. She couldn't risk it.

"Thanks, but no thanks." Olivia took a step back. "I need to do my job."

"By all means." He motioned with the glass.

"I don't need your permission." She hated how sharp and brittle she sounded. Hated that she could *feel* him watching her hurry over to the vacationers to refill their drinks. Most of all, she hated that she didn't completely hate the feeling.

* * *

Cillian drank his apple juice and watched Olivia work. She was as skittish around him as a wild animal. He'd been around the block enough times to recognize the desire written across her face when he'd talked about another night of uncomplicated sex, but she'd shut him down so fast, it was a wonder his head didn't spin.

Last night she'd said it was a onetime thing. That should have been the end of that, but that sex...fuck. It had been quick and dirty and hotter than it had any right to be, and even with what happened afterward, he couldn't get that bright spot in his memory to leave him alone. He knew it could be good between them if she'd give him a chance at a repeat.

*Doesn't matter. She said no tonight, and so I'm backing the fuck off.*

Even in his idiot party days he was a big fan of that little thing called consent. There was nothing that pissed him off more than watching some fool chase after a woman who obviously didn't want him, and seeing that slide from annoyance to fear on a woman's face...Yeah. Cillian had thrown down more times than he cared to count over that sort of thing when he was in college.

He didn't want her to feel uncomfortable. That was the *last* thing he wanted. This was her workplace, and he'd just made things worse by coming on to her after she expressly told him there wouldn't be a repeat. *I should leave, but I'm not ready to give up Jameson's. Not yet. Maybe not ever.*

There was no help for it. He'd have to apologize. It was the only chance to put them back on the right foot. Or it would have been if they'd *ever* been on the right foot.

He rotated on his bar stool and watched the bar. There'd be no trouble tonight. The energy of the place was low-key and comfortable, and he let it roll over him, wishing some of the atmosphere would rub off on him. It was a good place, nothing like some of the hole-in-the-wall pubs he'd ended up in over the years. He turned to find Benji watching him. "Hey, man."

"You know what I'm going to say."

Yeah, he did. "I'm going to apologize." An apology was just empty words, but it would make them both feel better. Theoretically, at least. "What's her story?"

"Didn't ask and she didn't offer." Benji's brown eyes didn't leave his face. "Don't pry. She's a good girl, and I'm not going to have you running her off." It was a variation of the same conversation they'd had six months ago.

It hadn't bugged Cillian then, but now it grated on him. "What do you think I'm going to do to her? Club her over the head and take her home with me?"

Benji didn't blink. "I like you, Cillian—you're a good kid for the most part—but trouble follows you around like stink on a pig. She doesn't need any more trouble in her life."

Which meant she already had some sort of trouble. Benji might play at the fun, lovable oaf, but he obviously knew more than he was saying—kind of like how he was on the O'Malley payroll and never mentioned it. Not high up, but there all the same. Cillian had found his name on the roster last week when he was going over the family finances, though he hadn't put much thought into it before now. Seventy-five percent of the business owners in their territory paid to one degree or another for various things—protection, favors, random shit that he was still having a hell of a time decoding. He'd spent the last six months with the old moneyman, Bartholomew, learning the various tricks of the trade—the kind of stuff you couldn't pick up in college. Now Cillian was officially handling the family's money; it was his job to keep track of that sort of thing as well as the investments that kept them flush.

But for Benji, the O'Malleys paid out.

He sat back. He was going to have to think about that. He could ask Benji, but he had a feeling the man wouldn't tell him anything useful. No, the answers would be found in the ledgers that were now Cillian's responsibility. All the O'Malleys' dirty little secrets were there, secreted in Bartholomew's code. He had the key. He just needed to buckle down and do the work to find the information he wanted.

The puzzle almost—almost—distracted him from the conversation. "I'm not looking to bring her trouble." That was the last thing he wanted. Too many people had already been hurt because of him. He couldn't stand it if anyone else bore the weight of his shitty decisions.

"You weren't looking to bring trouble to that brother of yours, either."

The words lashed him, leaving a blistering pain in their wake. No, he hadn't meant to bring trouble to Devlin. He'd thought it was an excuse to let loose a little with his brothers the way they used to, and he'd drank too much—as was his usual back then. Cillian gripped the bar as the room swayed around him. *No. I'm not doing this shit tonight.* The steel band around his chest tightened, making it damn difficult to draw a full breath. "Low blow, Benji."

The bartender held up his hands. "I'm sorry to bring it up, but I need you to understand this girl isn't for you. I don't know how else to make this clear to you."

A perverse part of him wanted to push just for the sake of pushing, but that wasn't the man Cillian was anymore. He released the bar and stood, wavering only slightly on his feet. "I got it. Loud and clear." It didn't mean he'd listen, but he wasn't going to start a conflict about it right now. He downed the rest of his juice and set cash on the bar next to the empty glass—enough to pay for the drink and a tip that was exactly thirty percent.

He pushed to his feet and strode over to where Olivia had just dropped off a set of drinks to the couple who looked half a second away from sneaking off to some dark corner and banging their brains out. He envied them, just a little. Their lives weren't shadowed by past traumas. All they cared about was the here and now and each other.

He focused on Olivia. "I'm sorry."

She stopped short. "What?"

"I was out of line, and I'm sorry. I haven't exactly been at my best lately." *Lately* being the last fucking year, with no signs of it getting better in the future.

She pressed her lips together, considering him. In their limited interactions, he'd noticed that she flipped between mouthing off and looking at him like she was half-sure he'd transform into a monster when she wasn't paying attention. Which one was the real Olivia? The cautious woman or the snarly spitfire? He wanted to know, even though he'd already promised himself he'd leave her alone.

Finally she propped her tray on her hip. "You're serious."

"Yeah, well, you made your position pretty clear, and I still came here tonight looking to change your mind. It was kind of a dick move, and for that I'm sorry."

"I see." But her tone said she still wasn't sure what to think of him.

He should leave it at that and walk away. But the old Cillian, the part he couldn't quite banish and wasn't sure if he even wanted to, piped up. "Don't get me wrong, the offer's still on the table if you change your mind. I'd love to spend a solid week making you scream my name while you come around my cock. Or a single night. Or somewhere in between. Your call. But I won't bring it up again."

Her dark eyes went a little hazy. "You're bringing it up right now."

"To make sure we're on the same page. I want you. You want me, too. You've got your reasons for not taking what I've offered, and I respect that." Or at least he was doing his damnedest to respect that. He shrugged, trying to work out some of the tension in his shoulders. "But if you change your mind, I'm all over it."

"I'm not going to change my mind." She didn't sound sure, though.

If he didn't miss his mark, Olivia would spend the rest of tonight thinking about the possibility of them fucking until they forgot their own names. *Good.* He permitted himself a grin. "I'll see you around, sweetheart." When he hit the street, even with the sticky heat of the July night trying to cling to him, he had the insane urge to whistle for the first time in too long.

# CHAPTER FOUR

Sloan O'Malley held her phone, staring at the caller ID while it rang. There was no name next to the number, but there didn't have to be. She knew who it was. *Carrigan.* Her thumb hovered over the end call button, but she couldn't do that any more than she could answer it. Some days she wished she could see things as black and white as her father did. To him, Carrigan had betrayed the family by dodging her forced marriage to Dmitri Romanov and falling in love with James Halloran instead. She did the most unforgivable thing of all—daring to choose a man over her family. To Seamus O'Malley, Carrigan was dead and gone the second she walked out the door. He'd done what passed for mourning for a few days, and then to all appearances, it was business as usual.

Though he hadn't mentioned marriage where Sloan was concerned.

Six months of waiting for the sword to fall—would she

have to take Carrigan's place to secure an alliance with the Romanovs?—and Sloan was just plain exhausted. But her father hadn't even breathed the word *marriage*, to Dmitri or otherwise, and she suspected she had Carrigan to thank for the reprieve.

Sloan set her phone aside, where it finally stopped ringing, and sent her sister to voice mail. They hadn't talked since she'd walked out of the house, leaving the rest of them to fend for themselves while she pursued her happiness. Sloan was a terrible person for judging her for that, but she couldn't seem to stop. Maybe if Carrigan's happiness had been tied up in anyone other than a Halloran it would have been easier to stomach. *Maybe*.

She still didn't understand. There were millions of men out there in the world, none of which was responsible—directly or otherwise—for the death of Devlin. Why couldn't her sister have fallen in love with one of them? That, at least, would be understandable.

Sloan left her phone on her dresser and slipped on her shoes. She had to get out of this house, which had started to feel a whole lot like a tomb. Her siblings were dropping off, one by one. Even those who hadn't left felt like they had a foot out the door. *They're all going to leave me. Maybe not today. Maybe not tomorrow. But it will happen.*

Cillian didn't chafe at the bit of familial responsibility, but he was half the man he used to be. Their father saw it as his growing up, but Sloan knew better. Part of the thing inside him that had been so vital and full of life was withered and dead. How long before the rest of him followed suit?

Keira...She wrapped her arms around herself as she hurried downstairs. She didn't know Keira anymore. The girl who'd been all sunshine and roses was something else altogether. The last time Sloan tried to talk to her, Keira *shoved* her. She was a ticking bomb, and it was only a matter of time before she exploded.

And Aiden…He might say and do all the right things, but Sloan could see how much it killed him to see his siblings hurt. It wasn't enough to push him to make different decisions, but the hurt was there all the same.

She was losing them.

The knowledge weighted her steps and made her head fuzzy. Everywhere she looked was a reminder that things were changing, faster and faster, until it was impossible for her to keep up. She slipped out the back door and inhaled deeply. The cool spring night eased her tension, but only a little.

A figure melted out of the shadows, and she tensed for a minute before she recognized her father's man, Liam. "I'm going to the church." She'd meant for the words to come out as a statement, but in reality they were closer to a question. She hated herself a little bit more for being so unforgivably timid.

Liam nodded. "I'll get the car."

"No." The word came out sharper than she intended, and she had to clamp her mouth shut to stem an apology. "I want to walk."

He hesitated, but finally nodded. "Okay."

It wasn't terribly far from the town house to Our Lady of Victories, but she couldn't remember ever walking it before. It was still early enough in the evening that there was plenty of foot traffic, people going on about their lives, each with their own stories and trials and tribulations. It made her feel small and unimportant, which was strangely comforting. She was just one more person in a crowd, going about her business and focused on her own problems. *I'm not that different from any one of these people.*

It was a lie. No matter their stories, she doubted these strangers had to deal with things like arranged marriages, or being part of a criminal family enterprise, or a father who had never quite made it out of the Middle Ages.

The feeling of oneness passed, making her feel even emptier than she had before. And significantly more overheated. The worst of the afternoon heat might be past, but that didn't stop her shirt from sticking to her back as she crossed the street. She tried to stop from wishing for the cool air-conditioning of their town car and failed miserably.

The O'Malleys might preach family before all, but it was to family that they were the cruelest. She wished she could set herself apart from that truth, but that would be a lie. Carrigan had been trying to reach her for months, and Sloan had ignored every single call, secure in her hurt and betrayal.

*Because she should have chosen* us. *Not a Halloran.*

There it was—the truth, petty and ugly. Once upon a time, Sloan had prided herself on her sensitivity and her willingness to listen and be the sole person who gave her various family members a shoulder to lean on. She wasn't sure when that had changed—maybe with Devlin's death, maybe even before that—but she was just as much part of the problem now as her father was.

The realization made her stomach lurch.

Needing to escape her own head, she focused back on the people around her. For all that Boston was famed for being a walking city, her family made a point of taking a car everywhere they needed to go. She'd never considered how elitist that act was, but as she stretched out her strides and walked down the sidewalk, she was faced with a startling truth—she'd missed out on a lot by taking those car rides. *Maybe I'm not as much of an odd duck within the family as I thought. Maybe I fit in all too well*. If that wasn't depressing, she didn't know what was.

Our Lady of Victories sat nestled on Isabella, just like it had for over a hundred years. There were countless buildings like that around the city—places that could trace their roots back to the 1700s. There were people like that, too, their family lines something they bragged about as if it actually meant something. It was the one area where the O'Malleys failed miserably. They hadn't come over on the *Mayflower* or been part of the first settlers who'd carved this city out of the so-called savage land around it.

As a result, the O'Malleys would always be "new money." And that wasn't even taking into account their criminal connections. No, if her mother had once dreamed of being the belle of upper society, those dreams had turned to dust over the years. She'd adapted well enough. What was that old saying? *I'd rather rule in hell than serve in heaven*. A life view her mother clung to.

Sloan strode up the steps and through the massive front door. At this time of night, the church was almost deserted. There was an older woman in the first row, but that was it. Sloan gave her a wide berth. She didn't want to talk to anyone tonight. She just wanted some kind of peace.

Ironic that she was looking for it here, of all places. Sloan had never felt a higher calling. She sank onto the pew three rows back and looked at the massive stained-glass window behind the altar. It was dark now, but with the morning light streaming through, it was one of the most beautiful things she'd ever seen. She'd spent countless

hours over the years tracing the patterns with her gaze while
Father Joe gave his sermons. There was something comforting in always knowing what to expect, what the next motion
would be. Mass was one of the few times in her life where
she didn't feel like she was spinning wildly out of control.

Since Father Joe often preached about giving up control
to God and having faith in His processes, she was failing on
multiple levels with her lack of trust. She sighed. *What am
I going to do?*

"Sloan?"

She tensed for a long moment before she recognized
the man who strode from the back of the church. *Teague.*
"What are you doing here?" Ever since her brother had married Callie Sheridan, he spent all his time with her. *Which
is normal. It would be weird if he kept hanging around the
house with a wife at home and a neighboring territory to
run.* But logic had no place in her head apparently, because
every day he didn't show up at the O'Malley town house
felt like another betrayal to her.

"Same thing you are, I'd bet." He sat next to her. "Sometimes it's nice to come here and just be. Mass is fine, but it's
not quite the same thing."

"I suppose." She knew she sounded sharp, but couldn't
help it. It was too great a coincidence that he was here now,
at the same time she was, and she'd stopped believing in co-
incidences a long time ago.

He smiled. "And Liam called me."

She turned around to glare at the man, but he was
nowhere to be seen. Not surprising. There were more shadows than light in the sanctuary right now. He could be
anywhere. She shivered. "Why?"

"Because I asked him to."

Now she turned in her seat to face him. "What's going on?" He wasn't there just so he could see her—he could come home any day of the week for that. That meant he had something he wanted to talk to her about that he couldn't do in the O'Malley home.

"Relax." He draped his arms over the back of the pew, looking for all the world like he was just in there for a friendly chat.

So why was her heart trying to beat its way out of her chest? She'd never feared her brothers before—though Aiden made her a little nervous these days—but the tang of bitterness on the back of her tongue was hard to ignore. "What did you do?"

"I didn't do anything." He drummed his fingers on the dark wood. "Have you given any thoughts to your future?"

She simultaneously wanted to laugh and cry. "What future? You know better than anyone that I don't have a choice. Father hasn't moved on any marriage prospects, but no doubt he has a little niche he'd like to shove me into when it suits his purposes."

"And how do you feel about that?"

"It doesn't matter how I feel about it, does it? There're no other options."

He was silent for a long time, silent and still. Finally he said, "What if there were other options?"

Fear unlike anything she'd ever known rose up and clawed at her throat. It was so easy for him to offer her *options*, and to talk about defying their father when he'd danced to Seamus O'Malley's tune. Despite his big talk while they were growing up, when push came to shove, *he* jumped when their father said jump. *He* hadn't taken any risks. *He* had done exactly as their father wanted and married Callie Sheridan.

And now he was asking her to...what? She shoved to her feet. *I don't want to know. I don't want to hear it. I'm not going to stick my neck out to make his guilt at leaving me behind more bearable.*

But what if she did?

The thought brought her up short. She'd spent her entire life being tossed from one wave to the next, with about as much control as a rowboat in a hurricane. All she had to do was look around to see her siblings taking control of their futures in whatever way they could. Even if it was destructive, they were *doing* something, which was more than she could say for herself.

Sloan made herself sit back down and turn to face him, even though every muscle shook with the effort to keep still. "What other options?"

"What if..." He hesitated, searching her face. "What if I could get you out—*really* get you out? You could have that little house in a small town like you've always dreamed of. You could leave the politics and danger and Boston behind."

It was almost too much to comprehend. She swallowed hard, a different kind of fear rising inside her. She might hate so much about her life now, but she knew the ins and outs and the risks down to the tiniest detail. To leave that all behind meant opening herself up to the greater unknown, which was scarier than she could have dreamed.

*If I stay here, it's only a matter of time before our father recovers from how things played out with Carrigan and tries to push me into an advantageous marriage.* When he did, she'd say yes. She always said yes. It would be the beginning of the end for her. She wasn't naive enough to believe otherwise.

So she took a deep breath and forced herself to nod. "Yes."

"Yes?" Teague looked like he was almost afraid to hope that he'd heard her right.

She nodded again, her voice so low it was barely a whisper. "Yes. Get me out."

* * *

"That everything?" Olivia finished balancing out the till and stuck the extra money into the appropriate zippered bag. It had been a good night. The businessmen bought enough alcohol to rival any frat boys, and they'd tipped well beyond that. She peeked out the back office to find Benji wiping down the last of the tables. Technically he should be the one closing the till, but he said he'd rather do just about any other job in the pub. Since she didn't mind the tedium in the least, she'd pretty much been doing this particular job since she started here.

The problem was that tonight the tedium had been her enemy. It gave her entirely too much time to think, which was the *last* thing she needed right now.

Benji stood up and wiped his brow. "Yeah, I got the rest of this covered. Your tips are on the bar."

"Thanks." She shouldered her purse and skirted around the boxes that would need to be taken out back. A quick count of the cash had her frowning. "Benji—"

"I don't want to hear it." He glared, though it was about as menacing as a teddy bear. She'd seen him muscle grown-ass men out of the pub more than once over the last six months without breaking a sweat, but his moods didn't faze her. She knew all about being pissy to force people to keep their distance, and normally she respected his space when he turned that expression on her.

But the last few days had pushed her tolerance almost to the breaking level. "Benji, this is nearly double what I actually earned tonight. Those guys tipped well, but not *this* well." She made her hands unclench from around the cash and set it back onto the bar. "I'm not looking for charity." Someday she might have to get the hell out of town without a word to anyone, and she'd hate feeling like she left the scales unbalanced behind her. Benji was too nice for her to take advantage of.

"Listen here, Olivia, because I'm only going to say this once. Are you listening?"

She sighed. "Yeah."

"You bust your ass. You're the hardest worker in this place, including myself. Now, I'm a firm believer that a good work ethic should be rewarded, and that's what I'm doing as your boss. It's not a handout, and don't you dare insult me by saying it is. I reward hard work in the way I see fit, and this is how I see fit. Got it?"

She swallowed past her suddenly dry throat—and the insane urge to hug the big man. "I got it."

"Good. I don't want to hear any of this nonsense again." He started to turn away. "Do you need a ride?"

"No, I got it." There was another half hour before she had to be down at Charles Station to catch the last red line home. She managed a smile. "Thanks, though. For everything."

"Don't go getting all mushy on me." He jerked his chin at the boxes. "Take those out back before you lock up."

This was more like the Benji she was used to. She'd never have thought it when she walked in here, determined to argue her way into a job, and saw the hulking owner behind the bar nearly making some poor guy piss his pants in fear, but she really liked working here with him. She grabbed the boxes and headed out back. *Attachments are dangerous, and you damn well know it.* Yeah, she did. Any relationship she formed was one that could be used against her if Dmitri ever decided to come calling.

*Which is exactly what he's apparently decided to do.*

It was enough to make her want to pack Hadley and their few important items and catch the first train out of town. *I can't live my life in fear.* Though some days, it seemed the smartest thing to do. If she kept moving, maybe she could outrun the shadow of his influence. The only thing that stopped her was the fact that it was no kind of life for Hadley. Her daughter was barely fourteen months old, and Olivia could see the strain their abrupt move from NYC had caused her, even though she'd been eight months old at the time. She wouldn't do that any more than necessary.

*The money...*

He should be goddamn *pleased* that she didn't want it. She grabbed a box cutter and started collapsing the boxes, putting a little more violence into it than strictly necessary. Dmitri didn't want her to have the money his father had put aside for her any more than she wanted to have it. But if he didn't get her to take it and return to the Romanov fold, he'd be going against Andrei's dying wishes. As Andrei had been so fond of saying when he was alive, a man didn't get by in their kind of life without having his own code of honor. While that didn't require him to be faithful to his wife or keep him from murdering the opposition or delving into the kind of illegal things that kept Olivia up at night, it *did* mean that his word was something he'd never break.

And that code was one Dmitri had inherited from their father.

So far Dmitri hadn't moved to force the issue, but if Sergei showing up last night was any indication, it was only a matter of time before he truly insisted she return to the family.

The boxes thoroughly demolished, she stuck the box cutter into her back pocket and gathered up the cardboard. It would take all of fifteen minutes to get rid of these and finish closing up, and then she'd be headed home to cuddle her daughter. Shutting a door between themselves and the rest of the world sounded like heaven right now.

But when she took the boxes into the back alley, she froze. There were three men in the alley. *Couldn't they find another damn place to do a drug deal?* She started to back into the pub, but raised voices caught her attention. Two of them backed the third into the brick wall, their stance aggressive and reeking of promised pain. *Go back inside, Olivia. This isn't your fight. Just call 911 and lock the damn door.*

One of the men punched the third, sending him spinning to the ground. She gripped the doorframe, torn between the need to run and the need to intervene. The second man stepped forward, his intention to kick the guy while he was down in every line of his body. *Damn it.* A boot could do fatal damage to the soft parts of a stomach. "Stop!"

"Stay out of this, bitch."

*I wish I could.* But she was already moving, ducking back through the door to grab the shotgun Benji kept hidden in the gap between counters. The first night she'd closed alone, he'd shown it to her and walked her through using it until he was satisfied she wouldn't shoot her foot off trying to defend herself. She could have told him that she was no stranger to using guns, but it was just easier to go along with it.

Olivia walked through the door, cracked the barrel to make sure it was loaded, and snapped it shut in a sound that only a fool wouldn't recognize. She lifted it, bracing the stock against her shoulder so it wouldn't knock her on her ass if she had to pull the trigger. "I said stop."

The two standing men exchanged a look, clearly weighing their options. She waited, though the shotgun was already getting heavy, the stock slick in her clammy hands. *Are they O'Malley men collecting payment?* A part of her didn't want to believe it. The rest of her knew exactly how families like that—like the Romanovs—functioned. She widened her stance, ready to do whatever it took to get them away from the guy on the ground. "I already called 911. They should be here any second."

The man on the left cursed long and hard and turned to the one on the ground. "Don't think that we'll forget Ricky, you piece of shit." Then he grabbed the other guy's arm and hauled him away.

Olivia waited for them to turn the corner...and then waited another twenty seconds to make sure they weren't going to change their minds. Only when the coast was a hundred percent clear did she rush to the fallen man's side. "Are you okay?"

"Aw, sweetheart, I didn't know you cared."

*Cillian.*

# CHAPTER FIVE

Cillian had taken a beating a time or two. He'd always had a mouth on him, and sometimes it talked him into more trouble than it talked him out of—and that wasn't even taking into consideration his upbringing and all that other shit. There was an ongoing threat of violence that existed in the background of all their lives from the time they were old enough to understand what their father really did to provide the lifestyle they enjoyed. For all that, he hadn't understood why two strangers chose tonight of all nights to jump him.

Not until they'd let slip Ricky Halloran's name.

*The sins of the past keep coming back to bite us in the ass over and over again, like a snake that's eating its own tail. We hate them for Devlin. They hate us for Ricky. And on and on it goes.*

He concentrated on breathing while he took inventory of his injuries. He'd have a black eye for sure tomorrow—Mother would love that—and more bruises than he cared to count, but nothing seemed to be broken. Thank Christ for small mercies. *Does James know his people are slipping his hold? Does Carrigan?*

A worry for another day. He braced himself and sat up.

"You shouldn't be moving." Olivia, his unexpected avenging angel, hovered nearly close enough to touch, but made no move to help him other than checking over her shoulder, presumably to make sure the Halloran men hadn't changed their minds and come back for round two.

"I'm fine." Mostly fine. The alley was spinning a little in a way that sure as hell wasn't natural. He touched the back of his head and winced when his hand came away bloody. "Shit."

She sat back on her heels, the shotgun carefully pointed at the ground away from him. "Let's get you into the bar."

The order surprised him. She obviously didn't like him that much, sex aside, but if she was the type of woman to charge into an alley to defend a man she barely knew, it stood to reason she'd want to make sure he didn't lie back down and die in that same alley.

His pride reared up and took control of his mouth. "I'm okay." It was only a few blocks back to the house. He should be able to make it there and convince one of the men to patch him up without telling anyone how bad he must look right now. They did this sort of thing all the time.

"You're bleeding from your head and weaving even though you're sitting down. You're not okay." She hesitated. "Look, I didn't actually call the cops, and if those guys come back, it'll mean trouble for both of us."

*That* got him moving. It was one thing to put himself in danger. It was entirely another thing to bring her into it. She was an innocent bystander, and even in his line of business, innocent bystanders weren't something to just mow down. *Devlin was as innocent as they come, and that didn't save him.*

*Fuck off.*

He used the brick wall to struggle to his feet, and nearly toppled over when the asphalt beneath him tilted. Olivia was there, sliding beneath his arm and keeping him upright. Cillian took a deep breath and got a face full of lavender and vanilla. How the hell did she manage to smell so good after working a full shift in a pub? He took a step, having to lean on her more than he wanted to. "Maybe I'm not completely okay."

"No, really?" She guided him inside, pausing to set the shotgun aside and lock the door behind her. "You don't have the sense God gave a toddler."

He wouldn't know. He didn't exactly spend a lot of time around kids since he'd stopped being one himself. He tried to picture a toddler and came up with a grubby little Tasmanian Devil. "I think you just insulted me."

"Only a little." She pulled out a chair. "Sit. I'll grab a rag and see if we can clean you up."

"Why are you doing this?"

She'd already turned away, but her shoulders tensed at his question. "Because if you bleed all over Benji's floor, he'll never let you through the door again."

That wasn't what he meant, and she had to know it, but she was already gone, disappearing into the back. He braced his elbows on the table and did his damnedest not to let the nausea that made his stomach lurch have control. She was right. The big bar owner would be pissed as hell if he showed up tomorrow to bloodstains on the wood floor. But there was more to it than that.

He waited until she reappeared with a few washcloths in her hand to say, "You didn't have to help me."

"I know." She set the cloths on the table. "This isn't going to be pleasant." She gingerly touched his head, sifting her fingers through his hair as she searched for the wound. He could have helped her find it immediately, but the feeling of her touching him—even in such shitty circumstances—felt too good to cut short.

*I'm a fucking creep. Enjoying her running her fingers through my hair when I'm bleeding and bruised all to hell. Classy.*

She found the spot his head had met brick wall and felt around. "It's a little gapey, so it might need stitches, but I should be able to get the bleeding stopped at least. Hold still."

Easier said than done. But he kind of liked her taking care of him, so he obeyed while she folded up a washcloth and pressed it carefully against his wound. It hurt like a bitch, but Cillian managed to keep his curse internal. Barely.

"You don't have to stay. I'll call someone." Though who, he didn't know. Both his father and Aiden would rip him a new one for letting those Halloran idiots get the drop on him—and then turn around and start plotting revenge. He wasn't interested in aggravating the issue. Things were already tense enough between the almost-war and then Carrigan defecting to their side. He wasn't going to be the one to light the match that made the whole thing explode. *I am going to have to give Carrigan a heads-up, though. She needs to know James is losing his hold on some of his men.*

"You know, for someone who was trying to get into my pants a few hours ago, you're sure ready to see the back of me."

"It's a seriously superior backside."

She surprised him by laughing and, *holy shit*, what a laugh. It was honeyed whiskey, and enough to have him thinking about things best done in private, the slide of skin against skin, his mouth on her. Her being so close didn't help, either. It didn't matter that he was covered in his own blood and had just had his ass handed to him. She smelled like heaven and looked like his favorite kind of temptation with those cutoff shorts over fishnets and a T-shirt of a band he'd never heard of.

Olivia bent down to look into his eyes. "You probably have a concussion, though I can't blame your lame jokes on that."

"Ouch. Here I am, trying to lighten the mood, and you're mercilessly cutting me down."

"I believe that was the men in the alley that I just saved you from." She hesitated, conflict written all over her face. Finally she used her free hand to sweep her hair off one shoulder. "What was that all about? I thought it was a shakedown, but it wasn't, was it? It was personal."

Even though he knew better, he found himself telling her the truth. It wouldn't endear him to her any, but it wasn't like he could make her opinion of him *worse*. "How familiar are you with Boston's underbelly?"

"Familiar enough." She shrugged. "O'Malley. Sheridan. Halloran. All chomping for a piece of the same bone, just like it is in every major city."

His curiosity almost got the best of him—what did she know about the crime scenes in other cities? He'd figured she'd have at least basic knowledge since she worked for Benji and he liked to keep his employees aware of any trouble that might come their way as a result of his being one of the main pubs the O'Malleys frequented, but there were some serious shadows in her eyes. He'd get into that later.

But she'd asked him a question, and he'd already decided to answer it honestly. "Well, it's not as crazy as it was a year ago. The O'Malleys and the Sheridans are tight now. I wouldn't say they actively work together, but they're not eyeing each other's backs and caressing their knives at the moment."

"I see." She leaned up to check the bandage, giving him an eyeful of her chest. He wasn't a saint enough to ignore that, so he looked his fill. Olivia was built slim, but from the outline of her T-shirt, her breasts were perfectly shaped. *Should have explored them at length when I had the chance.*

He clenched his teeth against the physical reaction trying to perk up. She was playing goddamn nursemaid right now. She wouldn't appreciate him popping wood in the middle of that.

Worse, she might stop touching him if he did.

To distract himself, he kept talking. "Technically the Hallorans and the rest of everyone are at peace, but there are some undertones that are hard to ignore. Plus, when shit goes sideways, it's hard to let that kind of thing go, even if the people up top demand it." Like Devlin. He didn't blame those assholes for wanting some revenge after Ricky died, though he knew for a fact it was an unsanctioned hit. Carrigan might be dead to the family, but she would never turn on them like *that*. And if she wouldn't, James wouldn't. From all accounts, that sadistic bastard Ricky was well liked by the men under him— most likely because James had kept him reined in as much as possible so they hadn't seen the destruction he was truly capable of—so it stood to reason that someone would come along at some point and decide to take their price out of enemy hide.

Except the O'Malleys weren't the ones who killed Ricky Halloran.

No, that was from an outside threat—Dmitri Romanov. He'd turned James's right-hand man and ordered the Hallorans' deaths. The guy had been only half-successful and, if anyone had asked Cillian which Halloran was less likely to send all the Boston families into a goddamn death spiral, it was James. So thank God for small favors.

"I can see that." She switched out the washcloth and added a dry towel over the top. "They say jump and expect everyone to jump and be happy about it."

Yeah, she'd *definitely* had interactions with a similar scenario. But who? She sure as hell wasn't associated with any of the three families in Boston. Part of his training for taking over for Bartholomew had been reading files on every major player under the Sheridans, the Hallorans, and even the MacNamaras, for all that they were extinct thanks to Callie's dad. There were extensive dossiers on anyone with more than a passing connection with any of the families. Even if she was using a different name, he would have recognized her from her picture. She wasn't there. He was sure of it. "You sound like you know a thing or two about it."

"Not in Boston." She took his hand and used it to replace hers on the towel. "How are you feeling?"

Like he wanted to get to know her better. He'd already wanted her—how could he not?—but now he wanted to do more than roll around naked with her. He wanted to actually sit down and have a conversation. It was tempting to play up his injuries to keep her here and touching him, but that would *definitely* put him in creep territory. "Nasty headache and I feel like I've been hit by a truck, but I'll live to see another day."

"You're probably concussed." She frowned. "But I'm hardly a doctor."

"You seem to know your way around head wounds." Which was another puzzle piece to add to the mystery that was Olivia. When he'd met her, he thought she was a beautiful woman with an attitude—and she was—but the more time he spent with her, the more he realized she was like the ocean—full of mysteries.

And just as likely to get him in over his head.

She shrugged. "I've seen a few in my day." Concern lit her dark eyes. "You shouldn't be alone right now."

Damn, he couldn't have asked for a better opportunity if he'd tried. But that was his old self talking. The man who'd go to great lengths to charm a woman into bed, who'd never met a challenge concerning the opposite sex that he wasn't willing to step up to the line with. He knew Olivia wanted him, even if she had something holding her back from going there again. A year ago that would have been like waving a red flag in front of a bull.

Now? Now he was tired and hurt, and there was a sick part of him convinced that having the shit beat out of him was nothing more than he deserved. Devlin had gotten a bullet from the Hallorans. Cillian had only gotten roughed up. If he could go back to that night...

But there was no changing history. There was no magic spell or time machine that would allow him to take his brother's place. There was only Cillian now, trying to do his damnedest to take it one day at a time and not let the vastness of the future overwhelm him.

* * *

Olivia hesitated, torn between wanting to kick Cillian's ass to the curb and wanting to make sure he was okay. He didn't *look* okay. Sure, she'd seen worse during the brief time she and Sergei lived together, but *worse* was a relative thing. And the look that had just come into his eyes made her shiver. It was the expression of the man staring death in the face and refusing to back down. "Cillian?"

He blinked at her, seeming to come back to himself. "Sorry, what did you say?"

Yeah, he was definitely concussed if he was spacing out in the middle of a conversation. What had he even been doing in the alley to begin with? He'd walked out the front door hours ago. Why was he still hanging around? Shouldn't he have some kind of protection detail with him? Dmitri never went anywhere without his goons. She bit her lip, looking around as if the answer would jump into being from the walls.

No such luck.

"Is there somewhere you can go?" She couldn't bring him home. Hadley loved people too much and, even though she was supposed to be sleeping, if she woke up and saw him, she'd be all over him in a hot second. And if Sergei saw her with another man, let alone an O'Malley...

She shuddered. No, she couldn't take him home.

If Olivia was smart, she'd wash her hands of this whole business and send him on his way. *Except you'll never forgive yourself if you see on the news tomorrow he was found dead on the sidewalk.* There had to be a better option.

He'd gotten paler in the last few minutes. "This might

sound childish, but I can't go home looking like this. I'm not willing to start a war over a few bruises."

He was suffering from a hell of a lot more than a few bruises. If he walked through the door looking like that... Yeah, she could see how it would send an already tense situation over the edge. *Damn it.* "Is there someone you can call? I can stitch you up, but it won't be pretty."

And everything about Cillian was pretty. Well, *pretty* was too feminine a word. But he was perfectly put together from his hipster hair to his tattoos to his expensive clothes. Though he didn't look particularly put together at the moment. His shirt was torn and had blood spattered over it, and his hair was totally screwed up. For the first time since they'd met, he looked almost... human. Approachable. She busied herself with folding another towel and making sure the bloody one wasn't leaving a stain on the table.

Finally, he said, "I think my phone fell out of my pocket in the alley."

She knew there *had* to be someone he could call. Ignoring the strange disappointment at the thought of sending him off with someone else, she straightened. "Give me a second."

"Wait." When she paused, he started to stand. "You can't go out there alone. What if those idiots come back? I'll go."

"You can't even stand." She gently pushed him back into the chair, slightly alarmed at how easy it was. Yeah, it was definitely time to call in reinforcements. "If I'm not back in two minutes, feel free to swoop in and save me."

It wouldn't be necessary. She could take care of herself. She'd been doing it since she was a child.

Olivia grabbed the shotgun and opened the back door cautiously. It was entirely likely that the Halloran men were long gone, but Cillian was right—no point in taking chances.

But the alley was empty.

She found his phone easily and hurried back into the bar, relocking the door behind her. Cillian was exactly where she left him, and he relaxed when she walked back into the room. "No trouble?"

"None." She wished she could chalk his concern up to self-preservation, but he seemed genuinely worried about her. It was . . . strange. She passed over the phone. "Call your people in."

"You're awfully sure I have people to call in."

"You're an O'Malley, aren't you?" The question came out harsh—harsher than she intended. It was as much to remind herself as anything else. O'Malley, Halloran, Romanov—it didn't matter. They were all the same. Dangerous and selfish and willing to do horrible things in the name of some higher cause that usually boiled down to power and money. She'd left that life behind, and she wasn't about to let it sink its claws back into her again.

Not even for this man who she was starting to see wasn't completely like she'd expected.

*You've known him a grand total of a few hours. You don't know a damn thing about him. He could be even worse than Dmitri.*

He shifted, leaning against the table as he paged through his phone with one hand. "You sound like you're holding a grudge. Did someone in my family hurt you?" The question came out deceptively simple, but there was tension in his shoulders.

*Would it matter if they did?* She managed to keep that thought internal, but she couldn't let him think that she'd been wronged by one of his. It just wasn't right. "No, nothing like that. I just know the type." Men like Dmitri. Men like Sergei.

She palmed her phone, cringing when she saw the time. There was no chance she'd make the last train now. *I'm going to owe Mrs. Richards in the worst way for this one.* "One second."

"Sure."

Mrs. Richards answered on the first ring. "Olivia, dear, is everything okay?"

The worry in the woman's voice made her feel even worse. But then a horrible thought struck. *Maybe I'm wrong about why Sergei is sniffing around. Maybe he was just waiting for me to leave the apartment to take Hadley.* She gripped the phone tighter. "Have you had any trouble?"

"No, of course not. Hadley wasn't too keen on bedtime, but a few times through *Goodnight Moon* was enough to change her mind."

Her breath left her in a whoosh, and she fought dizziness. Everything was okay. She was overreacting. Again. She cleared her throat, and tried to bring some calm back into her voice. "Good. I had a problem come up at work, so I'm running late."

"Don't you worry about a thing. I'm holding down the fort just fine. Do what you need to do."

Thank God for Mrs. Richards. She didn't know what she'd do if she had to leave Hadley with anyone else. No one in the world seemed as capable and able to deal with whatever complications arose without it ruffling her feathers. "Thank you."

"No need to thank me. Now, go take care of what you

need to take care of. We'll be here and waiting for you when you're done."

Olivia hung up, feeling slightly better. Whatever else came of tonight, her daughter was safe. That was all that mattered. She turned back to find Cillian watching her with an unreadable expression on his face. "Problem?"

"It's really none of your business." But she relented almost immediately. He'd bled all over her, and told her about the men who attacked him. The least she could do was answer a question or two. "It's my daughter. I had to let the person watching her know that I was going to be late." *And make sure Sergei hadn't done anything shady in the meantime.*

He blinked. "You have a daughter."

It wasn't quite a question, but she answered it anyway. "Yeah. She's fourteen months." *This will send him running for sure.* In her experience, the best way to turn away a man interested in hooking up was to mention that she had a kid. She didn't particularly like using Hadley as a barrier between her and those idiots, but it was a foolproof method.

"Cool." Just that. Nothing else.

*Guess he can't hightail it out of here when he can't actually walk. Way to go, Olivia.* She checked the towel he had pressed against the back of his head. It wasn't quite soaked through. At least the bleeding was slowing down. "Call your people, please."

He pressed a button and handed her the phone. "Tell them what they need to know."

The last thing she wanted was to become *more* involved, but she couldn't exactly hand the phone back when a gruff female voice answered. "What do you want?"

"Uh, I have Cillian O'Malley here with a head wound. He needs someone to come get him."

"Where the hell is *here*? I'm not a mind reader, girl. Speak up!"

*Wow.* She was tempted to hang up, but that would create more problems than it would solve. "Jameson's on Charles."

A pause. "Hold tight. I'll be there in a few." The woman hung up.

Olivia set the phone back onto the table. "Nice lady."

"Hardly. Doc Jones is as mean as a honey badger and twice as protective." He shot her a look. "I think you'll like her."

What did that say about the way he saw *her* if he thought she'd get along with that snarly woman? She moved around the bar to fill a glass of water for both of them. It shouldn't matter that he apparently thought she was mean. That was what she wanted, wasn't it? She worked hard to be as unapproachable as possible while she worked. It didn't affect her tips. People tended to like their bartenders one of two ways—mean as a snake or flirty as all get-out. The former had always come more naturally to Olivia.

So why did knowing that persona worked on Cillian bother her so much?

# CHAPTER SIX

Cillian knew he was in trouble the second Doc Jones walked through the front door. She was a big woman who looked like she came from a family of lumberjacks and bench-pressed trees for fun. Her orange-red hair was liberally streaked with gray, but she could be anywhere from forty to sixty. All he knew was that she'd been the family medic for as long as he could remember and, aside from the added gray hair that she liked to blame on the O'Malleys, she didn't seem to have aged a day in the meantime.

She took one look at him and snorted. "Always trouble with you, isn't it, boy?"

*I'm twenty-six. I'm not a goddamn boy anymore.* He bit back the instinctual response. It would only let her know exactly how much she got under his skin. Not that she needed the verbal confirmation. Doc Jones was one of the few people who talked shit to every member of his family from his youngest sister all the way up to his father, all without seeing any actual consequences. Probably because she was excellent at her job—and knew how to keep her mouth shut.

Olivia stood. "It's not his fault. He was jumped."

"Who's this cute little piece of ass?"

She started to bypass Olivia, but Olivia got right in the doctor's face. Nothing overtly threatening, but she didn't back up when the large woman got into her personal space. "I'm the one who saved his ass. So maybe before you go dismissing me, you'll ask me—the one *without* a head wound—for the details."

Cillian braced himself to stand and get between the two of them if it became necessary. No one—not even his father—talked to the doctor like that. But Doc Jones just grinned. "I like this one. Try not to fuck it up."

Right, because that was what he was worried about right now. The only reason Olivia was giving him the time of day was because she was afraid he'd fall down on the sidewalk and bleed out if she let him out of here unsupervised. It wasn't exactly the suave impression he'd wanted to make. After this, he'd be lucky if she looked at him with anything other than pity.

"He was jumped by two men. He's probably got a bunch of bruises, but the main issue is that he hit his head on the brick wall when he fell, and has been bleeding ever since." Olivia glanced at him. "He's been talking, but seems kind of out of it, so it's possible that he's got a concussion."

"Any vomiting?"

"No."

"That's something, at least." Doc Jones nodded. "You wouldn't believe the trouble this one gets into."

Olivia snorted. "Oh, I can imagine."

Cillian tried not to be too insulted that they were talking

about him like he wasn't in the room. Doc Jones took the towel off the back of his head and batted his hand away. "Don't move."

Since she had a history of smacking her unruly patients, he wasn't inclined to disobey. He'd already had his bell rung tonight—he didn't need it to happen a second time. "Yes, ma'am."

"Good boy." She prodded the wound, her touch much less gentle than Olivia's had been. "You don't even need stitches." She hefted her giant bag onto the table next to him and rifled through it, coming up with a handful of bandages. A few minutes later, he was wrapped up and feeling like one of those amnesia patients on the soaps his mother swore up and down and sideways that she never watched. "Good enough." Another dip into her bag brought up an orange pill bottle. "These aren't anything fancy—just extra-strength Tylenol. You're a grown-ass man, so you can handle a little pain, and I'm not giving you anything else until we know if you've got a concussion."

He ignored the bottle. "I don't need anything." Tylenol wouldn't knock him out like the meds he'd been given after he was shot, but his aversion to pain pills had only gotten stronger as time went on. He didn't want to take anything that might make him sleep too deeply—or take away his pain so he'd pass out. The nightmares were bad enough if he could startle himself awake easily. Being stuck in them…He wouldn't take the chance.

Doc Jones's eyebrows rose. "If you say so. Change the bandage once a day for a week, don't knock your head into anything in the meantime, and you should be fine. Call me if it starts bleeding excessively again."

"I will." He wasn't thrilled about the head bandage, but

it was better than stitches at this point. He fucking hated stitches.

She nodded, and turned to Olivia. "He can't be left alone tonight. So either take him back to the O'Malley house or take him home with you." Her dismissive tone said she couldn't care less which option the other woman chose.

"Wait—what? Aren't you going to take him?"

"Not my job. I made sure the idiot wasn't going to bleed to death. The rest is up to you." She grabbed her doctor's bag and marched out of the pub without a backward glance.

Olivia stared. "That's some bedside manner."

"She's always been like that. Comes in, patches us up, and is gone without any small talk." Doc Jones may not have been into the softer feelings, but she liked her money. So she didn't mind showing up at odd hours, fixing men who'd obviously been up to something less than legal, no questions asked. He was pretty sure she had her own clinic, funded in part by O'Malley money. Since he couldn't see her answering to anyone but herself, he figured the arrangement worked well for everyone involved.

"Wonderful."

He carefully moved his head from side to side. As expected, the bandages were a good fit and not going anywhere. Cillian looked at Olivia—really looked at her—for the first time since the attack. She wasn't exactly dragging ass, but she looked as exhausted as he felt. If it hadn't been for him, she already would have been home and safe and probably asleep.

*Way to go, asshole. If you hadn't been wandering the streets like a crazy person, this never would have happened.*

He carefully stretched. The aches and pains were more annoying than worrisome. "I can make it home on my own."

She shook her head. "I don't think so. It's late—or early, depending on your definition. I'll get you a hotel nearby and stay with you until morning."

"Sure. Thanks." Under different circumstances, he would have been happier than hell at this turn of events. As it was, he didn't have the strength to make a move even if she was willing. He was pretty sure pity was her sole motivation for helping him, rather than being so overwhelmed with his masculine sexuality that she couldn't wait to get him alone. *You are seriously knocking it out of the park with this woman.*

\* \* \*

This was a mistake. An epic mistake. Olivia should have just called him a cab and sent Cillian on his way. Instead here she was, checking them both into Beacon Hill Hotel while he leaned heavily on the counter next to her. Its nightly rate wasn't one she could afford, but it was the only hotel within walking distance.

Even though the night had cooled down to being nearly pleasant, she hadn't enjoyed one second of that walk. She kept flinching at every little sound, half-sure that the guys she'd scared off had come back to finish the job. Or, worse in some ways, that Sergei would melt out of the shadows and demand to know what the hell she was doing with Cillian O'Malley on her arm.

Maybe she should have just called the damn cab and sent Cillian home, but as stupid as it was, she couldn't help feeling kind of responsible for him. There was an old legend in a book that she'd read about as a kid that said if you saved another person's life, you became responsible for it. She'd found the idea tragically romantic as a little girl.

Now? Now she was starting to think it was a giant pain in the ass. She had enough to worry about. She didn't need some O'Malley with more charm than sense mucking around in her life.

*He offered to leave multiple times and you ignored him.*

*So what? That doesn't mean I want this.*

*It doesn't mean you don't.*

She cursed under her breath as the front desk agent passed over the hotel keys, very carefully avoiding looking directly at Cillian. Their room was on the second floor, so she slid under Cillian's arm to support him—not that he asked for it—to get him into the elevator and up to their door. He didn't say anything as she unlocked it and pushed it open. She stopped short when she caught sight of the single bed. "Damn it. I asked for a double."

"I'll call the front desk." He started to move toward the phone, but she grabbed his arm and steered him toward the bed.

"It's fine. I wasn't going to sleep anyway." Even though she was so tired, she was pretty sure she was weaving on her feet more than he was. Dealing with Sergei yesterday and then Cillian and those thugs and then Doc Jones on top of everything…

It was a lot. A whole hell of a lot.

She sat down next to him. "How are you feeling?"

"Like some asshole took a two-by-four to the side of my head."

"No, really?" She rolled her eyes. "Are you still dizzy? Nauseous?"

He started unbuttoning his shirt. "Just fucking tired."

"What are you doing?" She had to fight against the insane urge to slap his hands away and clutch the shirt together to hide the growing slice of skin on his chest the parting fabric revealed.

He didn't stop. "I'm covered in blood and feel like absolute shit. I can't do a damn thing about how I feel, but I can get this shirt off." He gingerly shrugged out of it, and then cursed when the dried blood made the fabric stick to his skin.

Olivia moved to help him, trying not to notice how freaking *good* he looked without a shirt on. The tattoos on his neck wound down, connecting with his sleeves and a giant mural over his left side, the ink only serving to accent a body that would have made her stop and take notice under any circumstances. Her fingers trailed down his chest as she finished unbuttoning his shirt, his skin almost hot to the touch. It was so strange that he'd been inside her but she hadn't touched him like this. She stopped when his stomach tensed beneath her touch. "Am I hurting you?"

"No, nothing like that."

She made herself stop stroking him and rocked back on her heels. "Right. Okay." The tattoos created such a strange contrast—the pretty boy and the multitude of artwork inked into his skin—that she wasn't sure what to think of him.

Hell, she hadn't been sure what to think of him from the start. Nothing he did was on par with what she expected. It was enough to make her head spin.

She pushed to her feet, needing some distance between them since the whole of a king-sized bed wasn't anywhere near enough. "Let me wet a washcloth and we'll see about cleaning you up, since a shower is out of the question." Doc Jones hadn't explicitly said that, but getting the bandages wet seemed like a pretty dumb idea.

"A sponge bath? Careful there, sweetheart—keep acting like that and I might actually start to think you like me."

"Yeah, yeah." She couldn't help a small smile as she ran the water until it was warm, and then wet the cloth. But her humor faded as she came back into the room, faced again with all that skin. *Just do it. Nurses do it all the time and it's not weird.* Sure, but she wasn't a nurse. She was a bartender who was having uncomfortable thoughts about a man who was injured.

Uncomfortable *sexy* thoughts.

Like the fact that they hadn't been this naked when they'd had sex. Or that just seeing him without his shirt was enough to have her reconsidering her promise to herself that it was a onetime thing.

Olivia debated how to go about it for half a second and then went to her knees in front of him. There were faint red tracks down his chest that had bled through his shirt, and his hair was matted on the one side. "Hold still." She ran the washcloth down his arm, figuring that was safe enough to start with. She bit her lip. She was sure she could feel the heat of his skin through the warm cloth. *I'm imagining things.*

What she wasn't imagining was how he tensed again the second she touched him. She froze. "Are you sure I'm not hurting you?"

He huffed out a laugh. "It's got nothing to do with hurt, sweetheart, and a whole lot to do with pleasure." Then he turned those dark eyes on her, and her breath caught in her throat. It didn't matter that he was walking wounded or that she wasn't even sure she liked this guy. He seemed to reach out and run his hands over her body without moving a single muscle. She tried to hold back a shiver and failed miserably. If he could do that with a look, what could he do if he actually touched her?

*Oh, right. You already know* exactly *what he can do if he touches you.*

*Bad idea. Really, really bad idea.*

It took far too much effort to break his gaze and go back to what she was doing. In an effort to distract herself, she said, "Tell me about your tattoos."

For a second, she thought he might not do it, but he sighed. "What you see is what you get."

Somehow, she doubted it. She focused on the ones wrapping his forearms. They were both pinups—an angel and a devil—but the angel was posed more like a porn star and the devil was downright demure. It made her smile despite everything. Things were rarely what they seemed to be, a truth that he apparently held as tightly as she did. Both women were framed by roses but, again, they weren't what she would have expected. They were the traditional colors—red for devil and white for angel—but the white roses were framed by deadly looking thorns, and the red were filled to the brim with green vines that were so lifelike, she reached out to run her finger along one.

The feeling of skin against skin, even so innocent a touch, was almost too much. She couldn't remember the last time she'd casually touched someone who wasn't Hadley. It had to have been Sergei, and that was more than a year ago. *A whole year.*

*That* had to be the reason she was reacting so strongly to this O'Malley. The reason she'd thrown caution to the wind and actually had sex with him. The reason she was having a seriously difficult time taking her hands off him.

*Focus.*

Right. Focus.

She took her hand back and went to work on his side. The tattoo there was massive, stretching from his shoulder over his chest and down his side to disappear into the band of his slacks. She paused. "A dragon." It was wrapped around a naked woman, but for the life of her she couldn't tell if it was protecting the woman or about to take a chunk out of her.

"Have you ever heard the story of Saint George?"

She glanced at him. "I'm not Catholic." The Romanov family was Eastern Orthodox, but she'd never been required to attend the Divine Liturgy and she hadn't felt the lack at all. What kind of church took money from people who were known criminals? A confession shouldn't be enough to absolve certain crimes. But as long as the funds kept flowing, no one said a single word. It was hypocrisy in the worst form as far as she was concerned.

"Saint George was a soldier for some Roman emperor or another, and was a pretty badass warrior. He decided that he didn't like the way the emperor was killing off every Christian he could get his hands on, so he told him so to his face."

She moved up his body to his chest, which held the head of the dragon—right next to a scar of what had to be a bullet wound. The scar didn't distort the tattoo, but it butted right up against the back of the dragon's head. "What happened?"

"Oh, he died. Torture and beheading."

She blinked. *Didn't expect that.* "Oh."

"Most of the saints went out in gruesome ways. Sometimes I wonder if it actually got them any extra cosmic points or if it was all for nothing." He gave himself a little shake. "But Saint George is my patron saint. Traditionally, the art depicting him shows him facing down a dragon to save a damsel in distress."

Olivia leaned back. There was no warrior in sight. "So where is he?"

"Not on me." He grinned unexpectedly. "See, the dragon typically represents the wickedness of the world, and I happen to be a big fan of wickedness—or at least I used to be. He's made up of the seven deadly sins."

He was? The scales of the beast were...She moved closer. There were scenes etched into his hide. Olivia silently counted them. Seven. His head was obviously lust, the depiction of the man and woman...and another woman...in a naked embrace so intricate it was a wonder she hadn't realized it was there before. "This artwork is amazing." Without thinking, she trailed her washcloth down to the woman. Olivia couldn't figure out if her face was frozen in fear or ecstasy. "And the woman?"

"She's supposed to be God's holy truth." From his smirk, he'd tweaked that meaning as well.

She went back up to his shoulder. The blood was almost gone now except for on Cillian's head, but she was hesitant to break this curiously intimate moment. *And maybe, just maybe, I'm prolonging the time I'm going to have to stop running my hands over his body.* "And what does your priest think about your interpretations of your patron saint?"

"Oh, I'm pretty sure he's resigned himself to my being fed to the fires of hell when I die." He shrugged. "But he never stops trying."

She finished with his neck and sat back on her heels. "I think your hair is going to have to wait until you can shower, so you'll have to talk to Doc Jones about that."

"Thanks." There it was again, that look that threatened to curl her toes. He reached out and took the washcloth from her and tossed it onto the nightstand. "I'm going to kiss you now."

She should object, move away, do something other than rest her hands on the top of his thighs and tilt her head up. *Stupid, stupid, stupid. Didn't the last few years teach you anything?* Apparently not, because she wanted Cillian to kiss her again, and she wanted him to kiss her *now*.

Truth be told, she wanted him to do a whole lot more than that.

Olivia licked her lips. "Okay."

His lips quirked up at the edges. "I can see I'm blowing your socks off. Let's see if I can do better." He cupped her face with one hand and then his mouth was on hers, soft and teasing, testing—nothing like the forceful kiss that started everything last night. She opened for him immediately, driven by the lightning dancing just beneath her skin. She wished she could blame it on being skin-starved, but the truth was that this man was doing more with a near-innocent kiss than Sergei had ever done with his entire body and hours at his disposal. *I am in so much trouble*.

Then Cillian's tongue stroked hers and she was lost. She gripped his thighs as he explored her mouth, giving herself permission to do some exploring of her own. He was all lean muscle, as if he'd been melted down and stuck in a forge, only to come out new. She ran her hands up his legs, stopping just short of his hips.

He took it from there. He ran his fingers through her hair and down her back, inching her closer until there was nothing more than a breath of distance between them. It would have been so damn easy to lean forward and touch him, pressing her body against his, but the separation was almost unbearably erotic. She shivered again, tilting her head back to give him better access.

She'd never been kissed like this, like she was something to be savored…valued. Like he had all the time in the world and he'd still never get enough.

Common sense tried to rear up and remind her that it was a goddamn kiss, not a lifetime commitment, but then his thumb feathered across the underside of her breast, and all rational reasoning flew right out the window.

He rested his forehead against hers, and groaned. "You're making it hard to be good, sweetheart."

*So don't be good.* She gritted her teeth to keep the words inside. If she started pressing now, it was a slippery slope to begging, and Olivia did not beg. So she closed her eyes and just took a second to enjoy the feeling of being wrapped up in him while maintaining some distance. Last night she'd pushed until she'd gotten her way. She could push tonight and he'd give in. She knew that in her bones.

But he was hurting, and going there with her might injure him further. She took a shuddering breath. "I understand."

"No, I don't think you do." He ran his hand down her side, slipping it beneath her shirt to rest on her hip. "I want you so bad it's killing me. But I'm not in a position to be able to take care of you how you deserve right now, with my head wound fucking me up." His thumbs traced circles on her skin. "And even if it wasn't…A few hours ago you were telling me that this wasn't what you want. When you change your mind for good—and you will—I want you to know you're not just coming down from an adrenaline high. You want me as much as I want you. It's not circumstantial."

*Oh*. That was the last thing she'd expected. She opened her eyes as he sat back. "It was just a quick fuck in an alley." A *really* outstanding fuck. Even if she'd been able to pretend last night was a freak thing…She couldn't do that now. Not when the chemistry was still sparking between them so hot, it was a wonder she didn't burn up with it.

"Sure it was." His low chuckle, so similar to the one he made last night before he was inside her, had her squirming.

It would have taken only the tiniest of pushes to take that kiss into the bed and lose themselves in each other. She was already poised on the brink and he'd barely done anything. Even now, it was a struggle to take her hands off his thighs and move away. She concentrated on stopping touching him. "Exactly. Nothing to write home to Mom about."

"Olivia."

She stopped backing away, her heartbeat picking up. "Yeah?"

"Let me take you out on a real date. It's obvious there's something between us. I don't know about you, but I sure as hell don't want to let it pass without exploring it."

Longing like nothing she'd ever known rose up inside her. *A real date.* She wanted to say yes, to put on a pretty dress and doll herself up and let Cillian take her somewhere nice. They'd spend the meal flirting and talking and then afterward, he'd kiss her again and, this time, there would be nothing standing in the way of taking things further.

Nothing except her past and his family.

*It's too big a risk, no matter how he makes you feel. Hell, the way he makes you feel only* adds *to the risk. This isn't some casual dicking around—this could be ruinous.*

"I can't." She stood. "I'm sorry."

"Can't or won't?"

*Both*. She walked to the nightstand where he'd tossed the washcloth, and picked it up, desperate for anything to distract her from the half-naked man watching her far too closely. "I have a whole lot of shit in my past that's just waiting to rise up and kick me in the face again, and you have…" She motioned in his direction. "Your life. Your family. Whatever you're running from. It would never work."

"I'm asking for a date, sweetheart—not a lifetime commitment."

Maybe, but there was nothing simple about her life right now, and she had a feeling he didn't know the meaning of the word, either. *I could lose myself in a man like this. That* was reason enough without everything else to stay the hell away from him. "It's not a good idea." No matter how much she suddenly wanted to say yes.

He gave her a long look. "Or maybe it's the best damn idea either of us has had. Life is too short, Olivia. Why not take your happiness where you can find it, even if it's not forever?"

She froze. When he put it like that… She'd been so busy running and trying to just survive that she hadn't taken a single thing for herself in longer than she could remember. Not until last night. What was one more night in the grand scheme of things? Even if it went well, he was right—it was one date. It wasn't like he was asking her to marry him.

*You're just looking for any excuse to say yes.* She unfolded and refolded the wet washcloth. "I don't know."

He didn't say anything else, just watched her with that heated look that made her want to cross over to him and crawl into his lap. She turned away, but it didn't help. She could *feel* him watching her, which made her think of that kiss...which led right back into imagining another kiss. More than a kiss.

*One night won't kill me. It might even give me the breathing room I desperately need.*

Flimsy excuse firmly in hand, she turned back to face him. "Okay. One date."

And she'd pray to the God she wasn't sure she believed in that she wasn't making a horrible mistake.

* * *

Sergei stood out on the street, looking up at Beacon Hill Hotel. He didn't like that his Olivia had taken the O'Malley there, and he liked it even less that she was still up there. When Dmitri sent him to Boston to keep an eye on her, he'd thought it was a reward, a chance to finally get close to her again. Now he wasn't so sure. It had been over a year since he could last call her *his* and mean it, but he still couldn't wrap his mind around the fact that she was walking into a hotel with that goddamn bastard.

He didn't like thinking about the possibility that his Olivia had turned into a whore.

His phone rang, a welcome distraction. Spending time thinking about what she was doing up there with that bastard made him want to march through the door and deal out the sort of pain he was known for.

He couldn't do that.

Dmitri didn't want Olivia to know he was watching her, and he'd be pissed if Sergei fucked up whatever plan he had going in that twisted head of his. "*Da?*"

"Where is she?"

Speak of the devil. Sergei might put the Romanov family

and its interests first, second, and last, but he still hadn't for-given the man for being the reason Olivia walked away. *He promised she'd be mine in the end. Remember that.* "She's with that O'Malley."

"I see." Dmitri sounded like he always did—cool and composed—but there was an underlying tension there. Apparently he didn't like that his little sister was going Irish any more than Sergei did.

"Do you want me to take care of it?" Sergei asked. He was the best at what he did and with good reason. No one fucked with him and his in New York. He'd worked his ass off to get that reputation and, if he sometimes enjoyed what it took to keep it...sue him. There was no shame in being proud that he was a man people thought twice about before crossing.

But this wasn't New York and he wasn't in charge here.

That didn't stop him from hoping that Dmitri would give him the go-ahead to fuck up the enemy who thought he could touch Sergei's woman.

Then Dmitri went and dashed all those hopes to hell. "No. You had your chance to deliver the message. Now your job is to watch her, and that's all I want done. No further contact, Sergei."

He clenched his jaw. Always with the orders when it came to Olivia. Everywhere else, Dmitri gave him plenty of freedom and trusted his judgment. If he'd done the same a year ago, Olivia would still be in Sergei's life and bed. "If you're sure—"

"I am." Just that. No explanation, but Dmitri never of-fered them. He was boss, and his word was law.

He was vulnerable to mistakes just like any other man, though. Sergei was sure this was one such mistake—just like the last time he'd gone head-to-head with the O'Malley family. If Dmitri had sent him to Boston six months ago to take care of business, they wouldn't be in their current clusterfuck. He would have handled things here just like he handled things at home, and that O'Malley bitch wouldn't have had a Halloran to run to.

But he couldn't say as much to his boss. If there was one thing Dmitri Romanov hated more than being disobeyed, it was being questioned. He had a plan, and he expected Sergei to fall in line and do what needed to be done without opening his mouth. "Got it."

"Call me if anything changes."

"Will do." His gaze flicked from one illuminated window to the next. Was she up there right now, sucking O'Malley cock? Or was she riding him, giving him the view of a god-damn lifetime? A sharp pain brought him back to himself. At some point, he'd pulled the knife from his pocket and engaged it, and begun running his finger along the edge. Sergei looked at the dark line of blood against his skin and imagined it was the man's throat.

When the time came that Dmitri was ready to get rid of the little shit, Sergei would be the first in line to get the job done.

# CHAPTER SEVEN

Stop pacing."

Olivia spun on her heel to face Cillian. Ever since agreeing to the date, she'd been full of nervous energy. It was all well and good to say yes to him, but the next few hours stretched out before them, and she wasn't sure what they were supposed to do to occupy themselves.

No, that was a lie.

She could come up with half a dozen solutions without even trying, all of which would probably reinjure his head. It didn't help that he sat on the bed, watching her have her little mental breakdown. She made an effort to stand still. "What do you do for fun?"

Cillian barked out a laugh that made her jump. He rubbed a hand over his face. "I'm sorry. That was unexpected."

Which only served to make her feel more awkward. Olivia threw up her hands. "I don't know how to do this."

"Do what?"

"This." She motioned between the two of them. "This isn't normal."

He laughed again, quieter this time. "What does normal look like?" When she balked, he held out his hand. "Sit down. You're making me twitchy with all the pacing. I'm not laughing at you. I'm laughing at the absurdity of this entire situation. So humor me and tell me what normal looks like."

She didn't know. That was the problem. Olivia wasn't sure she'd recognize normal if it hit her in the face. But she wasn't quite willing to share with Cillian exactly how messed up her childhood had been, outstanding chemistry or not. She inched closer to the bed and perched on the edge, but even with three feet between them, she felt like a lightning rod to his storm, full of vibrating energy and impending *boom*. She pulled at the edge of her T-shirt. "You know—we'd meet somewhere normal."

"We met at a bar."

"Most relationships don't start in a bar." She realized what she said and shoved to her feet. "Strike that. I didn't mean relationship. I just..." Not sure what she was trying to say, she charged on. "Maybe a coffee shop. You'd be behind me in line and say something witty, and I'd laugh and you'd spend the next ten minutes charming me until I gave you my number."

She was almost afraid to look at him and see his expression. His silence said it all. "That's stupid, isn't it?"

"No, not at all. It sounds nice."

Olivia faced him. "You're humoring me."

"Sit down." He waited for her to obey before he spoke again. "I'm not. It *does* sound nice." He carefully leaned back against the headboard. "So I charm your number out of you, huh? I must be pretty charming."

She shot him a look. "In this scenario, yes."

Cillian laughed. "Then I'd call you."

She edged over to sit on the other side of the mattress against the headboard. It was such a silly thing they were doing, but after how intense the rest of the night had been, maybe silly was exactly what they both needed. "A call instead of a text? I must have made an impression."

"More like I was determined to make the right impression. Texts are lazy, and you can't get a good read on someone that way. So I'd call."

She hadn't spent much time dating...well, ever, really...but even she knew that was different from the norm. "I'd think you were a freak for calling, but I'd answer because I was intrigued."

"We'd talk for a while, feeling each other out."

"More like me trying to figure out if you're a psycho."

He grinned. "Or that. I'd say all the things a normal guy would say. You'd be reassured that I wasn't likely to chloroform you and chain you up in my torture-slash-sex dungeon."

"That's...comforting."

"It would be, yes."

She laughed softly. "We'd set up a date at the end of the call."

"Somewhere nice and public and nonthreatening."

"Now you're getting the idea." She stared at the ceiling, part of her kind of weirded out at how well the conversation was flowing with him playing along. "Dinner, no movie. Movies are for people who are too intimidated by the thought of first-date conversation that they chicken out."

"The conversation would be titillating."

"You think so?" She rolled onto her side to face him, finding that he'd done the same. His bandage was a vivid reminder of why they were there in the first place. Olivia frowned. "How're you feeling?"

"That's not part of the game." He yawned. "So we'd drink pretentious wine that neither one of us liked and order things that we could barely pronounce and, at the end of it, we'd sheepishly admit that we didn't like either the drinks or the food, and we'd go find a food truck and laugh at ourselves."

It was an attractive picture he painted. Normal and kind of sweet and something she'd never have the option of doing. She made a face. "Instead, you wander into my bar because your family's territory encompasses it and we have a quick fuck in the alley." She should regret it. She knew she should. There were thousands of dating books and columns out there advising women to withhold sex until they had some sort of commitment.

Except she didn't regret a damn thing.

She'd seen what she wanted and she'd taken it. It might not have been the perfect version of events they were joking about right now, but there had been something empowering about it all the same.

"I like our way."

She smiled. "I kind of like our way, too. Simpler."

"Sweetheart, there's nothing simple about either of us, but it's pretty of you to say so."

She glanced at the clock. There were a good two hours left before she could safely leave him. She propped herself up on one elbow and grabbed the remote. "If I remember correctly, there's a *Justified* marathon going on right now. That should keep us occupied until morning."

"An artful dodge." He stretched carefully. "That's fine. Retreat. But don't forget that you already agreed to a date, and I fully plan on holding you to it."

As if she was in any danger of forgetting.

* * *

Cillian came out of the shower to find Olivia gone. He'd expected as much, though she hadn't said she was leaving. He sat on the bed and lay down to stare at the ceiling. What a crazy night. Getting his ass handed to him had been one thing, but everything that happened after almost made it worthwhile.

She'd said yes.

He sat up so fast the room spun around him, but the queasy feeling in his stomach was nothing to the crazy pounding in his chest. She'd agreed to go out with him. He grinned. Hell if that didn't add a silver lining to a seriously shitty night.

But he had things to take care of before he could even think about setting up a date to do Olivia justice. Their joking last night was just that—joking. He would never be that douche who took a date to some snotty, pretentious restaurant. Especially *this* date. She deserved a plan for something special.

But right now, his first priority had to be letting his family know where he was. It was tempting to just catch a cab home and slink up to his room while hoping no one noticed his newest fashion statement, but that was the coward's way out—something he would have done a year ago. Now it was time to face the music and deal with the consequences. He couldn't tell them it was Halloran men who'd attacked him, but he had to let them know he was attacked. He grabbed his phone. *Here goes nothing*.

Aiden picked up almost immediately. "Where are you?"

"I'm fine."

"Since you're calling me, I got that. So I'll ask again—where are you? I know you're fucking irresponsible sometimes, Cillian, but you missed a vital meeting this morning. Father's pissed."

He looked at the bedside clock and cursed. The Erickson meeting. He'd completely forgotten about it. "I'm sorry."

"Don't be sorry. Make sure it doesn't happen again. I don't care how things were when we were kids—I can't keep covering for your ass while you're out being a dipshit. It's time to step up like you've always said you would."

He gritted his teeth. "I understand. I need a car." He rattled off the hotel name and street.

Aiden cursed. "Goddamn it, Cillian. I hope she was worth it. You have our father to answer to."

It was damn near impossible to keep from snapping back, but a year ago, his brother's assumption that he'd blown off his responsibilities to party would have been right on the money. No one seemed to have noticed that he'd changed after Devlin's death, that he wasn't the same asshole who put himself before anyone else. But he understood. All of his siblings were so wrapped up in their own dramas and miseries, it was a wonder they realized he wasn't where he was supposed to be in the first place.

Their father...Time only seemed to be adding to the weight Seamus O'Malley carried—a weight Cillian had never recognized until he started carrying it himself. It didn't make the man any less of a bastard, but there was a level of understanding that had never been there before.

He took a deep breath. "Then I'll answer to him. Send the car." He hung up.

After using the bathroom, he stared in the mirror. One eye was blackened and, as he suspected, the bandage wrapping his head made him look like some soap opera trauma victim. "Sexy." It was a wonder that Olivia hadn't shoved his ass in a car and taken him to the hospital despite his arguments.

He owed her.

Hell, more than that, he actually liked her. He wanted to know more about her—about her past and her plans for the future. It might have started out because she was so different from any woman he'd met, but that superficial attraction wore off right around the time his head hit the brick wall.

When was the last time he'd had an actual connection with a woman?

He wasn't sure he ever had. Not really. There had been girlfriends in the past, but they were after the same thing he was—as much sex and booze and bad decisions that a person could manage on any given twenty-four-hour period. He'd always reasoned that he had to live it up because the shackle of family was going to snap around him eventually, but looking back, it was clear that he'd been running in the only way he knew how. If he drank himself stupid, he didn't have to think about how little freedom he really had—or what he might be asked to do once he was brought fully into the fold.

Well, he was there now. As the one running the

O'Malley finances, he now held secrets worth killing for, and hell if part of him didn't enjoy it. He liked working with the numbers and manipulating them to his family's benefit. He didn't even really have a problem with the fact that most of it wasn't strictly legal.

He just couldn't forget that it was familial politics that contributed to Devlin's death.

*That* was unforgivable.

The one thing he wasn't sure he could get past. Not that he had a choice.

He washed his face off as best he could and threw on his vest and jacket without bothering with the shirt underneath. It was ruined, and the bloodstained fabric would bring more attention than skipping it altogether. Once he was more or less presentable, he headed downstairs. This early, there was no one out and about—which was the reason they'd scheduled the Erickson meeting for this time. He was going to catch hell for missing it.

And rightfully so. He didn't have any business wandering into Jameson's last night in the first place when he knew there was an early morning meeting the next day. It didn't matter that he didn't drink anymore—the emotional hangover was almost worse than one driven by alcohol. He hadn't cared about that, though. He'd been too wrapped up in seeing Olivia again.

She was a distraction, and one he couldn't afford right now, but he wasn't about to let her go until they explored this thing between them. *Especially* since she'd actually agreed to a date.

Cillian walked outside as a black town car pulled up. The front window rolled down to show Liam. *Huh.* Apparently Aiden wasn't too pissed if he sent his most trusted muscle to scoop him up. Liam looked him up and down. "You're a mess."

Or maybe his brother just wanted to get the lectures started early. He sighed. "Rough night."

"So I see."

He started to get out, but Cillian waved him back into the car. "I can open my own door."

"From the look of you, I wouldn't trust you to wipe your ass by yourself today."

Considering how shitty he felt, he didn't blame the man. He just climbed into the backseat and did his best to relax. There would be questions, and he had to be prepared to answer them. His father would want to know why he'd gone to a hotel instead of back home, and if he didn't have a good reason, there would be even more hell to pay. He couldn't exactly say that he'd had an amazing woman playing nurse for him and he hadn't been willing to let that go.

All too soon, the car stopped on Chestnut, its familiar trees no more comforting now than they'd been since he was old enough to know what his fate held. *Christ, can you be any more melancholy? Your life is good—better than good. You always knew there were going to be sacrifices made and danger looming.*

Yeah, he just hadn't realized his brother would be the one to pay the price.

It was more than Devlin, though. Missing him was a near-constant ache, but it was nothing compared to the fear of something happening to another one of his siblings. He could comfort himself by saying Teague and Aiden knew the score, and even that Carrigan was no wilting flower. But Sloan and Keira? He didn't know if he could survive something happening to them. They weren't innocents—no one in the O'Malley family was—but they deserved better than to be a casualty of a war they weren't even allowed to fight in.

He climbed the steps to the front door and into the town house. It was eerily silent. He looked around. Nothing. So there was his choice—his father's office or his room to clean himself up a bit. Cillian looked down at himself. His suit was dark enough to cover up the blood spatter, but it still looked like he'd slept in it. Combined with his bandage... Yeah, Father wasn't going to be impressed.

The bedroom it was.

He started for the stairs just as heels clipped through the hallway. He froze, and that was all the time it took for his mother to come around the corner. She stopped short, her green eyes going wide in a rare show of surprise and then horror. "Cillian?"

"It's not as bad as it looks." It was exactly as bad as it looked.

She set aside the vase she was carrying and rushed over to him. "What happened? Does your father know?"

"I haven't seen him yet. There was a brawl down at the pub." He wasn't in love with the idea of perpetuating their belief that he was a worthless party boy, but it was better than the alternative. *They have enough reason to hate the Hallorans. I'm not going to give them one more—not when it might draw a line in the sand that Carrigan would be on the other side of.* "It's nothing—didn't even need stitches."

She moved around him, carefully poking and prodding until she was once again in front of him, her hand pressed against her mouth. It struck Cillian that Aileen O'Malley was getting old. Oh, she had years left of the beauty she was renowned for, but she suddenly seemed . . . fragile. He'd never thought of his mother as fragile before. There had always been something so iron-clad and unchangeable about her.

Except she'd gone and changed while he wasn't looking.

He tried for a smile. "It's really okay, Mother. Just a few punks with more beer in them than sense."

"You've got to be more careful. If anything happened to you . . ." She seemed to realize she was in danger of showing too much, because she straightened and threw her shoulders back. He'd seen his sister Carrigan make that exact move more often than he could count. Worried or not, they didn't make O'Malley women soft—at least not most of them. Aileen frowned. "Go get cleaned up before you talk to your father. He's not pleased."

No, he wouldn't be. Cillian nodded, wishing he could say something to comfort her, but anything that came out of his mouth right now would be a lie at best, and cold comfort at worst. "Will do." He started up the stairs, wanting to take them two at a time to get away from the uncomfortable realization that his mother was mortal.

"And Cillian?"

He stopped halfway up and turned to face her. "Yeah?"

"This has to stop." She pressed her lips together. "I can't have another—"

*Devlin.*

"I know. It will. This is the last time." But even as he said the words, he wasn't sure if he was telling the truth. He didn't exactly go looking for trouble, but that didn't stop trouble from finding him. And there was something about Olivia that screamed trouble. If he was smart, he'd send her a thank-you bouquet and leave well enough alone. Whatever was in her past had affected her deeply, and he wasn't without his own skeletons in his closet. Throwing the two of them together might not do anything, but he was too jaded to believe that. There would be fireworks—both good and bad.

He walked into his room and headed for his second shower of the day. Doc Jones be damned, he couldn't meet his father with his hair filthy with matted blood, and putting on the same dirty clothes after the last shower had negated its effects as far as he was concerned. He kept his head out of the direct spray as much as possible, but in the process of cleaning, he still managed to reopen the cut.

Cillian watched his blood circle the drain, letting the water beat against his back. He had to get his shit together. Now wasn't the time to let thoughts of Olivia and the pending date distract him. He'd screwed up with missing that meeting this morning, and he'd have to be held accountable. With a curse, he shut off the water and toweled off. It was a whole hell of a lot harder to wrap his head without help, but he managed. Barely. Once he was sure he wasn't dripping blood anymore, he went to his closet and got dressed slowly, piece by piece.

His clothing was just another indulgence, but one that had a purpose beyond spending insane amounts of money. Or at least it did now. Before, it was all surface value—he had the money, and spending it on clothes was fun. Now, he was all too aware of how people looked at him, summing him up based on his appearance. He didn't regret the tattoos, but the suit combated the instinctive judgment that some people had. How could he be a hooligan if he was wearing a ten-thousand-dollar three-piece suit?

*Just a mask.* He grimaced. Maybe, but it was a good mask. Putting on a suit made him feel like he was ready to face the world—like he was more than just a leaf being helplessly blown on someone else's wind. He finished buttoning up his vest—pinstriped blue to match the blue suit and gray dress shirt—and shrugged into his jacket. He was as ready as he was going to be.

Time to face the firing squad.

# CHAPTER EIGHT

Olivia managed a few hours of sleep while Hadley napped, but it was nowhere near enough. The only thing that got her through her day was the knowledge that she didn't have a shift for two days and could sleep through the night. To keep herself occupied, she went to work tidying up the apartment. It was old and there were some stains that were never coming out, but the smell of lemon cleaner never failed to make her feel more in control of her life.

Even if it was a joke.

Hadley toddled after her, and she handed over a clean rag. This was one of their day-off rituals. As she vacuumed, Hadley bounced around and ran the cloth over the walls and the television and pretty much every available surface she could reach. Then she went behind it with one of her sticky hands, leaving a trail. Olivia laughed and shook her head. There would be a day coming at some point where she'd have to force her daughter to help clean, so she always

focused on enjoying every moment she could of this innocence and fun.

That parental indulgence had never been a part of her life
growing up. Andrei barely acknowledged she existed until
she was around grade-school age, and her mother was even
worse in some ways. She wielded guilt like it was a bladed
weapon, a picture-perfect phantom of a woman who drifted
in and out of Olivia's life at the most inopportune of times.
Olivia would get to the point where she was *sure* she was
over wanting her mother to love her as more than a failed
bargaining chip to force Andrei to leave his wife and marry
her... And then her mother would deliver a few well-placed
barbs and she'd be a mess of emotion all over again. She'd
taken to avoiding the woman when she was all of ten, which
worked more often than not because her mother didn't like
seeing evidence of Olivia's existence any more than Olivia
liked seeing the woman responsible for bringing her into the
world.

She would never do that to Hadley. Her daughter might
not have been planned, but damn it, she *would* be loved.

Her phone rang three times during the course of the afternoon—all from Sergei—and she didn't answer it once.
Whatever he wanted, he could wait. She wasn't exactly riding high after her night with Cillian, but she felt a definite
buoyancy that made her turn up the music as she cleaned
and swing her laughing daughter around the room. She
wasn't ready to give up the rare good mood. Not yet.

"Mama! Again!"

She grinned and flipped the song back to restart. "My
baby girl likes LMFAO? I always knew you had great taste."
She wiggled in an exaggerated way that made Hadley let
loose a string of infectious toddler giggles. God, she loved

that sound. She spun a circle and dipped into the water-filled sink to grab a clean plate to dry next. The apartment didn't have a dishwasher, which wasn't terrible since there was only the two of them, but there were days when she felt the lack.

The phone rang again, and Hadley toddled over to it. "Wait!" But it was too late. Her toddler pressed the green button, answering it. Olivia dove for the phone, scaring Hadley in the process. Her daughter instantly started crying, but she couldn't do a damn thing about it right now. "Hello?" She slapped off the radio. "I'm sorry, I can't hear you."

"Olivia."

Her heart damn near stopped at the silky Russian voice coming through the line. She took the phone away from her ear and glanced at it. Yep, Sergei's number. It shouldn't surprise her that Dmitri used his favorite minion's phone to make this call—he wouldn't want any more strings connecting them than strictly necessary. *Why is he calling now?*

She took a shaky breath and tried to kill the panic creeping up inside her. "Dmitri." No need to ask what he wanted—he'd get around to telling her when he was damn well good and ready.

"I hear you've been making new friends."

She closed her eyes. *Cillian.* That had to be who he was talking about—he was the only thing that had changed about her life in the last week—but that didn't mean she was going to roll over and play dead. "New city, new friends. You know how it goes."

"Hardly." A pause in which she could perfectly picture him narrowing his eyes. "You haven't accessed the money I wired into your account."

She didn't ask how he knew that. New York might not be the Romanovs' in total, but enough people owed him allegiance that it wasn't surprising he had someone at her bank. What she didn't get was why he cared so much. She couldn't ask him. No one asked Dmitri Romanov a damn thing. "I don't want the money. I don't want the strings that come with it, either."

"Life rarely cares about individual wants. I'm surprised you haven't learned that by now."

She had. That was the problem. She hadn't asked to be born as Andrei Romanov's bastard daughter, and she sure as hell hadn't wanted his sudden change of heart. In a world where family was everything, she'd grown up as a barely tolerated individual within the realm of the Romanovs. It had sucked, but at least she knew she couldn't rely on anyone else but herself. To have Andrei suddenly decide that he wanted her to actually *be* a Romanov... No fucking way.

She rubbed the bridge of her nose, trying to ignore Hadley's wails. "If the money is so important to you, take it back."

"You know it's not about the money."

If it was, she might have just taken it. Maybe. Olivia leaned against the counter. If she could just get through to Dmitri, there was a chance he'd leave her alone. "I don't want to be a Romanov. That was never my place, and Andrei deciding it before he died doesn't change that."

He paused. "I gave him my word, Olivia."

*Damn you, Andrei. You didn't have time for me during your life. Was this just one final "fuck you" before you took that one-way trip to hell?* She closed her eyes, violating her determination to wait him out. "What do you want, Dmitri?"

His voice went hard. "Next time Sergei calls, you answer without hesitation. Is that understood?"

That wasn't an answer, but it was clear that he didn't really care about giving her one. Big surprise there. "You don't own me."

"On the contrary, I own everything about you. Your freedom is a luxury that *I* allow. If I choose to, I can snatch it back, and there isn't a single thing you can do about it. And your daughter..."

She gripped her phone so hard, it was a wonder it didn't shatter. "You can fuck with me all you want. I'm an adult. I can handle it. You come near Hadley, and I'll kill you myself."

He tsked. "You know better."

"This isn't about blood and this isn't about family. I don't owe your father a damn thing. He was nothing more than a sperm donor, which is a half step less than my mother was. You don't want me in New York, and I sure as hell don't want to be there. I don't care if you gave your word. Just let me go, Dmitri." *Please*. She didn't beg, though it was a close thing. The only thing that kept that final word on the right side of her lips was the knowledge that he'd capitalize on any weakness she showed.

"You know I can't do that." And hell if he didn't sound downright regretful. The worst part was that she didn't know if it was an act or if he was genuinely sorry he had to play these games.

*It doesn't matter. Either way, both Hadley and I lose.*

She opened her eyes. "Good-bye, Dmitri."

"Answer when he calls, Olivia. If you force my hand, you won't like the results."

She hung up without responding and set the phone on

the counter, her entire body shaking. Hadley immediately was there, her chubby arms raised, her face tear-stained. "Up, up."

"I got you, baby girl." She scooped her daughter into her arms and held her close, inhaling the scent of baby powder and clean toddler. Her entire life revolved around making the best life for Hadley that she could, and Dmitri thought he could threaten that...

Over her dead body.

*What if it comes to that? He'll kill me. He wouldn't even hesitate.*

It would leave Hadley even more adrift than Olivia had been growing up. Her mother had always been distant enough that she was little more than a stranger, wrapped up in the affair with Andrei, her owner and boss, all in one neat package. When Olivia found out she was pregnant—after several months of panic attacks—she'd promised herself that she'd never leave her baby alone in the world like both her parents had left her, albeit in different ways. No matter what it took, she'd be there.

Which meant she had to play by Dmitri's rules.

No matter how much she hated them.

*It's just a phone call here and there. Nothing crazy.*

She knew better. The request might sound simple enough on the surface, but her half brother did nothing without reason. Hadley cuddled up against her, and she rested her chin on her daughter's head. *What am I going to do?* Running sounded really great right about now—as far and as fast as she could—but it wasn't really an option. Dmitri had resources beyond what she could dream up, and besides that, she didn't have the funds to truly disappear without a trace.

*Not unless I tap into that goddam money.*

No. There had to be another way. Yes, Dmitri wanted something from her, but he was still talking. That meant she had time. Hopefully.

Hadley had quieted and gave one last pathetic super-fake sob. Olivia grinned despite herself. Her daughter had been a drama queen from birth, and that didn't look to be changing anytime soon. "It'll be okay, baby girl. I'll take care of both of us."

She just wished she knew what her half brother was up to.

\* \* \*

Cillian worked through the reports in front of him for the fourth time, and came up with the wrong answer again. "Something's off." He'd been working on getting things organized in an attempt to digitize their accounts. They were long overdue for a dose of technology, but Bartholomew was a purist at heart and had a borderline-paranoid distrust of all things computer related. Over the last six months, Cillian had spent every moment he wasn't with the old man working on a program Devlin had created that would encrypt their files digitally—once they were uploaded.

Now the only thing left was to wade through a couple decades' worth of accounts and do just that.

"Or maybe you're just hungover and shitty at math."

He glanced at his older brother sitting behind the desk on the other side of the room. Aiden had conveyed his annoyance for the last few hours by giving Cillian the silent treatment. Not that he minded. He had a wicked headache, and the last thing he wanted was yet another lecture on how irresponsible he was. The subject had already been ex-hausted between their parents.

He ran his finger down the math he'd gone through, barely resisting the urge to add it up one more time, and sat back. "It's not my math that's the problem. It's the numbers. They aren't adding up."

Aiden frowned. "Which numbers?"

At least he had his brother's full attention now. "Local. They each pay out fifteen percent, right? Except by these numbers, they're only passing over twelve. It's not a huge discrepancy, but across all the business, it starts to add up."

"That doesn't make any sense." Aiden stood and walked around to look over his shoulder. "Why would they be un-dercutting us? Do you think it's just bad bookkeeping?"

"No." He shifted the papers around until he found his list. "I could chalk one up to that—even three. But we're talking nearly every single business owing us loyalty in the Financial District. That's too many to write off as coinci-dence." He didn't know what it meant, but just seeing the list of places made the small hairs on the back of his neck stand at attention.

"Hmm." Aiden rubbed a hand over his mouth, his frown deepening. "Do you think it's Halloran?"

He almost reached up to touch the cut on his head, but managed to abort the move before it started. "I wouldn't necessarily rule it out, but I doubt it. Carrigan—"

"Don't."

*Jesus Christ.* She wasn't dead, no matter what their fa-ther liked to preach on the rare occasions when one of their siblings brought her up. Of them all, Cillian would have thought his older brother wouldn't stand to let her go com-pletely. She'd always been closest with Teague and Aiden, and it felt like yet another betrayal that Aiden was dancing to the tune their father set. Not surprising, but disappointing in a huge way.

Well, he wasn't going to dance. "It's not like saying her name three times is going to bring her crashing through the wall like the Kool-Aid Man."

Aiden clenched his jaw. "She betrayed our family."

"If that's what you want to call it." Cillian didn't chafe at the bounds as much as some of his siblings, but this was getting ridiculous. "The whole arranged-marriage thing is tired, don't you think? You can't blame her for ditching the Russian and going with her heart."

"Even if her heart led her to James Halloran?"

He looked away. *Those wounds are never going to close, not when we keep ripping them open to prove a point.* "I don't like it any more than you do. But she's still family, no matter what Father says."

"No, Cillian. She's not. She's a Halloran now." Aiden walked back to his desk and sank into the chair. "Don't bring her up again."

Fat chance of that happening. "My point is that James has been quiet these last few months. He's occupied with her and keeping control of their people. The only reason you even brought him up in the first place was because you're still pissed she chose him."

"That's not it."

Yes, it was. For whatever reason, Aiden took Carrigan's choice almost personally. Since Cillian knew for a fact his brother hadn't been thrilled with the Russian either, he didn't get it.

Damn it, that wasn't the truth. He understood it far too well. James Halloran might not have been the one who gave the order that resulted in Devlin's death, but he was still part of the family who did. That might not be enough to totally condemn him, but it didn't exactly win him any points, either. Cillian still had a hell of a time wrapping his mind around the fact that Carrigan had gone and fallen for *him* of all people.

But it was her choice. He respected it, even if he didn't understand it.

He leaned back, stretching his arms over his head. "If not Halloran, then who? We both know it's not the Sheridans." Teague and Callie might not share all their secrets these days, but they were allies. *That*, at least, he was sure of.

"I don't know."

The words settled between them, and the feeling of danger only got worse. Cillian straightened. "Well, we need to find out what's going on." It had to be a precursor to something else—something worse—but hell if he could figure out what it was. Even if all the businesses chose to revolt and throw a fit, there were other ways to do it. Better ways. Three percent was just…insulting.

It didn't make any sense.

"*I* will find out what's going on. *You* are going to stay out of trouble."

It was like his brother was talking to a child. Protesting that he hadn't gone looking for trouble just sounded like he was making excuses, which undermined his whole point. Pointing out that he'd danced to whatever tune Aiden and their father set wouldn't help, either. So Cillian sat there and glared—and felt childish for doing even that. "I can help."

"You found the discrepancy. That's helping." Aiden shrugged into his jacket and stood. "There's a family dinner tomorrow, and you're expected to be there."

"Wouldn't miss it for the world." It seemed like the only time he got to see all his siblings—Carrigan excluded, of course—was during the obligatory family dinner these days.

Aiden snorted and left the office. Cillian set his list aside and got back to work. Now that he'd brought all the accounts up to date for this week, it was time to go over the notes from the meeting he'd missed this morning. He rifled through the pages his brother had left him, cursing under his breath when he realized they were missing some seriously vital information. "Goddamn it."

"Problems?"

He glanced up to find Sloan standing on the other side of the desk. He knew she could be quiet when she wanted to, but he hadn't even heard her come in. "Hey, squirt. How's it hanging?"

She took the seat across from him and pulled her legs up to rest her chin on her knees. His little sister always seemed to do that—find a position to take up as little space as physically possible. She didn't look too great, either. She'd always been thin, but she was almost gaunt these days, her dark eyes huge on her face. It made him want to drag her down to the kitchen and make her a sandwich—except he knew it wouldn't really solve anything in the long term.

Still...

Cillian stood. "I missed lunch. Come on."

"If you insist." Her sigh was almost silent, but he caught it all the same. "What happened to your head?"

At least she asked him instead of just accusing him of brawling like everyone else had. He wrapped an arm around her shoulders as they walked down the hall toward the kitchen at the back of the house. "Oh, you know me, always leading with my head."

"Don't tell me you ran into a door."

He was about to make a joke, but the tight way she held herself stopped him. She was genuinely worried, and fuck if that didn't make him feel even worse than his parents and Aiden combined. "It was a wrong-place, wrong-time kind of thing. I know it doesn't help, but I wasn't out looking for trouble."

"Are you sure?"

He stopped short, and she made it another three steps before he caught up to her. "What kind of question is that?"

"I'm not blind, Cillian. Everyone else might be occupied with their own issues, but I've noticed that you come and go at all hours of the night, and most of the time it's on foot. It doesn't take a genius to connect the dots—you're out trolling for trouble." Her gaze rested on his bandage. "It looks like you finally found it last night."

"That's not fair."

She shrugged. "Maybe not. But I'm right, aren't I?"

Yeah, she was. Or she had been. He'd been a ship without an anchor, drifting wherever the current took him, until it was only a matter of time before he wrecked himself on the rocks. But things were different now. As cliché as it was, last night with Olivia had shifted things for him. He wasn't magically okay or any bullshit like that, but he felt like he had part of a purpose for the first time in over a year.

If he told anyone else in his family that, they'd laugh him out of the room. Sloan, though . . . Sloan might actually listen. "I met a girl, squirt."

"A girl." If anything, her voice went even flatter.

"Well, a woman." He pushed open the door to the

kitchen and held it for her. "She wouldn't give me the time of day. Not that I blame her."

"I can't decide if that makes her smart or a fool."

"Sit down." He waited for her to do so before he went to raid the fridge. Their cook usually left the makings for snacks tucked away in case any of them got hungry between meals. He opened the bottom drawer. Sure enough, there were three different kinds of deli meat and the good sliced cheese that had probably actually seen a cow at some point. *Perfect*.

He brought it all out and set it across from Sloan. "Turkey, ham, or beef?"

"I'm not hungry."

Yeah, he just bet she wasn't. He put on a stern face. "Well, I am, and you know Mother would smack me if I ate in front of you without making you one, too."

Some humor appeared in Sloan's eyes. "You must be thinking of someone else. Our mother doesn't lower herself to smacking."

"You're right. She'd just level one of *those* looks at us." He shuddered, putting a little extra shake into it for her benefit. "Don't throw me to the wolves, squirt. Let me make you a sandwich."

She sighed. "If you're going to insist, I'll take a turkey. No mayo, please."

"I remember." Ever since she was a child, his sister hadn't been a fan of condiments. He could understand some of the aversion—too much mayo was fucking disgusting—but she didn't even eat ketchup.

She waited until he had the bread laid out before she spoke again. "So . . . this girl. Tell me about her."

"She's about your age, I think, and she's a bartender

down at Jameson's." He slathered mustard onto one side of his bread. "She's got a kid. And a past, if I'm not wrong."

"You're joking."

"What?"

"A single mother? *Really*?"

He tried and failed not to be insulted by the shock in her voice. "What's wrong with a single mother?"

"Nothing." Sloan crossed her arms over her chest, her shoulders hunching even as she met his gaze. "But you're ... you. You have a history of dating blondes with bigger chests than brains—and that's if what you do could even be called dating."

She was right, but that didn't take the sting out of it. He carefully placed the meat on the bread, not looking at her. He'd known what his family thought of the way he'd gone about his life, and he'd never cared before. Now he did. He wasn't sure when that switch had been flipped, but he didn't like it. "I'm nowhere near as worthless as everyone seems to think, you know."

"Oh, Cillian, that wasn't what I meant at all. It's just that you like your freedom and you like to party, and it doesn't seem like a single mom worth her salt has much time for either of those things."

Another point to Sloan. He sighed and finished putting the sandwiches together. "It's just a date, squirt."

It didn't matter if no one had faith in him and his ability to be a responsible goddamn adult. He liked Olivia. She obviously felt that same connection. The rest would fall into place as they went. It was pointless to worry too much about it when there was so much unsaid between them. She knew what family he was a part of, and he got the feeling that she knew exactly what that meant, but they hadn't gotten into the dirty details. And she had a past that she'd obviously moved to escape.

Nothing was simple in life.

He'd known that since he was a kid, but the last year had really solidified that truth. In a perfect world they would have avoided war in Boston without any personal casualties—and if someone went out, it sure as hell wouldn't have been Devlin. And the fact that his older sister was with a man she was totally and completely in love with would have been a *good* thing, rather than something that got her banished from their family.

But that wasn't the world he lived in. He could only do what it took to make the best of things in this reality. For Cillian, that meant spending more time with Olivia and seeing if this thing with her would be ... Well, hell, he wasn't sure. *Something.*

He pushed Sloan's plate over to her. "It'll all work out. Just you wait and see."

# CHAPTER NINE

Two days passed, and then three. By the time the fifth day slipped by without seeing or hearing from Cillian, Olivia had convinced herself that their whole night together was a fever dream brought on by his head injury and her exhaustion. It didn't help her feel less hurt by his rejection—because, really, what else could she call him avoiding Jameson's as well as her?—but it was better than nothing.

And what if he wasn't avoiding her? Head wounds were tricky beasts, even under the best of circumstances. He'd seemed okay when she'd left the hotel that morning, but what if something happened in the meantime? She could have left him to die, and the only way she'd know about it was hearing a news report—which was why she'd been spending a truly unhealthy amount of time searching the local news outlets for anything about deaths with corresponding head injuries. It wasn't a perfect way to go about things, and knowing that only made her stress out worse.

"Why the long face, pretty girl?"

She grimaced and passed a beer to the guy across the bar. "Gas."

He jerked back, nearly knocking over the guy next to him. "Jesus. Sorry I asked."

It was too easy. Like shooting fish in a barrel. *That*, at least, she found some pleasure in. The men who came through this place were nothing to her, and for whatever reason, her pissy attitude had made her tips nearly double this week. It would almost be enough to change her mood if she didn't think about how worried she was about Cillian. It didn't help that Benji kept sending her worried looks.

She grabbed a rag to wipe down a spill. "I'm fine."

"I didn't say a word." He measured three different liquors into a shaker.

"You didn't have to. It's written all over your face." She wasn't sure why she was pressing this, let alone with her boss, but the need to talk to *someone* about what had gone down was nearly overwhelming. It didn't make sense. She wasn't a sharer. She'd been blown off before, and hadn't lost a second of sleep over it. But then she met that trouble-maker O'Malley, and now she was losing her damn mind.

Benji poured two martinis and passed them over to a pair of women chatting about their week at work. Then he turned to face her. "Do you want to talk about it?"

If she didn't, she might just explode. *I am so pathetic.* "The other night when I was taking out the trash and closing up, I caught two assholes beating the crap out of Cillian O'Malley."

His mouth tightened. "You need to stay out of those kinds of conflicts. I don't want you getting hurt." He held up a hand at an impatiently waiting customer without looking over. "You're tough, Olivia, but this is a whole different ball game from what you're used to."

That was the problem. It wasn't. She'd grown up around the casual violence and threats that came from underground crime, even if she'd been on the outskirts for the most part. It wasn't seeing those two guys beating Cillian up that spooked her so bad.

It was that she'd walked away from that night with all her convictions about the man questioned.

"It was fine. I scared them off with your trusty shotgun."

"This time." He took the order from the impatient guy and grabbed two Buds from the fridge below the bar. After the guy paid, Benji turned back to her. "Next time you might not be so lucky. You know what they say about heat waves—they bring out the crazy in people. That goes double for anyone under the umbrella of O'Malley, Sheridan, or Halloran."

How had this turned into him telling her to back off? She propped her hands on her hips. "I can take care of myself."

"These aren't common street thugs—not in this part of town, and not giving a beating to an O'Malley. Whoever it was won't forget that you intervened, and some of the families around these parts can have a long memory. If you're not careful, you might turn down a street one night and find yourself in more trouble than you can handle."

The sad thing was that if that ever happened, it wouldn't be a Boston family threatening her. It would be the Romanovs. She couldn't say that to Benji without explaining her past, though, and she wasn't willing to go there. Not tonight. Probably not ever. "I've got it covered. I promise. That wasn't even what was bothering me in the first place."

He frowned. "Then what's the problem?"

"I patched Cillian up and made sure he was okay and..." God, why was she even talking about this? She wasn't some high school girl with a crush. She'd already seen how that kind of thing worked out—with her in over her head and knocked up by a man who would never love her like she desperately needed. Olivia took a deep breath. "Never mind. It's not even worth talking about."

"Boy got under your skin, didn't he?"

Of course Benji saw through her. One didn't end up as a bartender as long as he'd been and *not* know how to read people. "Pretty much. It doesn't make any sense. He's so..." Gorgeous and broken and kissable.

"That boy has seen some things." Benji hand washed a few glasses, his gaze on the room. "A year ago, I'd tell you to steer clear of Cillian O'Malley—not that you'd need the advice. That boy was trouble personified, and he had no little liking for the ladies. That's all changed now, but you should still steer clear of him because of what family he was born into. He might mean well, but meaning well doesn't count for shit."

That's what she was afraid of.

"Benji, you're an awful friend. The first rule of being a wingman is that you don't warn the beautiful woman away from me."

Olivia turned, half-sure she'd misheard, but there he was. Cillian sat on the other side of the bar, every hair in place and almost masking the still-healing gash on the side of his head, a casual grin on his face, looking like he hadn't been beaten all to hell just a week before.

Like he hadn't completely blown her off since.

She pasted a neutral expression on her face, but from his expression, it wasn't all that neutral. "Can I get you something?"

"Your number."

*Good lord.* "Thanks, but I like to reserve my time for people who actually make time for *me*."

"I'm sorry, sweetheart. It took me longer to bounce back than I expected." He even looked sorry, like he regretted the absence as much as she had.

Her anger wavered, but she held on to it with both hands. *Being with him would always be like this—always me on a need-to-know basis and worrying my idiot self over him.* "It's fine."

"I may not be a genius, but even I know when a woman says *that* it means anything but." He looked at Benji. "How pissed is she right now?"

"*She* is standing right here."

Benji raised his hands. "I'm staying out of it. Olivia, holler if you need something." Then the coward fled.

She crossed her arms over her chest. "You're batting a thousand tonight, just like normal." Except for that single night last week when he'd been downright human. More than that, he'd been a person she actually understood on some level and wanted to know more about. Now he had his pretty boy facade firmly back in place, and his charm grated on her like sandpaper beneath her skin. It was a slap in the face after how worried she'd been about him. "Apple juice?"

"Please." He watched her grab a glass and pour the drink. "If it helps, I'm sorry I was gone so long. Things on the home front got away from me, and I had to take care of them before I could get back in here."

He was probably telling the truth, but that didn't really change anything. The fact of the matter was that she'd been right before—no matter how connected she'd felt to him

during that night, he wasn't all that different from Sergei—
or every other man in her life up to this point. He would always put his family obligations before her.

She couldn't go through that again. She *refused* to.

And to drag Hadley along with her? Unthinkable.

She passed the apple juice over. "Chalk my accepting
your offer up to temporary insanity. I'm not going out with
you."

"Olivia—"

"That'll be three-fifty."

He sighed. "I thought we'd gotten past this."

Hell, she'd thought so, too. But that night was a mistake,
and a mistake she didn't plan on repeating. No matter how
delicious he looked tonight in that three-piece suit. Who the
hell wore a three-piece suit to a pub?

*You're being petty and you damn well know it.*

*So what? I'm entitled to being petty.*

She really needed to stop having crazy-woman conversations with herself. At this point, she was a few short steps
from buying ten cats and holing up in her crappy apartment
with Hadley while they waited for the end of the world.

"I'd like to talk."

She shook herself out of her insanity spiral. "There's
really nothing to talk about." She hesitated. "I am glad
you're doing better, though."

"There you go again, making me think you might actually like me." His smile was wan. "A drink, sweetheart.
That's all I'm asking for."

It wasn't, though. Because it wouldn't stop with a drink.
She'd get drawn in by the chemistry that was *still* sparking
between them and, next thing she knew, she'd be crawling
into his lap and getting into all sorts of trouble. Olivia knew

herself well enough to know that. There was something about Cillian that was like catnip. Common sense didn't have a hold there.

Which was exactly why she needed to keep him at a distance. "No, thank you." A girl a few feet down the bar caught her eye and she moved away to fill that drink order, but she could feel Cillian watching her the entire time. It made her skin hot and tingly and, holy hell, it made her *want*.

Having sex with him had been a mistake. After over a year of celibacy, she should have known there was no way to keep her neat little boundaries in place, no matter how sure she was that she didn't particularly like Cillian. *That* was why she was responding so strongly to him. It had to be.

She turned around and nearly ran into Benji. He stopped her from mowing him over—or, more likely, bouncing off his chest—with his hands on her shoulders. "Whoa, there. You look a little out of it. Why don't you take a break?"

Taking a break would just give her more time to think, which was exactly what she didn't need. She was about to tell him that, but the girl behind her squawked. "This isn't a Cosmo! I ordered a Cosmo!"

Well, hell, there went all her arguments that she was fine. She *never* screwed up orders. Olivia glanced at the drink in the girl's hand, but she couldn't figure out what it was that she'd actually made. *Shit*. She forced a smile. "I think a break is a great idea." *Some air. I just need some air.* "I'll be back in ten."

"Make it fifteen." He softened the command with a smile. "You work hard, Olivia. Sit down and take a breather. I can hold down the fort."

Of course he could. He'd been doing it for years. She managed something closer to a real smile. "You're a good guy, Benji."

"Don't go saying that where people can hear you." He gave her a nudge. "Go on."

She went.

As soon as she stepped out into the cool night—a welcome relief from the heat wave that had hit during the last few days—she tilted her head back and took what felt like her first deep breath in a week. Cillian wasn't dead on the street or something equally awful. He was okay—an ass, but okay. *Great, now that you know that, you can move on with your life.*

Easier said than done.

"Olivia."

She turned; a secret part of herself that she'd never admit existed was simply thrilled at the sight of him. Cillian had cut quite the figure with his tattoos and expensive clothing every time they'd met, but knowing the meaning of those tattoos—and how extensive they were beneath his clothing—only made him more attractive. It really wasn't fair. She drank in the sight of him like a woman in the desert who finally caught sight of an oasis, not sure when she'd be able to do it again.

*You're putting distance between you two, remember?* Distance. "You shouldn't be back here."

"Neither should you." He glanced at the spot where he'd been beaten. "I would have thought that would go without saying."

"I can take care of myself." Maybe if she said it enough times, the men around her would start believing it. She almost snorted. *Unlikely.*

"And you can take care of me, too." He grinned, quick and easy, and she almost found herself grinning back.

It was an effort to keep any warmth from her voice. "What are you doing here?"

"Well." He moved closer, almost within touching distance. "If you won't go out with me, I thought we could talk out here." Something must have shown on her face, because he took another step. "I should have called. I'm sorry."

She caught herself staring at his mouth and jerked her gaze up to his eyes. "Really, I should thank you for dropping the ball so effectively. I needed the reminder." She took a tiny step back. "Now, please go. You're ruining my break."

"Do you really want me to leave?"

*No.* "Cillian..." Before she could think better of it, she grabbed his tie and hauled him the last step forward and against her. She went up on her tiptoes and kissed him. Instantly, his arms came around her, and one hand cradled the back of her head while the other yanked her even closer. He took charge of the kiss before she could process the sheer bliss of having so much of him pressed against so much of her.

He teased open her mouth, any hesitance gone as his tongue stroked hers. It wasn't the same kind of kiss that they'd shared in the hotel room. No, this was down and dirty and had her flashing back to the night in the alley, her legs around his waist and his cock buried deep inside her.

She arched against him, needing to be closer, needing to feel skin against skin. *This is such a bad idea.* She didn't care. She didn't want to think about anything except the next second and his mouth on hers. He backed her up two steps and pressed her against the brick wall. The cold provided a shocking counterpoint of the heat of him at her front, which only made her want him more. She rolled her hips, moaning when she encountered his hard length.

Before she had a chance to really enjoy it, he spun her around, forcing her to catch herself on the wall. "You are so damn determined to drive me out of my mind." He sounded as frustrated as she felt. "I'm trying to do this the right way, but that isn't what you want, is it?"

The only thing she wanted right now was exactly what he was giving her, his body against hers, his erection pressing against the small of her back. She shook her head, trying to clear it. "I'm not going to date you." *I shouldn't be doing* this. *Not here, not like this.* She felt like she was on a roller coaster, tipping over the edge of the first drop, past the point of no return.

And she didn't want to stop.

"You want me."

She used her leverage on the wall to roll her ass against him. "I want you."

"Fuck." His mouth came down on the back of her neck, the move somewhere between a bite and a kiss. "And if I shoved down that ridiculous excuse for shorts and took you right here, you'd love every fucking second of it. But you won't go out for one drink with me." His hand moved across her stomach, stopping at the top button of her shorts.

*Oh my God, is this really happening?*

She could stop it with a word...but that wasn't what she craved. No, what she wanted was exactly what his angry words were promising. She pushed back against him, silently demanding more. "Sounds about right."

"No."

She blinked, trying to focus through the haze wrapped around her mind. "What?"

"I'm not doing this again." He undid the button, and dipped his hand into her shorts, bypassing her panties and pushing a finger into her. "So goddamn wet for a man you're not even sure you like."

She rolled her hips, trying to take him deeper, but the damn shorts prevented it. "*Cillian*."

He kept kissing her neck as he pushed another finger into her. "No, sweetheart. I was down for exactly what you offered last time—a no-strings-attached quickie—but that's not what I want this time. Not now. Not like this." He pushed her shorts partially off her hips, giving himself some more freedom to move. "I like you, Olivia." His words were so soft compared to the harsh way he fucked her with his fingers. "I want to get to know you."

She was strung so tight, it was a wonder she didn't burst into a million pieces. He was here saying things she wasn't sure she wanted to hear while doing things that she most definitely *did* want him to do. "Cillian, please."

"You want to come?"

Her breath sobbed out. "I might die if I don't."

"Good." He stopped moving, his fingers still inside her, his breath heavy against her neck. "That's about how I feel right now."

She tried to focus, but he withdrew, sliding his fingers over her clit in a torturously slow movement. "Wait—"

"I'm not a toy you can just pick up when it suits you." He kissed the back of her neck again. "I'm sorry about the last week. It was a fucked-up situation, and you're entitled to be pissed. But you can't tell me to get lost and then practically jump me the second we're alone. It doesn't work like that."

He was seriously stopping this. She wasn't sure if she should throw something or cry. Olivia tried to keep her chin up as she turned around, her body sparking from the lack of distance between them and the denied pleasure that was so acute it actually hurt. "You're a bastard."

"Probably. But I'm the only one willing to say what you won't." He was still too close, his breath coming as fast as hers, his cock making a tent of the front of his pants.

"You want me. I don't...I don't understand." Any other guy would have taken what she offered, no questions asked. He *had* taken what she offered once before. Now here he was, riling her up and then backing down unless she agreed to go out with him. "This is blackmail."

"No, sweetheart. This is respect. I want more than sex, and I don't know how to prove that to you other than saying no."

*What am I supposed to say to that? Thanks? Fuck off? Please don't walk away when I want you so desperately, I'm about to break my own damn rule and start begging?* She crossed her arms over her chest, but the motion did nothing to combat the feeling of vulnerability creeping over her. What if this was it and she never saw him again? Fear that *that* was the truth forced words past her lips. "Cillian, please..." Her voice broke in the middle of the word, and she had to try again. "Please don't leave like this. I...I'm sorry."

He took half a step back, and then a look came over his face, something both fierce and apologetic at the same time. "Fuck."

And then he had her against the wall again, his mouth on hers, his hand burrowing into the front of her shorts. Two strokes of his clever fingers and she was at the edge again.

He pulled back enough to say, "A date, Olivia. Your next day off. I'll take you anywhere you want to go."

She looked up into his dark eyes. "If I say no, are you going to walk away again?"

"No." He pressed his palm against her clit, applying *almost* enough pressure to send her over the edge, and pushed a third finger into her. "But I want this, sweetheart. I want the conversations and the time, and then I want you naked in my bed so I can taste every inch of you before I fuck you." He pulsed his fingers, little strokes that set her blood aflame. "I won't leave you hanging tonight, but this is a onetime thing. It won't happen again."

"Are you sure?" She cupped the front of his pants. "You feel as out of control as I do."

"Maybe. Maybe not." He kissed her again, taking away her ability to argue, and then picked up his pace, ruthlessly pushing her to the edge and over, swallowing her moans as she came around his hand. And still he kept finger fucking her, drawing out her pleasure until her knees buckled and he was the only thing keeping her off the ground.

Then and only then did Cillian remove his hand and gentle his kiss. He took a step back, and then another, and pulled a card from his back pocket. "Call me. We both know you won't regret it." He pressed it into her hand, and then he was gone, striding off into the darkness and leaving her staring after him.

She licked her lips. "I'm pretty sure I already regret it."

# CHAPTER TEN

Cillian cursed himself for being an idiot and walking away from Olivia. But staying wasn't an option. He could still taste her on his lips and feel her coming apart because of *him*. It was all too tempting to turn around and finish what he'd started. He pulled on the edge of his collar, the move doing nothing to help him cool down. He couldn't even blame it on the warmth outside. It was all Olivia. She'd practically begged him for more.

That was the issue. *More* was exactly what he wanted.

He'd had no problem being a booty call in the past, but the thought of being only that for her left him feeling... dirty. And not in a good way. He couldn't blame her for being pissed that he'd pulled a disappearing act. He would be, too, in her situation.

A man stepped out of the shadows at the end of the alley, and Cillian jerked to a stop. *Stupid to get so distracted you aren't aware of your surroundings*. He frowned into the darkness. The guy was big and blond and looked like a serious bruiser with his sloped brow and nose that had been broken one too many times. Cillian couldn't claim to know every person on Halloran's payroll—though he knew most of them these days—but he didn't recognize this guy.

Then he spoke, and his Russian accent confirmed him as a stranger. "Cillian O'Malley."

What the hell was going on? He affected a relaxed pose, as if he wasn't considering his exit options. "You have me at a disadvantage."

"That woman Olivia. She is not for you."

He blinked. Of all the things he'd expected the guy to start with, that hadn't even made the list. "What's she to you?"

She'd mentioned a past, but he'd imagined an asshole family or maybe even an abusive ex. There was no reason to think this man might not be exactly that, but Cillian's spidey senses were tingling. He knew organized crime. Hell, he *had* to be able to recognize the signs. While it was entirely possible that this man asking about Olivia was a coincidence, when he thought about his family's history with the New York Russians...

Yeah, he didn't like his odds that this wasn't somehow connected. It was a crazily paranoid thought, but he couldn't shake it.

While he'd been thinking, the man seemed to have done his own inspection. "I don't know what she sees in you, pretty boy, but she is not for you."

"Yeah, you keep saying that. I think that's up to her."

Maybe he was wrong. Maybe this was all about Olivia and he was taking paranoia to a whole new level. The O'Malley family had had a shitty year, and no one could blame him for immediately jumping to the worst possible scenario. But if Olivia really *was* connected with a rival family, he had to find out about it. "Is there a reason you cornered me in a dark alley, or did you just want to chat?"

The man lowered his head, reminding Cillian of a bull about to charge, and held up a single finger. "One warning, O'Malley. That is all you get. Leave her alone, or you'll regret it."

"I'll think about it." *I have no intention of leaving her alone, though she and I obviously need to have another talk.*

The man considered Cillian for a long moment, then turned and walked away.

*That's it? No tossing me around to prove his point? How disappointing.* Cillian shook his head. He must have hit the brick wall harder than he'd thought the other day, because he was obviously off his game in a huge way if he was thinking that.

"Cillian? Are you okay?"

He turned around to find Olivia picking her way through the puddles in the alley toward him. He frowned. "I thought you went back inside."

"Considering your track record with this alley, when I heard voices, I thought I'd better make sure you were okay."

He glanced to where the Russian had stood. "It was just some drunk." He needed to know more about Olivia, but telling her that some meathead was warning him off her wasn't a good way to go about it. If she had a past like he was beginning to suspect—and all signs pointed to that—then it was entirely possible she'd spook and take off. Maybe for good.

He had to tell her. Just…not yet.

Cillian held his arms out. "See. I'm in one piece."

"I guess." She looked at him like she expected him to start bleeding from the head again. Considering what they'd been doing not too long ago, it was borderline insulting. But...

*She worries about me. That's not a bad thing.*

"Let me walk you back."

"Cillian, it's an alley. There are no entrances between here and there. I'll be fine."

She would, but he wasn't quite ready to leave her. "Humor me." He touched the small of her back, the tiny contact washing away his questions in a cascade of desire. It was all too easy to take a half step back into what they'd been doing not too long ago against that very wall. If he concentrated, he could feel the slide of his fingers against her soft skin and her hands digging into his shoulders.

Fuck, the things this woman did to him. They finished the walk back into Jameson's in silence. She stopped just inside the door and turned to face him. "Think you can manage not to get your ass kicked for the next few days?"

He shrugged, warmed by her concern, even if it was wrapped in barbs. "I make no promises, but I'm not going looking for trouble."

"Somehow, I think trouble finds you all on its own." She sighed. "I might have been...hasty...in shutting this whole thing down."

Hope flared, but he did his damnedest to not let it show on his face. "Oh?"

"You're right. There's something there between us." She fiddled with the bottom of her shirt, the movement flashing him a slice of tanned skin. "My days off are for my daughter, but if you want to get dinner or something before my shift on Friday, I'd be okay with that."

Despite everything, he let himself poke at her a little. "Just okay?"

"I'm saying yes, Cillian. Take it or leave it."

He grinned. "Oh, sweetheart, I'm going to take you in every way that counts."

* * *

Olivia paced through her room, staring at the piles of clothes she'd already tried and thrown to the side. She didn't do this. She didn't get nervous and twitchy and worry about what she'd wear on a date.

*How would you know? You've never been on a date in your life.*

She was really starting to hate that little voice inside her. The feel-good emotions from her last encounter with Cillian had worn off sometime around when she rolled into bed last night, and now all she had to focus on was all the things that could go wrong. What if he got into some kind of turf war while they were having dinner? What if they went out and then ended up staring at each other awkwardly over the entirety of a meal? What if Sergei showed up?

Sergei.

The tank top she held dropped from nerveless fingers. She hadn't heard from either him or Dmitri in nearly a week, and the end result was that she was constantly looking over her shoulder and jumping at shadows. It was only a matter of time before he showed up, and with her luck it would be when she was actually on the verge of moving on. The thought of Sergei and Cillian sharing the same space made her sick to her stomach.

"That's it. I'm calling the whole thing off. I knew this was a mistake, and I was right."

Hadley chose that moment to toddle into the room, wiping sleep from her eyes. She'd passed out on the couch in the middle of *Finding Nemo* an hour ago—long enough for Olivia to sneak a shower and lose her mind over nerves. She smiled. "Hey, baby girl."

"Mama." Hadley lifted her arms to be picked up, and Olivia was only too happy to comply.

Just holding her daughter settled something inside her. "It's us against the world. Nothing else matters." Not her ex, and not Cillian. "I'm going to cancel." That was the only choice. She'd been right to reconsider this the first time, and if she didn't go pathetically weak in the knees whenever he got too close, she would have stuck to her guns.

*I'll just have to make sure we aren't alone again. Easy.*

The sound of the front door opening had her peering out into the living room. Mrs. Richards slipped into her apartment, her arms filled with a wire grocery basket. "Hello, hello. Where's my Hadley?"

Hadley squealed and shimmied to be let down. Olivia set her back on her feet with a laugh and watched her daughter hustle over to the older woman. The way Mrs. Richards's face lit up warmed her heart. She'd told Olivia back when they first met that she didn't have any grandchildren of her own, though she'd always wanted a few to spoil. She was the kind of grandmother Olivia's mother wasn't capable of being—wasn't even interested in being. The woman had never even *met* Hadley. Even knowing what kind of person she was, Olivia had still managed to be surprised that her mother was so damn cold. Spending time with Mrs. Richards filled a void she'd barely been aware had existed.

*If we have to run again, we'll lose this.* She'll *lose this.* Life had been so much easier when she didn't have close ties or anyone to worry about but herself and Hadley. The knowledge that their absence hurt Mrs. Richards—that leaving the older woman behind would hurt both Olivia and Hadley, too—might make her hesitate when she needed to act. *Damn it.*

Mrs. Richards frowned at her. "Why aren't you dressed? I thought you said you're meeting him at six." She glanced at the ancient watch on her wrist. "If you don't hurry, you're going to be late."

"I don't think I'm going."

She frowned harder. "Olivia, you've lived in this apartment for six months, and the only time I've ever watched this little bundle of joy is when you're working. It's not healthy. You're only twenty-four years old, hardly the over-the-hill old woman you act like. You need to take time for you."

How was she supposed to do that when she had to work as many hours as possible to keep them afloat? Not to mention she didn't exactly have a stellar track record of picking people to care about. It made it hard to put herself out there and meet new people. Cillian was a perfect example. The first man she'd been attracted to in longer than she wanted to think about, and he was an O'Malley. She was batting a thousand when it came to her hormones getting the best of her.

She leaned against the doorjamb. "This guy is nothing but trouble. Just like my ex."

*I don't want that life for myself and Hadley. We got out. We're not getting sucked back in.*

"If he was, you never would have given him the time of day." Mrs. Richards set her basket down in the tiny kitchen and crossed over to take her hands. "I know it's hard to put yourself out there, especially when someone has been burned as badly as you have. But if you never take that first step, you're going to end up closing yourself off for good."

"That doesn't sound like a bad idea." At least then she could stay out of trouble that came with a penis attached. From the very beginning, there hadn't been a single man—family or otherwise—who was willing to put her first. She'd thought she'd found that with Sergei, but it had all been a lie. When she needed him most, when she was pregnant and terrified and Andrei was diagnosed with cancer and trying to find peace by forcing a father-daughter relationship with her, Sergei had chosen the Romanovs over her.

After that, she'd realized that she couldn't rely on anyone but herself—especially now that Hadley was in the picture.

Mrs. Richards shook her head. "Take it from an old woman who's seen too much of life pass her by—it's too short *not* to take a leap of faith every once in a while. This man lit something up inside you. Maybe it'll develop into something, maybe it won't. But it's guaranteed to wither and die if you don't give it a chance."

She tried to picture it—never seeing Cillian again. Never having him walk into Jameson's and give her that grin that made her toes curl. Never getting to know exactly what it was that put those shadows into his dark eyes. Never getting to kiss him again, never letting him sink between her thighs, never being able to follow through on the rough promise of his words and actions.

It made her stomach ache like she'd lost something valuable. It didn't make any sense. She barely knew the man—it shouldn't matter if he dropped off the face of the earth.

Olivia sighed. "One date. That's it."

"Good." She made a shooing motion. "Now, go get dressed. You don't want to be late."

Since she wasn't even sure she wanted to go in the first place, being late was the least of her worries, but she went back into her room and threw on the first thing she laid hands on—a pair of holey jeans, her boots, and a tank top that did great things for her minuscule chest. It wasn't fancy, but she had to work afterward, and that was more important... and she might just be digging in her heels in protest in any way she could.

She stopped in the kitchen to drop a kiss on Hadley's head. "Be good for Mrs. Richards."

"Tell your mommy that you're always good." Mrs. Richards grinned. "You look great. Now git."

Olivia shook her head and snagged her purse on her way to the door. "I'm closing tonight, so feel free to use the pull-out couch."

"I always do, dear."

She knew that. God, she had to stop micromanaging and get her ass out the door. "What would I do without you?"

Mrs. Richards smiled. "You'd do just fine. Now go meet your man and have fun."

"Night!" She waited at the door, just like she always did, to hear the click of the lock before she hurried down the stairs. Mrs. Richards was right. She'd cut things too close, and now she was going to have to catch a cab instead of the T. She tried not to think too hard on how many tips she'd have to earn to make up for this splurge.

*Cillian will pay it if you let him.*

No way. She wasn't going on this date to find a sugar daddy to take care of her problems. She'd picked Sergei because she thought being with him would make her feel whole, and look where it took her. No, fulfillment, whether financial or emotional, couldn't be found in another person. She'd make her own way or sink while trying.

She caught a cab down the street and rattled off the address Cillian had texted her earlier. As the cab pulled up, she discovered it was a tiny restaurant in the West End— close enough to Jameson's that she wouldn't have to take another cab, but also far enough away to be outside Beacon Hill. It struck her that Cillian had known this and planned it out like that—close to work but outside his family's main stomping grounds.

It still blew her mind that so much criminal activity went down in one of the most prestigious neighborhoods in Boston, but she shouldn't be surprised. The Romanovs rubbed elbows with thugs and politicians alike. There was no reason the O'Malleys wouldn't do the same.

*Stop it. Stop comparing them. They aren't the same.*

Weren't they? There was only one way to tell for sure, and she wasn't ready to throw herself back into that life on the off chance that she might be wrong.

She shoved her hair back. And if she waffled any more, she was going to have to douse herself in syrup and serve herself on a plate for Sunday breakfast.

This wasn't like Olivia. She usually knew what she wanted and she went for it. She didn't change her mind as the wind blew. What the hell was Cillian doing to her?

She paid the driver and stepped out onto the street. There was an eclectic mix of people moving on the sidewalks, their clothing anywhere from hers to the after-work special to hipster to half a dozen other things. She'd fit right in.

*He thought about this, too*, she realized. He picked a

place where they'd both feel comfortable. The thought-fulness of the gesture beat back some of her uncertainty. She checked the sign hanging out on the wall and ducked through the door into the restaurant. Inside it was dim and relaxed and cozily intimate, the walls lined with deep booths and a scattering of table and chairs across the open floor. Mouthwatering smells came from the kitchen and the tables that had already been served their food.

"Olivia."

She turned, a smile already slipping through her defenses when she saw Cillian. He wore yet another three-piece suit, this one in shades of dark gray with a lilac shirt. He looked perfectly put together and downright edible, and all she wanted to do was throw herself into his arms and then tow him to the nearest spot where they could be alone. *Down, girl.* "Hey."

"I hope you're hungry. This place has the best lobster rolls in town."

"I'm starving." And, suddenly, she was. She'd been too nervous to eat lunch today, and if anyone had asked, she would have been sure those same nerves would keep her from eating during the date itself. But as soon as he guided her to a table with a light touch at the small of her back, she inexplicably relaxed. Here, in his presence, it was harder to remember why this was such a bad idea. "How was your day?"

He pulled out her chair. "Tedious. The numbers are being difficult, which isn't a challenge that I thought I was going to have to deal with when I took over the accounts."

"Accounts." She blinked. "You're an accountant?" When she pictured accountants, she pictured tightly wound men in cheap suits who didn't get enough sun. Cillian couldn't be further from that image. "How...how did that even happen? You don't seem the type."

He grinned. "I'll take that as a compliment." He nodded as a harried waitress appeared with two glasses of water and disappeared just as quickly. "In my family, everyone has their place—their job. I'm the middle son of seven kids, so I had a bit more freedom than some of my siblings."

"So you decided to be an...accountant." Every time she said it, her disbelief deepened.

"If you prefer, you can call me the head of finances instead." His grin widened. "I like numbers. I'm good at numbers. And there's the added bonus that it puts me right in the middle of things without having to shoulder any of the responsibility that's crushing my oldest brother." Just like that, the grin faded. "Or at least, that was what I thought when I took on the job. Turns out, things are never that simple."

"No, they wouldn't be with your family." She regretted the words almost as soon as they were out. What the hell was wrong with her that she had to keep poking at this particular issue? "I'm sorry. It's none of my business."

"It's okay." He motioned at her menu. "Why don't you figure out what you want to eat and then we can skip straight to the hard stuff."

"Sure." It dawned on her that if he was willing to open up about his family and the "hard stuff," then he was going to expect her to do the same. She wasn't sure if she was ready for that. To distract herself, she looked over the menu. "You said they have amazing lobster rolls?"

"The best." He hadn't even picked up the laminated plastic menu.

She set hers aside. "That's enough of a recommendation for me. I'll get that."

The waitress must have been keeping her eye on them, because she swooped in, took their drink and food order, and was gone inside of thirty seconds. Then there was nothing standing between Olivia and all the questions she had for Cillian. Nothing except knowing she'd have to respond in kind. She used her straw to stir the ice around in her water glass. "Now that we're here, I'm not sure what to say."

"Should I have picked a fancy restaurant with unpronounceable entrées?"

She gave a brief smile in acknowledgment of the shared joke, but it fell away when faced with the reality of their situation. "I promised myself I'd never get involved with someone like you."

"Sweetheart, there is no one like me." He held up a hand when she burst out laughing.

"How about I give you the basics, and if you have any questions, you can ask them?"

He was actually offering to open up to her. It blew her mind. The Romanovs were all about their secrets and never letting the left hand know what the right hand was doing. She was pretty sure the only one with all the information was Dmitri. Everyone else was expected to take orders and keep their mouths shut. Olivia took a deep breath. *Cillian isn't Dmitri—or Sergei. How many times do I have to remind myself of that before it actually sinks in?* Apparently one more than she already had. "That sounds great."

"So you know I'm an O'Malley and that we're one of three families that run the majority of Boston. There are other players in the city, but they ultimately have to answer to one of us." He took a drink of water. "A year ago, we were on the brink of war because of, well, a variety of things. We managed to hash out an alliance with the

Sheridans, and we're also on pretty good terms overall with the Hallorans."

She frowned. "The Hallorans being the same men who were beating you in a back alley less than two weeks ago?"

"Yeah, well, nothing is ever simple. The people in charge might have decided on peace, but that doesn't mean that everyone feels that way. They did it without their boss's consent."

"You know that for sure?"

He shrugged. "I've passed word along and been assured that it will be dealt with. Since my sister is currently engaged to the guy in charge, I'm willing to take his word for it."

She blinked. There were a whole lot of undercurrents to what he just said, but she wasn't sure she was willing to delve deeper. "It sounds like things are good in Boston."

"As good as they can be." He straightened the paper-napkin-wrapped silverware. "That almost-war left a lot of scars and bullshit for us to work through. Our family still hasn't managed to get past most of it."

From the pain in his voice, she wasn't sure if he was talking about his family in general or him specifically. "I'm sorry."

"Don't be. None of it is your fault. It's just a by-product of the life we live." His mouth twisted. "Or that's the line my father likes to use."

"I've heard similar."

His dark eyes focused on her. "In that case, sweetheart, why don't you tell me a little about yourself?"

# CHAPTER ELEVEN

Cillian saw the exact moment she shut down. Olivia crossed her arms over her chest and wouldn't quite meet his eyes. *Damn it, I pushed too hard.* He sat back. "You know what? Never mind. You don't have to tell me anything you don't want to."

Her shoulders went even tighter. "No, it's okay."

"Obviously it's not." Which only made him even more curious. What was this woman hiding that she froze up at the mere mention of her past? He wanted to know. Fuck, he *needed* to know. If that meathead Russian was any indication, there was at least an abusive boyfriend in her past, but if it was something more complicated, it could be putting more than her in danger. "Look, Olivia, we all have secrets. It's okay."

"I just..." She still wouldn't look directly at him. "I grew up in a really rough family, and it took all the strength I had to get out—some days I wake up and wonder if I ever actually escaped or if it just bought me a stay of execution. It's hard to talk about."

"Then we won't talk about it."

She finally looked at him. "Just like that."

"Just like that. If you haven't noticed, I'm not looking for a quick fuck and run—not now. I'm willing to wait until you're ready to tell me." He kept his voice calm and easy, feeling like he was approaching a wild animal that would spook at any sudden moves. Not a deer or anything so mundane, but some kind of big cat—all claws and growls, but just as likely to run from what she thought was dangerous as she was to fight. He had a feeling that when her kid came into it, though, there was no hesitation. She'd go for his throat. "Tell me about your daughter."

She smiled, though it was a little shaky around the edges. "She's the best kid there ever was. I'm sure every parent says that, but Hadley is just . . . She's a little ray of sunshine. It doesn't matter what life throws at us, she bounces back with a grin on her face and so much energy I seriously wish I could bottle the stuff."

His chest gave a funny thump at the way her face lit up when she talked about her daughter. "How old is she?"

"Fourteen months." She rolled her eyes. "I don't know why they do that month thing up to eighteen months. Sometimes I think it's just to confuse people. So, yeah, she's a little over a year old."

Just a baby, really. He tried to picture what a fourteen-month-old looked like and came up blank. The last kid he'd spent any time around was Keira, and he was only seven at the time. None of his siblings had started their own families yet, and the end result was that Cillian didn't know a damn thing about kids. "That's great."

Olivia laughed. "Your eyes just glazed over. It's okay. I love my baby girl, and I could talk about her for hours, but I won't force you to sit through that."

He might be out of his element with the topic of children, but he liked how she lit up. "No, it's okay."

"That's sweet." She turned her smile on the waitress who walked up with their food. Once she was gone, Olivia snagged a fry. "I wasn't sure I wanted kids back in the day."

"Why not?" He took a bite of his lobster roll.

"With my history, family comes with more complications than benefits. I didn't like the idea of bringing a kid into that world. Plus, I was kind of the family outcast in a lot of ways, so adding to the list of things about me that they found wanting didn't seem like a good idea." She picked up her roll and took a bite. Watching the bliss spread over her face slammed him right back into that alley when *he* was the cause of it.

He shifted, trying to get his physical reaction under control. The whole point of tonight—in addition to getting to know Olivia better—was to prove to her that he wasn't just after a piece of ass. Dragging her to the bathroom to finish what they started the other night in the alley wasn't going to get that point across. He cleared his throat. *Keep her talking. The reaction will pass...hopefully.* "So what changed?"

"Hmmm?" She managed to drag her eyes open. "God, you weren't kidding about this being the best lobster roll place in town, were you? This is downright orgasmic." She shook herself. "Sorry, I'm getting distracted."

"I'm not complaining." He liked this softer side of her. It had started when she talked about her daughter, but it was even more pronounced now. The woman had more spikes than a porcupine, but once he got past those, she was...Hell, he didn't even know.

But he wanted more.

She shot him a look. "To answer your question, it wasn't exactly planned. I picked a guy...You know what? Never mind. You don't want to hear this."

It struck him that the goon he'd run into in that alley might be the father of Olivia's kid. Cillian wasn't sure why that bugged him more than the thought of the blond bruiser being an ex, but it did. He wanted to go back and punch the guy a few times for good measure. He took a drink of his water. "Do you still see him?"

"If I did, I'd be an asshole for sitting across this table from you, wouldn't I?" She shook her head. "No, he and I were over about halfway through my pregnancy, but we officially went our separate ways right around the time Hadley was born. We wanted different things."

*What different things?* And what the fuck kind of man left a woman who'd just had his child—especially a woman like Olivia? Cillian could barely wrap his mind around it. *What would she look like pregnant with* my *child?*

Damn it, that was out of line. He searched for something appropriate to say that wouldn't come across like he was a caveman pounding his chest before he dragged her back to his place by her hair. "I'm sorry."

"I'm not." She took another bite, her entire face relaxing as she chewed and swallowed. "He's not a great guy, but I got my daughter as a result. I know that sounds cliché—"

"It sounds like you love your daughter. That's nothing to apologize for." He tried to stop talking, but his mouth got away from him. "What you have with her is uncomplicated and that makes it even more special. You didn't have her for political reasons." Not like his parents had. They loved their children, though it hadn't been the warmest household growing up, but it was impossible to forget that a good portion of the reason they'd had so many kids was because they were actively building a dynasty. They might never be the old money that held power in Boston officially, but if Seamus O'Malley had his way, his descendants would be running a decent chunk of the criminal enterprises until the end of time.

Uncharitable? Probably. But that didn't make it a lie.

Her dark eyes were sympathetic. "Sounds like a cold reason to make that decision."

"I think there was more to it, but it was definitely something my parents considered. I mean, fuck, there are seven of us." He caught himself. "Were. There were seven of us." A year later and he was still stumbling over that fact. There would come a day when he wouldn't. He already mourned it.

"I didn't mean to bring up a painful subject."

"Life is full of painful subjects." He tried to make his voice light, but didn't quite pull it off.

Olivia saw. She'd have to be blind not to, but she did him the favor of changing the subject and not prodding deeper. "Do you want kids of your own?"

Did he? He took his time eating another bite before he answered. "I don't know. I guess I've never really thought about it. Up until a year ago, I was all about living life to the fullest and not slowing down for anyone, so kids weren't even on my radar."

"And now?"

Painfully aware that he was talking to a woman with a kid, he picked his words with care. But he couldn't lie to her. "I still don't know. I like the idea of eventually settling down and starting a family at some point in the future."

"You mean you aren't going to follow in your father's footsteps and try to repopulate Boston with more O'Malleys?"

He chuckled. "I think two or three would be much more manageable."

"And you don't have some sort of arranged marriage waiting in the wings?" She took a drink and held up her hand. "Sorry, that's not really my business."

"No, it's fine." Though he was now even more curious as to her connections to the kind of life he led. Most people considered arranged marriages a thing of the past—at least in this part of the world—so for her to broach the subject spoke volumes. He forced himself to temporarily let it go. She'd tell him when she was ready and not before. He wasn't going to ruin a good conversation by prying, especially since she was already cagey about coming out with him in the first place. "I'm not the oldest son, so I have some freedom from that sort of thing." His value lay elsewhere, in his bookkeeping skills.

She raised her eyebrows. "Your family sounds charming."

"You have no idea. There are definite perks, and they're mostly good people, but my parents don't let a little thing like emotional attachment get in the way of their plans."

"You don't sound particularly bitter."

"I'm not." Not really. Not most days. "Like I said—I made my peace with my place in the world a long time ago."

She tucked her hair behind her ears. "And what would your family think about you being out with me right now?"

He thought back to Sloan's response. It hadn't exactly been supportive, but that was more aimed at him than the woman across from him. He'd been telling the truth—when push came to shove, his skills with numbers were more valuable than any marriage he'd potentially make. That left him freer than most of his siblings. "It doesn't really matter what they'd think. I want to be here with you, so here we are."

For a second, she actually looked shocked before she managed to get an expressionless mask in place. Why was what he said so surprising? Sure, Irish mob families had a tendency to put family first and everyone else dead last, but as long as Olivia wasn't some kind of sleeper agent or spy intent on bringing them all down in flames, there was no reason his family should have a problem with them dating.

In theory.

But he meant what he said. The more he found out about Olivia, the more he liked. He wasn't about to give her up without a fight. Not now. Not until they'd had their fill of each other.

*And what if that never happens?*

He shoved the voice away. He'd cross that bridge when he came to it. "So, why don't we try something easy? Tell me about your hopes and dreams and fears."

She laughed again, the sound like the best whiskey. He could almost taste it if he closed his eyes. That night with her in the alley had been the first time he'd been with someone in...a long time. A seriously long time. Olivia picked up her water. "That's your idea of small talk?"

"Sure. What's wrong with that?" He knew damn well that it wasn't small talk, but he liked that she was teasing him. He liked it a lot.

"Oh, I don't know." She grinned. "Everything?"

"Sit back, sweetheart. I'm about to school you."

"This should be interesting."

She had no idea.

* * *

Sloan had never been a big drinker, but she was thinking now might be a good time to start. Keira certainly hadn't felt that five thirty in the evening was too early to begin tipping whatever was in her flask into her drink when she thought no one was looking. She caught Sloan's frown and grinned. "Don't look so disapproving. It's after five."

That logic was flawed in a seriously large way, but since her sister shut her down every time she tried to actually talk to her, Sloan turned to face the room. When Teague had invited her to the Sheridan residence, at first she'd thought it was going to be just the two of them going over the last details of her extraction. But, no, he'd invited all the O'Malley siblings.

She hadn't realized when he said all he meant *all*.

Carrigan caught her eye, and Sloan immediately turned back to Keira. "I can't believe he invited her."

"She's still our sister, even if she's pretty much a traitor." Keira swirled her drink, took a sip, and then added more from her flask. "Though Teague obviously doesn't agree with our parents on that."

Which was probably why their parents were noticeably absent tonight. She wasn't sure if they'd gotten an invite or not, but she understood why they'd chosen not to come if they *had* been invited. She might have done the same if she'd known Carrigan would be here. "She's with a Halloran. That's inexcusable."

"Is it?" Keira shrugged, taking another sip. "It doesn't make Devlin less dead, either way."

*"Keira."*

"What? It's the truth, isn't it? We're all so damn miserable. What's wrong with one of us dredging out a little slice of happiness for herself? Maybe that's why Mother and Father are so pissed—we're so much easier to maneuver when we're suffering."

She was about to tell her sister not to talk like that, but she stopped herself. Wasn't that part of the reason she was leaving? She was finally taking her future into her own hands and grabbing whatever happiness she could find. She nodded to where Teague stood with his arm around Callie's waist. "Not all of us are miserable."

"Well, duh." Another sip. "You want to know the other thing that stands out with those two lucky little shits? They got out. Oh, not *out*-out." Keira waved her hand. "But they aren't under our parents' thumbs anymore. Bet that helps with the whole happiness thing."

*It probably does.* But she couldn't say so out loud—not even here. No one could know she was planning on leaving. Their father couldn't risk forcing Carrigan back into the fold and provoking a true war with James Halloran, but Sloan had no such power in her corner. Teague could get her out, but his first priority would always be Callie and the stability of the Sheridans. "You need to stop talking like that."

"Why? Who's going to hear me?" Keira made a show of looking around, her whole body tilting unsteadily with the movement. "It's just us, Sloan." Then she frowned. "Where's Cillian?"

Sloan studied the room, only now realizing she hadn't seen him. "I don't know. Surely he was invited?"

"He's been wearing his cranky pants lately. Maybe Teague decided to leave him out of it."

She shot her little sister a look. "Because he was worried about you?" Considering her sister was obviously drunk and had decided that a pair of black leggings, combat boots, and an oversized white tank top that showed her black bra was appropriate attire for this dinner, Sloan wasn't sure she blamed him.

"It's none of his business. It isn't *anyone's* business." Keira's chin came up, a sure sign she was ready to fight. "He sent Liam after me, and I had to deal with a babysitter for the entire night. Talk about a buzzkill."

*Good.* She worried about her sister's nighttime activities enough as it was. It was good that Liam tailed after her when he could. Sloan was about to say as much, but Teague raised his voice. "There is a reason I asked you guys here tonight. If you'll sit..."

Sloan followed Keira over to the couches situated around the living room, carefully choosing one between her sister and the arm of the couch so she wouldn't risk sitting next to her *other* sister. She wasn't ready to face Carrigan. It didn't matter if every other one of their siblings seemed willing to forgive and forget—even Aiden from the looks of it. She wasn't.

Not now. Maybe not ever.

Teague stood behind the overstuffed chair Callie had taken, his hands on her shoulders. "I know we haven't always seen eye to eye in the past year—some of us more than others." His gaze temporarily rested on Aiden before he looked at the rest of them. "But I'm hoping that we can set all the baggage aside for a night because I have great news." His grin was downright blinding. "You're all about to become aunts and uncles."

Sloan blinked once, twice, a third time. Her mind churned, trying to make sense of his words, even though her gut already knew what he'd said. "You're...Callie's pregnant?"

Callie reached back to cover one of Teague's hands with her own. "Yes. We're due January eighth. I'm thirteen weeks pregnant on July fifteenth."

Four days from now.

*Oh my God.* She forced a smile. Teague had always wanted kids, and to have them with a woman he was so obviously head over heels for was his dream coming true. She watched Carrigan push to her feet and hug their brother and then his wife, her thoughts a buzz of white noise.

She *was* happy. But there were other, uglier, emotions in there, twisting that happiness until it was downright unrecognizable.

She wanted what Teague had, and at the same time, she resented him for having left her behind to gain it. It was selfish and horrible and she hated herself a little bit for feeling that way, even if she couldn't stop.

*I'm not even going to be here to see this baby. I'm going to miss it. I'm going to miss everything.*

She waited for something to rise in her, some sign that she should change her mind, but there was nothing but a growing determination to leave Boston and everything in it behind. *I'm a monster.*

She realized that most of her siblings had moved over to congratulate Teague and Callie, and forced herself to her feet. She had to fake it—for both of them. To do anything else would take away from his happiness today, and she wasn't anywhere near monster enough to do that. *Not yet. Because I'm leaving. They never have to know how conflicted I feel about this whole thing. How* jealous.

So she hugged Teague and cooed over Callie and managed to keep a smile on her face through the whole thing. They were so busy with everyone else that they didn't seem to notice she wasn't totally on board.

Which was good, because she was counting down the minutes until she put Boston behind her, once and for all.

# CHAPTER TWELVE

The rest of dinner went off without a hitch. In fact, it was going *too* well if Olivia was going to be honest with herself. Cillian was a perfect gentleman, and their conversation had only had the slightest hiccups through the meal. As he paid and rose to get her chair, she wasn't sure what the next step was. She hated being so unsure, but this was completely new territory across the board. Was this a date where he'd drop her off at work with a kiss? Or was he going to get back to what they'd started in the alley behind Jameson's?

She knew which one *she'd* prefer.

*Let's give him some incentive.*

She stepped to the side as they walked out onto the street, and grabbed his suit jacket, tugging him against her. Her back hit the wall behind her, the feeling making her shiver with memories from the other times he'd had her in this position. Cillian caught himself with his hands on either side of her, his body pressed against hers. "Hey there."

"Hey." She licked her lips, her gaze on his mouth, her stomach in her throat. It would be easy to make a joke and back off, and pretend this never happened. He'd let her. Hell, he was letting her take the reins right now. If she changed her mind, he wasn't going to blink. Knowing that only made her hotter. So she took a flying leap of faith. "I don't suppose you know somewhere we can go to be alone? I still have an hour before my shift."

"You mean someplace better than me dragging you into that alley?" His tone was flippant, but his eyes belied the joking. He'd do it. They both knew he'd do it.

And she'd enjoy every last second of it.

*Come on, Olivia. You're better than back-alley sex. No matter how much you like it.*

*Shut up.*

She ran her hands up his chest, taking her time and enjoying the way his muscles flexed beneath her fingers. "I don't know if that's a good idea."

"It's not." Still looking at her, he reached into his pocket, pulled out a phone, and dialed. "Yeah, Liam? Send a car around. One with a divider." He hung up.

"You're just going to do me in the backseat of your car? We're really moving up the class level, aren't we?" She gave a nervous laugh. "I don't even know how I feel about that."

Cillian leaned in, his breath brushing her ear. "You know exactly how you feel about it. And no, I'm not fucking you in the backseat, sweetheart."

Disappointment closed her throat. Of course he wasn't. Because he was classier than that, and it was becoming increasingly obvious that she wasn't. *She'd* been the one to haul him into that alley the first time, and if he'd been down for a repeat, she wouldn't have said a word otherwise. No, she would have dropped her pants right there in her desperation to have him. Shame rose to tangle with her disappointment. *God, I am so messed up.*

He leaned back enough to study her expression. "What did I say to put that look on your face?"

"It's nothing." Nothing except her mind being twisted into a tangle that she could barely navigate. He didn't have a problem with anything that had happened to date—*she* was the one creating the complications.

"I know what nothing looks like, and that's not it." He tipped up her chin. "Tell me, Olivia."

How was she supposed to deny him when he said her name in that tone of voice? A tone like he actually cared if he'd hurt her. Like he wanted to make it better. Every instinct she had demanded she close down and retreat to lick her wounds—opening up only gave the world more chances to stab her in the back.

Instead, she told the truth. "I'm just feeling awfully easy right now."

"Sweetheart, you're not easy." His brows dipped in a frown. "There's nothing wrong with seeing what you want and going for it—whether it's sex, money, or something else."

"You make it sound so simple."

"It is." He glanced over his shoulder as a black town car with darkly tinted windows pulled up to the curb behind them. "Come on."

"Cillian, I'm not sure this is a good idea…"

"Trust me." He stopped, and looked at her. "Just this once. This stops the second you want it stopped. Say the word and I get you to Jameson's—no questions asked."

*He's too good to be true.*

Maybe, but that didn't stop her from taking his hand and letting him lead her to the car. He ushered her into the backseat and climbed in behind her. Sure enough, there was a dark glass divider between them and the front seat, though it was cracked a few scant inches.

Cillian glanced at his watch. "Drive around for the next forty-five minutes, but stay in this general area."

"Yes, sir." The window closed before she could get a good look at the man in the driver's seat.

She crossed her arms over her chest, and immediately reversed the movement. "So, what now?"

"Now, sweetheart, we do whatever you want." He leaned back and draped his arms over the back of the seat. The position put his hand close to the back of her neck, and he trailed a finger across her spine.

She shivered. "Whatever I want."

"Exactly what I said." The tension in his body belied the ease of his words. "Normally...Well, it doesn't matter what would happen normally. We've played that game before and, I don't know about you, but I like the reality better than any alternative thing we could dream up. I like you, Olivia. I want to take you out again. So I'm willing to do whatever it takes not to spook you."

"I'm not a wild animal."

"Aren't you?" He traced some abstract pattern over her skin, drawing forth another shiver. "It's not meant as an insult. My point is that what happens in the next forty-five minutes is completely within your control."

"My control." She tasted the words, considering them, and then scooted closer. "Anything I want." She liked the sound of that. She liked it a lot. Maybe he was right—there was nothing wrong with seeing what you wanted and taking it. She might have been fighting it since that first time, but the truth was that she wanted Cillian.

"Anything you want." He didn't blink.

"Tempting. Very tempting." She ran a hand down the center of his chest, undoing the buttons one by one. It took a few minutes between the vest and the shirt beneath, but then she had his bare chest laid out before her. She spread his shirt, and then traced over the dragon. "How old were you when you got this done?"

"Eighteen."

She leaned down and kissed the dragon between his eyes. Cillian smelled amazing, like some kind of expensive cologne and, beneath that, the man she wanted more than she had a right to. "And the bullet scar?"

"Six months ago."

She traced it with her mouth. It must have broken his collarbone when it hit him, but she was suddenly so incredibly thankful that it hadn't gone near anything vital. "The person who shot you?"

"Dead."

"Good." The thought of some person wandering the world after putting a bullet in this man was wrong on so many levels. The gunman should have died for what he did, and she was glad to hear that he had.

She shifted down to the floorboard so she could kneel between his legs. "I like your ink. I don't know if I said that the other night."

"I like that you like it." In the darkness of the car, his eyes were pools of shadow. Even his voice sounded different, huskier and full of promises that she was only too eager to follow through on.

She undid his belt slowly, liking the way his mouth tightened, but didn't immediately go for the button of his slacks. Instead, she kissed his stomach, following the line of the dragon's back to his chest and then to his shoulder where its wings met the swallows bracketing his throat.

He rested his hands on her hips, not guiding or pushing, just touching her. She climbed into his lap to straddle him. "Touch me." She pulled her shirt over her head and dropped it to the side. "I want to feel your skin against mine." Leaning forward, she had to bite back a moan when her chest pressed against his, her bra the only barrier between them.

"You don't have to ask me twice." He ran his hands up her sides to cup her breasts. "Fuck, you're almost too good to be true." His thumbs feathered over her nipples, and this time she couldn't hold back her moan. Cillian dipped down and captured one with his mouth, sucking her through the lace.

"Oh *God*." She tried to get closer, digging her fingers into his hair and rolling her hips, but her jeans were too tight for her to get to where she needed. "More."

He looked up at her. "I'm going to make you come now."

She was already nodding. "Yes."

His grin was almost reward enough in and of itself. But then he hooked an arm around her waist and twisted, laying her down across the backseat and covering her. His weight settling between her legs was a whole new kind of heaven, but he didn't stop there. Cillian slipped an arm behind one knee and hitched her leg up and around his waist, so that the ridge of his cock rubbed right across the seam of her jeans and her clit. He kissed her as he rolled his hips, devouring her mouth. His tongue stroked hers and he slipped a hand down to cup her ass, bringing her more firmly against him. "You like this."

"Yes." A breathless laugh escaped as he licked and nipped across her jaw. "I feel a little like I'm necking in the back of some high school boyfriend's car, though."

He leaned back enough to meet her gaze. "Sweetheart, I'm a thousand times better than some fumbling teenager." As if to prove his point, he rolled his hips again, the friction nearly making her eyes roll back in her head. He lightly bit her earlobe.

She grinned even as she arched up to meet his thrust. "Oh, I guess you're pretty okay." There was something so goddamn hot about the fact that they were still wearing most of their clothes and yet her body was humming with more pleasure than she could have dreamed. He was right. He could get her off like this. She was already halfway there.

"Then I'll just have to up my game." He kissed her again, his hands digging into her hips and forcing her to meet his rhythm, stroke for stroke. Abruptly, he stopped, almost making her cry out in protest. "I changed my mind. These jeans have to come off."

A few seconds passed before she realized he was waiting for permission. "Yes."

"Thank fuck." He moved back enough to unbutton them and jerked them down her hips and off her legs. What in the world had possessed her to wear skinny jeans? Such a bad idea. But then they were gone and he was back between her legs. He lifted her again, resuming their original positions with her straddling him. She shot him a look, which he returned with another grin. "What? I like the view."

Sex had never been like this before—almost...fun. She liked it. God, who was she kidding? She liked *him*. Olivia braced her hands on the roof of the car and shifted against him, biting her lip when his cock rubbed against all the right places. "You're right. This is better."

He slid a thumb beneath the side of her panties, tracing down the dip where her thigh met her center and back up again. He was *so close* to where she wanted him, but he seemed content to tease her. "Your panties are soaked."

She angled her hips, trying to force him to touch her clit, but his grip tightened, holding her in place. "You promised me something." *Make me come again. Please.*

"I always keep my promises." His thumb stroked her clit and then spread her wetness up and circled it again. "This is what you want."

"*Yes*." She spread her legs even more, lifting herself up a little to give him better access, which he was all too ready to take.

He pushed a finger into her and groaned. "Fuck, sweetheart, the feel of you clenching around me drives me crazy."

He was doing a damn good job of driving her crazy right alongside him. She hooked the back of his neck and kissed him as she rode his hand, her orgasm looming closer with each stroke. He'd finish her like this if she wasn't careful and, as hot as that was, she wanted more.

Reaching between them, she dragged down his zipper and freed his cock. He was broad and long, and she shivered as she wrapped her hand around him. "I want to feel you."

"Then feel me." He had her down on the seat again before she'd registered the move, his cock lining up perfectly with her clit. He propped himself onto his elbows. "If I had a goddamn condom, I'd already be inside you."

She bit her lip to keep words she had no business even thinking inside. *I don't care about a condom.* But she did care. She had to. "I—"

Cillian kissed her, stealing her words. By the time he lifted his head, she had no idea what she'd been about to say. From the look on his face, he knew it, too. "Do you trust me?"

*No. Yes. I don't know.* She nodded. "Yes."

He kissed her again, his tongue sliding into her mouth as his hips moved, creating delicious friction between her legs. He kept their bodies sealed, offering no chance for him to push inside her, and a small, very stupid, part of her mourned the loss. But the rest of her body was too busy sparking with pleasure. She wrapped her legs around his waist, moaning against his mouth.

And then it was too much.

She clung to him as she came, kissing him with everything she had. He started to pull back, but she was having none of it. "No, don't stop." She arched against him. "Finish."

For a second, he looked almost shocked, but then the heat in his eyes doubled and he started moving with renewed purpose. He palmed her breast with one hand, keeping them tightly together with his other, his mouth on her neck.

Against all reason, she felt pressure building again. "Oh God."

"I can't get enough of you." He yanked her bra to the side and took her nipple into his mouth, all without missing a stroke. "You make me crazy, sweetheart. So fucking crazy."

She grabbed his hips, rising to meet each stroke as much as she could while being pinned to the seat. She could actually feel him swelling as his cock slid against her. "Come for me."

He cursed, his movements turning jerky, and she looked down in time to see him do exactly that, his semen hitting her stomach, so damn hot that it was a wonder it didn't scald her. She hissed out a breath, wondering how something like this could be so damn sexy.

"You're almost there." Without missing a beat, he slid down to the floorboard and pushed two fingers into her. "One more time, Olivia. I'm damn near addicted to the way you come so sweetly for me."

His eyes darkened further. "I've been dying for a taste of you." He dipped down and then his mouth was there, licking and tasting and *savoring* her. He kissed her there like he kissed her mouth—as if he'd never get enough.

That thought hit her as he fucked her with his tongue, and it was too much. She dug her hands into his hair and moaned his name as she came a second time. He kept going for a few seconds, drawing her orgasm out until it almost hurt. Then, and only then, did he raise his head. "Regrets?"

He was asking that *now*? Olivia managed a hoarse laugh. "No."

"Good." He moved up to sit next to her on the seat. "Then next Wednesday I'm taking you out again."

* * *

Sergei watched Olivia—*his* Olivia—get out of the town car, her hair mussed and a look on her face of supreme satisfaction. Every part of him rejected what his eyes were telling him, but then that Irish bastard leaned out, snagged the back of her neck, and kissed her like she was *his*. Sergei clenched his fists, fighting to remember his orders. He was not to intervene.

Not unless Dmitri changed his mind.

He fished his cell out of his pocket without taking his eyes off of them, and pushed the button to speed-dial his boss. Dmitri picked up almost immediately. "Now is not a good time."

"I was right. She's fucking that piece-of-shit O'Malley. The one with the tattoos."

A pause. "You're sure?"

Across the street, Olivia pulled away with a laugh, her entire face lit up with happiness. He hadn't seen her wear that expression in years, and *he* had been the last one to put it on her face. "Positive. They just fucked in his backseat, and he looks like he's ready to haul her in for round two." One well-placed bullet and he'd put that kid out of commission. Hell, it would be a waste of a bullet. He'd work him over with his fists.

Yeah, that was a much better plan.

He was so focused on all the ways he'd bring the enemy to his knees that it took Sergei a few seconds to realize Dmitri was still speaking to him. "I'm sorry, boss. I missed that last part."

"So I gathered." He didn't sound happy, his voice icy. "Keep your distance. I don't need you spooking her. I think it's time that I paid my darling sister a personal visit."

Damn it, that wasn't what he wanted. "That's not necessary. I can take care of it. No need to put yourself out."

"Wrong. And if you make contact before I get up there, I'll skin you alive. Do we understand each other?"

Sergei cursed long and hard, though no sound made it out of his mouth. He knew better than to cross Dmitri, but he'd always had a hard time keeping that in mind where Olivia was concerned. She was special. She alone had looked at him without fear—at least at first. It wasn't his goddamn fault that he was the best at what he did, and Dmitri had no problem putting him to work doing it. That was something to be proud of—not ashamed of like she was. He kept them safe. All of them—even her ungrateful ass. People heard the name Sergei Utkin, and it made them pause and think before they attacked the Romanovs.

And the money didn't hurt, either.

Dmitri's father had brought Sergei over from Mother Russia, where he could barely steal enough food to keep himself alive, and he gave Sergei everything he could need—more than he ever dreamed. He'd had money to blow, the best vodka, and any woman of his choosing. More than that, he had the respect and fear of every person he came in contact with. He liked his life, and he liked it even more with Olivia in his bed. It might have only been a year, but he'd gotten a taste for a woman of worth. He wanted her back. He wouldn't be able to pull that off with Dmitri looking over his shoulder.

"Sergei."

Damn it, he was so busy thinking, he wasn't paying attention to the other line. "Sorry again, boss."

"You're not comforting me right now. Do I need to bring a replacement when I come?"

And have another man watching Olivia? Not fucking likely. He cleared his throat, doing his best to sound curt and professional. "I've got it."

"You had better. She might be my father's bastard—for the moment—but she's still family. Don't cross me, Sergei. You know what happens if you do."

Yeah, he knew. He was usually the one Dmitri sent when that happened with someone else. "It's under control." Or it would be. He just had to keep a handle on his shit until Dmitri came and left—until he figured out what his boss had planned for Olivia. Because he had a plan. Dmitri always had a plan in place.

"I'll see you in the morning." He clicked off.

Sergei gave in to the need to curse aloud. What the fuck was Dmitri thinking? He should have hauled Olivia back to New York the second he realized she was gone. Andrei wanted her as a Romanov, and Dmitri had given his word that he'd see it done. Instead, he'd sat back and let her create a life for herself here. A life that didn't involve Sergei. Now she had some new cock she was fucking, and the fact that it was attached to the same family that had offered the Romanovs such disrespect barely six months ago...

He didn't like that. He didn't like that at all.

*A few more hours and I'll have answers. That will have to be good enough.*

And if he didn't like the answers?

Well, then he'd do something about it. He'd lost Olivia because of her half brother once before. He wasn't going to let it happen again.

# CHAPTER THIRTEEN

Cillian slammed into wakefulness, Devlin's name caught in his throat, his chest so tight it was a wonder he could draw a full breath, his entire body coated in sweat. He stared blindly at his ceiling for the space of a heartbeat, and then another, before his mind caught up with his instincts.

*Home. In my bed. Safe.*

He scrubbed a hand over his face, trying to convince himself that it was okay. He'd gone to bed so damn happy last night, still riding high from how well the date with Olivia had gone, better than he could have dreamed. Stupid of him to think that would be enough to keep his nightmares at bay.

With a groan, he climbed out of bed and stripped the mattress of the sweat-covered sheets. No one said anything about the fact that he was changing his bedding several times a week, but he knew the staff noticed. And if they knew, it was highly likely that his parents and probably even Aiden knew.

He wasn't sure if he appreciated their silence or resented it. No one talked about Devlin, and no one talked about the fact that everything was different now. It was a giant elephant in the room that only seemed to grow as time went on.

It took showering to finally shake the last of his nightmare and put him back on solid ground. He scrubbed his body, letting his mind wander back to how things with Olivia had ended in the car. It had been so fucking difficult not to bury himself between her legs, but she'd given him her trust—something he knew for a fact she didn't do lightly—and he couldn't betray that. He didn't want to.

It didn't matter. He had no intention of letting her walk out of his life and, as a result, there was plenty of time for them to work up to having sex again. For now, he had the dazed look on her face after her second orgasm to keep his demons at bay. He smiled and shut off the water. The things that woman did for him.

He walked back into his bedroom and froze when he realized he wasn't alone. *What the fuck?* "You know, Aiden, sitting here silently in my room isn't sexy. In fact, it's downright creepy."

"I need to talk to you. Since you apparently still don't give a fuck about anyone but yourself, I didn't dare wake you from your beauty sleep."

Not this again. Cillian walked into his closet and started pulling on clothes. "Last I checked, I haven't dropped any balls in the last week, so what crawled up your ass and died?"

"Where were you yesterday?"

*Yesterday*? He frowned. "I had a date." After buttoning up his shirt, he moved back into his room to select a tie.

Aiden shook his head. "A date. So you missed out on the announcement that you're about to become an uncle for a piece of ass."

He held up his hand and gave his brother his full attention. "Hold on, what? Uncle?"

"Teague and Callie are expecting." Aiden's mouth twisted. "She's due in March."

The room took a slow turn while he processed that information. "Another generation of O'Malleys is starting." He wasn't sure why that was so weird to him, but it was.

"Sheridan-O'Malleys."

"It might be the fact I was asleep like fifteen minutes ago, but you don't sound too happy about this."

Aiden sighed. "It's a good thing. Or it would be if all signs weren't pointing to us having an enemy—or multiple enemies—poking around Boston. Callie's going to be vulnerable, and Teague's going to be focused on her instead of all the things that could go wrong. It'll be up to us to pick up the slack."

"I don't think Callie's nearly as vulnerable as people might think." She'd managed to step up and take over the Sheridan family without more than a few ripples.

Aiden pushed to his feet and started pacing. "You know what I mean. Things aren't as stable as they should be. We still haven't heard from Romanov after the Carrigan disaster, and there's the three percent still missing."

"I thought you were going to look into that."

"I did. All the businesses claim that it was an accounting error made in innocence." Aiden turned on his heel and started another circuit around the room. "They even used the same language."

"You think they were coached." It made sense. If someone was crafty enough to slip in and steal from them, they had to be dangerous enough that the businesses affected wouldn't think to cross them. Considering how they felt about the O'Malleys, that made whoever it was a special kind of scary. Seamus was downright ruthless when it came to getting full and timely payments. It would start with a menacing visit, which was usually enough to bring people back in line—but if it wasn't, things would escalate quickly. Damage to the property. Damage to the property owner. He hadn't had to kill anyone since Cillian could remember, but when the O'Malleys first took over the territory, there had been more than a few people who tried to hold out.

If someone was managing to undermine them with *that* kind of fear present in their people, they were a threat—one that couldn't be ignored.

Suddenly, he was right on the same page as Aiden.

They needed that information, and they needed it yesterday. "We need that name."

"You think I don't know that? I don't have a lot of options available to me." Aiden ran his hands through his hair, making it stand on end. "Father wants to make an example of one of them."

Cillian shuddered. He knew exactly what that entailed. "Isn't that a little extreme? We've worked fucking hard to get these businesses to the point where they're cooperating with us instead of obeying out of sheer terror." They weren't exactly on the same page as the Sheridans, but the O'Malleys were still worlds better than the Hallorans. Or they had been before James took over. He had a softer touch than his father, and from what Cillian could tell, his territory had been benefiting from it.

"That's the point—they *aren't* working with us if they're

slipping money away to someone else." Aiden stopped short. "He says it's a good time of year for a fire."

And suddenly it all made sense. His brother had been stepping up more and more as time went on, taking over the day-to-day operations and phasing their father out. But, as far as Cillian could tell, that had mostly been the legal business. Now it looked like Father was handing over the other side of things.

He wasn't sure whether to comfort his brother or tell him to man the fuck up. They were O'Malleys. That meant that sometimes they had to get their hands dirty and do things that would have them waking up in the middle of the night, breathless and haunted, with demons still riding them. Then again, easy enough for him to say when *he* wasn't the one required to set fire to someone's property. "I'm sorry."

"Don't be sorry. It's the price of doing business. That poor schmuck who's going to lose his shop knows that as well as I do." His face went stony. "He better give me the fucking information after that."

Or he'd have to work the guy over... and maybe worse. *There's nothing to help in this situation. You just power through it and try to make it out the other side without too much damage.* "What can I do?"

Aiden turned to look out his window to the street below. "If I bring you their information and books, can you find the money trail?"

He was nowhere near the computer whiz that Devlin had been, but he wasn't a total disgrace. And he was learning fast. "Unless they're some sort of tech genius, I should be able to."

"Good." Aiden moved toward the door. "Keep your phone on you. I'm going to need you here as soon as I have it."

"I will." He watched his oldest brother leave, closing the door softly behind him, and couldn't shake the feeling that he was seeing what remained of Aiden's moral code ground to dust. It had been a long time in coming, but that didn't make it any easier to witness.

And there wasn't a damn thing he could do.

Hell, he wasn't sure he'd do it, even if there was. The sad truth was that a certain level of ruthlessness and willingness to get their hands dirty was required of any leader who wanted to *stay* a leader. Cillian had never been so glad that he wasn't the heir—or even next in line to the heir. Guilt rose. He shouldn't be happy one of his siblings was shouldering the burden so he didn't have to. He'd never avoided his duty to the O'Malleys, but then, he'd never been asked to do the things that were going to be a common thing for his brother as the one in charge. He fucking hoped that Aiden had it in him to do what was necessary.

If he didn't, then they were all in serious trouble.

* * *

Olivia managed to sneak two hours of sleep after her shift before Hadley woke up. Then it was time to throw together some food for both of them and figure out what they were doing with their day. She pulled her hair up into a ponytail. "What do you think, baby girl? Pancakes?" She usually saved them for a special occasion, but after last night, today was feeling pretty damn special. Things had been so unbelievably good with Cillian, and then she'd gone to work and had one of the best shifts since she started at Jameson's. There were two bachelor parties getting started there, and they'd tipped her well—all while ribbing the grooms they were with. She smiled to remember the way the one groom-to-be had blushed. Whoever he was marrying was a lucky woman. That guy was a serious winner.

Hadley hustled into the kitchen. "Cakes?"

"Yep. We're doing pancakes. Maybe I'll even try my hand at Minnie Mouse." She swept her daughter up and propped her on her hip. "Want to help Mommy?"

"Help!"

"I thought so." She moved around the minuscule kitchen, grabbing the pancake mix, vegetable oil, eggs, and milk. A quick check to make sure they had syrup and strawberries, and she was ready to get started.

Which, of course, was when someone decided to knock on her door.

"Damn."

"Damn!"

She froze. *Do not react. Do not react.* "Hadley, that's a grown-up word." Hopefully if she didn't make a big deal about it, her daughter would let it go. Keeping her face blank, she set her down and headed for the door.

Hadley laughed. "Damn! Damn! Damn!"

*Great.* She was going to have to explain to Mrs. Richards why her daughter was acquiring the vocabulary of a sailor. The older woman would just adore that. Olivia grinned as she unlocked the door. Well, it would make a great story later on in life. And she had four years to cure Hadley of the habit before she started school—plenty of time, at least in theory. She opened the door, and stared, her mind frantically scrambling to come up with a logical reason for what she was seeing.

There wasn't one.

Dmitri raised a perfectly shaped dark brow. "Are you going to invite me in, Olivia?"

*It's not a hallucination. He's really here.* "I'm seriously considering slamming the door in your face and calling the police."

If anything, he looked more amused. "You won't."

No, she wouldn't. They weren't in New York anymore, so there was no reason to think he had half the Boston police force in his back pocket the way he did back home, but that didn't mean they would side with her. She glanced up and down the hallway. "You're alone?"

"For the moment."

So his thugs were around, but he was giving her the illusion of privacy. Since that would only last as long as he indulged it, she stepped back and opened the door wider. Dmitri was more than capable of having one of his men kick down her door if she decided to be difficult, and she didn't want to deal with the questions—or the financial fallout—that would bring. "What do you want?"

He ignored her question, taking his time looking around the apartment. She tried to see it through his eyes, and cringed. The entirety of it could fit into his office back home, and the fading yellow paint now looked more like piss than the cheery sunshine she was sure the last tenant was aiming for. The carpet was old and frayed and a far cry from the thick ones that covered most of the floors in the Romanov residence.

*Stop it. You didn't invite him here. You're not responsible for impressing him. It's not even possible, and you damn well know it.*

He grinned when he caught sight of Hadley, the expression completely at odds with the carefully controlled way he normally held himself. The worst part was that she wasn't sure if it was feigned or not. With Dmitri she never could tell, and that scared the shit out of her. He crouched down. "How's my favorite Hadley?"

Hadley ran to him, her giggle filling the room as he stood and tickled her. It made Olivia sick, but she wasn't going to rush over there and tear her daughter from his arms. It was exactly the sort of emotional response that would please him, and she refused to give him the satisfaction. So she crossed her arms over her chest and waited. It only took a few minutes for him to finish playing with her daughter and set Hadley back on the ground. She immediately lifted her chubby arms to be held again. "Up."

"Ah, ah. Your mommy and I have something to talk about." He pulled a toy from his pocket, and Olivia nearly rolled her eyes when she saw it was a pretend cell phone. *Perfect.* "But I brought a surprise for you."

Hadley's face lit up. She grabbed the phone and toddled over to sit on the couch, her face a mask of concentration.

Only then did Dmitri turn back to Olivia. "This is what you left your family behind for? I never knew your penchant for playing the martyr went so deep."

This time she lost the fight not to roll her eyes. "Considering I was more like a stray dog that you let stay in the house than actual family, I don't know why you keep throwing that word around. I'm not family, and I never will be."

"Andrei didn't believe that."

She hated that the sound of their father's name made her flinch. "Yes, he did. Right up until he was on his deathbed. Chalk the change of heart up to dementia brought on by seeing his life ending, and let's move on."

"As delightful as it would be to keep beating this dead horse, that's not why I'm here."

She'd figured as much. "Then why are you here?"

He moved around the living room, which took him a grand total of three steps, and paused in front of a picture of her and Hadley. It wasn't anything fancy, but it was one of the tiny tokens that made this *home*. Dmitri picked it up, and it was everything she could do not to rush over and snatch it out of his hands. He looked at it far too long for her state of mind. "You aren't coming back."

God, were they really going to go around again? "No, I'm not coming back."

He nodded and set the picture down. She wasn't sure how to read the look on his face. He didn't like her. He never had. She was pretty sure if she was on fire, he wouldn't spare the energy to even think about putting her out. The only reason he was so damn determined to get her back to New York was because his father—*their* father— had insisted she take the Romanov name, and Dmitri had given his word that he'd see it done.

*Thanks, but no thanks.*

"I hear you have a new boyfriend."

She blinked. "I'm sorry, what?"

"And an O'Malley?" He tsked. "I knew your taste in men was questionable after Sergei, but this is taking things a bit far. At least Sergei was one of ours, if misguided at times."

Times like when he let Olivia seduce him. It had been a mistake—looking for love in all the wrong places—and she'd known Dmitri didn't approve, but this was the first he'd ever verbally acknowledged it. "I thought he could give me what I needed." *Why the hell am I trying to talk sense with this man? He doesn't care.*

"And you think this O'Malley will do the same?" He shook his head. "He won't. They're selfish beasts, every single one of them."

"As much as I've enjoyed this sibling bonding time, the day I start taking dating advice from you is the day hell freezes over."

"Then it's a good thing I'm here about business and not love, isn't it?"

Damn it, she *knew* he had a reason for showing up. "Then I'll ask again. What is it you want?"

"You might resist coming back to New York, but you're now in a unique position to be useful." The *for once* went unsaid. He touched her faded and worn second-hand couch and made a sound of distaste. "The O'Malley family and I have a complicated history."

*Oh no. No, no, no.* She held herself straight and still, the sound of her daughter playing in the next room a surreal counterpoint to what was going on in this one. "I don't want any part of it."

"That's unfortunate, Olivia, because this man of yours, Cillian, does the books for the family—"

"Stop. Just *stop.*" She wanted to cover her ears and curl into a ball to escape his words. She didn't want her borderline-evil half brother turning his attention on Cillian. She might have thought they were alike initially, but time had more than proved her wrong. Cillian wasn't a monster. He wasn't even close. "If you hurt him—"

"Darling sister, as much as I enjoy your willingness to think the absolute worst of me, I have no intention of laying a hand on the boy."

Which wasn't the same thing as saying he wasn't planning on hurting Cillian—or worse. She forced her expression to as close to neutral as she was capable of. If Dmitri had a plan, she needed to know what it was. "Then what do you want with him?"

"The information he has access to." He spread his arms, the very picture of innocence. She knew better. "They owe me a debt. I can collect it without harming anyone in any way—except financially, of course."

Just because he could didn't mean he would. The Romanov family might not have an official motto, but if they did, it would be something like "Never leave an enemy alive at your back." They were big fans of burning the ground and salting it behind them when they took out competitors. There was no reason to think that the O'Malleys would be any different. She shook her head. "Even if I wanted to help—and I very much don't—it's not like he's inviting me back to his office and leaving me unattended to dig through his records. What you're asking is impossible."

"Nothing's impossible with the right motivation." He turned back to the photograph and picked it up. This time, there was no mistaking the threat of his attention. "You have a very beautiful daughter—a daughter with Romanov blood in her veins no matter how much you wish to deny it."

"Stop it," she whispered through suddenly numb lips.

He ignored her. "I've been lax with you up until this point, but the truth is that she's the next generation. Our father had specific ideas of what that involved. If you insist on fighting those plans... You know how these things work."

Yeah, she did, but she still found herself verbalizing it. "You're threatening to take my daughter from me."

"Olivia, please stop with the dramatics." He set the photograph down, every move perfectly controlled. "I'm not the monster you like to pretend."

No, he was worse. *He's threatening to take my baby if I don't do what he wants. Oh God, what am I going to do?* She forced her panic down and tried to *think*. "Then what, exactly, are you being very careful not to threaten me with?"

"A child should know her family. That's all I'm implying. I would think you and I agreed on this." He paused, his dark eyes so cold it was a wonder there wasn't a layer of ice around his body. "Sergei deserves access to her."

"Over my goddamn dead body." This wasn't about Sergei and it wasn't about bringing a twice-bastard descendant of Andrei Romanov into the fold. It was about punishing her for not doing what he wanted. *Fuck that.*

"No need for that kind of talk." He smiled, the expression making her go cold. "Think about what I said, Olivia. I'm a patient man, but the time is rapidly approaching when you'll be required to make a decision—to declare your alliance, if you will."

"That's not fair." She was having a difficult time getting a full breath when it felt like he'd sucked up all the air in the room. This was the exact thing she'd left New York to avoid. *I should have run farther.* "I don't want any part of this. I'm not taking sides." She hadn't even been aware that there *were* sides when she started falling for Cillian. She should have known better.

"Then you never should have let the O'Malley boy so close." He moved to the door and paused as he opened it. "When it comes right down to it, all we have in this world is family, Olivia. You'd do well to remember that."

She waited for the door to close before she picked up the vase on the rickety end table and threw it at the wood. It hit the door but, being plastic, didn't shatter into a million pieces. She cursed and hurried over to pick up the scattered flowers before Hadley could come investigate. *What the hell am I going to do?* Dmitri might be content with careful non-threats right now, but that wouldn't last. The longer she didn't do what he wanted, the more explicit the consequences would be.

*He'll take Hadley. He wouldn't even hesitate. If what he said is any indication, he's already preparing for it.*

It was possible he'd started preparing for it the second he realized she'd never bend to Andrei's will.

"I never should have put Sergei on the birth certificate." She'd had a moment of sentimental weakness when he'd shown up at the hospital and held their daughter for the first—and probably only—time. Stupid. It wouldn't have ultimately changed anything, though. All he needed was a paternity test to prove that he was the father, and he'd have rights to Hadley. With the Romanov finances backing him, he'd be able to tie her up in court indefinitely.

And that was if they even bothered to go the legal road. It was just as easy for Olivia to go to work one night and come home to find Mrs. Richards incapacitated and Hadley gone to God alone knew where.

The band around her chest got tighter at the thought. *Oh God, oh God, oh God. What am I going to do?*

Running sounded like a really great plan, but she couldn't run on no cash, and if the ease that Dmitri found her with this time was any indication, she wasn't very good at it. They'd need new identities, cash to spare, and connections she just plain didn't have. He'd find them. It probably wouldn't even take him a month with his resources.

"Mama?"

She pasted a smile on her face and turned to her daughter. "Hey, baby girl. How about we watch some *Beauty and the Beast* while I make pancakes?" Some cuddle time might be able to beat back the panic making black dots dance across her vision.

"Up!" Hadley lifted her arms, and Olivia was all too happy to scoop her up, grab the throw blanket off the back of the couch, and get them set up in their favorite spot. She turned on the movie and settled in, letting the feel of her daughter, healthy and whole, in her arms relax her.

Her mind circled the problem as the movie progressed, but the solution didn't magically appear in front of her face. If anything, the more she thought about it, the clearer it became that she was in over her head in a big way. As much as she hated to admit it, Dmitri was right—there were only two options. She either had to obey him like a well-behaved lap dog, or she had to ask for help. She wasn't a fan of either option. Olivia had always taken care of herself, and the idea of needing to lean on someone stuck in her throat.

She looked down at Hadley. *For you, baby girl, I'll do it. I won't like it, but I'll do whatever it takes to keep you out of Romanov hands.*

Really, there was only one person she could ask for help who'd actually have the resources to do something effective. Cillian. She cuddled her daughter closer, considering. She liked him. She liked him a lot. That didn't mean she completely trusted him. Plus, trusting him with *her* and trusting him with Hadley were two very different things.

She'd told him that she had a past, but it was a big leap from having an abusive boyfriend like she'd let him believe and having one of the strongest cells of the Russian mob on the East Coast on her ass. It was entirely possible that he'd offer her something similar to what Dmitri had—his power for her information.

It was like choosing between the rock and the hard place. Neither of them was a great option.

*You believe Cillian is different.*

*Sure, but do I believe it enough to trust him with my life? Or, more importantly, with Hadley's?*

She didn't know. What she wouldn't give for a crystal ball to tell her what the right answer was. But, in the end, it didn't really matter. Dmitri wasn't an option. That meant she had to throw herself on Cillian's mercy. To do anything else would only postpone the moment when her half brother took Hadley away from her.

*I said I'd do anything to keep her away from the Romanovs. I meant it.* She took a shuddering breath and reached for her phone. *It's now or never.*

# CHAPTER FOURTEEN

Cillian set another stack of papers aside as his phone rang. He was almost pathetically grateful for the distraction. As much as he enjoyed his job, doing it for hours on end wasn't his idea of a good time. While Aiden was off doing what was necessary to get information that would help them figure out what the hell was going on, Cillian needed to clear off as much work as he could so he would be able to focus *solely* on that project when it showed up.

But a break wouldn't hurt him any now.

He grabbed his phone, grinning when he recognized Olivia's number. "Hey, sweetheart."

"Are you busy?"

He straightened at the tone of her voice. He'd heard her pissed and turned on and amused, but he'd never heard her sound so...vulnerable. Almost like she was scared. Every instinct he had demanded he go to her, but that was a damn problem since he didn't know what was going on or where she was. *Then find out, asshole.* "What's wrong?"

She laughed, the sound soft and broken. "I probably shouldn't be calling you right now. When push comes to shove, we barely know each other."

If he let her keep going, she was going to talk herself out of the original reason she'd called him. Cillian took a deep breath and made an effort to sound as calm and soothing as possible. "You can trust me."

"That's just it. I don't have a choice right now. You know that saying 'Better the devil you know than the devil you don't'? In this case, it's dead wrong."

He pushed to his feet, adrenaline spiking through him. She was in trouble. She wouldn't be talking this way if anything else was going on. "Where are you? I'm walking out the door right now."

"Wait." Olivia took a deep breath and, when she spoke again, she sounded more centered. "I'm sorry. I'm just rattled. That bastard always gets the best of me."

The roaring in his ears didn't abate one bit. Someone had threatened her—that much was clear. The realization didn't do a damn thing for his blood pressure. "Tell me what you need and it's yours."

"Just like that? What if I said I needed papers for me and Hadley to have new identities and enough money to disappear forever?"

That was one thing he could do. He'd had connections before he took over as the moneyman for his family, and now *he* was the one who would coordinate that kind of thing if any of their people needed to disappear. The thought of sending Olivia off and never seeing her again left a bad taste in his mouth, but she'd called him for help. From everything he knew about her, the fact that she'd even picked up the phone was a goddamn miracle. "Then I'd make it happen."

This wasn't about him and his needs. This was about a woman in trouble—a woman he cared about. He'd never considered himself a guy with a hero complex, but apparently some of Teague's white knight attitude had rubbed off on him, because he cared more about keeping Olivia safe than keeping her close to him. *Though if there's some other option…*

*No.* He'd spent the majority of his life thinking only of himself and being a selfish little shit. Now wasn't the time to backslide into that.

And she still hadn't said a damn thing. He rubbed the scar on his shoulder, wondering why the hell it decided to start aching right *now*. "Is that what you need, sweetheart? It'll take me a little time to put together, but I can make it happen." He had money of his own, though he rarely touched it for anything other than his clothing. It would be nothing to withdraw the amount she'd need to land on her feet somewhere else. He didn't have to think twice about it. The papers would be slightly more complicated, because he needed to keep that information out of O'Malley hands.

"You're being for real, aren't you? You'd just write me a check and let me go."

She sounded so shocked, he almost smiled. "Well, I wouldn't write you a check, since that shit can be tracked. But a duffel bag full of cash wouldn't be a horrible idea."

"I don't even know what to think of you, Cillian O'Malley."

Yeah, he didn't know what to think of himself most days, either. He leaned on the edge of his desk. "I just need the names you want the papers under and I can get started." He didn't want to. Fuck, it hurt just thinking about it—a whole lot more than he would have expected. He'd do it, though. For her, he was starting to realize that he'd do damn near anything.

*You're a goddamn sucker.*

Probably, but that was neither here nor there.

Something rustled over the line as Olivia shifted. "God, you have no idea how tempting that is. But I can't take you up on it."

It took him two seconds to process her words. She wasn't going to disappear. Relief was quickly followed by a strange mix of fear and anger. "If it's dangerous enough that you were thinking of running in the first place, then that's what you need to do. Letting your pride get in the way of your safety is fucking stupid, Olivia, and you damn well know it."

"I don't need to owe another man, okay? I'll find another way."

Damn it, he was fucking this up. He closed his eyes and counted to ten, protective instincts he hadn't even been aware of clamoring for him to do whatever it took to keep her safe. There had to be another way—something he could do that she wouldn't see as charity. A thought blossomed, one guaranteed to get him into a shit-ton of trouble with his family. He leaned against his desk. It wasn't like he hadn't been there before. He'd deal with the fallout, and it would have the added bonus of keeping Olivia close. "I have another idea."

A pause. "I'm listening."

"My family has a house out in the country in Connecticut. It's isolated and sits on twenty acres or some shit. It would be child's play to set up a perimeter with a few men.

No one could sneak in or out without us knowing, so it's as safe as we could get without you pulling a disappearing act."

"We?"

"Sweetheart, I'm going with you." Another thing his family wouldn't be happy about, though his taking a near-stranger there would overshadow pretty much everything else. The house in the country had come from his father's side of the family, and it wasn't used by anyone who wasn't directly related to them. Growing up, it had been that one oasis in the middle of the politics and shady dealings that he hadn't understood until he was older. Out there, even his father relaxed and became less of a hard-ass. He still wasn't going to win any Dad of the Year awards, but he'd actually cracked a smile on occasion.

Another pause, longer this time. He could picture her thinking it over, but the truth was that if she was calling him for help, she was backed into a corner and didn't have a damn thing going for her. She wouldn't have picked up the phone if she had any other option. He had no illusions about that.

Finally, she said, "I don't like this."

"If you're worried about owing me, I take payment in sexual favors."

She laughed. It was nowhere near her infectious one he'd heard the other night, but it was a start. "You're insufferable."

"That's what my mother tells me every day." He hesitated. He didn't want to push her, but it would take some maneuvering to get things in place if they were going to leave as quickly as possible. "What do you say?"

"You're not even going to ask what happened that made me need to rabbit?"

"It's irrelevant." And, yeah, he was definitely going to ask, but getting her to safety was more important than knowing all the dirty details. "You'll tell me when you're ready."

"I really don't know what to make of you most days."

Hell, he didn't know what to make of himself right now. He was still wrapping his mind around the fact that he'd offered to help her disappear without hesitation. So he waited while she thought it over.

A voice in the background sounded, a little girl. He couldn't make out what she said, but the innocence made his heart skip a beat. It was one thing to know Olivia had a kid. It was entirely another to hear evidence of her daughter. *She's going to be bringing that kid with her, so you better get used to the idea* real *quick.*

Her daughter—Hadley, that was her name—was part of the Olivia package. He'd already decided that he wanted her and everything that came with her, so he'd just have to deal with it.

She murmured something and then she was back. "Okay. I'll go with you. Tell me what you need from me."

He let go of the breath he hadn't even been aware he was holding. *She said yes.* "I need your address and an hour. Pack a bag with everything you need for you and Hadley and I'll text you when I'm outside."

"An hour." She cleared her throat. "Right. Okay. I can do that."

God, she sounded so shaken that he wanted to reach through the phone and hug her. "It will be okay, sweetheart."

"I . . . Yeah. You're right. Cillian?"

He was already up and walking through the door of his office. "Yeah?"

"Thank you."

His heart gave an alarming thump. "I'll see you in an hour." He hung up and immediately dialed the one person he knew he could talk to about this without it getting back to his father. The phone rang a few times before his brother picked up. Cillian took a deep breath. "Teague, I need a favor."

His brother didn't hesitate. "What do you need?"

Any of his other siblings would have demanded an explanation before offering—even Sloan. Maybe especially Sloan. Not Teague, though. He offered help without any strings attached. *It's a damn good thing that Callie has a ruthless streak, or they'd be in all sorts of trouble.* He hurried up the stairs and through the door into his room. "Do you still have keys to the Connecticut house?" Cillian had lost them sometime over the years, and he'd never needed to replace them since he never went out there alone.

"Of course."

"I'm going to swing by in a little bit and pick them up." After he'd figured out how the hell he was going to swing protection without anyone noticing that half the muscle were gone. He almost asked Teague, but that wasn't his brother's problem. Besides, having Sheridan men out there would be yet one more thing guaranteed to make his father blow a gasket. Better to waylay Liam and figure it out from there.

"Okay." The background sound muted, as if Teague had closed a door. "What kind of trouble are you in?"

"It's not me, for once. It's a...friend."

"You know you're going to catch hell for bringing this friend of yours out there."

"I know." She was worth it. She was more than worth it. "It's only a temporary arrangement."

"I'll have the keys ready."

Yeah, his brother's white knight complex had definitely rubbed off on Cillian. He grabbed a bag from his closet and started tossing clothes into it. "Thanks. I really appreciate it. And if someone asks..."

"I know nothing." He could almost hear Teague grinning. "Though if you change your mind about needing anything else, I'm only a phone call away. If you're in trouble—"

Everyone was so damn eager to assume he was the one with the sky falling down around him. Yeah, he'd been there more than a few times over the years, but fuck. "I've got it covered. Thanks, man."

"Understood."

"By the way, congrats on the pending member of your family."

"Thanks. We're pretty excited." The sheer joy in his brother's voice staggered him. Was that what came from being a father? He'd never associated happiness with kids, because their father never had taken much interest in them until they hit high school and became creatures he could reason with.

It was something to think about.

"I'll be there in a few." He hung up and immediately made a second call. This one had to be handled more delicately, because Liam might be the most sympathetic of his father's men, but he was still his father's man. As expected, Liam answered after the first ring. "Neale."

Here they went. "Liam, it's Cillian. I'm heading out to the country house for a while and I need protection duty. *Discreet* protection duty."

A pause. "Am I to assume your father doesn't know about this?"

Well, hell, he cut right to the chase. "Ideally, I'd like him in the dark for as long as possible."

"Fuck." Liam sighed. "You kids don't make my life easy, you know that?"

Considering Liam was Aiden's age and hardly an old man, Cillian only had so much pity. "At least life is never boring."

"That's the damn truth. How much heat am I likely to take over this?"

"I'll handle it. My idea, my order. You were just being a good employee."

Liam muttered something too low to hear, but it didn't sound complimentary. "I can spare five men."

Five men to cover twenty acres. Cillian bit back a curse. He couldn't have it both ways. He couldn't keep this under the radar and still take a small army with him. He went back to his closet and reached up to grab the .45 he kept there. He didn't normally carry it with him—too many things could go sideways in a conflict when someone pulled out a gun— but his father had made sure he knew how to use it. "That'll have to work. Can you have them ready in twenty?"

"Jesus. Yeah, I'll light a fire under their asses." He paused. "Do I want to know what this is about?"

"The less you know the better. Have them meet me in the garage."

"Will do." Then he was gone, off to coordinate.

Cillian checked the clip in the pistol, and then dug through the dresser to find the holster Aiden had bought him years ago when he'd bitched about the gun ruining the line of his suits. Shoving one into the waistband of his slacks might look cool in the movies, but it wasn't comfortable, and it was hardly safe. Cillian was rather fond of his ass—he didn't like the idea of shooting off part of it. Not to mention the chafing was a bitch.

He shrugged into the holster, fastened it, and then slipped the gun into place. A few practice draws were all it took to have muscle memory kicking in. As long as he kept his jacket unbuttoned, he'd have a clear line. He wasn't as good as the men they had on protection duty, but he wasn't a slouch, either.

One last walk-through of his room, and he had everything packed that he needed. There wasn't much need for three-piece suits in the country, so he'd unearthed a few pairs of jeans and T-shirts that he tended to forget he owned. He checked his watch. Right on time.

Down in the garage he found the five men Liam had promised him. Mark, Jacob, Grant, Rodger, and Finn. They were all solid guys, though he'd had the most experience with Mark. The man in question stepped forward. "Do you need an escort or do you want us to go straight there and get set up?"

The mantle of leadership wasn't one that Cillian craved, but there was a first time for everything. He thought quickly. He didn't know what danger there might be in the immediate future, but if Olivia wasn't panicked enough to be running without a plan in place, then there was no reason to think that he wouldn't be able to get her out of state on his own. "Go straight there. I'm leaving the city inside of an hour."

Mark nodded. "Got it. We'll watch for you." He and the other four men slid into one of the Hummers they kept for special occasions. The trio of vehicles were outfitted as small tanks—the kind of thing a person only took if they were expecting the worst kind of trouble. Since Cillian didn't know exactly *what* kind of trouble to expect, he appreciated Mark's choice.

For himself, he chose a Beemer. It was fast when the situation called for it, but it was nondescript enough that it didn't call attention to itself. Add in the customizations of bulletproof glass and a reinforced body and it was the best option. Cillian threw his bag into the backseat and headed out.

Technically, he was going by Teague's for the key, but the truth was he wanted a few minutes to talk to his brother and get a backup plan in place. Olivia might not like the idea of disappearing, but if she was scared enough to consider it, he wanted her to have that option. Maybe she wouldn't take money from him, but legitimate papers could go a long way. If Cillian was out of town, he wouldn't be able to get that ball rolling... but his brother could.

He just had to get him to agree to it first.

# CHAPTER FIFTEEN

Olivia checked her bag for the twentieth time. It had everything she could possibly need—which meant it had the majority of her and Hadley's possessions in it. Without her daughter's favorite toys scattered around the living room, the apartment looked dull and lifeless. It was almost enough for her to call the whole thing off. Maybe she was overreacting. Hell, she'd handled things herself before. She could do it again.

Except her version of handling it had bought her less than a year. Sure, she hadn't been trying to disappear completely, but there was no reason to think that if she ran again she'd be any more successful. If it had been just her, she wouldn't have hesitated.

But it was a whole lot easier to gamble with her life than it was to gamble with her daughter's.

She moved to the window and checked the parking lot again. The hour Cillian had given her was almost up, so he should be showing up at any time. He wasn't who she was watching for, though. The fear that brought her back to the window again and again over the last hour was that Sergei would appear. It wouldn't be Dmitri—she knew that much. He wasn't above getting his hands dirty, but he was a big fan of using the best weapon for the job. For this job, that weapon would be her ex.

She'd given up regretting her relationship with Sergei right around the time her daughter made her appearance in the world, but that didn't mean she was willing to forgive and forget. He'd already proven that he would choose the Romanovs over her. When she needed him the most—when she thought she had a chance to finally slip her leash—he'd let her believe he was leaving town with her...and then turned around and hauled her back to the Romanov residence, which resulted in her being under lockdown for the last four months of her pregnancy and the first two months of Hadley's life. Until Andrei died.

Her heart thudded at the memory. She'd barely waited for his death to be announced to leave, and that time she hadn't given Sergei a heads-up. She hadn't told *anyone*, though she'd seen her mother on her way out. The woman hadn't even glanced at Hadley, too wrapped up in playing the grieving mistress in her impeccable black couture dress.

*I wonder if Dmitri showed her the door as soon as our father's body was in the ground.*

She shook her head, letting go of the small shred of satisfaction that thought brought. There were bigger things to worry about right now—like Sergei showing up at the same time Cillian did...

*Oh God.* She'd brought Cillian into this. She'd never forgive herself if something happened to him because of her.

She hadn't even considered that as a possibility when she called him. All she'd been thinking was that she needed help and he was the one man who had the means to give it to her—and who might not hold it over her head for the rest of her life.

She checked on Hadley, but her daughter was sleeping soundly on the couch where she'd laid down with her favorite blankie while Olivia hurried around and packed their suitcase. *Thank God for small favors.* She grabbed her phone and dialed Cillian again.

He picked up almost immediately. "Did something else happen?"

"No. I just..." She braced herself. He was helping her because he was a better man than she could have dreamed. It wasn't fair to drag him into her mess. "Cillian—"

"Hold that thought."

A knock on her door had her spinning around. She approached the faded wood like it was a poisonous snake and leaned in to peer through the peephole. A gorgeous tattooed man in a three-piece suit stared back at her. "You're here."

"Open the door, sweetheart, and let's blow this joint."

"This was probably a mistake." She realized how stupid it was to be having this conversation on the phone when he was on the other side of her door, but she couldn't quite make herself unlock it. Not yet. "I would never forgive myself if something happened to you because of me."

"I'm a big boy, Olivia. I can take care of myself—and you and Hadley in the mix." He put his hand on the door, and she could almost feel his touch if she concentrated. "But if it makes you feel better, you can tell me everything. If I think it's too much after that, I'll turn around and bring you guys back to Boston."

Crazy as it was, that *did* make her feel better, even if she suspected he was just telling her what she wanted to hear. But that was a rational response—he'd hear her out and then he'd decide. She took a deep breath and unlocked the door. It was only when she opened it that she realized she still had the phone pressed against her ear. "Sorry. I'm just… rattled."

"It's okay." He waited for her to step back before he walked into the apartment. He glanced around, but then focused solely on her. "Where's your bag?"

"Here. And we should hook up Hadley's car seat before I pick her up. She'll probably sleep through the whole thing, but it will minimize the chance of a tantrum." Her daughter reacted to being woken up about as well as Olivia did.

He picked up the car seat and the suitcase. "Sit tight. I'll be right back."

She started to volunteer to help—hooking up the damn car seat sometimes felt like it required a degree in rocket science—but stopped. She couldn't leave Hadley alone. Sure, she'd be right there and have a direct line of sight to the apartment entrance… but she couldn't make herself do it. Dmitri's almost-threat was too close to the forefront of her mind. Her fear might be irrational in this situation, but it *wasn't* irrational in general. So she nodded. "Okay."

Then she stood and watched him from the window as he put her suitcase into the trunk and went to work on the car seat. It took him a few attempts to get it figured out, but he hooked it in faster than she had the first time she'd tried. Once she was sure he'd gotten it, she picked up Hadley and tucked the blankie around her. It was quick work to lock her door behind her, and she paused, part of her wondering if she'd ever see the shithole apartment again.

"Olivia?"

She turned to find Mrs. Richards peeking into the hall. *Mrs. Richards.* Shit, she'd forgotten to contact the woman. *Oh lord, I forgot to call Benji, too.* The latter would have to be dealt with on the way out of town, but she could take care of this now, at least. "We've run into some trouble."

The old woman frowned. "Trouble in the shape of that ex of yours, if I don't miss my guess."

"Yeah." She shifted Hadley into a more comfortable position. "I'm going to go out of town for a while until things calm down." *If* they ever did calm down. Dmitri could be dogged when it suited him, and she didn't see him letting go anytime soon. If ever. "If anyone comes looking—"

"Don't you worry about a thing, dear. I don't need to know where you're going—just keep that beautiful baby girl of yours safe." She walked out of her apartment and pressed a quick kiss to the top of Hadley's head. "Try to call and let me know you're safe once in a while."

"I will." Her eyes burned, but she blinked past it. This wasn't forever. She had a life here and, while it might not be particularly glamorous, it was *hers*. She'd fight tooth and nail to keep it. She just wasn't dumb enough to ignore the threat dangling right in front of her face. "I'll talk to you soon."

"Good. Now don't let me keep you. Go."

She went. Cillian met her at the bottom of the stairs. He did a double take at the sight of Hadley in her arms, but then he was next to her, his hand resting on the small of her back as they crossed the parking lot. She watched him out of the corner of her eye. He was too busy watching everything else to notice, surveying the area for a threat.

*He really came. He didn't demand an explanation. I called, and he showed up.*

It was a whole hell of a lot to wrap her mind around. She'd hoped—of course she'd hoped—but she hadn't really believed he'd come through for her, no questions asked, until he'd done just that. *Trust issues much, Olivia?*

*Only totally.*

With her track record, who could blame her? From Andrei right down the line to Sergei, not a single person had ever once dropped everything and come to her when she was in need. There were always conditions and power plays—if they even came at all.

She hooked Hadley into her seat, and then they were in the car and driving away from her place. She glanced back, but they'd already turned the corner, and the building was no longer in sight. Olivia sat back in her seat with a sigh. *It's not forever.*

It sure as hell *felt* like forever.

She shot another look at Cillian, but he was relaxed in the driver's seat...as long as she didn't pay attention to the way he watched the review mirror. "You think we're being followed?"

"No, but I've recently graduated into the 'better safe than sorry' mind-set. Going the roundabout way isn't going to hurt us any, and if we *are* being followed, it should throw them off."

"Oh." She pulled her knees to her chest, feeling seriously out of her element. She'd been so damn naive to think she'd left this life behind her. "I'm sorry."

"Stop apologizing." But he said it gently. "If I didn't want to help you, I wouldn't help. The offer to disappear still stands, by the way."

God, he was seriously too good to be true. She'd heard his conviction on the phone, but seeing it in person only drove that fact home. He wouldn't hesitate to give her a stack of cash and a set of papers and send her on her way. *So eager to see the back of me?* She shut the thought down. It was petty and downright wrong.

He was here…taking care of her. Shouldering part of the burden so she didn't have to go it alone. Her heart beat too hard at the realization. It was *nice* to have someone she could lean on—actually lean on—who would show up when she needed them, and was so damn capable while doing it. Because he wanted to be here. If he didn't—or didn't want to deal with her special brand of bullshit—all he would have had to do was tell her to fuck off.

As if reading her mind, he said, "I'm here because I want to be. No one held a gun to my head."

*Because Sergei wasn't here to see us make our getaway.*

She was just a little ray of sunshine today, wasn't she? Olivia checked on Hadley—still sleeping—and settled into her seat. "Let's get this Q and A out of the way so you know what you're getting into."

"It can wait."

"No, it can't." She already felt bad enough about bringing him into this mess. For him to do it without knowledge of exactly what the threat was would be unforgivable. "You remember how I said I have an ugly history?"

"I remember." He turned onto the turnpike, heading west.

"Well, I might have underrepresented that threat." The panic she'd been fighting ever since Dmitri left tried to close her throat, but she forced herself to breathe past it, even though the effort left her light-headed. "You ever hear of the Romanovs?"

His hands went white-knuckled on the steering wheel,

but his voice was still just as calm as it had been since he picked her up. "Out of New York? Run by Dmitri Romanov? Those Romanovs?"

"The very ones." Of course he'd be familiar with the family. People like him had to be aware of the threats around them, and Dmitri was nothing if not a threat. The next part was harder to get out than she'd expected. "Dmitri...He..." She took a shuddering breath and started again. "We share a father. He's my half brother."

"Half brother." That calm in Cillian's voice didn't waver, but his hands also didn't relax their grip. "I'm surprised he let you move to Boston."

"He didn't have much choice. I'm not exactly one of the inner circle—up until my father died, I was nothing more than a nuisance that he wasn't quite willing to turn out onto the street. But he wasn't too keen on interacting with me, either. It was an arrangement that worked out well for both of us."

Andrei had spent the first twenty years of her life doing an admirable job of pretending she didn't exist. He was too busy running his empire and raising Dmitri to be everyone's favorite sociopath. But, bastard or not, she was his blood, and he hadn't quite turned her out. She had a room in his obscenely large house and she never went hungry. Growing up, she'd been so damn conflicted over whether it would have been better to actually *be* his daughter—or to never know he existed. That half acknowledgment drove her to do some truly questionable things over the years.

Like Sergei.

It wasn't until Andrei had been diagnosed with lung cancer that he seemed to change, to focus on family more than his empire. He started requiring that Olivia attend weekly dinners with him, which she'd resented the hell out of. She hadn't needed a father in her life for the first twenty-one years, and she wasn't ready to fall at his feet in gratitude now that he was dying and decided she was worth a damn. *Too little, too late.* Except maybe it wouldn't have been if he'd lived longer. He wasn't exactly the warmest man on the planet, but a part of her couldn't help wondering if he'd have convinced her to come around given enough time.

And then she'd remembered the way he'd treated her mother—and herself—for the last twenty-one years.

*Daddy issues, thy name is Olivia.*

She realized she'd been silent too long. "When I was eighteen, I hooked up with one of his generals. It wasn't an intentional 'fuck you' but it came across that way." Cillian still didn't say anything, so she kept going. "It also wasn't a great love affair. Sergei was...I don't know. Uncomplicated. He wanted me, and I confused that with being in love with me. I was young and stupid and desperate for attention." Maybe she still was. Otherwise, why would she have let herself get so close to an O'Malley? "It was on again and off again for a few years, but when I got pregnant, I wanted to leave New York and everything Romanov behind. My half brother probably would have let me go, but Andrei seemed to take the whole thing as a sign that it was time to officially make things right. He wanted to formally adopt me and bring me into the fold."

"I take it you weren't a fan."

*Understatement of the century.* "Would you have been?"

Cillian glanced at her. "After being ignored for my entire life, it'd be a slap in the face."

"That's exactly what it felt like, though it was more than that. I might not have been involved in the inner workings of the Romanov enterprise, but I saw enough to know I didn't want my daughter raised that way. I told Andrei to take a long walk off a short pier, and made my plans to get out of town. Sergei came to pick me up, and it seemed like I might actually make this work."

It still hurt to think about, the words like shards of glass in her throat. "And then he drove me to the Romanov residence and basically carried my screaming, pregnant ass inside. I was under house arrest for the four months it took for Hadley to make her way into the world." And every day she'd had to deal with Andrei's forced shared meals. He'd talked about her mother, though she never graced them with her presence. It hurt to know that he'd seemed to truly love her mother, and that she loved him in return. Olivia didn't *want* to understand either of them, didn't want to know her mother was capable of loving another person more than she'd ever love the daughter she never stopped resenting, not when they'd put every other aspect of their lives before their daughter time and time again. It was almost a relief when he'd finally given in to the cancer and died, because it meant she wouldn't have to have the past neither one of them could change thrown in her face.

"Jesus."

"When Andrei died, Dmitri was so focused on stabilizing the power structure that he just wanted me out of his sight." Or maybe he didn't like the constant reminder of the fact that his father had seen her pregnancy as a deficiency of *Dmitri's* since he hadn't started a family of his own. "He didn't care that I was moving out of town, and so I hopped a train up here when Hadley was less than a year old." She hadn't had much in the way of savings, but it was enough to get her started at the apartment until she was able to find a job.

"So what changed? If he was fine with you leaving, you'd think he'd want to forget you even existed."

"If only." She picked at the hole in her jeans over her knee. "Andrei was obsessed with making things right, and for whatever reason, he decided that making me a Romanov was the way to go. He set up an account with a truly ridiculous amount of money that will be mine once I officially change my name and take my place in the family." He'd left her mother a villa in the South of France, which would have made a normal person happy, but all her mother had ever wanted was an official place at the Romanov table, and seeing Olivia granted that option—and rejecting it—was the final straw. She was under strict instructions never to contact her mother again—as if she was in danger of ever doing *that*.

"Except you don't want it." He didn't sound judgmental one way or another—just stating a fact.

"No, I don't want it." Maybe her life would be easier if she could just fall in line like a good little soldier, but that had never been her way. There might be more money than she could wrap her mind around waiting for her if she did what Andrei had wanted, but the strings that were attached with it were legion.

And those strings would pass down to Hadley.

Even if she was willing to take the hit for herself and choose a comfortable material life in exchange for... everything... she couldn't do that to her daughter. Hadley deserved to grow up in a world where she was able to make her own mistakes, without being used as a political pawn or exposed to the darker side of organized crime. That kind of thing was all well and good in theory or fiction, but the reality was that even on the outskirts, Olivia had seen things she wished she could wipe from her mind. She couldn't imagine how much more she would have experienced if she'd been treated like Andrei's actual daughter.

*No, thanks.*

The silence stretched on as they passed mile marker after mile marker. Finally, Cillian said, "So what changed? You've been in Boston for about six months by my count. Why are things going sideways now?"

She watched his face in the growing shadows, the lights of passing cars playing off his cheekbones. *God, he's too gorgeous to be real. It's not fair.* And she was heading off into the country with him. She called and he came, no questions asked. That made him even sexier, if that were even possible.

*Down, girl.*

She wasn't supposed to be lusting after her savior. She was supposed to be explaining the situation so he could change his mind about taking on her mess. Olivia studied his expression, but he gave her nothing to go off of. He wasn't freaking out, and he wasn't totally dismissive of it. It kind of blew her mind. If she'd found out that a person she thought was just an average Joe was actually connected to one of the most powerful crime families on the East Coast, she'd have at least muttered a few choice words under her breath. Not Cillian, though.

But then, he was a member of a family that could be classified in the same way. Maybe this was all in a day's work for him.

She looked out the window and settled back into her seat. Or tried to. Her muscles were so tense, she could already feel a headache starting at the top of her spine. "Before our father died, Dmitri gave his word that he'd see it done. He won't break it."

Cillian snorted. "He has no problem breaking his word."

It sounded like he had personal experience with that, which lined up with the comment Dmitri had made when he showed up to threaten her. Part of her wanted to know what the O'Malleys had done to earn his enmity, but most of her was just so damn tired. *It never ends.* "You're wrong."

"No, I'm not."

She sighed. "Look, I don't like Dmitri. I actually kind of hate him, but once he gives his word, he doesn't break it." She hesitated. "But he's as slippery as they come when it suits him, so it's possible that he manipulated the situation to meet his needs."

"That's as good as lying."

"I'm not arguing that." She went back to picking at her jeans. "But whatever his faults, he loved Andrei. He's going to do whatever it takes to see his last wish fulfilled, regardless of how I feel about it."

"Are you sure he doesn't want you back there because he actually cares about you?"

She snorted. "Dmitri can barely stand me. I'm like an itch he can't manage to scratch. It irks him." And here was the part that would make or break how Cillian felt about her. "He came to visit me today. Somehow he found out about us—though it's kind of too soon to call this an 'us' I think—and he . . . he wanted me to spy on you."

Cillian didn't look over. "It makes sense. Through me you'd have information on all of the O'Malleys' inner financial workings. It'd be enough to give your half brother a golden bullet to hit us where it would hurt most."

"I would never do that."

"I know." Again, there was no doubt in his voice. It was enough to make her wonder how the hell he was so confident about everything, because she felt like she was standing on a narrow cliff and there were earthquakes shaking the ground beneath her feet. He reached over and took her hand. The contact grounded her, his skin warm against hers, a reminder that she wasn't facing this alone. "He didn't like your answer, I take it?"

"No. He didn't threaten—Dmitri *never* threatens—but he made it clear that if I didn't fall into line at least on this, he was going to prompt Sergei to take Hadley." The fear that had her calling Cillian in the first place rose up and choked her. "I won't let him take my baby. I'd die first."

"I'm here, Olivia. You aren't alone." Cillian squeezed her hand. "We'll figure out a way around this."

She wanted to believe him. She really did. The problem was that Olivia didn't see a way around it. Every road led back to Dmitri being the one in power and taking what he wanted, just like he always did.

# CHAPTER SIXTEEN

They didn't talk much for the rest of the drive. Cillian kept a hold of Olivia's hand, and the little shakes that made it through that tiny point of contact worried him. He understood her fear. Even if Dmitri Romanov didn't have a reputation for being one cold son of a bitch, any family like theirs would fight tooth and nail to keep its members close and under its thumb. His included.

Hell, between his father and brother, they'd driven Carrigan away by trying to marry her off to none other than Dmitri Romanov. He wondered if Olivia knew that, though he doubted it from her comments about her half brother keeping his word. It was something Cillian would have to tell her, because it was one more reason to prompt the man to come after them. No wonder Dmitri had been downright delighted to discover she'd gotten close to Cillian. He was still pissed about how things had turned out six months ago. Dmitri hadn't done anything overtly threatening since then, but he also hadn't responded to Father's attempts to make things right.

*He could be the one behind the missing money.*

Cillian filed the thought away for later. Once he had the information from Aiden, he could figure things out one way or another. Coming up with wild theories wasn't going to help anyone—only facts would. Right now, he needed to focus on making Olivia and her daughter as secure and safe as possible.

That, at least, he could do.

He took the turn onto the dirt road leading out to the country house. His mother had wanted it paved years ago, but his father dug in his heels about it. It had been a dirt road since his childhood, and while he might allow a few upgrades in the house itself, he wanted the land kept as untouched as possible. It was one of the strange contradictions of Seamus O'Malley. He was unashamedly a city man who loved his luxuries, but when they came out here, it was like something relaxed in him. Like he was transported back to a simpler time before he became one of the three crime lords in Boston.

Naturally, it was only in the last year that Cillian had been able to look back and realize that. Growing up, he'd been more focused on cramming as many adventures into their time out here as possible. He wound through the trees, going slow to avoid some of the potholes that had developed over the years. It was like stepping into another world. He and his siblings had roamed these woods during the few weeks of each summer they spent out here. Oh, Sloan and Devlin had always posted up somewhere with a book and ignored the rest of their siblings' pleas to come play, but the rest of them had never been closer than when they were away from the city.

It wasn't like that anymore.

Time changed everyone. He knew that.

When Aiden finished high school, their father deemed him old enough to start the training his being heir required. He hadn't gone away all at once, but somewhere in the last decade or so, he'd become a near-stranger. And Teague... Teague had nearly disappeared into himself before Callie came along. Now Carrigan was dead to the family, Sloan was more ghost than woman, and Keira was on a path of self-destruction that worried even him.

And Devlin?

Devlin was six feet underground, his future cut off in the space of a heartbeat.

Cillian stopped in front of the house, but didn't turn off the engine. The building rose out of the clearing in the middle of the trees, a giant structure that looked like something out of the Revolutionary War. Since it had been built sometime around then, he figured that made sense. But it was home away from home.

He turned to Olivia. "Stay in the car. I need to check in with my men to make sure it's safe, and then I'll be back."

She nodded, exhaustion and stress written all over her face. The last twenty-four hours had taken a toll on her, and he wanted nothing more than to wipe it all away. Since that wasn't a real option, he'd do what he could—provide her a safe place where she could breathe until they figured out the next step.

The warm night air brought the sounds of crickets. He stopped for a second and just inhaled, letting clean country scents wash over him. Boston was home, but this was a close second. Forcing himself to focus, he climbed the steps to the front door.

Mark met him on the big wraparound porch. "All clear. There hasn't been anyone here since your sisters." When they'd been hidden away during the fallout of the conflict with the Hallorans.

"Perfect." He nodded. "And the rest?"

"I have the men stationed at the easy access points, and one of us will always be in the house." Mark jerked a thumb over his shoulder. "There's enough food to last until Monday, and I've scheduled a delivery for the morning."

In short, he'd taken care of everything just like Cillian asked. "Good." He glanced over his shoulder. "My friend isn't used to a bodyguard presence." And he wasn't sure how her daughter would respond. The little tyke had been sleeping through the entire drive. Olivia had enough to worry about without Hadley being scared by strange men looming in the background.

"Got it. I'll tell the boys to make themselves scarce." With that, he strode around the side of the house.

Cillian made his way back to the car and opened Olivia's door. "We're good. If you want to get Hadley inside, I'll grab your suitcase."

She climbed out and looked around. "When I think of the O'Malleys, I don't think of a place like this. It's a weird combination of peaceful and creepy."

"That about sums it up." He laughed softly. "It's an old family property by way of my father."

"I think I like it." She stopped in front of him, close enough that he could catch her lavender and vanilla scent. Olivia ran her hands up his chest and met his gaze. "Thank you. I know you didn't have to do this, and I'm bringing a whole lot in the way of baggage to the table, but you didn't hesitate. So...thank you."

He covered her hands with his, holding them in place. "No thanks necessary. I want you safe—both of you—and I'll do whatever it takes to make sure you are."

"Cillian…" She went up onto her tiptoes and framed his face with her hands. She kissed him, soft and sweet and lingering. "You are better than I deserve."

He stood there for a second after she'd moved away to the rear passenger door to unbuckle her kid, rooted in place by the sheer intimacy of the kiss. He'd dated, but he couldn't remember a single time that a girlfriend had kissed him the way Olivia just did—as something that was done just for the sake of itself, rather than a gateway to something more. It brought to mind casual weekday evenings spent lounging on the couch together and Sunday mornings spent in Mass.

*Slow your roll, man. One kiss and you're dangerously close to putting a ring on her finger. She's probably not even Catholic.* He snorted. Like that mattered to him. Sure, his family would shit a brick, but that was the least of his concerns right now.

*Devlin would like her.*

He waited for the inevitable flash of searing pain and breathlessness that thinking of his younger brother brought, but there was only a tentative warmth. Come to think of it, he hadn't had a daytime panic attack since he and Olivia started circling each other. Cillian watched her walk through the front door, still trying to wrap his mind around it.

Was he actually starting to heal? If he was, she was part of the reason, the thing that had shoved him out of his rut and back into life.

*I don't want to let that go. I don't want to let* her *go.*

He grabbed his bag and her suitcase and followed her into the house. Hadley chose that moment to wake up, blinking big dark eyes so like her mom's at him. She was an adorable little thing, all pudgy cheeks and curly brown hair, and when she sent him a grin, he saw she only had a handful of itty-bitty teeth. It was downright charming. He grinned back, laughing a little when she ducked her head under her mother's long fall of hair. "Cute."

Olivia glanced over her shoulder. "She is, isn't she?"

Mark had left the lights on leading through the formal living room and into the kitchen. Cillian set the bags at the bottom of the stairs. "I'm sure you're hungry."

"Not really, but Hadley probably is." She tickled her daughter. "Aren't you, baby girl?"

"Yes!"

"Thought so." She sent him a look that was half-nervous, half-unapologetic. "We'll be right back." She moved into the hallway, swooping down to grab a smaller pink bag that had been on top of the suitcase.

Left to his own devices, Cillian searched the cupboards. There were plenty of canned goods and nonperishables, and he found a jar of homemade jelly that he was damn sure no one in his family had actually made and a tub of peanut butter. Mark and the boys must have picked up a few things on their way up here, because there were several loaves of bread on the kitchen island, and three gallons of milk in the fridge.

And bacon. Lots of bacon.

He snorted. *At least they have their priorities in order.*

Since Olivia hadn't reappeared, he got to work putting together three PB&J sandwiches. It only took a few minutes and, after some consideration, he cut the crust off of one of them. He seemed to remember Keira going through a stage where she refused to eat crust on anything for years. Then he poured three glasses of milk. He wasn't a huge fan, but he figured Olivia needed the calories. Plus, little kids were supposed to drink a lot of milk, weren't they?

Hell, he didn't know.

She came back into the kitchen as he situated the plates and glasses on the little nook table set against the bay windows. It was getting dark now, but in the morning the sun warmed the whole room. He glanced over. "I hope you like milk and PB&J."

"I'm not really hungry." She set Hadley at the plate with no crust and smiled. "How'd you know?"

"Educated guess." He didn't have a whole lot of knowledge when it came to kids, but he was going to do his best. He pointed at the plate on the other side of the kid. "Even if you're not hungry, you need to eat. It's important to keep up your energy." Something his parents had taught him a long time ago. The O'Malleys had only been on the brink of war once that he could remember, but the risk was always there. It didn't matter what kind of crisis showed up, they were expected to keep functioning as if the world wasn't falling apart around them. It was great in theory, but he'd seen it in practice when Devlin died. There was something so *wrong* about moving on with life while the world was falling apart around them.

"I don't know."

He angled his body away from Hadley and ran his hand down Olivia's spine. As much as he didn't want to traumatize the kid, being this close without touching Olivia, even innocently, felt unnatural. "We might have to bolt with little-to-no notice. If you're ready to pass out from exhaustion and hunger, you're not going to be able to keep up." Yeah, it was harsh and, no, he'd never leave her behind, but he needed to get through to her. If she didn't take care of herself—or let him take care of her—they were going to be in trouble.

"Fine. I'll eat." She grabbed a sippy cup he hadn't noticed and poured Hadley's milk into it. After depositing that in front of her daughter, she dropped into her own chair.

"Good." He took the seat across from her and went to work on his own sandwich. Truth be told, he wasn't really hungry either, but since he'd just made a big deal about eating to Olivia, he had to follow his own advice. He watched Hadley out of the corner of his eye, amused that she seemed to be smearing more peanut butter and jelly on her face than she was getting into her mouth. She downed half her cup of milk and sat back with a burp that would have done any one of his brothers proud. Cillian grinned. "Nice."

For her part, Olivia looked horrified. "Oh my God, I'm sorry."

"Why? Compliments to the chef." His mother would have sent him a death glare if he'd belched at the dinner table, but he wasn't about to tell Olivia that. He sat back with a sigh. "So, what's next?"

"I need to get this one cleaned up, and settled in, but then . . ." Her gaze landed on him, a low heat kindling there. "Then we'll see."

"Olivia." He took a deep breath, trying to get his body's instant reaction to her tone under control. "Let's get you guys set up in one of the spare suites. That should meet your needs nicely." Though, truth be told, there was suddenly one specific need he was looking forward to meeting. He glanced at the clock on the wall. From the level of

Hadley's stickiness, he had a good fifteen to twenty minutes to touch base with Mark and do a perimeter check of his own before they settled in for the night. Hopefully that would be enough to keep him distracted from the fact that he and Olivia pretty much had the house to themselves.

He wasn't liking his odds, though.

* * *

Olivia stripped Hadley down as the bath filled, her thoughts a thousand miles away. Every time she turned around, Cillian was surprising the hell out of her. First, he'd put himself out there to get her somewhere safe, then he'd made sure she was eating and had taken care of Hadley. Taken care of *her*, right from the second she first reached out to him. She didn't know what to think of that.

No, that was a lie. She knew exactly what to think of it. She liked it. She liked it a lot. In a world filled with untrustworthy and downright murderous men, Cillian stood apart as a shining star of virtue. She snorted. Okay, maybe not virtue. Very little of what they'd done together since they met was virtuous, but that didn't change the fact that he had yet to betray her.

She looked around the bathroom, taking in the understated décor. The entire house was made up like that, comfortable and attractive and downright cozy now that night had set in. Something had changed in Cillian when they got out of the car below. He hadn't quite relaxed—she'd caught him putting himself between her and Hadley and any door or window to the outside—but he looked almost more at home out here than he did in Boston in his fancy suits.

Being out here with him was so...domestic. Well,

domestic with a dash of sheer insanity since her half brother and ex were no doubt figuring out right around now that she wasn't in her apartment. She'd called Benji on the way out here, so at least *he* wasn't going to worry about her.

That didn't stop her from worrying about everyone back in Boston, though. She hadn't meant to make friends and start to care about people. Her plan wasn't to be a pillar on her own, exactly, but she'd known that there was a decent chance Boston wasn't her final destination, so she'd tried to keep some distance between herself and the people around her.

She washed Hadley's back. Obviously, from the way both Benji and Mrs. Richards reacted, she'd failed miserably.

More than that, it hurt *her* to leave them behind. She hadn't realized how much she'd enjoyed her time in Jameson's until faced with the fact that she might never go back there. And Mrs. Richards was a saint put on this earth to keep her tethered to reality when her past got too close. What if she never saw them again?

She carefully poured a cup of water over her daughter's head. *It doesn't matter. I'll miss them, but Hadley is more important than anyone else. Keeping her out of Romanov hands isn't negotiable.*

And Sergei?

She dumped more baby bath wash into her hand and went to work on Hadley's unruly mane of hair. If she thought for a second that Sergei had any interest at all in their daughter beyond trying to please Dmitri, maybe things would be different. She'd grown up with one parent who borderline hated her, and the other who was almost completely checked out. She knew how important parents—

good parents—were. If Sergei actually loved their daughter, she wouldn't hide Hadley from him.

But he didn't.

At best, he saw her as a pawn to get Olivia back to his side. He didn't understand that Olivia would *never* be his again, or that he'd burned that bridge all on his own without any help from anyone else. Dmitri and Andrei hadn't ordered him to bring her to the house, but Sergei had known they wouldn't be happy if she disappeared, so he'd taken it upon himself to deliver her there. He'd used her freedom to propel himself even higher within the ranks. Even over a year later, it made her sick to think about.

She washed Hadley quickly, and sat back on her heels and let her daughter splash around in the water. As foolish as it was, she couldn't help comparing Sergei's actions to Cillian's. The latter stood to gain quite a bit once he knew who she was. Dmitri wanted her back, and he wanted her back badly. Delivering her to him would be a great way to foster goodwill between their families, and she didn't see how Cillian *wouldn't* benefit from that.

*He still might.*

No, he wouldn't. She was sure of it—as sure as she could be of anything. He didn't see her as a political piece to be moved around for his benefit—an asset to be leveraged. He saw her as a woman. It was a sad state of events that that was so novel, but there it was.

Or maybe she was wrong. Maybe she was so wrapped up in thinking the best of him that she was blinding herself to what was really going on.

But she didn't think so.

She drained the tub and wrapped Hadley in one of the

fluffy towels that hung next to the tub. "Your mama is a hot mess right now, baby girl."

"Mama!"

It was quick work to put Hadley into a diaper and her sleeper pajamas. Bedtime was still a bit away, but right now comfort was the name of the game. Olivia changed into a pair of yoga pants and a tank top. "Let's see if this place has a TV, huh?" She propped her daughter on her hip and made her way back downstairs.

# CHAPTER SEVENTEEN

The house was seriously surreal. It had all the modern amenities—especially in the kitchen—but the wooden floors and railing leading downstairs looked downright ancient. Olivia fully intended to explore tomorrow when things were a little more settled, because unless she missed her guess, this place had at least ten bedrooms and another half a dozen rooms. It looked like something out of a time warp.

She found Cillian sitting on a screened-in porch, his feet propped up. Her conviction from earlier that he was at home here was only cemented at the sight of him in a T-shirt and jeans. It was like he'd removed a few pieces of key armor and let her in, just a little. The way his face changed when she walked into the room made her heart skip a beat. He smiled, a wry grin that told her he knew how crazy this situation was but he didn't really care because he was here with her.

Or maybe she was just projecting.

Olivia moved through the doorway. No, she wasn't projecting. She had to stop doubting her instincts, especially when every part of her was clamoring that Cillian was here for her and her alone. His family couldn't be happy about this, but he'd shown up anyway.

For *her*.

He stood. "Hey."

"Hey." God, he looked good. Before, she'd wanted nothing more than for him to pin her against the nearest available surface—and, to be fair, she still wanted that—but there was a new layer there. Now she wanted to just walk into his arms and have him hold her and tell her everything was going to be okay. If he did, she might actually believe him.

*You're staring at him like a crazy person.*

He didn't seem to mind, though. He turned his attention to Hadley and smiled. "Hey there, cutie."

Hadley gripped Olivia's tank top, but she peered out at him while ducking her head. Cillian didn't seem bothered by it. He reclaimed the seat he'd been in and picked up a plate from the table next to it. "If your mama says it's okay, I have a chocolate chip cookie with your name on it."

Instantly, all shyness disappeared. She shot a pleading look at Olivia, who laughed. "Yes, but remember your manners."

She set Hadley on the tile floor and watched as she toddled over to him. He solemnly offered her daughter a cookie and it was taken just as solemnly. Then she rushed back to hide behind Olivia's legs. She laughed. "Sorry, she can't quite say 'thank you' yet."

"It's good." With one last grin at Hadley, he sat back. "I have a cookie with your name on it, too."

"I just bet you do." She took the seat next to him. This room was really nice. Better than nice. She'd lived in a city for her entire life, and the sheer amount of unrelenting darkness outside the screen should have been completely overwhelming. But it was so...full of *life*.

There was a pair of some kind of bird singing back and forth not too far away, and a buzz of some kind of insect in the background. It was peaceful. She checked to make sure Hadley wasn't getting into anything, but her daughter seemed content to peer out the screen at the country beyond, munching on the remains of her cookie. She'd been on her best behavior today, but it wouldn't last. Olivia just needed to keep an eye on her so when the indications of a full-on meltdown showed up, she could take Hadley upstairs. Cillian was being a borderline saint, but that didn't mean she'd be awful enough to subject him to her daughter's tantrums. If they were any indication of what kind of emotional roller coaster that the teen years were going to be, she was in for a world of trouble.

"What's got that look on your face?"

She twined a lock of her hair around a finger. "Just thinking that Hadley's going to drive me to drink when she hits thirteen."

"That little angel? No way." He held up the plate again. "Now eat your cookie."

"Yes way." She laughed and accepted the cookie. "Trust me, she might be all sugar and sweetness right now, but she's capable of shattering glass with her shrieks when she doesn't get her way."

"My baby sister used to do that." He stretched in his seat, drawing her eye to the long line of his body. There was so much strength there—strength to lift her against an alley wall and drive her out of her mind, strength to keep going after he'd seen unfathomable loss, strength to stand between her and Dmitri and all of his men. She got the feeling from some of his throwaway comments that he didn't see it, but it'd never been more clear to her than it was right now. Cillian was a good man. The best kind of man.

He kept going. "Truth be told, I'm surprised she got through her teen years without my mom sending her off to a convent. I think the subject was actually on the table for a while."

The obvious love he held for his little sister made her smile even as her heart ached a little. "Your family is very Catholic, aren't they?"

"The most Catholic. My oldest sister actually put off the whole marriage conversation for years because she pretended that she was seriously considering becoming a nun. I think my father was so supportive because he figured that a nun in the family might somehow balance out our karma."

Unless she'd gotten her facts confused about his siblings, that would be the sister who was supposed to marry Dmitri. "I didn't think Catholics believed in karma."

"Karma. The Golden Rule. Tomato-tomahto." He shrugged. "But, yeah, Keira was a holy terror. Hell, she still is." Something crossed his face that she had no name for. "She used to want to go to art school. She's an amazing painter, though I've seen her do things with crayons that would blow you away. It seems like anything she gets her hands on, she turns into these stunning pieces that don't *look* like anything, but somehow you can stare at one and it dawns on you that you're seeing joy, or happiness, or some other emotion. It's crazy."

He couldn't have sounded prouder, but she frowned. "Used to?"

"She was supposed to start school last fall, but she dropped out of all her classes."

"You're worried about her." It shouldn't be such a novel thing—he was her brother, so of course he was worried about her—but it kind of blew Olivia's mind. Dmitri didn't care about her mental health as long as she was doing what he wanted. What would it have been like if he was a brother more like Cillian?

*I never would have left New York. It would be me and him against the world.*

But that wasn't her reality.

Cillian shrugged. "I'm hoping it's a phase she's going through. Keira's always been one to take her own path— and tell anyone who doesn't like it where they can stick it."

There was something he wasn't saying. "But?"

"But after our brother died..." He rubbed a hand over his mouth. "It changed all of us."

She couldn't begin to imagine. She reached over and touched his arm. "I'm sorry."

"It's okay." He put his hand over hers, his gaze a million miles away. "No, actually it's not. He was a good kid. My brother Teague used to say Devlin was the best of us all, and he wasn't wrong. He was brilliant and sweet without being a pushover, and he had the world at his feet."

She squeezed his arm. "We don't have to talk about him if you don't want to."

"It's just...this life has costs. Growing up, I knew that— we all knew that. Some of my siblings fought against it, but I always found it kind of comforting to know exactly what my future held. I was a cocky little shit, to be honest. And then one night it all went sideways. Everything changed and nothing at all changed, and sometimes wrapping my mind around that is damn near impossible."

He looked at her, his dark eyes stark. "The world should change if someone like my brother dies. It should mourn and cry, and the face of it should be altered. Except none of that happened. It kept on spinning and we were expected to do the same. So we're all in our private little hells and no one talks to anyone else and it's just this giant clusterfuck that I'm sure a shrink would have a heyday with."

There was nothing she could say to heal the pain lurking inside him. Hell, even if there was some easy fix, he was right—it took away from his brother's death to just slap a Band-Aid on it and keep moving like nothing had happened. Even Andrei's death had affected her, so she couldn't imagine what it would be like to go through the death of someone she actually loved.

Hadley chose that moment to plop down and start wailing, preventing her from having the chance to figure out what the right thing to say was. Olivia checked the clock on the wall behind her—sure enough, bedtime was fast approaching. "Duty calls. Give me a few?"

"Of course. Take as long as you need."

* * *

Cillian could really use a cigarette. Or a beer. Or both. It didn't matter that he'd quit smoking right around the time he'd quit drinking. Night finished falling as he waited for Olivia, but the peace he'd glimpsed when he'd first stepped out of the car was nowhere to be found. Too many things circled around in his head. He had to tell his family where he was. And he had to tell them about Olivia and her connection to Romanov. It was a risk, and they needed to be aware of it.

But first he'd get her permission.

She'd been pushed and pulled even more growing up than he had. He wasn't going to be yet another person who tried to make decisions about her life without talking to her. *And if she says no?* Well, then, he'd deal with that problem when he came to it. He didn't want to have to choose between her and his family, because he wasn't sure what choice he'd make.

Either way it'd be the wrong one.

His phone chirped and he sighed. *Aiden.* It had only taken him a few hours to figure out Cillian was gone. "Hey."

"You know, when I said you needed to stay out of trouble, that didn't mean take a fucking vacation to the country."

"The air out here helps me think."

"You're full of shit." He cursed long and hard. "I need you in town, Cillian. I have the information we were looking for, but I need you to decipher it."

He sat back in his chair and propped his feet up, trying to ignore the worry taking root inside him. "That was quick." And Aiden sounded tired—really tired. *It might be a necessary evil, but it's killing part of him.* "Everything went off without a hitch?"

"I don't want to talk about it."

*Shit.* That wasn't good. That wasn't good at all. He frowned, trying to decide the best way to approach this. "It might be a good idea to talk about it with someone, even if it's not me." Otherwise, Aiden would end up like a volcano, just waiting for the right moment—or the wrong one—to explode. That was dangerous under the best of circumstances, but with him now functioning as the leader of the O'Malleys on most of the day-to-day things, it could be downright deadly.

"Fuck off."

Cillian rubbed the bridge of his nose. Aiden wasn't going to talk to him and, if he kept pushing, his brother might actually hang up. Since Aiden was right and no one could get to the bottom of this information faster than Cillian, he needed to not push him past his limits. No matter how worried he was about him. "E-mail me what you found. I'll get to the bottom of it."

"It would be better if you were in Boston."

He knew that, but he'd have to make do. "I'll get it taken care of. Just send me the files."

"Why are you out there? Liam didn't say a damn thing other than you took a few men and left town."

Thank God for Liam's discretion. Mark would have reported to him, so he'd know that Cillian wasn't alone out here, but he'd kept it to himself. He understood why Liam had reported at all, though—there was only so far he'd put his neck out there. *Far enough to have it cut off if this goes sideways.*

He hesitated. Easy enough to come clean now and give Aiden a heads-up that Romanov might be a more active threat than they could have anticipated. All he had to do was open his mouth and say the damning words.

Instead he forced a laugh. "You know me, big brother. I had a lark, so I ran with it."

"I thought you were past all this craziness."

"Apparently I'm not." Even hearing it now was a bone in his throat. He wasn't that irresponsible dickhead anymore, but he'd play the part for Olivia. Right now the most important thing was making sure he could keep his promise to keep her safe. The rest would fall into place one way or another.

Aiden sighed. "Call me when you have the information I need."

"Will do." He hung up before he could change his mind. If, after he talked to Olivia, she was fine with him sharing with his family what she'd told him, then he'd call Aiden back. If she wasn't... Well, it wasn't like this would be the first secret he'd ever kept.

A board creaked, and he looked up to find her standing in the doorway to the porch, looking like heaven. Her dark hair had started in a ponytail when he'd picked her up, but strands of it had come loose in the intervening hours, softly curling around her face. Every other time he'd seen her, she'd been in her bar getup—crazy ripped jeans and equally ripped T-shirts—but now she wore yoga pants that fit her like a second skin and a tank top that looked loose and comfortable. It made him want to hold her close.

*Why not?*

Still holding her gaze, he held out his hand in a silent demand.

She took a step forward, hesitated like she might change her mind, and then crossed the distance between them to slip her hand into his. He pulled her into his lap, the feel of her there settling something in his chest he hadn't even been aware was broken. It felt good. *Right.*

And he was going to fuck it all up with what he had to ask her. "Sweetheart—"

She lifted her head. "I think we've talked enough for one night, don't you?"

This close, it would be the easiest thing in the world to

kiss her. And, fuck, he wanted the taste of her on his tongue more than he wanted his next breath. It was only sheer self-control that kept him from taking her up on the invitation blazing across her face right then and there. "Hadley?"

"She's sleeping." She made a face. "Though you're right. I'd feel a lot better if there was a locked door between us and her."

God, she was killing him. "Sweetheart, I didn't bring you up here for this." But he wanted it. Holy hell, he wanted it more than he'd wanted anything in longer than he cared to remember.

"I know." She climbed out of his lap and tugged on his hand.

Still, he held off. "You're sure?"

Olivia rolled her eyes. "Do I have to spell it out for you? I'm tired of waiting for our chance to come around again, Cillian. I want you. You want me. Life's too short. Let's do this."

He pushed to his feet. "And they say romance is dead." He picked her up and tossed her over his shoulder.

"Hey!"

"I said it before, sweetheart. We do this, we're doing it my way." He smacked her ass for good measure, grinning when she cursed. The nearest room with a door that had the ability to lock was the rarely used study. He walked into it, locked the door behind him, and then shut the curtains. The O'Malley men might be discreet, but he didn't want anyone getting an eyeful of Olivia except him.

Only then did he set her on her feet. She opened her mouth, but he kissed her before she could get a word out. Instantly, she melted into his arms, pressing her entire body against the front of his. He ran his hands down her back and grabbed her ass, backing her up and lifting her onto the desk. The extra height lined her up with his cock, the yoga pants a sad excuse for a barrier between them. He thrust against her, holding her hips in place so he could get the same angle he'd had in the car.

She gripped his shoulders, her head falling back, and a moan escaping her lips. "Cillian."

"Sweetheart, next time you say my name like that, I'm going to be inside you." He skimmed off her shirt and tossed it to the side, quickly followed by her bra. She leaned back on the desk and lifted her hips, helping him get the damn pants off.

And then there was only Olivia, naked and waiting.

For him.

He cupped her breast, his cock so hard, it was a wonder he could string two thoughts together. "You're fucking perfect." He stroked down the front of her body to cup her between her legs. He traced her opening with a single finger, teasing her. "So hot and wet and ready for me. I've been dying to taste you again."

"What are you waiting for, then?" She spread her legs wider, boldly meeting his gaze even as her body shook.

*Fuck.* She was such an intoxicating mix of attitude and vulnerability. He stepped back, slowly pulling his shirt over his head. The look on her face made the new distance worth it. She devoured him with her eyes the same way he was devouring her, in an almost physical touch. He started to unbutton his jeans but stopped.

Olivia pointed. "Stop teasing me and lose the pants."

"I haven't even *started* to tease you yet." He went to his knees in front of her. "You might want to cover your mouth."

"What—*oh my God*." She slapped a hand over her mouth as he licked up her center, his gaze never leaving her face. Watching the play of emotions there—shock, pleasure, a growing need—was almost as good as the taste of her on his tongue. Almost. He gripped her hips and jerked her to the edge of the desk and then licked her again, exploring her slowly with his tongue and reveling in the little sounds coming out of her mouth, muffled by her hand. He wanted her to come like this, against his mouth and spread out over this desk. *For him*. Because of what *he* was doing to her.

He didn't have a right to feel possessive of her, but he didn't give a fuck. All that mattered was being the only one she could focus on for the next few hours. Cillian sucked her clit into his mouth, working her as she went wild around him, her cries growing more frantic with each pass of his tongue. He'd joked about teasing her, but he could no more deny her an orgasm than he could deny himself the pleasure of giving her one. He picked up his pace, flicking her clit, holding her thighs wide even as her body shuddered and went tight. *Jesus.* He gave her one last long lick and sat back on his heels.

She stared down at him, her dark eyes wide. "I...uh... wow."

He stood. "*Now*, sweetheart, I'm losing the pants."

# CHAPTER EIGHTEEN

Olivia wasn't sure when her life had been turned upside down, but right now she didn't care. All that mattered was the man in front of her, slowly unbuttoning his jeans. He shoved them down his hips, and all she could do was stare. She'd had his cock in her hands in the back of that town car, but somehow seeing it like this made everything so much more real. He was long and thick, and her hands itched to stroke him again.

But he took a step back.

She frowned. "No more teasing."

"Trust me, teasing is the last thing I want to do right now. But condoms are a necessity, and I just realized that mine are up in my room."

She bit her lip against the insane urge to tell him that it didn't matter. It *did* matter. He was right. They had to be smart. Even if there weren't diseases to think about, she wasn't on birth control. She hadn't been since she got pregnant with Hadley. She nodded. "Okay."

Cillian yanked on his jeans and then he was on her again, kissing her like his life depended on it. She tasted herself on his lips, which was unbearably erotic. *Maybe we could do it. Just this once…* He grabbed her hand and pressed it between her thighs, exactly where she needed him most. "Touch yourself. I want you hot and ready for me when I get back."

"I'm already hot and ready for you."

He used a finger to push one of hers inside her, the double penetration making her eyes go wide. "If you're not fingering yourself when I get back down here, I'm going to put you over my knee and spank you." And then he was gone, striding away and leaving her naked on the desk.

She held her breath for a second. *No way was he serious. He's not going to spank me… is he?* She idly stroked herself, picturing the look on his face when he'd placed her hand there. Wild and barely controlled and full of so much desire, it was a wonder they both didn't burn in the inferno of it. God, he was so sexy, it drove her wild even when he was making her crazy. More than that, though, she liked the moments of quiet strength he showed. She'd never met anyone like him, and she was starting to come to realize that she could travel the world for the rest of her life and never meet another man who held up against the comparison of Cillian.

*Stop it. Stop thinking so much before you ruin it.*

Determined to sideline her thoughts, she circled her clit, but even the pleasure wasn't enough to distract her. *There's no future with him, Olivia. You know that. Even if he wanted one, his family would never accept you, and you haven't worked so hard to get you and Hadley away from the Romanovs just to switch them out for the O'Malleys.*

The door opened, slamming her back into the present. She made a sound of relief when Cillian walked through and locked it behind him, his dark eyes hungry for her. *Yes, this. This is simple and exactly what I need.*

*Liar.*

It didn't matter, though, because he'd shucked off his pants and rolled on a condom while she was arguing with herself. Then he was there between her legs, pulling her back to the edge of the desk so she had to cling to him to avoid falling. "Miss me?"

*Yes.* She flipped her hair out of her eyes and put as much attitude as possible into her voice. "You were gone five minutes. Plus, I was occupied."

"Mmm." He reached between them and pushed a finger into her. "Guess you don't get a spanking. This time."

"Arrogant."

"You know it." He notched his cock at her entrance, and paused.

She grabbed his chin. "If you're about to ask me if I'm sure, don't bother. I'm about to drag you to the floor and have my filthy way with you." Then she kissed him, because the fact that he was checking to make sure she was okay every step of the way only made her heart ache for him more.

Thankfully, Cillian took her at her word. He held her hips tightly and pushed into her. The intrusion had her gasping, stretching her almost uncomfortably. She opened her eyes to find him watching her face, his gaze intent on her. "Lie back."

"What?"

He let go of her hip with one hand and gently pushed on her shoulder, guiding her down onto the desk. "Relax, sweetheart. I've got you." He pushed into her another inch, a muscle jumping in his jaw. "I'm not going to hurt you."

Hurt her? She was pretty sure she might die if he didn't keep doing exactly what he was doing. She wiggled until he let go of her hip and then moved, propping one leg over his shoulder and looping the other around his waist. The position shifted him a bit deeper and she moaned.

Cillian froze. "Olivia?"

She used her new leverage around his waist to slam down onto him, taking his cock the rest of the way inside her. "There!"

"Damn difficult woman." He pulled out a little and pushed back into her. "I'm trying to be gentle with you, and you're determined to make me lose my damn mind."

"Gentle isn't what we are." It wasn't what she wanted right now, no matter how much she appreciated the thought.

"It could be." There it was again, that look on his face that she didn't have words to describe.

It was too much, and somehow not enough. There was no way this could be uncomplicated—they'd burnt that bridge ages ago—but she didn't want any deep discussions in this moment. She reached over her head to grasp the edge of the desk, loving the way he followed the movement, zeroing in on her breasts. "Are you complaining?"

"Sweetheart, I'm inside you again. Things can't get better than this." He pulled out and slammed back into her. "Actually, I lied. The only thing that could make this better is feeling you coming around my cock. I've been losing sleep revisiting fucking you in the alley, and I'm craving that feeling like the best kind of whiskey."

It wouldn't take much. Her earlier orgasm had her primed and ready, and the friction of him sliding in and out of her only heightened the sensation. She grabbed his hand and pressed it against her clit, mirroring what he'd done to her earlier. "Then make me come, Cillian."

She hadn't thought his eyes could get darker, but they did. "Your wish is my command." His thumb stroked her clit as he pounded into her, making her breasts bounce and forcing her to cling to the desk to avoid being fucked right off it.

She loved every second of it.

Pressure built low in her stomach, spiraling through her with each combined stroke of his cock and thumb. She thrashed, but he had her pinned in place, and all she was capable of doing was taking it. "*Cillian—*"

"I've got you." One more circle of her clit and she was at the edge. Another one and she was tumbling over, releasing her death grip on the desk to hold a hand over her mouth and muffle her cries. The pleasure went on and on, until she was sure she couldn't take another second of it. She was vaguely aware of his strokes becoming more irregular, and his hands gripping her hips tightly as he came, her name on his lips.

He slumped over her, his ragged breathing a match for hers. "Five minutes."

It took her brain a few seconds to catch up. *Surely he doesn't mean…* "You just made me come twice. *You* just came."

"Yeah." He pressed a kiss to first one breast and then the other. "But I've been wanting to get inside you again since that first time. You didn't really think that once was going to be enough, did you?"

He sucked her nipple into his mouth, and against all reason, her body started readying itself for round two. *Oh my God.* She dug her fingers into his hair as he leisurely explored first one nipple and then the other. Olivia was starting to fear that she'd never get enough of this man.

Which was a damn problem, because there was no way this thing between them could be permanent.

\* \* \*

Sending Olivia to bed alone was one of the hardest things Cillian had ever done. But duty called, and Aiden would blow a gasket if he didn't get some kind of answers soon. He ran his hand down her spine as they walked into the bedroom, and pressed a kiss to the back of her neck. "I've got some work to do."

"Sounds good. I've got some sleeping to do." She climbed into bed and pulled the covers over her head. It was the cutest thing he'd ever seen.

It was official. He'd gone and fallen for Olivia Rashidi, half sister to a man who was emerging as an enemy to the family.

He shook his head and pulled on a pair of sweats, going through all the reasons it was a totally legit choice to climb into bed with her. Ultimately, it was the desire to let her sleep while she could that had him padding out of the room and down the stairs to the study. He grinned at the desk, the memory of what they'd been doing a few short hours ago flashing through his mind. *We'll have a repeat later.*

The computer took a few minutes to boot up. They'd replaced the old dinosaur last year with a laptop, so it was quick work to open his e-mail and find the documents Aiden had sent him. Apparently the business owner, Mr. . . . Cillian checked the files . . . Mr. Diaz, had kept elec-

tronic records of everything. There were the profit/loss reports for the last year, and they were detailed right down to
the last dollar. That made his life a little easier. As Devlin
had taught him, the Internet was forever. Once something
was uploaded, it was damn near impossible to erase it.

Lucky for him. Not so lucky for Mr. Diaz.

He cracked his knuckles and got to work. It was a
slow and tedious process to peel away the layers, but
he'd never be a hacker like his little brother had been.
What Devlin could do in twenty minutes took Cillian
nearly a full damn day.

Several hours later he sat back and sighed. Getting into
the bank records wasn't difficult because he had their guy's
name and account numbers, but the account the money had
been sent to was a dummy one. *Why didn't they just take out
cash? Pretty stupid to do a wire transfer, even if it's routed
through several accounts.*

It didn't make any sense. *None of this* made any sense.
It was almost like they were being left a trail of bread-
crumbs to follow. Since Cillian knew how *that* story ended,
he wasn't optimistic about what he'd find at the end of this
search. He stood and stretched, trying to decide what the
next step was. Even if the account was a shell, the money
had to go *somewhere*. It was just a matter of tracking where
it ended up.

A smell had him turning toward the door. Bacon. He
walked out of the study, moving slowly because he could
hear Olivia chatting with her daughter. Well, she was chatting. The kid was giving enthusiastic answers that might or
might not have been English.

He stopped in the doorway to the kitchen and watched
Olivia move around the kitchen. She'd found stuff for

pancakes somewhere and had one that looked suspiciously like Mickey Mouse going on the frying pan while another pan cooked bacon. Hadley danced around the kitchen, singing some melody that he might have been able to place if half the words weren't mumbo jumbo.

The whole picture made his chest ache.

*What would it be like if this was my life and every day started like this?*

Olivia turned and smiled. "Hey, I hope you don't mind. We were hungry, and I had the sneaking suspicion that you hadn't eaten anything."

He stepped into the kitchen. All he wanted to do was pull her into his arms and reacquaint himself with her body, but he was conscious that they weren't alone. It wasn't his place to set the limits on their relationship when it came to what went down in front of Hadley. So he stopped a few feet away, willing to take his cues from her. "Is Mickey Mouse for me?"

Hadley tugged on his sweats. "No!"

"That's right, baby girl, it's Minnie Mouse." She gave him a stern look. "Cillian isn't educated on the finer points of Disney characters, but we'll get him up to speed, won't we?"

She turned those inky dark eyes on him, and said in a serious voice as she raised her arms, "Up."

There was no mistaking that meaning. Hoping like hell that he wasn't stepping on any toes, he bent down and picked her up. She arranged herself against him and then turned that adorable grin his way. He grinned back. This wasn't so hard. When he glanced at Olivia, he found her watching him with a strange look on her face. "What?"

"Nothing." She turned back to the stove and flipped the pancake. "I hope you like your bacon borderline burnt."

"Works for me." What had he missed? He shot a look at Hadley, but she was busy tracing his tattoo with one chubby finger, a look of concentration on her face. Obviously he'd be getting no epiphanies from that corner. He shifted the kid into a more comfortable position. "Anything I can do to help?"

"Just keep doing what you're doing. Not having her underfoot really helps." There was still something off in her voice, but he didn't think now was the time to call her on it.

Maybe she was regretting the sex? Or maybe she was worried about her ex and Dmitri? *Fuck.* He didn't know how to do this. He'd always gone out of his way to keep things uncomplicated in the past, and Olivia was complicated on more levels than he could count. "Sure." He caught movement out of the corner of his eye and walked out of the kitchen to meet Mark on the back porch. The man didn't look like he'd spent the night hoofing it through the woods around the house, but who knew? "Anything?"

"We're clear."

"Good." It didn't mean that someone *wouldn't* follow them, but so far so good. When he'd checked the perimeter last night, he'd been more than satisfied with how they had things set up. It wasn't a rock-solid wall between him and Olivia and the rest of the world, but for someone who didn't know these woods to get past them, it'd be a challenge most enemies wouldn't be up to. "You and the boys want something to eat?"

"We got it covered. Thanks." Mark's gaze went to the toddler on his hip. "It's not my business—"

"You have an opinion. Let's hear it." He already knew what it was about—Olivia. Better to get it out there than to let Mark ponder on it and have the subject fester. Or, worse, talk about it with the other men and risk some distorted version of the truth getting back home before he had a chance to do damage control. *If you told them first, you could spin this however you want.*

No. Not yet. He had to talk to her first. He refused to do anything else.

Mark fell into an at-ease position. He'd done a few stints overseas, but when it came time for him to come home to Boston, he'd had a hell of a time adjusting to civilian life. It was Aiden who heard he was having trouble—from Mark's cousin, Liam—and offered him a job. The O'Malleys weren't exactly the military, but they sure as hell weren't civilians, either. It turned out to be a weird limbo that Mark flourished in. The man focused on a spot just over Cillian's shoulder. "If this woman is someone who might be putting your family in danger, then you should think long and hard about keeping them in the dark."

Olivia wouldn't hurt his family. But that didn't mean she wasn't a danger. It was a distinction he wasn't comfortable thinking about, but that he'd have to face sooner rather than later. Cillian sighed. "I've got it covered."

"If you say so, sir."

Hell, Mark had to be really uncomfortable for him to start calling Cillian *sir*. There had to be something he could say to make this right. He thought hard. "I'm giving you my word, Mark. Nothing I'm doing here is going to hurt the O'Malleys." He hoped.

"Good." Something in the man relaxed a little. "In that case, I'm going to go relieve Grant."

"Just make sure you're getting enough sleep, too."

"Sleep is for the dead, Mr. O'Malley."

Cillian watched him walk away, wondering if he'd just

made a promise he had no way of keeping. Coming out here hadn't gotten them a pass on the danger—only a reprieve. They still had to figure out a solution that would keep Olivia off Dmitri's radar and prevent a conflict between his family and the Romanovs. With the Sheridans and possibly the Hallorans backing them, they'd most likely win. But "most likely" wasn't a sure thing, and he already knew too well what war sometimes cost.

He walked back into the house. In the kitchen, Olivia had the Minnie Mouse pancake dismantled and covered in syrup. Whatever had been wrong before was apparently resolved, because she smiled when she saw him. Damn it, he hated that he was about to wipe the joy right off her face. "We've got to talk, sweetheart."

# CHAPTER NINETEEN

Sergei turned around the empty apartment, cursing in Russian. The only evidence that someone had lived there was a half-full laundry basket and some mostly clean dishes in the sink. There was nothing to indicate where Olivia had gone. *Nothing*. Certain he'd missed something, he stalked through the tiny space again, but it was just like the first two times, and no new evidence magically showed up. "Fucking bitch."

Bad enough that she'd run before. He could almost understand it in the wake of how things went down with Andrei. The entire family had been in turmoil, and that meant everyone connected with them was off, too. But to run now, when Dmitri had specifically hunted her down to bring her home? Un-fucking-forgivable.

Dmitri.

He had to report, and he had to do it soon. Failure burned his throat like acid, rage creating a buzzing in his ears that was almost welcome. *I'll find you, Olivia. And when I do, I'm making damn sure that you're not walking away from me again.* He'd tried to be patient. He'd tried to be understanding. But nothing had changed.

And now she was fucking that bastard O'Malley.

He could have forgiven her even that. It would have been damn near impossible, but he could have. But she'd gone and run from him.

Obviously it was time to take a firmer hand with her. She'd always been rebellious. He'd seen it from the time he first started noticing her when she hit sixteen and seemed to turn into a beautiful woman overnight.

Sergei could take strong measures when given the motivation—something she'd just done. If she needed a harsh hand to bring her back to heel, he'd be more than happy to give it to her.

He heard a sound and spun around. The ancient bitch from next door stood in the hallway, glaring at him. "What are you doing here?"

"Where is she?"

"Gone, and out of your control. You'll never get your filthy hands on her again."

Red danced across his vision. This old bat knew something. He was sure of it. If Olivia trusted her enough to watch Hadley, she would trust her enough to tell her where she'd hid away like a rat fleeing a sinking ship. "Where. Is. She?" Each word was a step forward.

The woman realized the danger too late. Her eyes went wide and she tried to duck back into her apartment. Sergei caught the door before it could shut. "You will tell me where she is."

"I don't know." She dove for the phone.

He ripped it out of her hands. He closed her apartment door behind him and locked it, the sound of the bolt sliding home a click of finality. He needed to find his Olivia, and this woman was the key to doing so. "Now, now. We're having such a nice chat. Let's not end it so soon, *da*?"

* * *

After getting Hadley fed, dressed, and set up playing in the grass in the backyard, Olivia turned to Cillian. "What do we need to talk about?" Was he already regretting the sex last night? She really, really hoped not, because it had been quite possibly the single hottest night of her life. Even with everything else going on around them, she wanted more. He looked so serious, her heart lurched. "What's going on?"

"I need you to hear me out before you react. Can you trust me enough to do that?"

*Nothing good starts out this way.* She did her best to quell her knee-jerk reaction. He hadn't done anything to make her question him up to this point. The least she could do was give him the benefit of the doubt for a single conversation. She held her breath and nodded.

He didn't seem any more reassured than she did. "You know this is one of my family's homes, and I'm using their resources to guard us."

*Don't react. Do* not *react. Hear him out.* "I'm aware."

"You also know we have a history with the Romanovs." He held up a hand, obviously reading the distress she could feel working through her. "I'm not plotting or planning or going to use you against them. Breathe. There'd be no damn point of getting you out of town if I was asshole enough to dangle you like bait in front of Dmitri Romanov. That's not what I'm saying."

Her fear took hold of her vocal cords. "Why not? It'd be a smart thing to do, and you'd probably be a hero to the O'Malleys."

His brows slanted down. "Sweetheart, I don't need to be a damn hero for anyone. I can be a cold bastard sometimes, but if you missed the fact that I care about your contrary ass, you're being intentionally thick." He shook his head. "What I'm asking you is permission to give my family the heads-up that the Romanovs are in town and gunning for us."

Permission. She waited, but he didn't say anything else—anything beyond the fact that he cared about her too much to use her as bait or leverage, and that he was asking her before he so much as talked to his family about a very real threat that *she* had brought to their front doorstep. *Olivia Rashidi, you are an idiot.* She cleared her throat. "That's it?"

He nodded. "I can't promise they won't want more information, but I won't tell them anything you don't want me to."

She wrapped her arms around herself and watched Hadley toddle through the long grass. Someone must be on the payroll to keep this place maintained, because the longer she was here, the more sure she was that this was all a dream. It was too damn good to be true.

Just like the man next to her.

Finally, she huffed out a breath. "Tell them what you think they need to know. As much as I want to stay under the radar, if I'd wanted to keep you and the rest of the O'Malleys out of it, I never should have called you."

"Olivia." He grabbed her hand. From the look on his

face, he wanted to pull her into his arms, but he glanced at Hadley and just squeezed instead. "I'm glad you called. Never think otherwise."

How could she argue with him when he was looking at her like that?

She couldn't.

She opened her mouth to say...God, she wasn't even sure...but her phone chose that moment to ring. With a frown, she hurried over to where she'd left it inside the screened porch. It was a Boston number, but not one she recognized. "Hello?"

"Is this Olivia Rashidi?" A woman's voice, somehow managing to be both apologetic and official at the same time.

*What the hell?* "Yes?"

"We have you listed as Deborah Richards's emergency contact. Does that sound right?"

She blindly reached for the doorframe as the room went sideways on her. *Mrs. Richards.* "Is she okay? What's going on?"

"There was an attack last night—a home invasion. I don't have the specifics, but she's in the hospital right now." The woman paused, as if realizing just how cold she sounded. "She's going to be okay. She's suffering from several broken bones and a few other minor injuries, but she should make a full recovery."

Broken bones. Home invasion. Olivia tried to focus. *What are the chances this is a coincidence?* "Is she awake? Can I talk to her?"

"She's under heavy sedation at the moment, but she should be waking up in the next hour or so. She was incredibly determined to call you when she was brought in—

she tried to refuse surgery until someone would give her a phone."

*Not a coincidence, then.* The only thing that would make Mrs. Richards *that* determined to get a hold of Olivia was if she had something important to tell her—to warn her about. "Thank you for calling me."

"My name is Jessica Randolph. I'll be on shift for the next few hours, so feel free to call and ask for me if you have any questions or concerns." She sounded like she was reading off a script. It was enough to make Olivia wonder how often this woman had been forced to make calls like this. Probably too many times. "She's a nice old lady. Stubborn, but nice."

"Thank you. I'll call to check on her in a little bit."

"Great. Have a good day."

Having a good day after receiving this news was impossible. She hung up and carefully set her phone down, even though she wanted to throw it across the room. The only reason she'd brought the damn thing in the first place was so Mrs. Richards or Benji could get a hold of her in case of an emergency. She just hadn't thought that there would *be* an emergency.

Or that she'd be the cause of it.

"What's wrong?"

She went to Cillian and wrapped her arms around him. After half a second, he returned the embrace, holding her so tightly, it was hard to draw a breath. It was exactly what she needed. She buried her face in his chest, trying to stop the shaking starting in her body, but it was no use. "It's my neighbor, Mrs. Richards. She was attacked sometime last night."

"Oh, sweetheart, I'm so sorry."

"It's my fault." She hugged him tighter. "She was brought to the hospital, and even though she had broken bones that needed *surgery* to fix, she was demanding to call me. The only reason she would do that was to warn me."

She half expected him to tell her that she was being paranoid and crazy. Hell, she kind of wanted him to. She really, really didn't want this to be her fault. Mrs. Richards was a friend and had been there for her since the day she moved in. She had become like the mother Olivia always wished she had—at the very least, a beloved aunt. For her to be hurt because of *Olivia*...God, she could barely breathe past the guilt.

Cillian stroked a hand over her hair. "Would they do something like this?"

She didn't have to ask what "they" he meant. Dmitri. Sergei. She started to answer, took a shuddering breath, and forced herself to actually think about it. "Dmitri isn't usually so...blunt. He would have gone over there, had tea, and threatened her with a smile on his face. Honestly, he's smart enough to have figured out within a few minutes that I hadn't told her where I was going, so he'd move on and wouldn't waste the energy."

But Sergei? He'd always had a temper. He'd never turned it on her, but there had been a few fights where she'd seen his fists clenched and wondered if that would be the day he'd finally hit her. There was a reason he was one of the most feared men in the Romanovs' employ, and part of that was because he didn't have the same boundaries that other men did. To Sergei a job was a job. It didn't matter what the job required—he'd do it and never lose a minute of sleep afterward.

He was a dog on Dmitri's leash, but as much as she

wanted to lay this sin at her half brother's feet, she just couldn't see him ordering Sergei to rough up an old woman on the off chance that Olivia had told her something important. It didn't make any sense. "I just don't know."

"I can find out."

*Don't leave.* She lifted her head. "How?"

"Your apartment is in O'Malley territory. I'm not going to pretend we're do-gooders who investigate every little thing that goes on, but if this is connected to the Romanovs, then it's not a simple assault." His mouth twisted. "I can't believe I just said that. Let me make a few calls, and I'll see what information I can dig up."

"Thank you." There weren't words to describe how grateful she was to have Cillian basically holding her hand through this. She couldn't imagine getting that news alone. Her guilt was awful enough as it was—it was too tempting to rush back to the city and check on Mrs. Richards. To see with her own eyes that the old woman really would be okay.

Which would be exactly what Sergei and Dmitri would want if they were really the ones responsible for this.

She turned in his arms to watch Hadley roll around in the grass. *That* was her endgame. She had to keep her eye on the ball and keep her daughter safe. Even if that meant holing up here and possibly putting the few friends she had in the world in danger. "Benji!" She jerked away. "I have to call Benji and warn him."

Cillian stopped her with a hand on her arm. "I'll take care of it, Olivia. Though, to be honest, Benji has seen worse than the Romanovs could bring to the table."

If he could say that, he hadn't seen their worst. She had. Or at least she'd been on the borders enough times to hear more than she ever wanted to know. But he was right. There wasn't much more she could do other than call him. She took another step away from Cillian, and tried to put on a brave face. "Make your calls. I'll be out here with Hadley."

He hesitated. "I'd prefer it if you both would come inside. We can put on a movie until I know something and then we'll make lunch."

Because they couldn't guarantee that someone wouldn't come for her. God, how had this turned into such a mess? All she'd wanted was her freedom. She didn't realize it'd come at the cost that the people around her would be forced to pay. It was so damn wrong.

"Yes, you're right." Truth be told, she didn't really want to let Cillian out of her sight, either. Her phone rang again, and she frowned at yet another strange Boston number. Maybe it was the hospital again? "Hello?"

"Olivia."

Her whole body went cold at the rough Russian voice on the other line. "Sergei." Instantly, Cillian was at her side. She shook her head when he motioned for the phone, but took his hand instead, his warm grip keeping her grounded and the panic at bay. Barely.

"You've been a naughty girl. Tell me where you are, and I'll forgive you."

God, how had she ever convinced herself she was in love with that bastard? She glanced at Hadley, still playing happily, and then at the forest around the property. Suddenly the backyard felt horribly exposed, like danger could be lurking beneath any of the trees framing it. "Leave me alone, Sergei."

"I can't do that, and you know it. You're mine. And if you think I'll let what's mine walk away from me, you're as fucking stupid as your brother says you are."

She jerked, the sheer violence in his tone like he'd reached across the distance and slapped her. Cillian squeezed her hand, his hard expression letting her know he heard every word. She swallowed hard, fighting to get the words out. "I'm not yours. And I'm hanging up now."

"I'll find you, Olivia. It would be better for you and that little brat if you just come to me willingly. If you don't, things will get ugly...Like they did with that old bitch."

*Mrs. Richards*. She gripped the phone, her head going fuzzy. *He really was the one to hurt that poor old woman.* "You're a monster."

"I do what's necessary. I always have."

Why was she even talking to him? Nothing she could say would change the way he felt, and if Dmitri had given his blessing... *Wait.* "Does my half brother know what kind of shit you're pulling in O'Malley territory?"

"Let that bastard enjoy you while he can. I'll be taking back what's mine soon." He hung up.

She stared at her phone. "These things can be tracked, can't they?" And she'd had hers on for the entire time that she'd been here—plenty long enough for Sergei to figure out where she was.

She started to take the battery out, but Cillian stopped her. "Call the hospital first and give them my number."

"Right. Of course." She should have thought of that herself. It took five minutes to get a hold of the nurse she'd talked to earlier and give her Cillian's phone number as a contact to call, but they felt like the longest five minutes of Olivia's life. She kept picturing Sergei staring at his phone, watching her GPS as he traveled ever closer. As soon as she hung up, she yanked her battery out. It was probably too late, but on the off chance that no one had already tracked her down, there was no reason to make it easier on them. *So damn stupid. Getting rid of your phone is Running 101.*

"It will be okay."

Maybe if he said that enough times, she'd start to actually believe it. Olivia let him draw her into his arms. Cillian rubbed a hand down her back and up again. "I promise it will be okay. I'll keep you both safe no matter what it takes."

"Mama?"

*Keep it together, Olivia. If you don't, you're going to scare Hadley, and that's not going to do anyone any favors.* "I'm here, baby girl." She extracted herself from his arms to find Hadley offered her a handful of dandelions. She sank to her knees next to her daughter and made a show of examining them. "What have you got there? Flowers for your mama?"

Hadley presented them to her solemnly, and then split into a grin wide enough to make Olivia want put all her problems on the back burner. She climbed to her feet. "Come on, baby girl. Let's get these flowers in a vase." Cillian's presence at her back was almost enough to steady her and make her believe that everything would be okay.

Almost.

# CHAPTER TWENTY

Sloan stared at the little house, the sound of the ocean in her ears. She'd done it. She'd really done it. It had taken her the majority of two days to get here—first a plane to Denver and then a rental car to LA and a *different* rental car north to the little Oregon town of Callaway Rock.

She rubbed her hands over her arms, the sea air distinctly chillier here than it was back in Boston. *I've been alone more in the last two days than I have in the last five years.* There had been no one looking over her shoulder or checking up on her or drawing her into some plot that she wanted no part of. There had just been her and the open road. It had been... terrifying.

*This is how the rest of my life is going to be.*

She wasn't sure if the thought was scary or exhilarating. Sloan pulled the flip phone out of her purse and turned it on. Teague's instructions had been detailed to the point of being tedious, but he knew more about putting people in hiding than she did, and she wasn't about to take any risks that her family could find her. She pressed one, speed-dialing the only number in the phone. Two rings later and her brother's voice came over the line. "You're there?"

"Yes." The house was dark, not even the exterior lights on. "I thought there was someone already here." The whole reason they'd picked this place to begin with was because Callie had some distant aunt who owned it. Sloan fully expected to have to deal with that once she arrived, but the place looked deserted.

"She's out of town, but she'll be back in a few days—a week at most. You have enough money to get you started in the meantime. I can always wire you more if you need it."

"I won't need it." She was going to get a job and provide for herself. Teague had already put himself out there too much for her. She wouldn't let him take any further risks—or give her any more handouts.

"If you do—or if you need anything—I'm there for you." He paused. "I've got to go, but there will be a package showing up in the next day or two with phones to contact me. Don't ever use the landline."

"I won't. And, Teague, thank you." She hung up, took a deep breath, and started up the narrow walkway to the front door. She reached for the key she'd shoved in the inner pocket of her purse, when the sound of a foot on the gravel had her turning around. She squinted, trying to make out the details in the darkness. "Hello? Is anyone there?"

A shadow detached itself from the corner of the house to the left of her, and Sloan had to cover her mouth to keep from shrieking as it formed into a hulking brute of a man. He had shoulder-length hair and a close-cropped beard and looked like he was capable of the kind of acts that would put someone into prison for the rest of their life. "Stay back."

"Trespassing is against the law."

*What is he talking about?* She backed up a step, hating the fear that clogged her throat. "I'm renting here."

"That's impossible." His voice was so low, it was almost lost in the nearby sound of the waves hitting the shore.

*Get a hold of yourself. You can't spend the rest of your life jumping at shadows. Now's the time to discover your spine.* She lifted her chin like Keira tended to do before a confrontation, though the move made her feel like an imposter. "Hardly. I have a key." She turned, resisting every instinct that screamed she was an idiot for presenting *that* man with her back, and inserted the key into the lock.

Or she tried.

A hand covered hers and, this time, she couldn't fight down a small shriek. The man used his hold on her hand to turn her around. Being faced with the fact that he towered over her made her literally shake in her boots. *Show no fear.* "Get your hands off me." Instead of coming out harsh, the words were small and weak.

He didn't answer, just turned her and used the hand not touching her to point at a house about fifteen feet away from where they stood. The lights were on and it appeared downright cheery. "That's where you're going." When she just stood there, shivering, he cursed. "The O'Connor place. That's the only empty house on the street."

Callie's aunt's name was Sorcha O'Connor. There was no way it was a coincidence—which meant he was right and she was most definitely trespassing. She tried to jerk away, but he held on to her for several seconds—long enough to make it clear he was choosing to let her go. In that second, she could have sworn his thumb traced a line across her inner wrist, but it had to be her imagination, because his expression was just as forbidding as it had been since he appeared.

*Show. No. Fear.* She took one cautious step back. "I guess that makes us neighbors. I'm Sloan."

He didn't respond, didn't so much as grunt, so she carefully made her way down the steps and back toward the relative safety of the street. He said something, and she turned around, nearly impaling herself on what looked like a rosebush. "I'm sorry?"

"I'm Jude." She made it a few more steps before his gruff voice carried the rest of his words to her. "Now stay the fuck off my property."

*That* would not be a problem. She didn't want to spend any more time with that horrible man than she already had. Sloan hurried over to the correct house, kicking herself for mistaking the address in the first place. She wasn't the most social of creatures, but even she wouldn't have reacted like that man—Jude—had to an honest mistake. It wasn't as if she'd been peering into his window and taking pictures.

She let herself into the house and locked the door behind her, that barrier between her and the rest of the world allowing her to take her first full breath since she stopped on this street. The hallway led straight into a small living room. It should have felt cramped, but with the dainty couch and coffee table facing the wall of windows, it didn't. She stopped in front of the windows, trying to see past the glare and into the night. It was no use, so she opened the sliding glass door and stepped onto the back porch.

The sound of the ocean was louder here, the reason obvious once she moved past the lights illuminating the porch.

There was a narrow path leading right to the beach, her property and the sand separated by an uneven white picket fence. She almost laughed at the sight. *It's perfect.* She didn't need to see the rest of the house to know that.

All the same, she went back inside to explore. There were two bedrooms, both decorated in shabby-chic beach style, and two massive bathrooms that overlooked the ocean. There were windows everywhere, which should have made her feel like she was living in a fishbowl, but she suspected the views they'd offer in the morning would make it more than worthwhile. She glanced through the nearest window to where her cranky neighbor's house stood. *I wonder what his story is.*

"No. Absolutely not. You've gone out of your way to leave danger behind, and if there's one thing that man is, it's dangerous." She yawned. Tomorrow would be soon enough to unpack and settle in. Tonight, she was going to take a walk on the beach. Sloan smiled. She'd taken the first step—the most important step. Now all that was left was for her to press forward and make a life for herself here.

A life where she could truly be happy.

* * *

Despite how the morning started and the sheer volume of the calls he'd had with both Teague and Aiden, the rest of the day went off without much drama. Cillian moved his work into the living room and kept pulling on the leads that he'd gotten from the shell corporations while a Disney movie about Rapunzel played in the background. Hadley couldn't quite sing the words, but she had the tune of every single song down pat. Even Olivia managed to relax a little, though she got up every half hour to wander the room and look out the windows.

Sometime around Rapunzel using her hair to save the hero, Cillian got sucked back into the numbers. It took longer than he would have liked to crack the shell, only to find another shell within it. *What the fuck?* That was a lot of work for a measly three percent—which added up to a few grand a quarter from this particular business. Even with all the other businesses that seemed to be paying it, there was barely a hundred thousand dollars missing. It wasn't exactly chump change, but in their line of work, it wasn't enough to put this level of effort into.

It just didn't make any sense.

"Are you hungry?"

He looked up from his computer and frowned. The light had changed in the room, the shadows getting longer as the sun went down. "How long have I been working?"

Olivia shrugged. "Three movies' worth of time."

Damn it, he hadn't meant to zone out on her like that. "Sorry. I didn't mean to get so distracted."

"It's okay." She shot another look at the nearest window. "I'm just jumpy. You're sure he couldn't track my phone?"

He set the laptop aside and stood, stretching. "Chances are that he wouldn't have the tech to do it, since you have a prepaid phone. Even if he *can*, we're still better set up here than we would be anywhere else. Small hotels have too many entrances and exits to cover with five men. My men know this area, and they know this house. No one is going to get close without them seeing."

She didn't look completely convinced, but she nodded all the same. "Okay. I'm just...I'm not good at sitting on my hands while other people do the work."

He understood that. If he hadn't had the money mystery occupying him, he'd probably be in the exact same headspace as she was. "It will be okay. Between Teague and Aiden, this isn't going to get away from us." He'd even called in a favor with Carrigan—and, through her, James. With all three families in Boston uniting, even Dmitri Romanov would think twice before coming after Olivia. "They have a meeting set up for tomorrow. They'll make him back off."

"I'm sure you're right. It just seems like I should be there." She held up a hand. "I know I can't and that might be playing into his hands, but it doesn't change the fact that I'm having trouble with all this."

He'd done what he could do to stack the whole thing in their favor, but obviously he'd missed a step when it came to comforting her. Cillian stepped closer, until they were almost chest to chest, and lowered his voice. "What can I do to make this easier for you?"

Her smile was almost real this time. "You're a strange man, Cillian."

"It's been said before." And it would no doubt be said again. As it was, he now owed serious favors to three of the most powerful men in Boston. It didn't matter that two of them were his brothers and one would eventually be his brother-in-law. Family meant a lot, but he'd put Olivia in front of family, and that wasn't something they were going to forget anytime soon. It wouldn't stop them from helping him, but he'd have a whole hell of a lot to answer for once this all died down.

The only one who *wasn't* actively pissed at him was Carrigan, and that was only because, as she'd said on the phone, she'd told everyone that they hadn't seen the last of Dmitri

Romanov six months ago when he disappeared from Boston. Their father hadn't listened, and neither had Aiden.

Well, they were listening now.

He took her hand. "You said something about food?"

"I did." She led him out of the living room and down the hall to the kitchen, where Hadley was staring intently at the stove. "Hadley and I have prepared a very glamorous and high-end macaroni and cheese for dinner thanks to your men delivering a truly outstanding amount of food."

"Kraft?"

She laughed. "Is there any other kind?"

"Not as far as I'm concerned. I'm a fan." Always had been, much to his mother's annoyance. But then, plenty of shit Cillian had done over the years put that look of disparaging frustration on her face. One would think she'd finally accept it. But not Aileen O'Malley. She just kept right on trying. *I wonder what she thinks of all this*. He cringed. *On second thought, better not to know*.

Olivia dished up two large bowls and a much smaller one, and set them on the table. "Dinner is served."

He didn't realize he was starving until he took that first bite. Cillian smiled at Hadley. "You did a great job with dinner."

She ducked her head and stuffed a massive spoonful of food into her mouth—or mostly in her mouth. A girl after his own heart. He glanced at Olivia to find her watching him with that strange look on her face again. "Do I have food in my teeth or something?"

"No. It's just... Never mind. It doesn't matter." She took a bite.

He almost pressed, but decided that it was possibly something she didn't want to talk about in front of her daughter. This whole dealing-with-a-small-human thing was full of more pitfalls than he could have guessed. Once dinner was done, he sat back and really *looked* at Olivia. He'd seen the anguish on her face this morning when she realized that her neighbor had been hurt by her ex, and he knew all too well that it wasn't gone, no matter how good a face she tried to put on it. "Why don't you go take a bath and try to relax?"

The look of disbelief she gave him would have been comical under other circumstances. "A bath."

"Yeah." He got up and started the water running. "Hadley and I'll do the dishes and get the kitchen all squared away."

"You...I..." She shook her head. "You don't have to do that."

He knew, but he also knew that Olivia would run herself into the ground if she didn't stop and take a little time for herself. And the reality was that if he wanted something more with her, he'd have to get to know her daughter, too. He might as well take out two birds with one stone right now.

But Cillian waited, because if she didn't trust him with Hadley, he wasn't going to push. She'd proven herself to be a fierce mother and she'd already gone through hell trying to create a better life for her daughter. It would hurt if she didn't want him spending time alone with her, but he'd understand.

Finally, Olivia nodded. "I guess a bath would be nice."

He let loose a breath he hadn't even been aware he was holding. "We'll hold down the fort, won't we, Hadley?"

The cheese-covered toddler grinned and waved a spoon, sending more cheese sauce flying. Olivia sighed. "Are you sure you don't want me to clean her up first?"

"Nah. We got this."

With one last lingering look, she stood and walked out of the room. He waited until he heard the board at the top of the steps creak to turn to Hadley. There was some advice he'd read once that showing fear to either young children or wild animals was a recipe for disaster, so he just charged right in. "How about we get you wiped down and then you can help me rinse?"

She stared up at him with those inky eyes like she wasn't quite sure what to think of him. Hell, he didn't blame her. Cillian wet a washrag and walked back to the table. He carefully extracted the spoon from her chubby hand and moved the plate out of reach. "This was my least favorite part as a kid, but we can't have you cleaning dishes with messy hands, now can we?" He didn't hesitate. He wiped down her hands, making silly noises that seemed to amuse her, and then went for her face. She sputtered a little, but she didn't start crying, so he called it a win. Cillian lifted her and brought a chair over to the sink. She could barely get her hands into the water, so maybe that would minimize the mess.

Hadley squealed and splashed both hands into the sink, sending a wave of water onto both her and Cillian. She froze, her eyes getting shiny and her face screwing up into what promised to be an epic meltdown.

"No, no, no." He moved fast, grabbing a cup and handing it to her. "A little water never hurt anyone. Now we're ready to really get to work." He took her hand and guided it into the water, rinsing off the plastic cup. "See—easy. Isn't this fun?"

Frankly, he didn't know what the fuck a fourteen-month-old found fun other than princess movies, but she gave him a tentative grin and dunked the cup again. He stayed close in case she somehow managed to get *into* the sink and went to work on the pot. Hadley seemed completely content to splash around with her cup, making little noises that might be words in a few months.

He set the pot to the side and picked up the first plate. "I really like your mama, Hadley. And you're pretty cute, too." She was adorable enough to get away with murder, which was something he'd have to keep in mind, because she turned those liquid eyes on him and he handed over a plate without thinking. *Damn*. But he'd do what it took to keep her happy and distracted from what was going on. He doubted she was aware enough to realize the full extent of it, but in case she was, he needed her to know that there was nothing to be afraid of. "I'm going to keep you and your mama safe. No matter what."

\* \* \*

It took Olivia longer than usual to get Hadley down for bed, but that was as much due to her distraction as her daughter being riled up from "helping" Cillian with the dishes. She kept going back to dinner, to his insistence that she take a little time for herself. As much as she hadn't wanted to admit it, he was right—that bath had helped relax her and fend off the panic attack that she'd had brewing all day. Then she'd come downstairs to find both Cillian and Hadley soaked and doing more playing in the sink than actually washing dishes. He turned a smile her way that had actually made her skip a step.

She finished the story she'd been absently reading and

looked down to find Hadley sleeping soundly. *This is how it could be. This is how it's* supposed *to be.*

Olivia sat on the edge of the bed, staring into the darkness. A truth stared back at her that she'd been doing her damnedest to ignore.

She was in love with Cillian O'Malley.

It had snuck up on her somewhere around the time he offered his help without expecting anything in return, and how he'd been interacting with Hadley only solidified it. Though he obviously didn't spend much time around kids, he didn't patronize her daughter or dismiss her, and he didn't so much as blink at the kind of help a toddler offered. He'd been so incredibly respectful of Olivia's boundaries and careful when interacting with her in front of Hadley.

Not to mention the sex was out of this world.

She traced the floral pattern of the bedspread. Her heart might be all tangled up in him, but that didn't mean she had to do anything about it. She snorted. *Right*. Because going through life alone and playing the martyr was so much more attractive than finding a man who'd actually be a partner—one who'd love both her and Hadley.

*Getting a little ahead of yourself, aren't you? You don't even know how* he *feels.*

No, she didn't. But a few times today she caught him looking at her with some indefinable expression on his face, and she couldn't help feeling that he was as caught off guard by the thing growing between them as she'd been. Yeah, he'd wanted to take her out, but a date and riding in to whisk her off to his out-of-town fortress to keep her safe were two different things.

He hadn't hesitated.

She double-checked on Hadley—still sound asleep—

and carefully moved her to the Pack 'N Play. Just because she realized she loved him didn't mean she had to tell him right away. They had time. Hopefully. If she said anything right now, it would look like she was responding to the fact that he'd brought her here or, worse, that last night had gone to her head.

She wandered back downstairs, and stopped in the doorway when she caught sight of him. He'd changed out of his wet clothes at some point since she went upstairs, and was now frowning at his computer just like he had been most of the day. "Trouble?"

"Troublesome, for sure. My father is going to blow a blood vessel when he finds out." He sighed and closed the laptop. "But I'm not going to get any more done tonight, and the conversation can wait until morning." He set it aside and held out his hand, just like he had last night, in a silent command for her to come to him.

Since she was only too happy to obey, she walked over and slid her hand into his, letting him pull her into his lap. "Have I said 'thank you' recently?"

"It might have come up." He stroked a hand down her back. "Hadley's asleep?"

"She fought it hard, but she's out like a light now. I suspect her bath in the form of helping with dishes had something to do with it."

He chuckled. "It's tiring work."

She waited, but he didn't seem like he was going to do anything other than rub her back. As good as it felt, she had her epiphany rattling around in her head, preventing her from totally relaxing against him. She straightened. Though she wasn't willing to start throwing around four-letter words, she could *show* him how she felt. "Come on."

He let her pull him to his feet and lead him down the hall to the powder room. It had a fancy pedestal sink and little else, but it was more than big enough for what she had planned. More importantly, it had a door that locked and a massive mirror that went almost floor to ceiling. She locked the door and pushed Cillian until his back hit the wall across from the mirror. His gaze jumped from her to the wall behind her. "I like where this is going."

"Good." She unbuttoned his slacks. "Don't move."

He raised his eyebrows. "You can have your way—for now. But in approximately five seconds, I'm going to strip you naked, spread you out, and fuck you in front of that mirror so you can see me sliding in and out of you until you come."

*Holy shit.* She shivered and went to her knees in front of him. "Try to hold out for more than five seconds." Though she meant the words to come out amused, they were breathy instead. She pulled his pants down just enough to free his cock. She stroked him with one hand, looking up his body to meet his eyes as she did. The picture he presented made her hot in ways she never could have dreamed, and knowing *she* was the cause of the expression on his face was the icing on the cake.

She ducked down and took his cock into her mouth, rolling her tongue against him as she sucked him deep. His curse was music to her ears, and his fingers lacing through her hair made her moan. She might be in charge, but it was only because he allowed it. The combination of power and submission made her head spin, and so she didn't think about it. Instead, she gave herself over to doing whatever it took to make him curse a blue streak. When his hips started pumping to meet her strokes, she knew she had him.

Which was right around the time he dragged her up his body and kissed the living hell out of her. She fisted the front of his shirt, her tongue tangling with his, the feel of his body against hers better than the best vodka. Cillian spun her around and jerked her shirt over her head. "My turn, sweetheart."

# CHAPTER TWENTY-ONE

Cillian watched Olivia's face as he stripped her. Her dark eyes were glazed, and her chest rose and fell with the quick breaths she took as each inch of skin was revealed. She loved this as much as he did. He kicked her yoga pants to the side. "Don't move."

As he stripped, he couldn't take his gaze off her body, the curve of her waist seemingly made for his grip, her small breasts, her legs that went on for days. And that hair. Fuck, her hair was as wild as she was. It fell around her shoulders in a dark mass that his hands itched to dig into. So he did just that, stepping up to press against her back, wrapping her hair around one fist and tilting her head to the side so he had access to her neck. He kissed her there, taking the time to nibble on the sensitive skin until she was writhing against him.

Then he reached around her with his free hand to cup one breast and then the other, playing her nipple between his fingers. All the while he watched her face, watched her watch him in their reflection. "You like this."

"I love this."

He tightened his grip on her hair when her eyes started to drift shut. "Eyes on me, sweetheart." He dipped between her thighs, groaning when he found her soaking wet. "Did that blow job do it for you?"

"Yes." She hissed out a breath as he pushed a single finger into her. "Because it was you."

*Fuck*. He pumped his fingers a few times, mostly because if he entered her right now with those words ringing in his ears, he'd lose his shit. But he couldn't quite let it go, either. "Because it was me."

"Mmm." She arched against him as much as she could, watching him with heavy-lidded eyes. "Knowing I was the one making your voice go hoarse while you cursed... Yeah, that was hotter than hell."

"Damn, sweetheart, you shouldn't say shit like that if you expect me to be able to let you walk away." He pushed a second finger into her, the very idea of her leaving him sparking the anger that he never truly got rid of these days. "But then, I wasn't going to."

She leaned forward and braced her hands on either side of the mirror, the long line of her back making his mouth water. "It's not your choice."

"No, it's not." He grabbed a condom that he'd stashed in his pocket earlier and rolled it on. Then he was at her entrance, pushing into her in one slow, smooth movement. "But I'll tell you a secret."

"What's that?" Her voice was as harsh as his, her hips already shoving back to take him deeper.

He wrapped her hair around his fist again, arching

her back so that he could see every inch of her in the mirror—and every inch of his cock disappearing between her legs. Cillian's lips brushed her ear. "You don't want to leave. You want to be kept as much as I want to keep you." He thrust into her, using his free hand to stroke her clit. "Which is a good goddamn thing, Olivia, because I'm never letting you go."

She gasped, her body going tight as she came, her pussy milking him until it was everything he could do not to follow her over the edge. He refused to, though. He was nowhere near done with her.

When the last shudder racked her body, he pulled out of her and spun her around, lifting her and carrying her to the sink. He set her on the edge and spread her legs wide. "Any objections?" Before she could answer, he went to his knees and buried his face between her legs, devouring her like he'd been dying to do all day. Her muffled cry was music to his ears.

And if she was too busy coming again on his mouth to tell him that she wasn't his, well, that was too damn bad. He sucked on her clit and fucked her with two fingers, ruthlessly driving her into another orgasm. It didn't matter that she hadn't actually disagreed with him. He knew Olivia. He knew that she wouldn't let herself be caged again—even by him. What he needed her to understand was that he wasn't offering a cage. Fuck, he was offering whatever she'd take, because the thought of her walking away from him had become unbearable sometime in the last twenty-four hours.

"Say it." He stood and shoved into her again, holding her close so he didn't fuck her right off the sink. "I want to hear you say it, sweetheart."

She wrapped her legs around his waist and kissed him

like her next breath was in his lungs. "I'm not leaving." She moaned. "I'm yours."

The words were a balm to a wound he hadn't even been aware of. He dug his hands into her hair and kept fucking her while he kissed her. This time when he sent her hurtling over the edge, he was powerless not to follow. He pumped into her, coming so hard it felt like the top of his head blew off.

Cillian braced himself on the sink with her draped around him and tried to relearn how to breathe. He opened his mouth, then shut it again. There was nothing else to say. She could claim all day and night that what she'd said during sex didn't count, but it did. She wanted him as much as he wanted her. He dropped his head to her shoulder. "How about a shower and a bed?"

"Sounds like heaven." She ran her hand up his back, stopping when she found the scar from the exit wound. "What happened here? You've told me about your tattoos, but not this."

He straightened, and helped her off the sink. "There's not much to say. My sister was in trouble. Well, actually, the guy she was head over heels for was in trouble, and she needed help."

She frowned. "This would be the same sister who was supposed to marry my half brother?"

"Yeah." What an incestuous little bunch they were. He pulled on his pants. "She couldn't ask for official help because…politics." And at first he hadn't wanted anything to do with the whole mess. It didn't take much to slide back into the past, to Teague's wedding, to him and Aiden finding her and Halloran in the damn storage closet together. The betrayal lay thick against the back of his throat. Hell, it still did. But Carrigan was still his sister, and when she needed help, he was there for her.

"So you helped her."

"Me, Teague, and a bunch of Sheridan men. It ended up being a clusterfuck on multiple levels. We got the girls they were trafficking safe, but Halloran had been double-crossed by one of his own men." He shrugged, trying not to let his muscles tense as the memories of that night washed over him. He hadn't even been there to see James's right-hand guy turn the gun on him. By that point he'd already been on the ground, bleeding from a Romanov bullet. He grabbed the rest of his clothes off the floor—Olivia had already dressed. "The universe is kind of a funny place sometimes."

"Why do you say that?"

"Because it was your half brother who had put the whole damn thing into motion that night. It was his men who showed up to support the double-cross, and it was them that we ended up fighting." He touched the scar. "The bullet went through. Hurt like a bitch, but it didn't hit anything vital. I was lucky." A whole hell of a lot luckier than Devlin. That night Cillian lay there on the cold concrete, the world a blur around him, and wondered if karma had finally come calling. If this was his punishment for being part of the reason his brother died. If it was finally his time.

But then he didn't die.

Part of him had wondered if that was a mistake. Now he knew it wasn't. If he'd died on the docks that night, there would have been no one for Olivia to call when she got backed into the corner. For the first time in longer than he could remember, he had a purpose—and a noble one at that.

She opened the door and walked out of the room, still frowning. "I didn't know."

"There was no reason for you to. It's not like Dmitri shared his plans with you—and you were in Boston by that point." He could still remember the first time he'd seen her, and how she wouldn't give him the time of day. It made him smile to think about it now. "It's the past."

"Except it's not. Dmitri still has his claws in Boston. My half brother doesn't like to let things go."

If what he'd found with the accounts was anything to go by, she was right. He wasn't a hundred percent sure that the money was going to the Romanov bastard, but he was sure enough to bring the information to Aiden and his father. Convenient since they had a meeting with the man himself tomorrow. Whatever the guy was up to, it wasn't going to stop with three percent from a handful of small-time businesses. Obviously he hadn't let go of the insult of Carrigan ditching his ass—or the fact that Halloran hadn't rolled over and played dead like he was supposed to. No, Dmitri Romanov had plans for Boston. And Cillian had to make sure his father and brother were prepared to face that.

He stopped at the top of the stairs, most of him wanting to follow Olivia into the bedroom, but the pull of family digging deep. "Start your shower, sweetheart. I have a quick call to make."

She nodded. "I'm sorry I brought all this trouble to your door."

"You didn't. It was here already. You just helped shine the light on the extent of it." He pressed a quick kiss to her lips and retreated back downstairs to the study. After closing the door, he locked it for good measure. It was late, but someone would be up at the house back in Boston. They always were.

Sure enough, when he called, his father picked up. "I'm not pleased, Cillian."

The last thing he wanted to do was have a go-round with Seamus O'Malley when he was worked up. As tempting as it was to mouth off like he normally did, he kept his tone perfectly polite and professional. "I know you're not happy with how I've handled certain things—"

"'Not happy' is a vast understatement. I was under the impression that you'd left your wayward habits behind, and then I'm informed that you picked a piece of ass over your family. You've used O'Malley resources and put our people in danger, and for what? Throw the woman back to Romanov and good riddance. She's not our problem."

He gritted his teeth, fighting for calm. "She's an innocent."

"She's half-Romanov—she's no more innocent than you are. She knew the risks when she ran, and she dragged trouble straight to our door. Hell, that's the best-case scenario. She could very well be leading you around by your dick, and you wouldn't know until it was too late."

*Jesus Christ.* "Enough."

"I know you're impulsive, Cillian, but this is taking things too far."

"*Enough.*" He took a deep breath, but his calm had gone up like a puff of smoke. What was the point of doing every single thing his father ever asked of him if the second he veered off the chosen track, he was being accused of thinking with his cock? "I'm not calling about Olivia. I'm calling about the missing money."

A pause. "Taking that tone with me is a mistake, boy."

"Unless you're planning on declaring me dead to the family like you did Carrigan, there's not a damn thing you can do about it. I'm doing what I think is best— for both the family and Olivia—and that's all I can do.

Give me some fucking credit, shut up, and listen to what I have to say."

There was a rustling, and then Aiden's voice came over the line, speaking low and fast. "Whatever the hell you just said to him, you need to make it right. He looks like he's about to drive out there and throttle you with his bare hands."

Considering he'd never talked to their father like that, his response wasn't surprising. Hopefully Aiden would be more rational. "I know who's been skimming off of us."

*That* got his brother's attention. "You should have led with that."

It was kind of impossible to do that when their father started in on him the second he answered the phone, but Cillian didn't say that. It was an excuse, and a stupid one at that. "I'm not one hundred percent, but I'm pretty damn sure it's Dmitri Romanov. Or at least one of his people."

Aiden cursed long and hard. "That bastard keeps popping up like a goddamn weed."

"Yeah, well, you have a chance to bring it up tomorrow when you meet with him. The money was routed through half a dozen shell accounts, but it links back to a bank in New York—a branch in Manhattan. It's not exactly a smoking gun, but unless we have another person in that area aiming for us, then it's him."

"You're sure it's that bank."

"As sure as I can be." Devlin would have been able to pinpoint it. Cillian just didn't have the skills to take it further. Frankly, he was fucking surprised he'd managed to get *this* far. "Whatever this is about, it goes beyond money."

"You think I don't know that?" Aiden cursed again. "Okay. Send me what you have and we'll deal with it."

Cillian tightened his grip on the phone. Part of him wanted to be there, but it wouldn't make a difference. He wasn't one of the decision makers in the family. There was nothing he could add to that meeting that he hadn't already done. Plus, Olivia needed him here. Going back to Boston would be just a selfish way to pat himself on the back for being clever. He was beyond that shit now. He had to be. "Will do."

"And Cillian?"

"Yeah?"

"Don't think for a second that the conversation about this woman is over. The *only* reason we aren't handing her back to Dmitri gift-wrapped is because I hate that bastard. She's still a threat, and she still needs to be dealt with one way or another."

*Over my dead body.* "No one touches Olivia. You so much as try, and Dmitri Romanov will be the least of your worries." He hung up before his brother could say something else that would start to burn the bridge between them. Cillian turned for the door, but reconsidered. He dialed quickly. "Teague."

"Do you know what time it is?"

"It's not like you were sleeping." Even if his brother did sound distracted. "I know it's only been two days, but have you made any progress on the papers I asked you for?"

"I should have them ready in a day or two." A female voice said something in the background, but then a door closed and it was so muffled Cillian couldn't make out her words. Teague spoke, distracting him, "You're worried about how things will go down tomorrow?"

"Yeah." He couldn't tell Teague about the missing money. He might be Cillian's brother, but ever since his marriage to Callie Sheridan, his first alliance would always be to her. Handing over a potential weakness wasn't an option. But he *could* talk about Olivia. "Romanov isn't going to give her up without a fight." And every time the man let the O'Malleys get one over on him, he was potentially weakening his position. It wasn't something a good leader would allow, and that was if things *weren't* personal.

"I'll call you as soon as the meeting is over and let you know how it went. If you have to get her and her daughter out of town in a hurry, you'll at least have some warning."

Since he doubted either Aiden or their father would be eager to do him the favor of a progress report, he appreciated the offer. "Thanks. I owe you."

"You don't owe me shit. You're my brother, and you're doing the right thing. If I can help with that, I will in any way possible." The voice sounded in the background again. "I have to go, Cillian. I'll talk to you tomorrow."

There was nothing else that could be done tonight. He walked through the house, turning off most of the lights and locking the doors. Mark appeared when he walked into the kitchen. Cillian paused. "Everything good?"

"Yeah. Quiet." He patted his side where his gun was holstered. "We got this. Get some sleep."

"I'll have my phone on."

"I know."

There was nothing more to say. They were as covered as they could be given the circumstances. He trudged upstairs, feeling a hundred years old. He'd known his father was a stubborn son of a bitch, but he'd foolishly thought that the old man would support him in this—after all, Dmitri was using Olivia to threaten the O'Malleys—but of course all Seamus saw was the threat *she* posed. It seemed like he'd only gotten stricter and more brittle since shit went sideways with Carrigan. Everything was black or white. Gray would not be tolerated.

Well, that was too damn bad.

Cillian meant what he'd said to Olivia earlier. He wasn't giving her up without a fight. He had serious feelings for the woman going on, and that kind of thing didn't come around often enough to shit it away. He poked his head into the room she'd set up for Hadley, making sure everything looked good. The little girl was curled into a ball in the little portable crib thing that Olivia had packed, hugging a blanket to her chest. He shook his head and partially closed the door, then padded down to the room he'd shared with Olivia last night. She was asleep on the right side of the bed, one arm flung over her head and the other clutching the sheets to her chest.

He showered as quickly as he could, and then slipped into bed next to her. Cillian propped himself up onto his elbow and smoothed her hair back, staring down at her in the moonlight. *She's so fucking beautiful, it actually hurts.* He traced his thumb over her bottom lip, and her eyes opened. She smiled. "Hey."

"I'm sorry I woke you. You need to sleep." But he wasn't sorry. Not with her naked in his bed and gazing at him with that happy, sleepy look in her dark eyes. He cupped her face and pressed a light kiss against her lips. "Let me make love to you, sweetheart." He kissed his way across her jaw to her neck.

"Yes." Just that. Nothing more.

But he didn't need more. She was here, with him. They might not be exchanging vows, but there was something real here, something he wasn't about to let slip past him.

If Cillian had learned anything in this life, it was that you couldn't take a damn thing for granted. He ran his hand down her side to cup her hip. "You are so beautiful, inside and out." He shifted down her body, trailing kisses as he went. "I meant what I said earlier. I have no intention of letting you go—either of you."

"Good." Her word was little more than a moan.

He sucked one nipple into his mouth, palming her other breast, working her until she was writhing beneath him. And then he switched breasts. He wasn't rushing things tonight, not when nearly every sexual encounter they'd had to date was wild and nearly a frenzy. He liked it. Hell, he loved it. But he wanted to show Olivia exactly what she was coming to mean to him.

He nipped her hip bone and then soothed the spot with his mouth. She made a frustrated noise and lifted her hips, a silent demand he had no intention of ignoring. Cillian licked up her center, circling her clit. Her fingers laced through his hair, holding him in place. Like he wanted to be anywhere else. There was nothing like the feeling of this woman coming apart and knowing *he* was the cause.

"Wait."

He froze. "Yes?"

She tugged on his hair. "I want you inside me when I come."

Cillian paused to grab a condom from the drawer and roll it on, and then he settled between her legs. As he slid into her, it was a little slice of heaven here on earth. Olivia wrapped her legs around his waist, arching to meet each slow stroke. They moved in sync, almost like two halves of a whole.

It was good—too good.

He rolled onto his back, taking her with him. She caught herself on his chest with a soft laugh. "Changing positions?"

"I want to see you." The only light in the room was the full moon, and it traced down her body in a way that could only be described as lovingly. He followed its path with his palm, ending on her hips. "Ride me, sweetheart. I want to see the look on your face when you come."

"So demanding."

"Only about things worth fighting for."

She opened her mouth and seemed to reconsider. Before he could ask her what she was thinking, she started moving, rolling her hips and taking him deeper. With her hands on his chest and her body moving over his, it was almost unbearably intimate. Almost. He hooked the back of her neck and brought her down to kiss her, sealing their bodies together. The slow slide of her skin against his had him fighting for control, fighting to keep this going as long as possible.

She kissed him, the desperation of that point of contact a direct counterpoint to the way she rode his cock. He could feel her tightening around him, her movements becoming irregular, and he grabbed her hips to force her to keep the same rhythm that was going to send her over the edge. She gripped his shoulders, her nails digging into his skin. "*Cillian.*"

He barely waited for her to ride out the aftershocks before he flipped her onto her back and hitched her leg up over his arm. "You look so fucking sexy when you come, sweetheart. I'm never going to get tired of that." He gave in to the instinct demanding that he pound into her, his control slipping further with each stroke. "And the feel of it. Fuck, it's too good to put into words."

"Then don't." She kissed him, and it was too much. His whole body went tight, his orgasm sweeping away everything but the feel of her. Cillian shifted to the side of her and drew her against his side.

Olivia gave him a sleepy, satisfied smile. "Careful. I could get used to this kind of wake up."

*Good.* He kept the word inside, though it was a close thing. She was going through so much right now. He wasn't willing to be yet another man putting demands on her. He'd said he had no intention of letting her go, and he meant it. There was no point in pressing her about it—not while they were still dealing with the looming threat of her ex and half brother.

After? That would be a completely different story.

He got up and went to the bathroom to dispose of the condom. By the time he got back, Olivia was asleep again. She turned toward him as he climbed back into bed, and he pulled her against his chest, wrapping his arms around her and letting the sound of her steady breathing ease what remained of his earlier tension. This was what it was all about.

He'd do damn near anything to keep this woman in his life.

# CHAPTER TWENTY-TWO

Olivia woke to the sun on her face. She stretched and sighed, feeling better rested than she had in weeks. She sat up and rubbed a hand over her face. *Hadley must have been more tired than I thought if she's still sleeping.* She glanced over Cillian to the clock on the nightstand. "*Ten?*"

No way.

A frisson of fear iced its way down her spine, but she did her damnedest to ignore it as she climbed out of bed. It had been a crazy few days. It was absolutely logical that Hadley would be overtired and just had one of those random days that rarely came around and slept in. She'd thrown a horrible tantrum yesterday, after all, and she only did that when she was exhausted beyond all reason.

Olivia threw on a sweatshirt over her tank top and padded down the hallway to the room her daughter slept in. She pushed open the door. At first, relief nearly sent her to her knees. There Hadley was, all cuddled up under her blanket like she preferred to sleep. *Way to overreact, idiot.* She almost turned around and let her daughter keep sleeping, but something made her walk over and look into the portable crib. She tugged down the blanket, frowned, and tugged it down further.

It took entirely too long for her tired mind to understand what she was seeing.

A pillow.

She picked the pillow up, half-sure that somehow she'd missed something and Hadley had snuggled down beneath it, but there was nothing below it except more blankets. Frantic now, Olivia stood and tore the blankets off the bed itself, as if her daughter had somehow climbed out of the crib and fallen asleep somewhere else. *She has to be here, she has to be.*

Nothing.

"Hadley?" *She just escaped her crib. She's done it before. She's in the house. I just have to find her.* "Hadley! Come out, baby girl, you're scaring Mama." She nearly ran over Cillian as she rushed out into the hallway. "I can't find Hadley."

He didn't waste time with cold comfort or telling her that she must be mistaken. He just nodded. "We'll find her."

They tore the house apart looking for her, every second that passed solidifying the horrific truth in Olivia's mind. *Hadley is gone. My baby girl is gone.* She opened the front door.

And screamed.

Instantly, Cillian was by her side. He pulled her against him, burying her face in his chest. "Don't look, sweetheart."

But it was too late. She already had the image of the dead man imprinted on the back of her eyelids. *So much blood.*

The panic she'd been mostly able to hold at bay rose up and punched her in the face. *Someone killed our guard, and my daughter is gone.* "Hadley—"

He led her into the living room and guided her down onto the couch. "Listen to me, Olivia. Are you listening?"

It was harder than it should have been to focus on his face. "I'm listening."

"I need to check on the other men."

*He thinks he's going to find more bodies.* "But—"

"I'm not leaving you here alone." He squeezed her hands, his touch gentle despite the command in his voice. Though part of her wanted to argue that she wasn't helpless, the rest was trying to come to terms with the fact that her daughter was *gone.* Someone had come in here, killed at least one person, and taken Hadley.

Fear and panic crystalized inside her, morphing into rage between one breath and the next. *They took my baby girl. I'm going to* kill *them.* "It was Dmitri."

Cillian's expression didn't change. "Get what you need. We won't be returning."

"Okay."

She followed him upstairs, eerie calm settling around her. Dmitri might have threatened to do just this, but a naive part of her had assumed that he wouldn't follow through on it. Not like this. Not without warning. Not in the middle of the night and killing at least one person along the way. She changed into a pair of jeans, a T-shirt, and her boots, conscious of Cillian standing between her and the doorway, his dark eyes narrowed as if he expected an attack at any moment. She could have told him it was no use, that Hadley was gone, but she'd obviously been wrong about the lengths Sergei and Dmitri would go to before, so she might be wrong about this, too. Olivia repacked her bag, her hands lingering over Hadley's clothes. *I'm getting you back, baby girl. Just hang in there. Mama's coming.*

"You got everything?"

She looked around the room, part of her hoping that this was all a mistake and that her daughter would appear with an infectious giggle. But it wasn't a mistake, and she didn't appear. Olivia stood on shaking legs and forced herself to nod. "Yes."

She must have been more out of it than she realized, because Cillian had managed to dress in one of his suits and pack his own bag while she was working on hers. He pulled her into his arms and hugged her so tightly, it was as if he was afraid she'd break apart into a million pieces. "We will get her back."

"Cillian—"

"We will get her back, Olivia." He pressed a kiss to her temple and stepped back. "Stay close."

He didn't take her hand, and she belatedly realized it was so he could be free to draw the gun she could see in the shoulder holster. The similarities between Cillian and Dmitri were never more pronounced than in that moment with that deadly glint in his eyes. This was not the man who made love to her last night and told her he had no intention of letting her go. This was Cillian O'Malley, a man who'd seen unfathomable loss in his life, a man deadly in his own right.

There must have been something on her face, because he stopped on the stairs. "Do you trust me?"

"Yes." There was no hesitation. He might look like a near-stranger right now, but this was still the man who she'd spent the last few weeks getting to know. He might be an

O'Malley, but that wasn't *all* he was. She just had to re-member that.

Cillian nodded. "Then let's go."

She followed him out the back door. He hesitated, almost like he wanted to tell her to stay in the house, but then gave himself a shake and started for the tree line. She kept close, all too aware of how exposed they were out here. Yes, he kept his body between her and potential danger, but that wasn't a guarantee of shit.

They found the second body propped up against a large tree just inside the forest. She made herself look at the wounds, made herself memorize the face of the man who'd died while on protection detail for *her*. She was so focused on his face, it took her several seconds to understand the wound pattern. "Knife?" *Sergei.* That bastard always had liked his blades—at least when it wasn't efficient to use his hands.

"It looks that way." He stood and took a step back. "I'm going to have to move the bodies, but we need to check on the others first." He waited for her to nod before he started moving again.

They found the next man alive. Cillian went to his knees next to him. "Mark."

"Fucked up." The man held both his hands to his stomach. "The blond Russian bastard caught me off guard."

There was no way she could pretend Sergei wasn't involved. Her stomach lurched, and for one second she thought she might lose it completely. "I'm sorry."

"My mistake. My fault."

But he wouldn't be here if it wasn't for her.

Cillian looked at her. "Can you get him to the barn? I need to check on the last two men."

She nodded, and they ignored Mark's protests that he would be fine while she levered him off the ground and wedged herself beneath his arm. He didn't seem to be actively bleeding, which was a relief. She already had the deaths of at least two men on her head. The trip to the barn seemed to take forever, each step accompanied by Mark's wheezing breath. She started to say something half a dozen times, but what could she say that wouldn't be spitting in his face? "I'm sorry."

She pushed the door open to the barn and helped him hobble over to a bench shoved up against the wall next to the empty stables. Mark let out a pained sigh. "Like I said—not your fault."

"Do you want me to check that?"

He shook his head. "If it hit something vital, I'd be dead by now."

That was a good point. She looked around for a phone. "We should call 911."

"Olivia." The shock of hearing him rasp her name stopped her cold, and she turned to face him. Mark leaned his head against the wall and closed his eyes. "Let Cillian handle it."

Cillian slipped through the door, supporting another man. This one was a ghastly shade of white and looked about ready to pass out. Olivia helped him to the bench next to Mark. "You have to call someone."

"Doc Jones has a colleague in the area. She's on her way, but the guy she vouches for will be here in fifteen." He crouched in front of Mark. "Can you hold on for a little longer? The other three…They're gone. I'm sorry. I have to see to the bodies."

Mark nodded. Cillian took Olivia's hand. "Come on."

He waited until they were halfway across the yard to say, "We're going back to Boston."

"Dmitri." He would be there in a few hours, and he was the one who held the answers. She rested her hand on her purse, the comforting bulge of the pistol there. Every heartbeat was a reminder, each second ticking by another where her daughter might be wondering where she was, might be scared and confused. *Hadley, Hadley, Hadley*. She'd find her. She had to.

Cillian nodded. "He has a lot to answer for. Hadley's your daughter, just a little girl. She didn't ask for any of this." He stalked out onto the driveway. "And those were my men. The only reason they're here at all is because I asked them to be."

Three more deaths for him to shoulder. There wasn't a damn thing she could say to that, either. They might have known the risk when they signed on to work for the O'Malleys, but no one had expected Sergei. *Those deaths are as much my fault as they are his*. She followed him to the car. "We both asked them."

"This isn't your fault, sweetheart." He shook his head. "Give me a minute."

She watched as he combed the car, searching the front, back, trunk, and undercarriage. He even spent some time on the engine. *Checking for bombs*. Olivia shuddered. As much as she didn't like to contemplate death, if Sergei wanted her dead, he had plenty of opportunity while she slept. So she wasn't surprised when Cillian gave the all clear. "He didn't even slit the tires."

"He wants me to follow." He'd get his wish. There wasn't another option. She just hoped and prayed to any god who was listening that he managed to take care of

Hadley in the meantime. She was only a baby. She needed diapers and cut-up food and... *Stop. You're going to start panicking again, and that won't help Hadley or you.*

Cillian took the bag from her. "We'll get her back."

"I know." There was no other option.

"Stay here. I'll be back in a few."

*The dead men.* She climbed into the car and did her best not to think too hard about everything that could go wrong as he disappeared around the side of the house. Part of her chafed at the delay, but those men had given their lives trying to protect her and Hadley. The very *least* they deserved was to be kept safe until someone could be sent to deal with them properly.

A car passed hers and drove straight to the barn. She watched Cillian appear to talk to a man who couldn't have been more than twenty-one. They hurried into the barn and shut the door behind them. She wasn't sure how much time passed before he reappeared. It could have been five minutes or five hours with how her growing panic distorted everything.

Cillian walked out of the barn, his expression bleak. It took him mere seconds to cross to the car and slide into the driver's seat. "Mark and Rodger will live."

A small comfort. Part of her wanted to reach out to him, but she couldn't afford to have her calm shattered, and Cillian's touch would definitely do that. So she stared straight ahead and clutched her purse. "We need to be at that meeting today." The only way she'd get to Dmitri was if he wasn't expecting her, and he sure as hell wouldn't think that she'd show up to something with the O'Malleys.

"I know." He entered the freeway and picked up speed. "We'll make it."

She put her phone back together, trying not to notice how her hands shook. If Sergei was waiting for a call, she'd damn well give it to him. She scrolled through her old numbers and called him. The line rang and rang and rang, finally clicking over to an answering service. *Damn it*. She dialed Dmitri next, with the same results. Wherever they were right now, they wanted her hurting and worrying and generally driving herself insane. That would do plenty of damage and they wouldn't have to lay a finger on Hadley. She hoped.

That didn't stop her from trying to call both men repeatedly as they crossed state lines back into Massachusetts. Nothing. Nothing, nothing, nothing. It was enough to have a scream fighting to make its way into the world. A scream and horrible accusations.

*You promised we'd be safe. You promised you'd keep them from us. You* promised *this wouldn't happen.*

*If I hadn't been so determined to sex him up, I would have run and taken Hadley with me. It wasn't a perfect plan, but they wouldn't have caught up to me so quickly. I let my personal desires get in the way of my daughter's safety.*

*I am the worst mother ever.*

"Whatever you're thinking, stop."

She didn't look at him, her gaze on the highway, as if she could will them over the distance faster if she just concentrated enough. "It's my fault."

"It's not your fault."

"It is. If I'd just fallen in line, he never would have taken this step." She'd effectively chosen Cillian over her own daughter. Just like her mother had chosen Andrei over Olivia over and over and over again from the time she was born. The one thing she'd promised herself she'd never do—the lowest bar she could have possibly set for herself—and the first man who gave her a bit of attention had her throwing all those good intentions right out the window.

Now Hadley was suffering for her choices, just like Olivia had suffered as a result of her mother's.

"You got out. That's not something most people in our life can say."

"If I'd actually gotten out, this wouldn't be happening right now. I should have run as soon as I realized he wasn't going to leave me alone." Weeks wasted. It made her sick to her stomach.

"Olivia, look at me." His voice was so harsh, she instinctively obeyed. The expression on his face was even harsher than his tone. "We don't have time for the pity party you're indulging in right now."

She tensed. "You don't get to tell me how to feel. That monster has *my daughter*."

"And you're so wrapped up in blaming yourself that you're going to play right into his hands." His grip tightened on the steering wheel. "The past is the past. You can't go back and change it. You can only move forward and ensure that the mistakes you made don't define you."

"Pretty to think so."

"No, it's not. It's fucking hard. You think I'm not tearing myself up over the deaths of those men? They are *my* fault. You said that Romanov might know where we were, and I ignored the potential threat. That's on *me*." He wound through slower traffic, the speedometer approaching triple digits. "I'm going to have to be the one to tell their families that I was too goddamn cocky, and they died as a result."

Just like his brother had. Her chest tightened, but she couldn't afford sympathy. Not yet. Maybe not ever.

Instead, she focused on what she'd do once they reached their destination. It seemed to take forever and no time at all to get back to Boston. Cillian drove them straight to Beacon Hill, stopping in front of a town house that looked like every other town house on that street—massive and expensive. The trees lining the sidewalk barely did anything to soften the look. She got out of the car and stared at the wide door that would be at home in some lord's castle halfway across the world.

"Let me do the talking."

She nodded, though she had her own plan. Olivia slipped her purse over the crook of her arm and walked with him up the stairs and into the town house. The interior was just as intimidating as the exterior—possibly more so. From the home in Connecticut, she'd gotten the feeling of a building well loved by the family that lived there. Here, everything was stark and expensive and uncomfortable, as if it had been designed to remind visitors just who they were dealing with.

As if she could forget.

He led her into a study filled with people. She recognized Cillian's sister, Carrigan, and her...whatever he was. They weren't married, but calling James Halloran her boyfriend seemed juvenile. Next to them was another O'Malley—judging by his dark coloring—and a blond woman. From the possessive way he stood behind the chair where she sat, as if ready to spring into motion at the slightest moment to protect her, she'd guess this was Teague and the Sheridan heir. Then there were the two men standing on the other side of the desk, as if trying to put as much distance between themselves and the rest of the room as possible. The younger man was nearly a carbon copy of the older—Cillian's older brother and father.

Neither of which looked happy to see them.

His father glared. "Aiden specifically told you to stay the hell out of Boston while we cleaned up this mess."

"The circumstances have changed." Cillian shrugged, and if she wasn't a step behind him, she wouldn't have noticed how tense his back was. "I need to have a word with Dmitri."

"Convenient that I'm here then, isn't it?"

Olivia moved before she had fully processed the silky Russian voice. She grabbed her gun from her purse and spun, shoving him against the wall and the gun against the hollow of his throat. The only reaction she got was a slight widening of his eyes. "Little sister."

"Half sister." The response was automatic, and she pushed the gun harder against his skin. "Where is she?"

"Where is who?"

She was vaguely aware of raised voices behind her, but she trusted Cillian to keep them off her while she got answers. *You think you would have learned after last night. Apparently not.* Pushing the thought away, she focused on Dmitri. "Don't play games with me, you bastard. Where is Hadley?"

Confusion played across his face, but she'd seen him use the tiniest expression to manipulate people around him. She wasn't going to fall for that shit. She moved in closer, the gun growing warm in her palm. "You ordered Sergei to take *my daughter*, and you're going to order him to bring her back to me, or I'm going to blow your fucking head off."

"What are you talking about, Olivia?" His accent thickened, and he switched to Russian. "I don't have your daughter."

"*Stop lying!*" She wasn't sure if she was speaking English or if she'd made the switch along with him, because all she could see was the growing anger on his face. "You threatened me, and when I didn't do what you wanted, you followed through on it. Stop playing games."

"I never—"

"I swear to God, if you say you never threatened me, I will do something unforgivable." Her breath was coming faster now, but she couldn't dial it back in. "We both know what your intent was even if your words weren't exactly that. Where. Is. She?"

"I. Don't. Know." He glared. "I didn't order this. If it was Sergei, it was done without my knowledge."

"*Liar.*" She jerked back to hit him with the gun, but then arms were around her stomach, hauling her off him. Olivia screamed and fought, but they were iron bands holding her in place while someone else took her gun.

"Sweetheart, stop." Cillian's voice in her ear, angry but a thousand times calmer than she felt. "We'll get answers, but if you kill him, we aren't getting shit."

"He's not going to tell you the truth." She lunged for Dmitri, more animal than human, but Cillian jerked her back again.

Then Seamus O'Malley was between them, managing to look down his nose at everyone in the room. "If you can't control yourself, I'll have you locked in a room until this is over. Decide."

*That* got through to her. No one cared as much about Hadley as she did. It wouldn't be personal to them. Even if they decided to help her, it would just be a job. She couldn't afford to be shut out. So she let Cillian guide her to the other side of the couches—though she never took her gaze off Dmitri. *I'll kill him if anything happens to Hadley. Him and Sergei and anyone who gets in my way.*

Seamus sent her a disgusted look, as if he could read her thoughts, and turned back to her half brother. "Explain yourself."

"I don't have to explain anything to you." He'd taken the few seconds everyone was focused on her to straighten his suit, his calm mask firmly in place once more. "This is family business. I'm sure you understand."

"I'm equally sure that you've been dicking around with us for months, Russian. The girl might be your sister, but she's in *our* territory with *my* son. That makes it my business."

"As I told my *sister*, I know nothing about that." He looked directly at her. "You know how I work, Olivia. You know what I'm saying is true. If I was going to take her, it wouldn't have been like this."

She didn't want to agree with him. In fact, all she wanted was to get out of Cillian's arms so she could go over there and follow through on hitting him with the damn gun. But...he was right. She stopped struggling. If he didn't order Hadley taken... *Oh my God.* "Sergei is off the rails."

"It would seem that way." He gave a shrug that meant nothing at all. "I do apologize, Seamus, but one of my men has decided to take matters into his own hands—without my knowledge, of course. There's little I can do."

Cillian hugged Olivia tighter. "Where is he?"

"How should I know? I'm not the man's keeper." That one moment where Dmitri might have been a real human being was dead and gone. He adjusted his cuff links. "If that's all…"

"It's not." Seamus glanced around the room, his brows slamming down. "Everyone out except the Russian. We have other business to attend to."

# CHAPTER TWENTY-THREE

Cillian kept a hold of Olivia until they were out of the study and had a closed door between them and Romanov. He didn't think the man was lying, though things would have been a whole hell of a lot easier if he was. If he hadn't ordered Hadley taken, then there was no telling where her ex was.

Carrigan sauntered over. "Your kid is gone?"

"Yes." Olivia didn't sound like she was about to leap into a blackout rage, but Cillian hadn't expected her to go after Dmitri, either. He'd known she had a gun, but it never even crossed his mind that she might use it. *Stupid.*

His sister nodded. "We'll help however we can." She glanced at James, who crossed his arms over his chest. "We're not huge fans of people who prey on the weak."

That was all well and good, but the chances that Sergei came back to Boston after taking Hadley were slim to none. Olivia must have realized the same thing, because she gave a brittle smile. "I appreciate the offer, but I think I need to search beyond your reach."

Teague approached, his arm around Callie. "We can help, too."

Callie took Olivia's hands. "I can't imagine what you're going through. If your half brother didn't order this, where would this man have gone?"

"If I knew that, I'd be there instead of here." Olivia stepped back, extracting herself from his sister-in-law's grip. "If you'll excuse me." She walked down the hallway away from them, checking each room and then ducking into the bathroom and closing the door. He wanted to follow her, to wrap his arms around her and tell her that everything would be okay. Maybe if he did that, *he* would actually believe it.

Because things were starting to look pretty fucking stark. He turned to Aiden. "Dmitri Romanov's man came to our house in Connecticut, butchered three of the men I had watching the house, and then abducted a fourteen-month-old toddler. I don't care what our father says—this is personal."

"Why are things never simple with you?" Aiden shook his head. "You know what, don't answer that. Nothing is simple anymore."

That was the damn truth. Even if Olivia hadn't ended up in his life, Dmitri Romanov still would have been skimming off their top. Everything was so twisted up, it was a wonder he could keep any of it straight anymore. *I don't have to keep shit straight. The only thing that matters is getting that little girl back.*

With that driving him, he walked past his siblings and slipped into the office, locking the door behind him. His father sent him an aggravated look. "We're talking business, boy. Get out."

"I have business with Romanov." He ignored his father and crossed to stand in front of Dmitri. Not close enough to be in the man's space, but close enough that he had no choice but to focus on Cillian. "That little girl is your niece."

Another of those goddamn shrugs. "As my sister is so fond of telling me, she's only *half* my niece."

Maybe. But he could read the tension in the man's shoulders. Whatever he thought of Olivia, she was right that his promise to his late father was weighing on him. If he wanted to honor Andrei's wishes, letting Hadley be hurt—or worse—was a shitty way to go about it. "Do you really think this Sergei can take care of a toddler?"

Dmitri's mouth went tight. "I told Olivia, and now I'm telling you—I don't know where the man is. If I did, *I* would take care of things. I don't tolerate disobedience."

*That* was the button to push to get the information he needed. "A man like that doesn't have a whole lot going for him that isn't connected to you and your people. Where would he go?"

He crossed his arms over his chest. "What interest do you have?"

"He killed three of my men. I don't like that." He couldn't believe how calm he sounded. It felt like there was a creature inside him, shredding his heart and lungs and stomach, but nothing showed in his voice.

"You care about my sister. If I don't miss my guess, you love her." Dmitri's brows rose. "Fascinating."

Hearing that word—that *truth*—from an enemy's lips made his blood pressure rise. He hadn't had the luxury of exploring his feelings for her, not beyond knowing that he had no intention of letting her go. To have this man call him out like that . . . Cillian took a step forward. "Think hard, Romanov. Because otherwise Olivia and I are going to work our way through your people, and you're not going to like the results."

"You threaten me?"

*"Cillian."*

He ignored his father and focused solely on Romanov. "No, I'm telling you plainly what will happen. You think three percent is a way to undermine our operations. Let's see how you feel when I start chipping away at yours."

"Impossible."

"You can take that risk, or you can fix a problem that you're partly responsible for. Call Sergei. He'll answer." Cillian hoped. If the man was as loyal as Olivia said, there was a decent chance he'd pick up before he had a chance to think better of it if Dmitri was calling. He might have gone off the deep end, but old habits died hard.

Dmitri gave a put-upon sigh. "Fine." He pulled a phone out of his jacket and dialed. After a second, he switched it to speaker so all three of them could hear.

*"Da?"*

"English, Sergei."

"Yes?" The man on the other end sounded tired. Exhausted, even.

"You've displeased me." Dmitri *looked* displeased. But then, he would be. A king was only in power as long as he was obeyed without question. The second someone started doing things without permission, everything started falling apart. It was why such drastic measures sometimes had to be taken to ensure loyalty. If everyone saw some dickhead disrespecting the one in power, they might start doing the same damn thing.

The background noise was the type you'd find when someone was driving, which meant he could be anywhere. "You don't understand, boss. Olivia was *fucking* that Irish bastard. She has to be taught a lesson."

It was everything Cillian could do to keep his mouth shut. That piece of shit might disrespect Olivia, but the endgame was more important than the fact that he wanted to reach through the phone and strangle him.

For his part, Dmitri didn't seem to like hearing that, either. "That's for me to decide."

"You were taking too long."

And he was losing Sergei. If he didn't do something to reel the man back in, they wouldn't get the information they needed. Cillian crossed his arms over his chest, which made Dmitri raise an eyebrow. "Tell me where you are so we can fix this."

"You should have let me keep her. If you had, none of this would have happened. It's *your* fault she left me."

"That may be so, but stealing her child isn't the way back into her heart."

"I don't want to be back into her heart. I just want her to suffer as much as she's made me suffer." A child wailed in the background, and Sergei cursed and spat out something in Russian.

Then the line went dead.

*Fuck.* That had been their one chance of finding out where the bastard was going, and they'd just blown it. Cillian ran a hand over his face. "What a clusterfuck."

"Hardly." Dmitri slipped the phone back into his pocket. "I know his destination."

"How in the hell did you figure that out?"

"He's not coming in, which means he won't be with any of my men or in any of the various locations I have control of." He straightened his tie. "He'll be going south, to Philadelphia. He has an aunt there that he doesn't think I'm aware of." But of course the man was. He didn't seem like the type to let much get past him. He grabbed a pen and scrawled an address on the notepad on the desk. "If we're done here?"

"Go." Seamus spoke from the spot he'd taken behind his desk. When Cillian made to follow, he said, "Not you."

He waited for the door to shut to turn and face his father. "I know this isn't what you wanted, but I'm not going to let a little girl suffer for your politics and pride."

"So I gathered." Seamus steepled his fingers and tapped them against his chin. "You care for this girl enough to challenge me and the rest of your family."

"Yes." No point in denying it now.

"Go. Take Liam and as many men as he thinks you need."

He could barely believe what he was hearing. "What?"

"I might be a cold son of a bitch, but even I have lines that shouldn't be crossed. As long as the woman feels the same way about you that you do about her, she's controllable and only a minor threat. Go get the child." He leaned back. "And when you're home again, you will dismantle every connection Dmitri Romanov has in our territory. The man is a snake, and I refuse to give him so much as a toehold. You were right when you threatened him—his money is where a hit would hurt the most. So that's what we'll do."

Cillian rocked back on his heels. "He cooperated."

"He did the bare minimum—only after bringing this

mess to our front door. He's the one who's been skimming from us, undermining our authority with our people. He's the one who lost control of his man, which resulted in the death of three of ours. That can't be allowed."

No, he supposed it couldn't be. A slow satisfaction expanded inside him. Dmitri had made Olivia's life a living hell. It didn't matter if he seemed to regret what Sergei had done—he'd been the one to put the man in a position where he'd be able to act. Cillian smiled, well aware that it was as ice cold as the expression on his father's face. "It would be my honest-to-God pleasure."

* * *

Things happened quickly after Olivia came out of the bathroom—barely having gotten control of herself—to find that Cillian had somehow garnered Dmitri's support and had an address where Sergei was most likely taking Hadley. She hadn't even known he had an aunt, let alone one in the country. It was entirely possible that her half brother was sending them on a wild-goose chase, but Cillian didn't seem to think so. Trusting him was so incredibly hard, but she didn't have another option.

So to Philly they went.

She glanced into the rearview mirror for the millionth time, silently counting the black SUVs trailing behind them. One, two, three. All jam-packed with expressionless men with murder in their hearts. They hadn't taken the news of their friends' deaths lightly. She had no illusions that they were there for her. They weren't.

They were out for blood.

Cillian hadn't said anything since they started driving

four hours ago. At first she was grateful for the silence. Her nerves were strung tight, and she wasn't capable of small talk. Not when Hadley was in danger. But the longer it stretched, the more uncomfortable she felt.

Finally, when they hit the city limits, she turned to him. "Thank you. I...I couldn't have done this without you."

"You could have. It would have just taken longer." His voice gave her no indication of how he was feeling.

*He's right. Keep your emotions in check until you know Hadley is safe and Sergei is dealt with. Everything else can wait.* She sat back. "I have to be the one who goes in. Anyone else tries, and he might hurt Hadley."

He hissed out a breath. "I don't like it."

"But you know I'm right. It's the best shot we have of pulling this off."

"If something happens to you..." Silence for a beat, and then two. "You're right. Damn it, I know you're right. Just don't do anything to get yourself killed."

Her heart tried to beat its way out of her throat. "I won't." Now wasn't the time to play the hero, and the suit had never been something Olivia aspired to. She wanted a quiet life. A home. A family. A man who loved her and her daughter more than he loved anything else.

It seemed so simple, and yet it was an impossible dream.

She was Dmitri Romanov's half sister. No matter what else she did with her life, that would always be there, hanging over her head. There was no escaping that particular identity, no matter how much she wanted to. Even if she changed her name, it would always be lurking, ready to take her out when she least expected it.

*First Hadley. Then deal with everything else.*

They wound through neighborhood after neighborhood,

the houses getting smaller and in poorer repair. Finally, he pulled up at a curb. "She's two blocks down. Yellow house on the right."

It was slightly cheerier than its neighbors. Though the paint was fading and peeled, there were flowers in a pot on the front porch and curtains hanging in the windows—something floral and bright. It said something about the kind of woman Sergei's aunt was. In different circumstances, maybe she would be someone Olivia could have connected with.

It didn't matter. If she was helping Sergei, then she was as much the enemy as he was.

She took a deep breath, but it didn't do anything to calm her. "Okay."

Cillian stopped her with a hand on her arm. "You go in the front door. You have five minutes before we bust down the back, Olivia. That's it."

It wasn't much, but in reality, a lot could go wrong in the space of five minutes. Lives could change. Lives could *end*. She gave a jerky nod. "Okay."

"Get Hadley and get down. We'll take care of Sergei." From the grim way he said it, he meant permanently.

*Good.*

She slipped out of the car and walked down the sidewalk, every step taking her farther away from Cillian and closer to danger. She had the sudden insane urge to run back to him and tell him that she loved him. *What if that was my chance and I'll never get another one? What if Sergei kills him? What if he kills* me? She'd spent too much time around the man to underestimate how dangerous he was. There might have been a time when he'd hesitate to hurt her, but it had disappeared right around when he'd stolen Hadley from her bed. All bets were off now.

It took entirely too little time to make it to the yellow house and walk up the steps. She knocked before fear could paralyze her. There were heavy footsteps on the other side and she barely had time to brace herself before the door was flung open and she was face-to-face with Sergei. His blue eyes went wide. "You."

Everything that she'd been trying so hard to control came rushing to the fore. "Me." Olivia shoved past him and into the house. "Where is she?"

She barely made it three steps when he grabbed her arm and spun her to face him. "How did you know about this place?"

"Dmitri. How else?" She laughed, the sound high and nearly hysterical. "You didn't really think you could hide anything from him, did you? If anyone should know better, it's you."

He tightened his grip. "Who else is with you?" He moved to the window, dragging her behind him, and peered outside. "Where is that boyfriend of yours?"

*Hopefully sneaking up to the back door right about now.*

She ignored the question and looked around. Despite the floor plan, the décor was bright and downright cheery. This place was obviously well loved. "Where is Hadley?" She wanted to call out for her daughter, but if she wasn't here, she wasn't in the line of fire of what was about to go down. "What have you done with her?"

"You really think I'd hurt a child?"

That wasn't a damn answer. She shoved at him, but he only gripped her tighter. *I'll be wearing those bruises tomorrow if I survive this.* "You forget. I *know* you. Do you really want me to answer that?"

He shook her hard enough to snap her head back. "Don't be a bitch, Olivia."

"You first, Sergei."

He started to turn a mottled red color, a sure sign of violence to come. "You always had a smart mouth on you. Maybe it's time to teach you a lesson once and for all." He glanced at a hallway—if it could be called that. It was barely three feet deep, ending in two closed doors.

*Hadley*.

He was talking about hurting Hadley.

*No.* "You're right. I did." Somehow she managed to keep talking despite the pain radiating from where he held her. *Keep focused on me, you piece of shit. You leave my baby girl out of this.* "You know, I always suspected sex was so boring with you because you had to hurt a woman to get it up. Looks like I was right."

He yanked her closer and gripped her throat with his free hand, her death in his eyes. "You always were a bitch."

"No argument there." Each word was fire inside her, his hand tightening until black spots started dancing across her vision. *This is so very, very bad.* She kicked at him, but he dodged easily, something like arousal on his face. So she went for his eyes.

She barely had a chance to rake her nails across his face when he slammed her into the wall hard enough to stun her. "This will be easier if you don't fight me, Olivia."

No telling what exactly he was threatening, but she didn't really want to know, so she fought harder, almost thankful for his hand around her neck because it made screaming impossible. *Stay where you are, Hadley. Please, God, whoever's listening, let her stay where she is.* She kicked and clawed, nothing seeming to have any effect on Sergei, even though she could see the blood running down his arms.

He shook her again. "Enough."

"You're right." The voice came from behind him.

Sergei was ripped away from her, and Olivia fell to the floor. She shoved to her knees in time to see Cillian land a punch that sent her ex staggering several steps back. He pistol-whipped him, knocking him to the ground. She froze. She'd never seen Cillian look like that, almost... soulless. He kicked Sergei in the face, flipping him onto his back. "You will never put your hands on her again."

"You can't stop me." Sergei drew a gun from his ankle holster, pointing it at her.

Cillian didn't hesitate. He pulled the trigger of his pistol twice in quick succession.

Olivia crawled over to Sergei in time to see the life leak out of his pale blue eyes. She touched his chest, part of her disbelieving that it was over as easy as that, but it didn't draw breath. *No pulse, no breath, eyes staring at nothing. Can't fake that.*

It didn't stop her from wanting to empty a clip into his chest to make sure.

"Olivia." Strong arms wrapped around her and pulled her to her feet. It was harder than it should have been to stay standing, so she clung to Cillian, her gaze never leaving Sergei. "He's dead."

"He damn well better be. He might have been a tough son of a bitch, but no one can survive two bullets to the heart." He turned her slowly away from her ex, and framed her face with his hands. "Are you okay, sweetheart? When I came through the door and saw his hands around your neck..."

A full-body shudder worked through her. "I'm fine." Her voice was so raspy, the words were damn near indistinguishable. It hurt to talk. Hell, it hurt to breathe.

But she wasn't done yet. She turned toward the closed doors. "Hadley."

"Why don't you—"

"No. Not until I know she's okay." *Please be sleeping.* If he'd done something to her baby girl, she'd bring him back to life so she could kill him again. *Not good enough. Not by a long shot.* Olivia slipped out of Cillian's arms and crossed the living room in a daze. It had all happened so fast. One second Sergei was there, his larger-than-life presence threatening to smother hers. The next, he was dead and gone. He'd never be able to hurt her again.

She opened the first door, but it was just a bathroom, as tiny and clean as the rest of the house. The next door was locked. Her heart skipped a beat. She rattled the lock. It was one of the old ones that could be popped with a bobby pin—which was something she didn't have.

"Let me." Cillian gently nudged her out of the way and set his shoulder to the thin wood. She glanced back to find dour-looking men filing into the living room. Without a word, one produced a tarp, and they set about wrapping Sergei's body in it. It took seconds, and then there was only a small stain on the faded blue carpet and the cracked plaster where her head had met the wall. Another man came through the door with a bucket of what looked like cleaning supplies. *They've done this before.*

*Yeah, no shit. When you do illegal things, people get hurt, and it's necessary to cover it up.*

She turned as Cillian hit the door again, cracking the wood and sending the part still attached to the hinges slamming into the wall behind it. Olivia saw the familiar flash of a gun and *moved*, slamming him into the wall and covering as much of his body as she could with hers. Fire exploded across her back, the burning fury a match to her throat. "Gun."

"Got it." He pulled his out again and peered around the door, nearly taking a bullet to the face. "We're not here to hurt you. We came for the girl."

A torrent of angry Russian was his only answer. Olivia frowned, trying to concentrate enough to translate the words. "She's not happy that we're here."

"I gathered." He peeked around the door again. "Hadley's there. She doesn't seem to be hurt."

Relief made her light-headed. Or maybe it was the blood she could feel soaking her back. She slumped to the ground. "Get my baby girl, Cillian. Please."

She hit the ground, his answer sliding through the darkness blotting out her vision. "I will. I promise. Just hold on, sweetheart."

# CHAPTER TWENTY-FOUR

The sight of Olivia on the floor, her dusky skin too pale, made Cillian's mind go blank. All he wanted to do was scoop her up and get them both the hell out of there. But she trusted him to take care of the crazy Russian in the other room and save her daughter.

He caught Liam's eye and motioned over his shoulder. So far the woman was solely focused on keeping them out of the room, rather than hurting the little girl she had in her arms. If she didn't have that damn gun, he'd just rush her, but he couldn't take the risk that she'd turn the weapon on Hadley.

Liam frowned, and then made a circling motion with his hand. He didn't wait for Cillian's nod to take another man and disappear out the back door. They'd slip around to the window behind her. He just needed to wait for their signal.

It didn't take long.

The sound of breaking glass was his cue. He rushed

into the room. The older woman had turned her gun toward Liam, and Cillian wasted no time grabbing her arm so the shot went wide. She was strong, but he was stronger. He wrestled the gun away from her and then turned both on her. "Put the child down."

She spat something he couldn't understand, but she set Hadley down on the mattress. The little girl was awake, her tear-stained face enough to make his heart ache. Her lower lip trembled. Cillian shoved his gun into his holster and motioned to her with his free hand while he kept the other gun trained on Sergei's aunt. "Come here, baby girl."

"Mama?"

"She's here, too." *Unconscious on the floor.* He couldn't afford to think about that. Not yet. Hadley had to come first. He went down on one knee. "Let's get you home."

Hadley slid off the bed and toddled over to him, shooting terrified looks at the woman behind her. What had she done to the little girl? It was almost enough to make him pull the trigger right then and there. Only the fact that it would add to Hadley's trauma stayed his hand. He picked the toddler up and stood. "We're leaving now. I highly suggest you stay in this room."

Cillian backed out the door. Liam must have come back around, because he was at his side instantly. "Your woman was hit?"

"Yeah." He wanted to pass Hadley over and be the one to pick up Olivia, if only to comfort himself with the fact that she was going to be okay, but Hadley had a death grip on his neck. *She's terrified and you're the only person in this room she knows.* He cuddled her close, trying to comfort her while he focused on the situation at hand. "Her back. We need to get her out of here now, before someone comes to investigate."

"On it." Liam pulled out his phone and gave terse orders to whoever was on the other line. Then he went to his knees next to Olivia and carefully prodded her. "Bullet took a chunk out of her back, but it was a graze. Nothing vital hit."

He released the breath he hadn't realized he was holding. "Let's get out of this fucking hellhole."

"Yes, sir." He picked Olivia up carefully and led the way out of the house. Their train of vehicles now idled at the curb directly outside.

Liam glanced back. "The little one isn't going to be letting go of you anytime soon."

Considering the shakes rocking her tiny body, he didn't want to risk traumatizing her further by forcing her to do anything other than bury her face in his neck. It was only because she was clinging to him so tightly that she hadn't seen Olivia yet. A small favor, but he couldn't drive and hold Hadley and sit with Olivia at the same time. Cillian nodded. "Put her in the backseat and drive."

He moved around the back of the car and got into the other side. Keeping a hand on the back of Hadley's head, he accepted the towel Liam had gotten out of the trunk. Between the two of them, they got it folded and propped behind Olivia, and then buckled her in. He didn't like how pale she was, but they didn't have much in the way of an alternative. Right now the main goal was to get the hell out of Dodge.

So he sat back and stroked Hadley's hair and back until her little sobs abated. He kept checking Olivia, but her breathing was steady and so was her pulse. *Nothing you can do.* "Have Doc Jones ready for us."

"She's meeting us halfway."

*Smart.* He glanced down to find that Hadley had fallen

asleep, her tiny fists clenched in his shirt. Aside from being scared out of her mind, she didn't seem to be injured, but that would have to be confirmed by the doctor, too. Either way, both she and her mama would recover.

*And then what?*

That was the question, wasn't it?

The threat of Sergei had been effectively removed, but there was still Dmitri to think about. He wasn't the type of man to take defeat lying down, and the O'Malleys had one-upped him twice now—three times if Cillian did what his father had asked of him. Dmitri would be coming, and he'd be coming for blood. That need for vengeance might encompass Olivia, or it might not—there was no way to tell until the hit came.

As long as she stayed with him, she was potentially in danger. He looked out the window, every fiber of his being trying to reject that truth, to find a way for them to be together that wouldn't put her at risk.

There wasn't one.

Even if he left with her, the full force of his father's wrath would follow them, and then they'd have twice the enemies to dodge. Those weren't great odds, not with the amount of money and power both the Romanovs and O'Malleys could bring to the table. She'd have a better chance of disappearing if it was just her and Hadley.

*Fuck.*

He didn't want her to go. They'd only known each other a few weeks, but she'd completely rocked his worldview in that short amount of time. He couldn't imagine his life without her in it.

*You have to. For her. For Hadley. To do anything else is unforgivable.*

Olivia stirred, her eyes flying open and a gasp on her lips. "Hadley!"

"I've got her." He gently pressed on her shoulder to keep her from lurching forward. "We're safe. Sergei's gone. How do you feel?"

"That's a stupid question." She touched her throat and winced. Then her gaze landed on Hadley, and the sheer love there rocked him. *What would it be like if she looked at me that way?* He shut it down before it could take root. He'd already come to terms—as much as he ever would—that Olivia couldn't be his. Torturing himself with what-if questions wasn't going to do anything but make her inevitable leaving worse.

He passed over the sleeping toddler. "Careful. You took a few hits back there."

"It was worth it." She kissed Hadley's head and closed her eyes. "We're going back to Boston?"

"Yeah." *For now.* He had to sit her down and talk about the escape plan he'd worked into place with the help of Teague, but now wasn't the time. For one, Liam could hear everything they said. The man might be loyal to a fault, but he was loyal to the O'Malleys—not Cillian, and definitely not Olivia. He needed as few threads connecting her new life with her old one, which meant the fewer people who knew about it, the better.

"Good." She reached over and took his hand without opening her eyes. "I haven't said 'thank you' yet. So thank you."

"Don't thank me. I'm part of the reason this happened."

"No." She pinned him with a look. "You have plenty of guilt to carry around, deserved or not. You don't get this, too. I knew what the risks were every step of the way, and even I didn't see Sergei doing what he did. If you want to blame someone, blame him." Her voice dropped. "You saved me, Cillian. Don't take that away from either of us."

It was too easy to step back into that room and see everything going down as if in slow motion. Sergei had been a big guy, but he looked even larger towering over her. Cillian shook his head, wishing he could shake the memory as easily. He was going to have nightmares for the rest of his life about what would have happened if he hadn't gotten there in time. He squeezed her hand. "Try to rest. We're meeting Doc Jones to get you and Hadley checked out." Then he'd talk to her about the next step.

"Doc Jones. You spoil me."

Despite everything, he grinned. "I remembered how much you liked her last time."

"Smart-ass." She gave a small smile and closed her eyes. This time, she didn't open them again. He held her hand and listened to her breathe, and tried to tell himself that losing her was worth it as long as he knew she was alive and well in the world.

* * *

"You two are nothing but trouble."

Olivia winced as Doc Jones tightened the bandage wrapped around her chest. The bullet had taken out a chunk of flesh, but it hadn't so much as chipped a bone. And her throat was horribly bruised, but nothing seemed to be broken there, either. She had a few stitches and would have to be careful lifting Hadley for a little while, but it could have been so much worse.

She held her breath while the doctor looked over

Hadley, her gruff demeanor changing into something much softer. It felt like forever, but it was only a few minutes later that she looked up. "She's still shaken and scared out of her mind, but aside from a few bruises, she's physically fine. The best thing for her is going to be getting back into some kind of routine. Expect nightmares. They'll pass, though." Her blue eyes hardened. "The bastard that did this is dead?"

Cillian nodded. "Yeah."

"Good. I can't abide monsters who hurt kids." She pushed to her feet, and pinned Olivia with a look. "Those stitches will have to be taken out, so make sure you either call me or go to your normal doctor. If you don't, it's going to be a mess, and there's no damn reason for it."

"Okay."

She crossed her arms over her chest. "If that's all you need?"

"Yeah. Thanks, Doc." He stood and walked her to the door. Hadley looked up as he came back, and lifted her arms in a clear demand for him to pick her up. Cillian didn't hesitate, tucking her against his side and rubbing her back as if it was the most natural thing in the world. He came to sit down next to Olivia. "What a day."

"You can say that again." She leaned her head against his shoulder. "I never thought I could be so tired."

He tensed, which didn't make any sense. "I'm going to send most of the men home and get us a hotel. You two need to rest, and another three hours of driving isn't going to accomplish that."

There was something off in his voice, but when she looked at his face, he gave her nothing. Olivia frowned, but he had a point. She was exhausted. They all were. A full night's sleep might be just what they needed, and then they could start fresh in the morning. "Okay."

He passed over Hadley. "Give me a few to arrange everything."

She held her daughter tightly, and watched him walk away, unable to shake the feeling that she was missing something vitally important. *Get a grip. He just killed a man. That's enough to shake up anyone.* The explanation should have made her feel better, but it didn't.

The feeling only got worse as he drove them to a hotel and got them checked in. All the while, he wouldn't quite look at her. *Maybe he blames me for getting him into this mess. Can't hate him for that.* But it hurt to think that he wouldn't look at her like she was something special again.

That he might never love her like she loved him.

Hadley had fallen asleep again, no doubt exhausted from her trauma, so Olivia tucked her in. At some point she'd be able to walk out of the room without fearing that Hadley wouldn't be there when she got back, but that day wasn't today or any day in the near future. It was hard enough to use the bathroom, even knowing Cillian was sitting on the opposite bed, in plain view of her daughter. *It's over now. Hadley's safe and you're safe and he's safe, and Sergei is gone for good. You couldn't have a better result than that.*

So why did she feel like the other boot was about to drop?

She came back into the room to find Cillian looking out the window. "Are you going to tell me what's going on, or do I have to guess?"

He turned, a manila envelope in his hands. Without a word, he handed it to her. She tore it open and dumped the contents onto the bed. Passports, birth certificates, social security cards—two of each—a driver's license, and a truly impressive wad of cash. "What—?" But even as she asked, she knew. "I told you I didn't want this."

"That was before." He scrubbed a hand over his face. "I can't keep you safe, not completely. Fuck, Olivia, you have no idea how much I wish I could. But if the past few days are any indication...I can't let something happen to you because I was too selfish to let you go."

A week ago she might have taken the documents and run as fast and far as she could. But...so much had changed since then. She tried to focus on his words and not the fact that he seemed to be shoving her and Hadley out the door as fast as he could. A knee-jerk reaction wasn't going to do either of them any favors. "Selfish."

If anything, he got more agitated. Cillian laughed harshly. "Karma is a serious bitch, because that's the only way to explain that the one woman I fall head over heels in love with is the one I have to let go in order to keep her safe. I couldn't deal with it if something happened to either one of you because I tried to find a way to let you stay, and failed." He paced from one end of the room to the other. "Fuck, what am I saying? You want to go. So that makes me even more of an ass for wanting you to stay."

"Cillian, stop." She crossed to him and put her hands on his shoulders. "That was a seriously impressive monologue, but how about you let me get a word in edgewise?"

"What else is there to say?"

"Oh, I don't know. You can start by asking me what I want."

He looked down at her, agony and love written all over his face. "What do you want, sweetheart? Tell me and I'll do my damnedest to make it happen."

Her heart lurched in her chest. She'd run before. It hadn't been far or fast enough, but those weren't the deciding factors. The truth was that fleeing her problems wasn't a good way to deal with them. She might hold them off for months, or even years, but in the end they'd find her. And she'd have to deal with them alone.

Or she could take a different path.

Cillian wasn't Dmitri. Every step of the way, he'd done what he could to put her before his family. He'd fight tooth and nail to keep her and Hadley safe—to keep them out of the line of fire. What was more, Olivia couldn't imagine her life without him in it. She didn't want to.

"I love you." She wanted to hug him, but she needed him to see the truth on her face. "I never planned on it, and I still can't quite wrap my mind around it, but I love you so much it hurts."

"That would be the injuries Sergei gave you."

She smacked his shoulder. "I spent my entire life learning that I could only depend on myself, and then you've come along and shot that all to hell. You've been there when I needed you—when *we* needed you. I know I'm not exactly undamaged goods—"

"Olivia, stop." There was something terrifyingly like hope on his face. "What are you saying?"

"I'm saying I choose you. I know Dmitri is still a potential threat, but I've dealt with him up to this point, and I'll keep on doing it—if you're willing to hook up with the half sister of a Romanov."

"Sweetheart, if you stay, I'm going to make damn sure that bastard can never get to you." His expression turned to one of concentration. "In fact..." He pulled out his phone and dialed. He was close enough to her that she heard a familiar Russian voice pick up the other line.

*"Da?"*

"Romanov." Cillian met her gaze, his voice cold. "I have a proposition for you, and don't make the mistake of thinking it's optional."

"Cillian O'Malley. Such a pleasure to hear from you once more." A pause. "I'm listening."

"You will leave Olivia alone. She wants no part of the Romanov name, no matter what your father willed. In exchange, I'm willing to offer that the O'Malley family will let go of the fact that you tried to undermine us."

A longer pause. "And if I choose to turn down this less-than-beneficial agreement?"

"War." Cillian's gaze turned contemplative. "I happen to know that you haven't magically found a wife in the last six months since my sister very publically chose an enemy to her family over you. That made some of your business partners a little nervous, didn't it?" The silence on the other end was confirmation enough. Cillian snorted. "Yeah, I thought so. You can't afford a war right now and you damn well know it."

Dmitri's silky laugh made the small hair on the back of her neck stand on end. "While you're not completely incorrect, I have a counteroffer."

"And what's that?"

"I am prepared to let my darling sister settle in with you—which is what I assume you're planning, otherwise you wouldn't be calling me—in exchange for two concessions."

Of course he couldn't just take what Cillian was offering. Olivia didn't even know if Cillian had the authority to make that threat in the first place, but if he said they would go to war over her, she believed him. And he was right—war wasn't something Dmitri could afford right now, not with him only having full control over the Romanovs for less than two years. Her heart beat harder. *This could actually work.*

Cillian frowned. "What concessions?"

"You, Cillian O'Malley, will owe me a favor. It will not in any way undermine your loyalty to your family, but other than that, it is a free favor that I can call due at my convenience."

*No.*

"Deal." Cillian didn't look at her. "And the other?"

"I would like to see my niece a few times a year." His voice warmed to just this side of freezing. "I know you're listening, Olivia. No threats. No bargaining. No underhanded maneuvering. But I will come to Boston and I will see Hadley for a few hours on an arranged date."

*No.* She took a deep breath and stamped down on her initial knee-jerk reaction. Cillian was still watching her, waiting for her answer. She held out her hand for the phone and he passed it over. "Why?"

"She's family." Such a simple answer, and yet incomparably complicated.

Olivia took a deep breath. "If I agree to this, I can call off these visits at any point without repercussions from you or anyone associated with the Romanovs."

"Only if I violate my part of that agreement."

*No threats. No bargaining. No underhanded maneuvering.* She didn't like it. She had a feeling he was going to be holding that position in the Romanov family for her daughter as a way to keep his word to Andrei. But . . . She took a deep breath. There would come a time when Hadley would have to know about her history. Andrei waited until it was too late to try to start a relationship with Olivia. Was she any better than he was if she denied Hadley a chance to know her uncle—especially if he was earnest in his intentions?

She thought hard, trying to see this from all angles. The thought of leaving Dmitri in the rearview forever was an intoxicating one, but she couldn't expect to stay in Boston without some kind of agreement in place. This was as fair as it was going to get. "I will be there for every second of the time you spend with her. I want your word that your intentions are true." It wasn't a foolproof guarantee, but it was as close to one as she'd get.

"You have it."

She released her pent-up breath in a rush. "Okay."

"Good-bye, Olivia."

"Good-bye, Dmitri."

She hung up the phone and passed it back, hardly daring to believe it. "He's not going to try to force me to come back. He gave his word." A smile pulled at the edges of her lip, and she let loose a giddy laugh. "I can't believe it."

"You didn't have to agree to let him see Hadley. We could have found a different way."

She didn't think so. But, beyond that, her gut said that Dmitri wasn't making a power play with that request. "He's alone, Cillian. Andrei is gone. His mother passed away when he was in high school. Hadley and I are the closest thing to family he has, and while that wasn't enough to stop him from playing dirty to try and bring us back into the fold, he realizes that this is the only way to fulfill his promise to our father." And she had his word. It was as close to a sure thing as there was in this world.

She laid her head on Cillian's shoulder. "I don't know

what the future will bring, but I *do* know that I want you in my life in a permanent way. The rest will figure itself out."

"I love you so fucking much, it blows my mind."

She lifted her head so she could see his face. "Then kiss me, Cillian O'Malley. We won today, and we're safe. Tomorrow will figure itself out."

Don't miss the next book in the
O'Malleys series....

Sloan may no longer be in Boston, but
that doesn't mean she's safe. Especially
when it comes to her new neighbor, Jude.

Please turn the page for a preview of

# *Forbidden Promises*!

Coming in Summer 2017

# CHAPTER ONE

You have no job experience. In anything."

Sloan O'Malley did her best not to wring her hands when faced with the incredulous expression on the face of the woman sitting across from her. Her potential future boss. Around them, the little diner bustled with early morning customers, either coming in before their day got started or ending their night shift. It felt like every single one of them was staring.

She realized she hadn't answered the question that wasn't a question, and cleared her throat. "I'm a hard worker and I learn fast." She hoped it was true. She'd never had cause to put herself to the test, and it was slightly horrifying to realize just how sheltered she'd been when it came to actual real life. "Please. I need this job."

The money her brother Teague had sent would last for a few more weeks, but she didn't want to lose that precious cushion. What was more, she was so incredibly *tired* of sitting around while life passed her by. That was why she'd escaped her family, slipping out like a thief in the night and traveling across the country without a word to anyone. They would look for her—she'd be a fool to believe otherwise— and that meant she had to ensure Teague didn't have cause to send her more resources.

She had to stand on her own two feet for the first time in twenty-four years.

She just hoped she wasn't about to fall flat on her face.

Taking a deep breath, she tried her hand at a convincing smile. The woman across from her, Marge, did not look convinced. What could she possibly say that would make the woman hire her? "Marge—"

"Here's the deal." Marge sat back. She was an older woman with a no-nonsense face creased with laugh lines that spoke of a life well lived. Her graying hair was pulled back into a bun and she wore serviceable clothes and a nondescript apron and looked like someone who could take anything life threw at her. "You look like trouble, and the last thing either I or this town needs is trouble."

Sloan tried not to wilt at that, but Marge wasn't through. She sighed. "But I have a thing for strays and you're nothing if you're not that. I'll give you a shot. You screw up, you're done. You're late, you're done. You bring any unnecessary drama to my door, you're done. Got it?"

She could hardly believe what she was hearing. "You're hiring me?"

"Isn't that what I just said?" Marge shook her head and pushed to her feet. She had to be nearly six feet tall and she was built like a linebacker. "Show up tomorrow morning at seven. Dress comfortably, because I'm not going to be sending you home because your shoes pinch your feet. You complain—"

"I'm gone."

A small smile graced Marge's lips, gone as soon as it'd come. "Yep. Now, get lost. You're distracting the menfolk and these fools have places to be." She turned and walked across the diner to the counter and snapped her fingers at the cook through the gap in the wall where the food was delivered. "Hurry up, Luke. You know damn well that the Judge has places to be and he'll be wanting his breakfast as soon as he walks through the door."

Sloan got up and hurried out the door. *I got the job.* Her first impulse was to call Teague and tell him, but the only reason she was supposed to call was in case of an emergency or if she was in serious trouble. This was neither.

She headed for the beach, needing to burn off her pent-up energy. With the way the interview had gone, she'd been sure Marge was going to tell her to get lost. She'd even prepared herself for it. To have the woman do exactly the opposite made her head spin. *She's taking a chance on me and she doesn't even know me.* She could hardly believe it. In her world, people didn't take chances on strangers like that.

Except that wasn't her world anymore. This was.

The salt air cleared some of the static in her head. She'd grown up in Boston, but the ocean felt different on this coast. Wild. Free. Vast beyond comprehension. She slipped off her shoes and dug her toes into the sand.

Callaway Rock was about three miles from one side of the town limits to the other, all of it stretched out along the beach. The little house she was living in was on the southern outskirts and the diner was smack dab in the middle. It might have been smarter to drive down here, but she liked the walk. There might come a time when she didn't crave the sand beneath her feet and the ocean breeze in her face, but that day wasn't today.

Her shoes dangling from her fingertips, she started walking, letting her mind wander. The last week had been the first time she truly lived alone, and the learning curve was...strange. There were so many little things she'd taken for granted, things she'd never bothered with because they had a full-time staff to do everything from cook to clean.

It turned out Sloan wasn't much of a cook.

*I'll figure it out. All I have is time.*

She missed her family, too. She hadn't counted on that. All she'd ever wanted to do is get away from that life, to remove herself from the playing field where she'd never have control. And she had, with Teague's help.

Unfortunately, she couldn't turn off her brain, and she kept wondering how Keira was doing, and if Aiden was holding up under the increasing pressure he must be feeling as heir. And Cillian. Last time she'd heard, he'd been off in Connecticut with that woman. Had things turned out? They must have, because if something happened to Cillian, Teague would have called her.

She hoped.

She trailed off to a stop, staring blindly at the tide coming in. Then there was Carrigan. Her big sister. The one she couldn't quite forgive, no matter how much time or distance was between them. It wasn't fair and it wasn't right, but Sloan couldn't let it go.

*Maybe someday...*

She inhaled deeply and started walking again. Mentally flogging herself by wondering what her five siblings were up to wasn't going to do her a single bit of good. And thinking about Devlin, who was rotting away six feet beneath the ground... That way lay madness.

Up ahead, the bright green door that signaled her house appeared. She'd woken every day for the last seven days thinking that would be the day when Callie's aunt, Sorcha, showed up, but the woman hadn't made an appearance yet. Frankly, a part of Sloan was relieved by that. She didn't know much about the woman except that she owned this house and seemed willing to do her niece a favor by housing Sloan indefinitely.

Against her better judgment, Sloan's gaze drifted to the house directly north of hers. *Jude.*

If she never ran into him again, it would be too soon.

If she was a more curious woman, she'd wonder if perhaps he was hiding something behind those closed curtains and barred shutters. *Who owns a beach house and keeps all the windows blocked?*

"None of my business." She had enough trouble without borrowing more.

As she passed, the back door opened and the devil himself emerged, a coffee cup in his hand. Sloan jerked to a stop, unable to tear her gaze away from him. His long dark blond hair was in a bun at the back of his head, which should have made him look feminine, but there wasn't a single thing feminine about the man staring at her. His jaw might as well have been chiseled from stone, and though she couldn't see his blue eyes across the distance, she knew they were icy and intense.

But what he was wearing...

Or, rather, *not* wearing.

Sweatpants hung low on his hips, and he'd misplaced

his shirt somewhere. Every muscle was defined, his body too perfect to be real. She blinked, but he didn't vanish like she'd half expected. Instead he lifted his mug to his lips, drawing her attention to his impossibly broad shoulders that tapered to a narrow waist and, good gracious, what were those muscles called that created a V leading directly into his sweatpants?

Her face felt impossibly warm despite the mild July morning and she was suddenly sure that she was blushing furiously. *Keep walking. Just put one foot forward and keep walking.* She couldn't move. She couldn't do anything other than stand there and stare at him until he nodded briefly at her, turned around, and walked back into his house.

*What in God's name just happened?*

\* \* \*

Jude MacNamara left his place as soon as night fell. He didn't like moving around Callaway Rock during the day. Fuck, he didn't like small towns in general. Everyone had too much time on their hands and felt like it was their God-given right to stick their noses into their neighbors' business. He'd had to run off over a dozen attempts to welcome him into town since he moved here three months ago, and that hadn't done a damn thing to dissuade anyone. If anything, it made the locals *more* determined to figure out everything there was to know about him.

They were wasting their time. He was here for a job. He sure as fuck wasn't staying.

He stalked onto the beach, pausing only to make sure no teenagers had decided it was a brilliant idea to have a beach fire tonight. It was clear. Unlike the towns further north,

Callaway Rock didn't get much in the way of tourists. Maybe if they had, he wouldn't have had to actually buy a house here while he waited for his target to reappear.

Jude lifted a pair of binoculars to his eyes. In his dark clothes and with the ocean at his back, he was damn near invisible on a night like this, with clouds covering the moon. He gave the beach to the north and south of him a cursory look to reconfirm that there was no one but him out tonight and then he turned to his real target.

The O'Connor house.

It had sat unoccupied for two and a half months, but a little over a week ago, a woman had moved in. She was about fifty years too young to be Sorcha O'Connor, and the coloring was all wrong regardless. This woman—Sloan—had both dark hair and eyes, not the blond hair and blue eyes that ran through Sorcha's family.

He paused at each window, taking in the little changes that had come with the new resident. After he'd moved to Callaway Rock, he'd broken in and gone through the entire house, looking both for clues to where Sorcha currently was and familiarizing himself with the layout in the event that he'd need to return. There was nothing of the former, and the latter was laughably easy. With the massive windows and fact that the curtains and shutters were never closed, he hadn't had to set foot in the place to figure out everything he needed to know. But it paid to be thorough.

What he couldn't figure out was who the hell this Sloan was and how she was connected to Sorcha O'Connor.

For a second, right when he found her peering into his windows that first night, he'd half convinced himself that she was actually Callista Sheridan, come to visit her long-lost aunt. A coup like that...It made his adrenaline spike just thinking about it. What better way to make Colm Sheridan suffer than removing his beloved daughter from the struggle for power among the big Boston families? She was the only child he had left, after all...

But as soon as Sloan had stepped into the light, he'd realized his mistake. Even if her coloring could be faked, this wasn't Callista. He'd seen her a time or two over the years, and she carried herself as a woman used to having her orders followed without question, even before she took over the Sheridan empire.

Sloan? She seemed to have her shoulders perpetually hunched, as if expecting a blow. He couldn't tell if it was an abusive ex or something else, but she was fleeing something. *And it's none of my fucking business if she is. She's not my target. Sorcha O'Connor is.*

Every light was lit inside the house, and he watched Sloan walk through it, pausing to touch the marble kitchen counter, the thick mantel over the fireplace, the back cushion on the couch facing the massive windows. Then she disappeared, reappearing in the guest room, her hands going to the buttons at the front of her dress.

Jude's body sprang to attention when he realized what was happening. *Put the damn binoculars down. Sorcha isn't there, and this girl isn't your mark.* But he didn't. Instead, he watched as she shrugged out of the dress, leaving her in only a pair of silk white panties and an equally white bra. She looked innocent, untouchable, and he could barely wrap his mind around it.

It took considerable willpower to lower the binoculars as she reached behind her to unhook her bra, but he wasn't a goddamn Peeping Tom. Jude laughed softly. *Sure, stand on your high moral horse. You fucking kill people for a living and you're going to be honorable about watching some woman who you've met once undress.*

*There have to be lines. Even if they don't always make sense.*

And, mystery past or not, that woman *was* an innocent. It was...odd. These days, most of the people he spent any amount of time with were either contacts to further his goals or people in the same life. Every single one of them had seen things, same as him. They didn't blink at the choices he'd made or the path that had brought him into it.

He didn't have many dealings with innocents.

He'd seen the way she looked at him this morning, though. Even across the distance between them, the hunger in her eyes had been readily recognizable. It made him hot just thinking about it. What would she do if he walked up to her front door right now and knocked? Would she answer in a robe? Would she submit if he closed the distance between them and kissed her?

Jude cursed long and hard, his cock so hard it was a wonder it didn't burst out of his jeans. He had no business thinking things like that, not while he was on a hunt and sure as fuck not about a woman who had some kind of connection with his target.

*An innocent.*

He was half surprised he could even recognize that trait in another person. He hadn't ever been one. He hadn't had a chance to be. That opportunity had been taken away the moment Colm Sheridan declared the death sentence on Jude's father and brothers—the same death sentence he would have delivered to Jude's mother if he'd known she was pregnant.

No, there was no room for innocence in his life.

There was only revenge.

# Fall in Love with Forever Romance

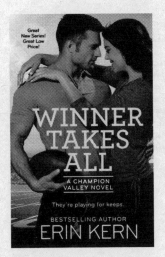

## WINNER TAKES ALL
### By Erin Kern

The first book in Erin Kern's brand-new Champion Valley series, perfect for fans of *Friday Night Lights*! Former football player Blake Carpenter is determined to rebuild his life as the new coach of his Colorado hometown's high school team. Annabelle Turner, the team's physical therapist, will be damned if the scandal that cost Blake his NFL career hurts *her* team. But what she doesn't count on is their intense attraction that turns every heated run-in into wildly erotic competition...

## LAST KISS OF SUMMER
### By Marina Adair

Kennedy Sinclair, pie shop and orchard owner extraordinaire, is all that stands between Luke Callahan and the success of his hard cider business. But when the negotiations start heating up, will they lose their hearts? Or seal the deal? Fans of Rachel Gibson, Kristan Higgins, and Jill Shalvis will gobble up the latest sexy contemporary from Marina Adair.

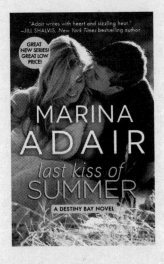

# *Fall in Love with Forever Romance*

## MEANT TO BE MINE
### By Lisa Marie Perry

In the tradition of Jessica Lemmon and Marie Force, comes a contemporary romance about a former bad boy seeking redemption. After years apart, Sofia Mercer and Burke Wolf reunite in Cape Cod. Their wounds may be deep, but their sizzling attraction is as hot as ever.

## RUN TO YOU
### By Rachel Lacey

The first book in Rachel Lacey's new contemporary romance series will appeal to fans of Kristan Higgins, Rachel Gibson, and Jill Shalvis! Ethan Hunter's grandmother, Haven, North Carolina's resident match-maker, is convinced Gabby Winter and her grandson are meant to be to-gether. Rather than break her heart, Ethan and Gabby fake a relationship, but if they continue, they won't just fool the town—they might fool themselves, too...

# Fall in Love with Forever Romance

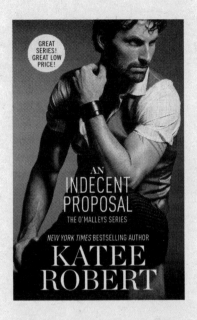

### AN INDECENT PROPOSAL
### By Katee Robert

*New York Times* and *USA Today* bestselling author Katee Robert continues her smoking-hot series about the O'Malleys—wealthy, powerful, and full of scandalous family secrets. Olivia Rashidi left behind her Russian mob family for the sake of her daughter. When she meets Cillian O'Malley, she recognizes his family name, but can't help falling for the smoldering, tortured man. Cillian knows that there is no escape from the life, but Olivia is worth trying—and dying—for...